RESCUING ELLENA (SPECIAL FORCES: OPERATION ALPHA)

BRAVO SERIES BOOK 4

ANNA BLAKELY

Dear Readers,

Welcome to the Special Forces: Operation Alpha Fan-Fiction world!

If you are new to this amazing world, in a nutshell the author wrote a story using one or more of my characters in it. Sometimes that character has a major role in the story, and other times they are only mentioned briefly. This is perfectly legal and allowable because they are going through Aces Press to publish the story.

This book is entirely the work of the author who wrote it. While I might have assisted with brainstorming and other ideas about which of my characters to use, I didn't have any part in the process or writing or editing the story.

I'm proud and excited that so many authors loved my characters enough that they wanted to write them into their own story. Thank you for supporting them, and me!

READ ON!
  Xoxo
  Susan Stoker

This book is for all of my fellow Susan Stoker fans. Like most of you, I've read Susan's amazing stories for years. Also like you, I've fallen in love with every single hero she's created. To be a part of her world is an unbelievable honor, and I'm grateful to each and every one of you for giving my stories and characters a chance. I look forward to sharing even more exciting tales of love and suspense with you in the future.

XOXO
Anna

PROLOGUE

Three years ago...

"Put the gun down, Campbell. You don't want to do this." With his heart lodged in his throat, Master Chief Gabriel Dawson somehow managed to hold his own weapon steady. Finger next to the trigger, he kept his gun trained on the man he'd once considered to be a brother.

"Wrong again." His former teammate chuckled. "I *do* want to do this. I want to look into your eyes while I rip away the only thing you've ever really cared about. Just like you did to me."

Though he wanted to—*God* did he want to—Gabe refused to look at Ellena. If he did...if he saw her fear and allowed himself to think of everything he stood to lose...his control would shatter.

"She's not the only thing, Vic." He stared at his former teammate. "I care about every man on our team."

"Except it's not *our* team anymore, is it?" Vic's upper lip curled into a vengeful sneer. "It's *your* team, Dawson. Judd, A.J., Neil... they walk around in your shadow like a bunch of fucking puppies searching for some tit. And you"—he snorted—"you lead 'em around like you're the head of the goddamn pack."

"I'm just doing my job. As the team leader it's my duty to—"

1

"As the team leader, you're supposed to protect us!" The man's face turned red, the barrel of his gun pressing against Ellena's head even harder.

Gabe's trigger finger twitched. "I did protect you."

"You threw me under the fucking bus!"

"I told the truth."

"You ended my career."

"Wrong." Gabe clenched his jaw. "You did that all on your own the second you killed that man in cold blood."

"He was a terrorist!" Spittle flew from Vic's mouth as he spoke.

"He was an unarmed prisoner on his knees with his hands bound behind his back."

Two weeks ago, the team had been sent to Pakistan to stop a group of men who'd invaded and terrorized a small village just outside Karachi. Hamza Hassan, the man Vic had murdered, was among those captured.

"Hassan raped and murdered a woman while her six-year-old son hid under the bed. I did the world a fucking favor, and you damn well know it!"

A vein in the middle of the unstable man's forehead bulged, anger and resentment turning the skin there a dark reddish-purple. Sweat beaded and fell from Vic's temple.

Gabe knew he needed to tread carefully. For the past month, he'd been worried about his teammate's mental wellbeing. Concerned the darkness of the world they lived in was too much for the young SEAL to handle.

He was right.

"You disobeyed my direct order to stand down," he reminded Vic.

"It was just you and me, man." Vic stared back at him. "You could've looked the other way."

"No." Gabe shook his head slowly. "I couldn't."

Vic smirked, but his crazed eyes held no humor. "Always a fucking boy scout. You couldn't wait to run your mouth and tell everyone what happened."

"I didn't have a choice."

2

"Yes, you did! You could've chosen to have my back like all those times I had yours. Instead, you looked me square in the eye and tore that patch from my chest. That patch meant everything to me, man. *Everything!*" A tear leaked from the corner of Vic's eye, the silver streak mixing with the thin sheen of sweat. "You destroyed the only family I'd ever really known. How could you…" His voice cracked. "They want to send me to prison, Gabe. Fucking Leavenworth."

"I know."

Because that's where the Navy sends murderers.

"You were supposed to have my back!" Vic yelled again as another tear fell. "How could you do that to me?"

"You're right," Gabe lied. The man wasn't even fucking close to being right but agitating Vic even more than he already was could be a fatal mistake for Ellena. "I should have, and I didn't. That's on me."

"You're damn right it's on you!"

Keeping his voice steady, Gabe inched a step closer to the man holding his entire world hostage. "I know that, now. And you have every right to call me out, but this is between us, Vic. Ellena had nothing to do with it."

"But I wanted her to be involved," Vic revealed as he backed up slowly, toward the door leading from the kitchen to the back yard. The other man glanced down, his next words spoken directly to Ellena. "I wanted them to send me to you for my psych eval, but they wouldn't."

"They couldn't, Vic." Ellena's swallow was audible. "I'm your team leader's wife. I-it would've been a conflict of interest to have m-me be the one to evaluate you."

For the first time since walking in on the horrifying scene, Gabe allowed himself to glance at his wife. The tremble of fear in her sweet voice made him want to put a bullet between his former teammate's eyes.

"Elle, look at me." Gabe stared into Ellena's frightened baby blues. "It's okay, sweetheart. Everything's going to be okay."

Her bottom lip quivered as her bow-shaped lips attempted to form a smile. "I know."

That smile turned into a wince as Vic pressed the barrel of the gun even harder against Ellena's temple.

"You're wrong," the angry man growled back at him. "Everything's not going to be okay. It's never going to be okay, and it's all *your* fault."

As if she could sense Vic was about to pull the trigger, Ellena blurted out, "I'm pregnant!"

Vic froze. His cold, dark eyes shot to Gabe's.

"It's true," Gabe confirmed the news, barely resisting the urge to end the other man for daring to touch what was his.

"Bullshit."

"It's not bullshit, Vic." Ellena tried to convince him. "Look at the fridge. Look at the picture hanging there. That's a copy of the sonogram I had last week. I'm only eight weeks along, but I was h-having some cramping, so my doctor ordered the test. Just to m-make sure everything was okay."

Gabe watched the man's eyes slide to the appliance on his left. Hanging by a thread, he waited while Vic studied the blurry, black and white image.

Vic's voice filled with an accusing tone as his focus shot back to Gabe. "You never said anything."

"Because I asked him not to," Ellena responded quickly. "I-I wanted to wait until we'd made it past the three-month mark."

"Please, Vic," Gabe pleaded. "Just drop the gun so we can talk about all of this."

"Talk." Vic chuckled. "I don't want to *talk*. I'm sick to death of fucking talking!"

"Okay, fine." Gabe nodded. "Then let Ellena go. She and the baby"—Gabe had to swallow to keep his own voice from cracking—"they're innocent in all of this. You were right before. This is all on me. So if you want to kill me, fine. But not them. Please, man. Just let her go."

"No!" Ellena shook her head vehemently. The blues in her eyes darkened with anger. "You are not going to sacrifice yourself."

Gabe's heart swelled, even as it began to shatter. "That's my job, baby." He smiled sadly. "I'd sacrifice myself a hundred times over if it meant keeping you safe."

She was shaking her head again even before he was finished. "I won't let you do it."

His eyes softened. "Not your choice to make."

"Yes, it is." Ellena stared back at him with a sudden determination. It was clear she was trying to tell him something more.

The blood in his veins grew cold with fear as he realized what it was. "No, it's not," he tried to get through to her.

Ellena licked her lips nervously before whispering, "I love you."

Knowing there was nothing he could do to stop her, Gabe prepared to defend her and their child—with his life, if necessary.

In what he hoped was an indiscernible move, he curled his finger around the gun's trigger.

"It's my decision," his wife stated again. A message he received loud and clear. "And I'm making it...*Now!*".

The scene became a slow-motion movie as everything happened all at once.

His daring wife spun her head to the side—away from Vic's gun. Simultaneously, she used her right hand to push his arm upward as she threw herself to the floor.

A deafening *boom* filled the air as Vic pulled the trigger. Pieces of drywall and paint rained down on them from where the bullet pierced the ceiling.

With a maddening fury, the unstable man's eyes went from being wide with surprise to a narrowed, venomous glare.

"You bitch!" Swinging his gun back around toward Ellena, he made his intentions clear.

Gabe didn't hesitate. He pulled the trigger, his bullet hitting its mark with perfection.

The sound of the shot barely registered as Gabe watched as his teammate's body jerked. The man's brain matter and blood splattering on the door behind him. A second later, Vic fell against it before sliding down to the tiled floor below.

He was dead before he ever hit the ground.

"Elle!" Gabe shoved his gun into his waistband against his lower back and rushed to where his wife lay.

Shaking, Ellena pushed herself into a sitting position. "I-I'm okay."

Despite her words, Gabe frantically ran his hands down her arms and back up to her shoulders. He cupped both sides of her face, his own hands trembling. "Did he hurt you?"

"No." Tears fell from her eyes, her face crumbling as she glanced over at Vic's lifeless body. "Oh, God."

"Baby, don't." Gabe gently forced her focus back on him. "Just keep looking at me."

Shoving his hand into his pocket, he yanked out his phone and dialed 911. He kept one hand on her face, his thumb caressing her precious skin as he reported the shooting to the police.

Hanging up, he immediately made another phone call. This one to his commanding officer.

When the authorities arrived, he and Elle were separated to give their official statements of the events. Gabe hated to leave his wife's side for even a second, but he understood the reasons behind the protocol.

Several minutes later, he was still in the kitchen speaking with the lead detective and his CO when the officer taking Elle's statement came running into the room.

"Your wife needs you," the young man blurted loudly, his wide eyes staring directly at Gabe. "I've already called for an ambulance."

An ambulance?

Gabe's pulse spiked as he shoved past the kid and ran into the living room where Elle had been taken. His heart nearly stopped altogether when he saw her down on her knees, hunched over and clutching her stomach.

"Elle!" He ran to her for the second time in as many hours. Dropping to his knees beside her, he asked, "What is it? What's wrong?"

"I-I don't know." Tears fell from her eyes, sorrow filling her beautiful face. "I was telling the officer what h-happened, and I got this sharp p-pain. Then I felt the b-blood, and I..." She squeezed her eyes shut, crying out as another pain hit.

The baby.

Please, God. Don't take the baby!

But when he saw the blood seeping through Ellena's jeans, Gabe knew his silent prayer had come too late.

CHAPTER 1

Gabe opened his apartment door. Distracted by the ghosts of his past, he almost missed the fact that the light he'd left on in his apartment—the one he *always* left on to give him a clear view of the space when he returned—was off.

The place was pitch black...almost.

In one fluid motion, he pulled his gun from its place at the small of his back and flipped the safety. After spending several years as a Navy SEAL, and the last few as the leader of an elite private security team, the weapon was like an extension of his body. And even better than his American Express.

Never fucking leave home without it.

"I'm armed," Gabe warned whoever was there. "And I will not hesitate to shoot."

"I know." A man's voice rumbled low from the right side of his living room. "That's why I turned off your light."

Christ. He was *not* in the mood for this shit. "You picked the wrong apartment to rob tonight, my friend."

"Oh, we're not friends, Dawson." The man chuckled. "Not even close."

Gabe's lamp turned back on, and it took a millisecond for his eyes to adjust. Even then, he couldn't believe what he was seeing.

Sitting in his favorite recliner as if he didn't have a care in the world was the man Bravo Team had been itching to find.

"Hello, Gabriel." Adrian Walker tipped his head. "It's been a while."

What the actual fuck?

Gabe's finger slid down to his trigger as he took a large, advancing step toward the traitorous bastard. "What the hell are you doing in my apartment?"

"Now that was almost *exactly* how I imagined this little reunion playing out."

Arrogant bastard.

Gabe took another step closer. "I'm about two seconds away from putting a fucking hole in the middle of your forehead, so I suggest you cut through the bullshit and tell me why you're here."

"Ellena."

The name was like a physical blow. One that nearly sent Gabe stumbling backward.

Terror for the woman who would forever own his heart filled him with an icy cold.

Gabe's trigger finger twitched, his voice turning low. Deadly. "What did you just say?"

"You heard me, Dawson."

Slowly, Walker pushed himself to his feet. The second he did Gabe took two, large strides across the carpeted floor, nearly covering the distance between them.

Gabe's next warning escaped as a deadly hiss between his teeth. "Don't you fucking move, or I swear to *God* I will pull this trigger."

"Easy, Dawson." The other man put his palms up. "I'm not on the job. On the contrary, I came because I have information that I know will interest you."

"Why did you say her name?" Gabe bit out sharply.

"Because she's in trouble. And the man after her, well...he plays for keeps."

Another unexpected blow that left Gabe's mind whirling. "Why should I believe you? You're a goddamn traitor. A killer for hire who's aided in the abduction and near murder of *two* of my teammates' wives." Walker had also shot and nearly killed two of Gabe's men. "Now you break into my apartment and try to tell me my—"

"Guilty on all counts," the man interrupted with a shrug. "I can assure you it was pure coincidence that my professional path crossed with your team on those other two occasions. But this time, it's different."

"Different how?"

"The man after your Ellena?" Walker's brown eyes darkened. "He's a special kind of twisted."

The ice in Gabe's veins melted as a heated fury took over. Schooling his expression, he swallowed that damn fear and said, "I want a name."

"Go to her, Dawson." Adrian ignored the request—and Gabe's gun—and started for the door. "She needs your protection."

With his mind filled with a whole slew of what-the-fucks, Gabe's reaction to the other man walking away was slightly delayed.

Turning around, he and his gun caught up with Walker. "I said don't move!"

"You won't shoot me." The cocky fuck was almost to the door.

"What makes you so sure?"

Walker sighed loudly, his body shifting to face him even as he was reaching for the doorknob. "One, you're a fucking Boy Scout. Yes, I'm in your apartment uninvited, but I haven't touched you or made any threats toward you. Hell I'm not even armed."

"My ass."

No way a guy like Adrian Walker goes anywhere without at *least* one gun.

"Do you see a weapon?" The man smiled. "I know you, Dawson. You won't shoot an unarmed civilian without just cause. Not even me."

The fucker was right. *Goddamnit*, he was right.

"And two," Walker continued, "I still hold the answers to all those questions running around inside that brilliant brain of yours. Like how I even know about the gorgeous Doc with the long, blonde hair and adorable dimples."

"You son of a bitch!" Gabe took a step forward. He'd never had to work so hard at *not* pulling the trigger as he did in that moment.

Except that day with Campbell.

Walker glanced down at the gun now pointed at his heart and smirked. "See? I know you won't shoot me, because you're a smart man. As the great English writer, Samuel Johnson, once said... 'curiosity is one of the most permanent and certain characteristics of a vigorous intellect.' And you and your team are some of the most vigorous men I know."

"Why bother to even come here if all you're going to do is speak in fucking riddles?"

"You a card player, Dawson? First rule of poker, never show the other players your cards until the hand's over." Walker opened the door and faced him again. "I give you everything now, you probably *will* kill me. At the very least, you'll turn me over to the authorities. Not that I could blame you. But either one of those happens before we talk again, you'll lose your chance at ever learning what I know."

"You've already told me someone's after Ellena. Why do I need you for anything else?"

Adrian's lips curled up into a smug grin. "Because I know who is after her and why. The knowledge she has will help you and your team stop them, but you need to get to her soon." He glanced at his watch. "It may already be too late."

The man vanished, then, leaving Gabe alone in his apartment to try to make sense of what had just transpired.

You let the asshole go. That's what happened.

"Fuck!" Gabe slammed the palm of his hand against the door. His chest rose and fell with heaving breaths, his booming voice echoing through the modest space.

He had him. He fucking *had* him. What the hell had he been thinking?

You were thinking about keeping Ellena safe.

From the moment Walker uttered her name, Gabe hadn't been able to think of anything else.

His instinct to protect her had always been strong. It was that same innate need to keep her safe that had been the driving force behind his decision to leave her.

But now...

If Walker was telling the truth—and Gabe's gut said the asshole was—Ellena was in danger. Again.

He was well aware that this could all be part of some big, elaborate set-up to take him and the rest of Bravo Team down, but he couldn't think about that now.

All he was worried about...all he *cared* about...was the woman he'd spent the last three years trying to forget.

I need to call her!

Praying she still had the same number, Gabe shoved his gun back into his waistband and pulled his phone from his jean's pocket. Muscle memory took over as he dialed the number he hadn't called in ages.

It started to ring.

He waited.

It rang again.

Come on, baby. Pick up!

It rang a third time and then, "You've reached the voicemail of Dr. Ellena Dawson." Gabe's chest tightened, her sweet voice stealing every ounce of oxygen in his lungs. "I'm unable to come to the phone right now, but if you'll leave your name, number, and a brief message, I'll return your call as soon as possible. If this is a medical or mental health emergency, please hang up and dial nine-one-one."

Gabe held his breath. As he waited for the beep, he tried not to think about the fact that these would be the first words she'd hear from him since he'd walked away from her years before.

"Take care of yourself, Elle. I'll see you in my dreams."

That was the last thing he'd said to her. It was what he always told her when his SEAL team would leave for an op. That and...
I love you.

But Gabe hadn't said those three little words when he'd left for the last time. Not because they weren't true. They would always be true.

Until the day I die.

Gabe had purposely chosen not to tell Ellena he loved her right before he walked away because he knew she no longer believed him.

Wrapped up in the particularly shitty memory, he nearly missed the beep's end. Gabe swallowed hard and began to speak.

"Hey, Elle. It's me." He cleared the trembling fear from his throat and spoke quickly. "Listen, I know it's been a long time, and this is going to sound crazy, but I think you're in danger." God, he hated to just blurt that shit out. Mumbling a curse, he ran a hand over his salt and pepper scruff before continuing, "I'm sorry to drop this on you out of the blue, and I promise I'm not trying to scare you, but…look, I'll explain more when I get there, okay? I'm leaving Dallas tonight, and I'll call you as soon as I land. Do me a favor and don't go anywhere. Keep your doors locked and don't answer them or the phone unless it's me. Call me when you get this." Because he knew how much she hated being bossed around, Gabe added a quick, "Please."

He barely got the message out before the phone beeped again, ending the recording. Rushing down the short hallway to his room, Gabe frantically began to pack.

Uncaring of how wrinkled his wadded-up clothes would be, he filled the large duffle with enough to last a week, along with all the necessary toiletries. He was zipping it closed when his phone began to ring.

Heart pounding, he snatched the phone from his mattress and answered it on the first ring.

"Ellena?" He was met with silence.

Frowning, Gabe held the phone away and looked at the screen. The area code matched hers, but the call was from a number he didn't recognize.

He put the phone back to his ear. "Hello?" He spoke a little louder.

"Uh, yes. Is this Gabriel Dawson?"

His heart sunk. The female voice on the other end of the call didn't belong to his Elle.

She's not yours anymore, remember?

Ignoring the annoying prick-of-a-voice, Gabe answered the woman. "That's me."

"Mr. Dawson, my name is Amy Hallowell. I'm an emergency room nurse calling from the Naval Medical Center in San Diego."

It was the same hospital where Ellena works. Except Ellena worked on the mental health floor, and this woman had said emergency room.

A ball of dread settled in Gabe's stomach. "Yes?"

"Sir, I'm calling because Ellena Dawson was brought in as a patient a few hours ago, and you are listed in her chart as the person to contact in case of an emergency."

"Is she okay?"

"Sir, Ellena was in a pretty bad car accident. She's currently unconscious and listed in serious but stable condition."

Ah, God.

Gabe grabbed his suitcase from the bed and raced down the hallway. "I'll be there as soon as I can." Walker's warning ran through his head. "Do *not* let anyone other than hospital personal in her room."

There was a pause and then, "Sir?"

"Amy, I need you to listen to me. I am a retired Master Chief Special Warfare Operator." Because she worked in a Naval hospital, she *should* understand what that meant. "Less than five minutes before you called, I was made aware of a threat to Dr. Dawson's life." He stepped out of his apartment, locked his door, and jogged to his truck. "I'm in Dallas now, but I'll be there as soon as I can. In the meantime, Ellena needs security posted outside her room. Do you understand?"

Obviously flustered, the woman attempted to respond. "I-I...um..."

Shit. He needed to make her understand. "Amy?"

"Y-yes?"

"I'm going to give you a phone number, and then I'm going to hang up. I want you to wait three minutes and call that number."

"Who am I calling?"

Gabe got into his truck and started the engine. Tires squealed loudly as he tore out of the parking lot and headed for Jake McQueen's ranch.

More specifically, the private airstrip located on his boss's property.

"The number I'm giving you is a direct line to Agent Jason Ryker with Homeland Security. I want you to tell him what's going on and that I told you to call him. He'll be able to verify who I am and that this is not a hoax or some type of prank. The threat to Ellena is very real, and I need for your hospital to take it seriously." He rattled off Ryker's number. "I'm going to hang up now, Amy. Please. Call the number. Ask for Agent Ryker. He'll take care of the rest."

Gabe started to end the call when he heard the nurse's voice again.

"Wait!"

Shit. "Yeah?"

"How will I know this man really is a Homeland agent?"

"Trust me. You'll know."

There was another short pause and then, "What exactly is your relationship to the patient?"

Gabe swallowed before answering, "Ellena's my wife."

CHAPTER 2

"You're *married?*"

Feeling like a doomed man facing a firing squad, Gabe stared back at his boss and his team. With his hands shoved deep inside his denim pockets, he stood in front of the large, stone fireplace and blew out a breath.

"Yeah, Carter." Gabe nodded to the former Naval Intelligence officer. "I'm married."

"Whoa." Nathan Carter, Bravo Team's technical analyst, looked like a cartoon character as he blinked his wide eyes and plopped down onto the leather couch.

"Holy shit." Kole looked just as surprised. "I don't...I don't even know what to say to that."

"Nothing to say," Gabe told the young sniper who was sitting next to Nate.

"Oh, there's plenty to say, Dawson." With a shake of his head, Zade grunted. "I'm just trying to decide where to start."

Gabe looked over at Zade, who was sitting in one of the room's two leather recliners. The former Marine lifted his ballcap and ran a hand through his short, dark hair before readjusting the hat back into its rightful place.

"Tell me about it," Matt spoke up from the recliner positioned on the opposite side of the cozy space. "Between that major bomb drop and Walker showing back up, I've got so many what-the-fucks going through my head right now, I can't even think of a response."

Matt's confusion wasn't unexpected, given the white lie Gabe told his teammate months before. An elaborate excuse for why he and Ellena were no longer together.

Fuck!

"There's a first," Nate teased the other man.

Nate wasn't wrong. As a former Pararescueman and Bravo Team's medic, Matt was as badass as they came. He was also a total smartass who always seemed to have some sort of quippy comment ready and waiting.

He now also knew his team leader was a damn liar.

On a major time crunch, Gabe nodded. "I'm married. So what? It's really not a big deal."

"Oh, it's *such* a big deal." Matt stared back at him.

Gabe gave him a look that said they'd sort their shit out later.

"Turner's right, Dawson." Nate gave Gabe a pointed look. "How is it this never came up in conversation?"

"Seriously, man," Zade agreed. "I mean, we've had how many weddings between the four of us so far? Not *once* have you ever mentioned having a wife of your own."

"Because we're not together anymore," Gabe bit out harshly. Pulling his hands free from his pockets, he ran one over his scruff-covered jaw and blew out a breath. "Look, I get that you guys are probably pissed that I didn't tell you about Elle before now, but we can hash that shit out later. Right now, I need you to focus on the possible threat to her, and I need to get my ass to San Diego."

"He's right," Jake spoke up. Standing between the edge of the couch and the recliner Zade was in, their boss rested his hands on his hips and addressed the entire group. "We all know what kind of man Adrian Walker is, and what he's capable of."

"He's a fucking traitor," Matt spit out the words, his focus now off of Gabe's previous deception and onto the man in question.

"And kidnapper," Nate added angrily.

Zade's expression hardened. "Don't forget cold-blooded murderer."

Each of the three men had a personal connection to the former Marine. Matt and Walker had been working on the same Fleet Anti-terrorism Security Team—or FAST—when Walker vanished. After a lengthy search, the military assumed he'd gone AWOL. It wasn't until later that they discovered the bastard had actually switched sides.

Working for the highest bidder, Walker had played an intricate part in the kidnapping of Gracie, R.I.S.C.'s office manager and Nate's wife.

The fucker had shot Nate before handing Gracie over to a bastard who'd nearly killed her. A few months later, Walker showed up again when he kidnapped Matt's wife, Katherine, and shot Zade and left him for dead.

Thankfully both of Gabe's men pulled through, and with the help of a kick-ass Delta team, Bravo was able to bring both women back home safely.

Now the fucker was back and this time his woman was the one being threatened.

You keep forgetting she's not yours, Dawson. Not anymore.

"Adrian Walker is all of those things and more." Jake's voice drew Gabe's attention back to the topic at hand. "Most importantly, the man is smart. He doesn't do anything without purpose, which means we have to assume what he said about Dawson's wife is true."

Nausea filled Gabe's gut for what felt like the millionth time since Walker had mentioned Ellena's name. "Ellena and I…" He started to explain but stopped to swallow down the knot of regret filling his throat. "We've been separated three years, and our divorce will be finalized soon." The thought clawed its way into his broken heart. "But she's still—"

"Important," Zade finished for him. The man gave him a knowing glance. "We get it, Gabe."

"We all do," Nate chimed in.

Looking around at the other men in the room, Gabe realized his teammates were right. At one time or another, every single man staring back at him had lived with the woman they loved being threatened.

And every single one of them was willing to die to protect the ones they loved.

Just like me.

His and Ellena's future may have been destroyed long before now, but he'd still fight death itself if that's what it took to keep her safe.

"Just tell us what you need, Gabe." Matt looked back at him solemnly. "We've got your back. No matter what."

"We all do," Jake assured him.

A new lump formed in his throat, but Gabe swallowed it down and schooled his expression. Emotions had no place in this room. Not now.

Ellena was lying in a hospital bed this very minute, and the faster they came up with a plan of action, the faster he'd be by her side.

"Okay." He gave his boss and his team a nod. "Here's what I need from you."

Less than four hours later, Jake and Gabe were landing R.I.S.C.'s company jet onto a private airstrip located in San Diego. The rest of the team had stayed behind in Dallas with orders from Gabe to be ready at a moment's notice.

From the pilot's seat, Jake turned and faced Gabe. Concern crossed over the man's dark blue eyes. "You sure you don't want me to stick around?"

Gabe shook his head and unbuckled his seatbelt. "I've got this. Besides, I think it's probably best if I ease Elle into the idea of having a bodyguard before springing an entire team on her."

The entire flight here, Jake had tried talking Gabe into going ahead and bringing in his team. Gabe understood his boss's concern. Anytime Walker came into the picture, shit usually hit the fan.

Luckily, he'd talked Jake down by pointing out the fact that if Adrian Walker wanted to hurt him, the bastard would've taken his shot earlier. The second Gabe stepped foot inside his apartment.

Despite his boss still not being too keen on the idea of dropping him off and flying back out, Jake agreed to do just that. Why? Because they were R.I.S.C., and the trust and respect they had for each other was thicker than blood.

"I don't like it, but I get it. First sign of trouble, though..."

"Don't worry. You'll be the first person I call."

"Good. In the meantime, I'll contact Ryker. See if he's heard any recent chatter involving Walker."

Jason Ryker was an agent with Homeland Security. He ran a covert team out of the Dallas branch, and was also R.I.S.C.'s handler for when they took on jobs for the agency.

"Might give Ghost a call, too. Sometimes those guys find shit out before the suits."

Keane "Ghost" Bryson was the captain of one of the best Delta Force teams in existence. He and his men were as solid as they came. They'd also been invaluable assets in the rescue missions involving Nate's, Matt's, and Zade's women.

And if that right there isn't a reason to keep Elle away from my world...

If Gabe didn't know any better, he'd think the men of Bravo were destined to fall in love with women in peril. Just another example of why he'd made the right choice to walk away from Elle when he did.

"Good idea," Jake agreed. "I'll put feelers out with them both and let you know what I find out."

With a firm handshake and a nod, Gabe thanked his boss for the ride and exited the plane. He wasn't sure when the formidable man had found the time, but the guy had even arranged for a cab to be waiting when they landed, ready to take him straight to the hospital.

For the entire duration of the drive, Gabe's mind was filled with a lifetime of memories. Both good and bad, they were all moments he'd shared with the woman he was about to see.

Moments he'd never forget.

"Sir?"

The gravelly voice snapped Gabe's attention back to the

present. From the back seat, he met the driver's gaze in the rearview mirror.

"Sorry, what?"

The man pointed toward something outside. "I said, we're here."

Gabe turned to look out his window. The sight of the large, brick building caused a familiar ache to spread painfully inside his chest.

The last time he was here had been the beginning of the end.

Pushing the past away, Gabe dug some cash from his wallet and paid the driver. Sliding his way out of the car, he grabbed his bag from the leather seat and shut the door.

Huge red letters shone brightly over the hospital's emergency entrance. After a moment's hesitation, Gabe sucked up his pride and headed for the automatic doors.

His Ellena was in there, somewhere. And she needed him.

She's not fucking yours, Dawson. Get that through your thick skull.

The tiny voice was right, but Gabe knew it didn't matter. He had always thought of her as his. Always would.

Which was why he'd dropped everything to come here.

For reasons he still didn't understand, Adrian Walker had broken into his apartment for the sole purpose of telling him Elle was in danger. Less than five minutes later, the phone call came about the accident.

If it really was an accident.

Either way, Gabe was bound and determined to find out what the hell was going on with his estranged wife. But first things first...

I need to make sure she's okay.

It was going to be hard as fuck to see her again. To see and hear her again. To not touch her.

To not be able to hold her and tell her how much I missed her.

How much he still loved her.

That ship hadn't just sailed. The fucking thing was drifting a world away, far out of his desperate reach.

But there was still one thing Gabe could do for her—one

thing he'd always do—and that was protect her. So he'd focus on doing that.

Nothing more. Nothing less.

Not that he really had a choice in the matter. Even if he wanted to try and mend what he'd torn apart, it was clear Elle wanted nothing to do with him.

The papers he received two days ago were proof of that.

With that in mind, he put on the mask he was so good at wearing, lifted the strap of his large duffle over one shoulder, and walked through the doors and straight to the patient check-in desk.

He must not have controlled his emotions as well as he thought, however, because the young nurse sitting behind the table appeared alarmed when she spotted him.

Wide, round eyes stared up at him from behind the glass. "M-may I help you?"

"Ellena Dawson."

The woman's eyes grew a bit rounder at his gruff tone. "I take it she's a patient of ours?"

No shit.

Doing his best to stay calm and not scare the girl even more, Gabe bit back the smart-ass retort and nodded. "Dr. Dawson was brought in a few hours ago. I'm listed as her emergency contact. My name is—"

"Gabe!"

He swung his head around in search of whoever had just said his name. His chest tightened a bit when he spotted a familiar face.

Wearing a pair of light blue scrubs, Jenna Shaw—an emergency room nurse and Ellena's best friend—hurried toward him.

"I was told you were coming."

"Hey, Jenna."

Without hesitation, the woman reached out and wrapped her arms around his waist. She pulled him in for a tight hug.

It felt a bit awkward given the situation, but Jenna had always been a hugger. She'd also been a friend of his, too, back when he and Elle were still together.

"Hey, Jenna." Gabe gave her a little squeeze before pulling away. "How is she?"

She stepped back and dropped her arms at her sides. "Conscious, thank goodness. She took a pretty good knock to the head and her left shoulder had to be put back into place. But her vitals are stable, and she's coherent and responsive." The sweet nurse exhaled loudly, her concern for her friend obvious. "She was lucky."

"What happened?"

"We don't know for sure."

"What the hell do you mean you don't know?" Gabe demanded as he readjusted the bag's strap.

Jenna crossed her arms at her chest and shrugged. "Elle doesn't remember anything about the accident."

His brows rose. "Nothing?"

She shook her head. "She remembers heading to work this morning, but the rest is a blur."

Muttering a curse, Gabe ran his free hand over his jaw. "Was there another car involved?"

"It was a hit and run." The other woman rolled her lips inward, looking nearly as pissed as Gabe felt. "I have a friend who works for SDPD. He said the report points to someone running a stop sign, t-boning Elle's car on the driver's side, and then taking off. The officers who worked the accident blew it off as some punk who either had a warrant for their arrest, was drunk, or just didn't want to stick around for the ticket."

He didn't miss the underlying tone of her voice or the frustration in her green eyes.

"You think there's more to it."

With her long, red ponytail swishing from side to side, Jenna looked around as if checking to see if they had an audience. The waiting room was surprisingly sparse, but the nurse behind the desk was unabashedly staring up at them.

Noticing this, Jenna grabbed his elbow and led them both away. "Come on." Her long legs moved quickly. "We can talk on the way up to her room."

More than ready to see with his own eyes that Ellena was in fact okay, Gabe followed the woman without argument.

When the first of the two elevators opened, a couple with a young child who'd been waiting stepped inside. Gabe started to get on but stopped when Jenna pulled on his arm.

She shook her head. "We'll take the next one."

Seeing that there was more than enough room for them all to fit, he looked back at Jenna questioningly.

"Trust me, the conversation we need to have should be a private one."

Jenna had worked in the Naval Medical Center's emergency room for as long as he'd known her. She was smart, funny, and had been there for Ellena when he couldn't be.

When you should've been.

Ignoring the direction in which his thoughts seemed hell-bent on traveling, Gabe listened to the woman and waited.

Her insisted privacy did nothing to ease the massive ball of worry settling in his gut. But Gabe knew she must have her reasons for wanting to wait to discuss whatever was going on with Ellena.

Finally, after what seemed like an eternity, the second elevator opened. He released the breath he'd been holding when he saw there was no one else waiting.

Thank fuck.

The minute the doors closed, Gabe turned to Jenna.

"Okay, talk."

Despite her obvious need to share, a slight trepidation seeped into her suddenly unsure gaze. "Elle's gonna kill me if she finds out I told you any of this, so you can't let on that you know."

The fuck? "Know what?"

"I'm serious, Gabe." Jenna crossed her arms tightly at her chest. Determination replaced her brief uncertainty as she stared up at him. "The only reason I'm sharing this with you is because I'm really worried about her."

His stomach fell, and his brow furrowed. "But you just said she was going to be okay."

"I'm not talking about what happened." Jenna shook her

head. "I mean, I guess I am, but..." Trailing off, she bit her bottom lip as if she were contemplating some big, important decision. "Promise you won't tell her I told you?"

Hanging on by a thread, Gabe drew in a slow, deep breath and prayed for patience. He let it out slowly as he tried to not bite the well-meaning woman's head off. "Jenna, just tell me what you know."

After a second's worth of hesitation, his wife's friend blurted out, "I think someone's after Elle." She licked her lips and added, "And, after what happened today, I'm pretty sure they're trying to kill her."

Smacking his palm against the elevator's emergency stop button, he brought the moving cart to an abrupt halt. Despite Walker's ominous warning, Jenna's words sent an entirely new rush of fear coursing through his system.

Not wanting to add to Jenna's obvious concern, Gabe kept what he knew to himself and calmly asked, "What makes you say that?"

Jenna's knowing eyes studied his. "You don't seem surprised. Am I right? Is someone really after Elle."

His refusal to neither confirm nor deny was all the answer his wife's intelligent friend needed.

"*Damnit!*" Jenna huffed out a breath. The tips of her ponytail flung from side to side as she shook her head with frustration. "I knew I should've called you sooner."

Okay, so that *did* shock him. "Why me?"

"Um...hellooo." She looked up at him as if he'd lost his mind. "You're a freaking SEAL."

"Former SEAL."

"Whatever." Jenna waived his clarifying words away. "All that alpha male hero stuff is engrained in guys like you forever. Which is why your stubborn wife *should* have called you the first time someone tried to hurt her. But you know Elle. No matter how hard I tried to get her to call you, she wouldn't—"

"First time?" Gabe exclaimed loudly. Placing his hands on his hips, he frowned. "Has something like this happened before?"

"Not like this. I mean, it's the first time she's actually gotten hurt, but it's not the first accident Elle's had. Not that I believe for a second either incident was an accident. Although she refuses to—"

"Jenna!" Gabe's voice boomed inside the confined space. He waited until he was sure she'd finished rambling, then in a quiet, gentler tone said, "Take a breath and tell me what the fuck's been going on with my wife."

Despite his angry outburst, Jenna didn't so much as flinch. Unlike most women he came across, she'd never been intimidated by his size or gruffness.

It was probably why she and Elle got along so well. They were both strong, confident women who didn't take shit from anyone.

They were also both stubborn as hell.

Glancing toward the emergency button, she raised a brow before looking back at him. "You know, that won't keep us locked in here forever."

"Then I guess you'd better talk fast."

Jenna smiled wide. "God, I've missed you. I know Elle's going to kill me for this, but she probably won't tell you herself, and I really think it's something you need to know—"

"Jenna," Gabe warned, his patience damn close to becoming non-existent.

"Okay, here it is. A couple weeks ago Elle called and asked me to meet her for lunch. When I got to the restaurant, I could tell right away that something was off. When I asked her what was up, she told me she felt like someone had been following her. Like they were watching her from a distance or something."

Two fucking weeks ago.

Jesus.

Gabe kept his expression the same and said, "Go on."

"By the end of lunch, Elle had convinced herself it was nothing more than stress-induced paranoia. Or something like that. Whatever shrinky term she used, I wasn't buying it. Then two days ago, she was riding her bike on the Old Mill trail. Which by the way, I told her not to do alone anymore. You remember that place, right? Anyway, she was riding along like she always does when her tire blew out."

"Was she hurt?"

"No, but only because she got really lucky."

"Lucky how?"

She frowned. "It happened right before the bridge, Gabe."

Gabe did remember the trail. He and Elle had ridden it together several times back in the day. He also remembered the bridge Jenna was referring to.

It was the only one on the long, gravel path. A hundred feet below it was a shallow, rocky creek bed. If Elle had fallen over the drop-off near the bridge's edge…

Sonofabitch.

"Thankfully, Elle managed to keep control of the bike long enough to get herself to the railing," Jenna continued. "Otherwise, she would've gone off the edge of the trail and fallen down that steep-ass embankment to the creek below."

He ran his fingers through his hair and thought a moment. "Okay, I'll agree she was damn lucky, but bikes blow tires all the time, Jenna."

"They do." The petite redhead agreed. "Lord knows I've had my fair share of flats over the years. The thing is, this was different than any other ruined tires I've seen in the past."

"How so?"

"Elle called me after she got home. She tried to play it off, but I could tell she was still a little shaky. I stopped by her place to make sure she really was okay." Jenna licked her lips nervously. "I looked at the bike, Gabe. The tube inside had clearly blown out, but there was a small, almost perfect hole in the sidewall. The edges of it looked melted, like something hot had punctured it.

Small hole. Melted edges…

His heart slammed hard against his ribs. "You think someone took a shot at Elle?"

Jenna gave a slight shrug, but he could see the answer behind her emerald eyes. "I don't know what to think. But you know Elle better than anyone. She's one of the most cautious women out there, and in a few days' time she's had two 'accidents.'" The woman made air quotes. "And either one could've easily been fatal."

When he didn't immediately respond, Elle's friend tilted her head as if to study him a moment. "Is that why you came so quickly? Did you already know someone was after her?

Shit. The last thing he needed was for Jenna to worry even more than she already was. That happened, and she was bound to say something to Elle before he had the chance to explain what was going on.

Not that I even know what the hell is going on.

But he would and soon. No one fucked with his woman and got away with it.

She's not...

"I got a call saying my wife was in a fucking car wreck," he interrupted his own pointless thought. "The nurse said Elle was hurt, and she'd been taken to the hospital. *That's* why I'm here."

Jenna's lips curled into a slow, knowing smile.

"What?" Gabe asked, confused by her reaction to his gruffness.

"You called her your wife."

"We're still technically married, Jenna." He blew her comment off.

"Only because you don't have the balls to sign the papers," she unabashedly called him out on his bullshit.

Another similarity the woman had with his...with Ellena.

"And"—she added with a knowing expression—"there's never been anything *technical* between the two of you, and you know it."

Well fuck. "She uh..." Gabe cleared his throat. "She told you she filed for divorce?"

"Of course." She grinned. "Elle tells me everything."

The corners of his mouth turned upward. "Glad to see some things haven't changed."

"If you look closely enough, I think you'll find there's a lot that hasn't changed."

Gabe stared back at the sassy woman. "And here, I thought Elle was the shrink."

Jenna chuckled. "Maybe being friends with her all these years has caused some of her shrinkness to rub off on me."

"Yeah well, don't get any bright ideas about the two of us. I'm just here to make sure she's okay. Besides, I'm pretty sure she'll try to kick my ass out of her room the second she sees me."

"*Try* being the operative word in that sentence." One of her auburn brows arched high. "And you'd better not even think about letting her get away with it. You do, I'll kick your ass."

"Don't worry." Gabe reached out and pressed the emergency button. As the elevator began to move again, he stared back at his wife's closest friend.

"I think you're right. I think someone's trying to hurt Elle, and I'm not going anywhere until I find the son of a bitch."

"And then?"

Looking as serious as he'd ever been, Gabe vowed, "I'm going to end them."

CHAPTER 3

Ellena was dreaming again. She had to be. Her dreams were the only place she could still hear *his* voice.

She usually had no problems finding him. She'd simply close her eyes, fall asleep, and Gabe would be there. But something about this time was different.

The subtle spice of Gabe's intoxicating scent was much stronger than in dreams past, and his deep, familiar voice reverberated through her system. It was all so real, almost as if he were actually near.

But why can't I see him?

At first, dreaming of Gabe had been her favorite pastime, but it hadn't taken long for Ellena to resent her longing, subconscious mind.

Some nights her dreams were filled with smiles and laughter, while others brought with them all the love and passion she'd been living without for the past three years.

Nights like those were both a blessing and a curse. A stark reminder of what she'd once had…and all that she'd lost.

Then there were the nightmares. They occurred less often now, but occasionally, the haunting memories of her past still managed to slither their way in.

No matter which kind—good dreams or bad—Ellena always found her way to him. Then the inevitable would happen and she'd wake up. When she did, Ellena always felt even more empty and lost than before.

The truth was, most days—despite the fact that she was a successful, respected psychologist and self-sufficient woman—Ellena felt as though she were living half a life. Simply going through the motions while she waited for the universe to right itself again.

Deep down, she knew that was never going to happen. Something that had taken her nearly three years to accept.

In that time, she used her knowledge and energy to focus on other people's problems rather than her own.

It was a classic avoidance tactic, but whatever worked, right?

At least she loved her job. Not many people could say that.

Helping people, especially those who'd risked their lives for their country was the most satisfying career imaginable.

In many ways, being a counseling psychologist for the military was cathartic for her, as well. Helping the men and women in her care reminded Ellena that her problems weren't all that significant.

Not compared to theirs, anyway.

"I think she's waking up."

Gabe's voice reached her ears once more. He sounded so close.

So real.

The meds the doctors had given her when she'd woken up earlier—after they'd nearly poked and prodded her to death—were still weighing her down. Desperate to see his handsome face at least once before she woke up, Ellena tried following the sound through the dense fog.

She wanted to scream with frustration.

For the first couple of years after Gabe left, Ellena had *lived* for her dreams. She'd watched the clock incessantly, counting down the hours to those few, stolen moments with him.

Moments that only existed in her head.

It was a pathetic excuse for a life, but thankfully, with the help of her own therapist, she'd finally started coming to terms with reality.

Her husband wasn't coming back.

In her head, she understood it was time to move on. Her heart, however, was having a much harder time letting go of the dream that he'd return. A dream only she wished would come true.

Maybe you're not the only one.

No, she couldn't go there. Not again. Her future with Gabe died a long time ago, and if she didn't stop holding on to the past, she'd never have any kind of future.

So why hasn't he sent the papers back yet?

Ignoring the voice determined to sabotage her need to move on, Ellena gave up the search and opened her eyes.

Just like when she'd first woken up after the accident—she had no idea how long ago that had been—everything in the dimly lit room appeared fuzzy. The hospital's familiar antiseptic smell mixed with Gabe's lingering, masculine scent.

Great. Now I'm smelling him even after I've woken up.

Elle blinked several times, frowning when she saw the person sitting in the chair to her right.

"Shouldn't you be working?" Her voice sounded rough from sleep.

Jenna smiled back at her. "My shift ended forty-five minutes ago."

"So why are you still here?"

Her best friend shrugged in that casual, laid-back way of hers. "I wanted to come by and check on you. How do you feel?"

"Tired." Ellena glanced down at the gray sling holding her arm in place. "Shoulder's sore and a little achy, but my head no longer feels like it's going to explode, so that's something, at least." Grunting, she began scooting herself up the noisy mattress and moving the bed into a more upright position.

Jenna shot to her feet. "Here, let me help."

"I've got it," Ellena insisted, already sitting up straighter. She glanced at the clock on the wall in front of her and frowned. "It's really late, Jen. You should go home and get some rest."

"I see that bump on your head did nothing to ease your stubbornness."

Ellena scowled at her equally stubborn friend who was in the process of settling back down into one of the room's two plastic chairs. "Independence does not equal stubbornness, you know. I'm just..." She cut herself off, confused when she spotted the man standing outside the room. "Is that a security guard by my door?"

Jenna gave her an unapologetic nod. "It is."

Ellena exhaled loudly. "I know you mean well, Jen, but I told you before. No one is after me. This was an accident. Plain and simple."

"I know that's what *you* think." Jenna added a mumbled, "Even though you can't remember anything that happened."

Ignoring that last bit, Ellena gave her friend a look. "Well if you know that, then why did you request a guard to be posted outside my room?"

"I-I didn't."

The sudden change in Jenna's demeanor gave Ellena pause, but she blew it off. Hating how the lingering effects of the drugs were still muddling her thoughts, she asked, "Then who requested the—"

"I did."

The breath in Ellena's lungs froze, and she could feel her eyes growing wide as she stared back at her friend. A friend who now looked like the Cheshire cat after eating a big, fat mouse.

No.

At first, Ellena was sure she'd imagined the voice. That it was some sort of drug-induced conscious dream stemming from her earlier thoughts.

But then she saw Jenna's eyes shift to something to Elle's left, and she knew.

"Hello, Ellena."

Oh, God.

This wasn't some medication-induced hallucination nor was it a figment of her imagination. It was the voice from her dreams, only this time, she was very much awake.

Ellena started to swing her head around, but the movement

—and the man she now realized was standing in the shadows by her room's large window—made her dizzy.

She closed her eyes and waited for the nauseating wave to pass. When she opened them again, she met a worried gaze.

"Are you okay?" Gabe asked, sounding genuinely concerned.

"Gabe?" She'd whispered his name with utter disbelief because, holy shit.

He's actually here.

Stepping out of the shadows and into the dim light, the man who'd once vowed to stay with her forever stared down at her. "Hi."

Her heart stuttered, and her mind whirled. For a moment all she could do was stare.

In some ways, he looked exactly as she remembered. In others, it was almost as if she were staring back at a total stranger.

Physically, Gabe still looked like the same tall, handsome SEAL she'd fallen in love with years before. Even more fit than she remembered, his dark gray t-shirt stretched over a sculpted chest and a set of strong shoulders.

The same ones she'd held onto countless times while they made love.

His shirt loosened around his narrowed waist, and though she couldn't see them, Ellena knew there was still an impressive six-pack hiding behind the thin material.

Lowering her gaze, she noticed the way his taut thighs stretched a pair of well-worn jeans, and damn. Denim should *not* be that freaking sexy.

And then there was his hair.

Tearing her eyes away from his lower half—and memories of how those same legs used to press against hers as he drove himself deep inside her greedy body—Ellena found a bit more salt in his short, dark tresses and trimmed beard than was there before.

The frustratingly handsome man could've coined the phrase 'silver fox', and for some reason, the thought made her want to cross her arms and stomp her feet like an angry child.

Good thing you've got a sling and a hospital bed to stop you because that would be very embarrassing.

Okay, so her thoughts may be a little higher on the pity-party scale than usual but come *on*. The guy could've at least made this a little easier on her by going bald and gaining a couple hundred pounds.

Not that she ever thought that would happen.

Gabriel Dawson had always been handsome and fit, but staring into his dark eyes now, Ellena realized he'd somehow become even *more* attractive over the last few years.

It was something she would've sworn was impossible. It was also ridiculously unfair and frustrating as hell.

There was one thing, however, that was exactly as she remembered.

Something that had nothing to do with his body or hair. Something that made her heart hurt for him. For *them*.

It was there, dulling his perfect, gorgeous eyes.

Despite his having been a big, bad Navy SEAL, Gabe's dark chocolate eyes had always been filled with his passion for life...and his love for her. But that was before.

All Ellena saw now was the same closed-off expression he'd worn the day he told her he was leaving. The one that screamed 'Keep Out'.

As memories of the past collided with his being here, now, Ellena's stuttering mind tried to make sense of what she was seeing.

This wasn't some pointless dream or fantasy. It was real. After all this time, Gabe had finally come home.

What she didn't understand was why?

For years, Ellena had prayed for his return. She'd begged God to bring him back to her and make the sexy, strong protector see that what happened all those years ago wasn't his fault.

From the guarded look on his face, she knew instantly that wasn't the case. So why *was* he here?

Is it possible?

Her heart beat a little harder, the incessant beeping in the background picked up its pace.

Had her accident finally snapped him out of whatever self-imposed hell he'd sentenced himself to three years ago, or was it something else?

The papers.

The thought hit with a crushing blow. Of course, that's why he was here. He came to finalize the divorce.

If she wasn't already sporting a shiny new gash there, Ellena would've face-palmed herself right in the middle of her forehead.

You know, Doc. For such a brilliant woman, you really can be an idiot.

"Elle?" Gabe took a hesitant step forward but stopped before he got too close. His dark brows turned inward with concern. "Sweetheart, what is it? Are you hurting? Do we need to get the nurse to bring you more pain meds?"

His barrage of questions, along with the alarm in his voice, snapped her out of the emotional delusion. Part of her couldn't help but relish in the fact that he was so worried after all this time.

The other part wanted to tell him to go to hell.

Gabe had no right to be concerned about her well-being or any other aspect of her life. Not anymore.

He gave up that right the day he walked out the door and never looked back.

"W-what…" She cleared the crackling sound from her throat. "Why are you here?"

Of all the things she'd thought to say to him if and when the time ever came, and *that's* what she'd come up with? Seriously?

She'd thought of *so* many brilliant one-liners and smart, witty comebacks. All created during the fabricated conversations she'd imagined over the years.

While she'd stood alone in the shower, crying and missing him so much she thought she'd physically die from the pain. During her evenings and weekends when she'd be cleaning her house or folding and putting away the laundry.

Hundreds of imaginary conversations had taken place, and in every single one Ellena had said exactly what she wanted to say, when she wanted to say it.

But now that he was here, in the flesh, all she'd come up with was 'Why are you here'?

The only solace she had was that Gabe looked even more uncomfortable than she felt.

Serves him right.

He shoved his hands into his pockets, his troubled stare remaining locked with hers. "The hospital called. Apparently, I'm still listed as your emergency contact."

God, she'd missed that voice. Just hearing it again was almost enough to make her want to...

Wait. *What?*

"No, you're not." Confused, Ellena slid her gaze back to Jenna's. "You are."

The hospital updated their entire system a few months ago requiring all employees to re-enter their information. Including emergency contacts.

Changing hers to Jenna had been the second official step Ellena had taken in her attempt to move on from her failed marriage. The first step had been taking off her wedding rings, which had nearly shattered her.

"No one called me." Jenna shrugged innocently.

Too innocently?

"A nurse named Amy Hollowell called." Gabe's deep voice rumbled through the tense air. "Told me you'd been in a car accident."

Ellena knew Amy. She was a good nurse and a sweet girl. Still...

I'll have to have a little talk with Miss Hollowell.

"She shouldn't have bothered you." Ellena forced herself to look back at him. The fingers on her good hand fidgeted with the sheet covering her lower body. "I'm sorry you came all this way for nothing."

"She didn't bother me, Elle, and you're sure as hell not 'nothing.'" His Adam's apple bobbed with a hard swallow. "I'm glad the nurse called me."

A familiar fluttering swirled inside her lower belly, but she ignored it. "Why is that?"

His dark brows turned inward. "Why am I glad?"

"Yes." It wasn't like he'd cared enough to check up on her before now.

The wrinkles in his forehead deepened even further as he inched closer. "The nurse said the wreck was bad."

"I'm fine."

"You were unconscious."

"I said I'm *fine*," she repeated herself sternly, praying he'd believe her and go away.

These past few years without him had been hard. Almost unbearable, at times.

But what Ellena hadn't realized—what she had no way of knowing until this exact moment—was that seeing him again would be so much worse.

Gabe crossed his muscular arms, the American Flag tattoo covering the upper half of his left arm bulging with the movement. Raising an arrogant brow, he stared down at her but remained silent.

Memories of the way she used to lazily trace that tattoo with her fingertips flashed through her mind's eye. As quickly as the images formed, Elle was blinking them away and focusing instead on the look he was still giving her.

It was the same one he'd always gotten when he knew he was right. And just like when they were still together, Ellena found herself defenseless against it.

She sighed loudly. "I have a mild concussion and my shoulder will be sore for a few days. But that's all."

"That's *all?*" Both of his brows arched high.

"Yes, Gabriel. That's all." She shifted on the uncomfortable mattress, refusing to wince when she accidentally tweaked her bad shoulder. "Look, I appreciate you coming all this way to check on me, but unless there's another reason you're here, there's really no need for you to—"

"There is," he cut her off. "Another reason."

A sliver of hope left her heart thumping, but it was almost instantly replaced with a mound of disappointment that shouldn't exist. After all, she was the one who filed for divorce.

Finally making it official was a good thing. The *best* thing, really.

At least that's what she'd been telling herself ever since she'd first spoken with her lawyer.

"Right. Of course." Pushing away the confusing onslaught of emotions, Ellena lifted her chin and forced herself to appear aloof. "If you just want to leave the papers with me, I'll make sure everything is taken care of."

A look she couldn't decipher crossed over him briefly. "This isn't about the papers."

"You didn't bring them with you?"

"Nope."

The same blasted hope returned, creating a sudden sense of anger. Damn it, she was *trying* to move the hell on, already. He clearly wanted nothing to do with her, so...

"Why didn't you bring them?" Ellena demanded to know.

His expression intensified. "I had other things on my mind."

"Like what?"

He scoffed. "Like wondering whether or not you were going to be okay."

It was her turn to raise a brow. "You expect me to believe you were so worried about me you didn't think to grab them before flying all this way?"

"Yes." He dropped his arms to the side, moving close enough he was almost right next to the mattress. Gabe looked her square in the eye when he said, "That's exactly what I expect you to believe."

Ellena took a moment to study him. He was worried about her, sure, but her gut said there was more to his being here than he was letting on.

"Why are you really here, Gabriel?"

His eyes darkened, just like they used to when she'd use his full name. He slid a quick glance in Jenna's direction, but when his gaze found hers again, the cold shield that was there before had returned.

"Tell me about the bike."

"How did you…" Ellena felt nauseated as the disappointing realization finally settled in.

He may not be here to put an end to their estranged marriage, but he wasn't here to fix it, either. In typical Gabe fashion, he thought she was in trouble and had swooped in to save the day.

The man was nothing if not protective.

It was like he seriously couldn't help himself. If someone needed the kind of protection he could offer—especially a damsel he believed to be in distress—Gabriel Dawson didn't hesitate to rush in and save them.

His alpha heroism was as engrained in him as breathing.

If Ellena was being perfectly honest, it was also one of the many reasons she'd loved him.

You still love him.

Ignoring the useless thought, she turned to her friend. "You told him, didn't you?"

"Gosh." Jenna stood and smiled back at her with a little too much enthusiasm. The other woman made it a point to glance at the clock. "You know, you were right. It's really late, and I have to work again tomorrow, so I really should be going."

"Jenna," Ellena warned.

"As you, yourself pointed out earlier, I've been working all day and…" Her friend feigned an exaggerated yawn. "Man, I'm beat."

More pieces of the crazy reality she'd woken up in began falling into place.

Gabe being called instead of Jenna.

His knowing about the bike.

The guard outside her door.

I'm going to strangle her. "Oh, no you don't." Elle gave her friend a stern look. "You're not leaving here until you tell me the truth about what's going on."

With an innocent tilt of her head, Jenna asked, "What do you mean, sweetie?"

"Don't you sweetie me. I know very good and well that *you* are listed as my emergency contact person because I changed that when we got our new system a couple of months back. Not to mention, the only way Gabe could know about what happened with the bike is if you told him, because you're the only person *I* told." Ellena's gaze bounced back and forth between her soon-to-be-ex and her frustrating best friend. "Somebody had better start talking. Now."

Looking as if he were fighting a smile, Gabe looked across the bed at Jenna. "Go on, Jen. I've got this covered."

"I'm sorry, *this*?" Ellena balked at the comment.

Gabe's eyes found hers once more. "The situation," he carefully clarified.

"There is no 'situation'. I was in a car wreck caused by a careless driver."

"From what I understand, you can't remember what caused the wreck. So there's no way you could know that."

It wasn't just the wreck. She'd nearly lost an entire day. "It was an accident Gabe. End of story."

He shrugged. "I disagree."

"Well you can disagree all you like, but that doesn't mean you're right."

Jenna interrupted their bickering with a gentle side-hug. "I'm going to give you two some time to catch up."

Despite Ellena's continued objections, her friend bid them both a goodnight with a promise to come by before her shift the next afternoon.

Seconds later, Jenna was gone and Ellena was alone in a room with her husband for the first time in what felt like forever.

For several, long seconds neither said a word, the awkward silence in the room deafening.

Part of her knew she shouldn't be so angry with him. After all, he had clearly dropped everything to come here because he thought she was in danger.

On the other hand, that was one of the biggest reasons *why* she was so upset.

While it was true Gabe didn't come to California to end their marriage, he sure as heck hadn't come here because the accident had made him realize he still loved her…as she'd first hoped.

No, the only reason he'd stormed back into her life was because he thought she needed his protection.

Didn't he get it? She didn't need nor did she want his protection. She only wanted *him*. Or at least she used to.

God, she hated feeling like this. Truth be told, Ellena didn't have a clue what she wanted, other than to not *hurt* anymore.

Unfortunately, there wasn't a medication on the market that could ease the chronic pain in her heart.

The sound of a chair scraping across the tile floor drew her attention back to the object of her frustration. Sitting next to the bed, now, Gabe leaned his elbows on his thick thighs and let his loosely connected hands hang between them.

"Look, Elle." He spoke more softly than before. "I know my being here isn't easy for you."

Um…understatement, much?

At least he didn't go on about how hard it was for him, too. He made his bed, then he left her alone in it.

"Then I'll ask you again." Ellena stared back at him. "Why are you here? And why did you arrange for a guard? I mean, I know Jenna means well, but I promise you, she's blowing my almost-bike-wreck way out of proportion. You know how she is with all her conspiracy theories."

"I'm not here because of the bike," he interrupted. "Although I do want to take a look at it later."

Gabe hesitated, then. Something the man only did when he was either nervous or about to deliver some bad news.

Great. "I know that look, Gabriel. Just say whatever it is you came here to say."

Drawing in a long, deep breath, he slowly released the air from his lungs before locking his gorgeous, tormented eyes with hers. "I have reason to believe someone is trying to kill you."

Ellena laughed, but then winced when her reaction caused

the throbbing in her head to return. "Come on, Gabe. Just because I had a couple of accidents, that doesn't mean someone's intentionally trying to hurt me."

"It's not just that." He shut down her attempt to rationalize the situation. There was another slight hesitation and then, "I had a visitor earlier tonight, Elle. Just before the hospital called. This person who came to see me is…well connected."

She started to furrow her brow, but a quick, sharp pain reminded her of the cut on her forehead. "Connected how?"

Gabe shook his head, his tone serious when he told her, "You don't want to know."

Something about the way he said it made her believe him. "Okay, so can you at least tell me what this *visitor* said?"

He started to reach out, almost as if he were going to rest his hand on her leg but stopped himself. "He told me someone very dangerous is after you."

The discontentment she felt from his not touching her was more than a little disturbing.

Refusing to let it show, she gave him an incredulous look. "And you believed him?"

His single nod and somber expression were enough to make her stomach turn. "I believe him."

A few seconds passed before Ellena responded with a head shake that reminded her she needed to stop moving her head altogether. "You realize how crazy that sounds, right?" She stared back at him. "I'm a psychologist, Gabe. I talk to them and then I go home. I sometimes stop at the grocery store on the way, and every great once in a while, when I get a wild hair or two, I meet Jenna for dinner or drinks. But for the most part, I lead a very normal life."

Some would call it a normal life. Jenna calls it sad and boring.

And she'd just admitted as much to Gabe.

Head throbbing again, Ellena didn't bother to hide her agitation when she asked the obvious question. "Who in their right mind would want me dead?"

Gabe's eyes turned cold. "I don't know yet, but I promise you I will find out." He did reach out then, his large hand resting gently on her blanket-covered thigh. "No one's going to hurt you again, Elle. You have my word."

"Gabe..."

"I wouldn't have come here if I didn't take what this man said very seriously."

The comment was a crushing reminder of the reason for his impromptu return.

"I know you wouldn't have." She forced herself to keep eye contact. "Your noticeable absence the last three years has proven that."

The flash of guilt on his face should've made her feel better. Instead, Ellena felt worse.

She really needed to get control of her emotions. Better yet, maybe she needed to make an emergency, in-hospital appointment with her own shrink.

"Sorry." Using her good hand, Ellena rubbed her fingertips along her right temple. "This is just a lot to take in. Plus my head hurts, and my arm's starting to ache again, which is making me cranky, and I..."

She stopped talking when Gabe leaned over the bed's railing and pressed the button to contact the nurse. She also stopped breathing, refusing to let his mesmerizing scent influence her in any way.

"What are you doing?"

"Getting you some more pain meds."

"I don't need more medicine. It makes me loopy."

"It will also help you rest, which is the best way for your body to heal."

Ellena barely held back the low growl building inside her chest. A lot of things may have changed between them, but Gabe's innate need to take care of her clearly hadn't.

Too bad that's no longer his job.

"Listen, Gabe. I appreciate your concern, but I don't need you coming in here and taking over everything. I've gotten along just fine on my own since you left."

"I know you have." A flash of pain filled his eyes, but it was gone as quickly as it appeared.

"And exactly how would you know that?"

He opened his mouth to respond at the same time the nurse walked in. Despite what Ellena had said to him, she found herself more than ready for those drugs to be administered into her IV.

For what seemed like forever, she'd wanted nothing more than to see him again. Now all she wanted was to get away from the frustratingly confusing man.

If a medically induced nap was going to be the only way to accomplish that, so be it.

As the cool liquid hit her veins, she nearly laughed at how unfair life could sometimes be.

After years of wishing the love of her life would come back to her, he was finally here. Still close enough to reach out and touch, even.

God, she'd wanted to. Every night since he walked out on her, Ellena had wanted nothing more than to feel his warm body next to hers.

To hold and comfort him, and to let him know he wasn't alone in his grief.

More importantly, she'd prayed for the day he'd finally accept the fact that what had happened back then wasn't his fault.

That day never came.

When the nurse left and they were alone once more, Ellena looked over to find Gabe staring back at her. Try as she might, she still couldn't read his expression.

"So what's the plan, sailor?" The naval-inspired endearment she always used to use slipped out before she'd even realized it.

Damn, those drugs work fast.

Gabe leaned a little closer. "The plan is, I stick around until I can figure out who has you in their sights and stop them before they can hurt you anymore than they already have."

Ellena gave up trying to convince him the wreck was a simple accident...for now. Instead, she asked, "What're you gonna do...be my personal...bodyguard?" Her lids were getting heavy, and her words were starting to slur.

"Pretty much."

She closed her eyes then blinked them open again. "I'm too tired...to argue about this...now." Another long blink. "Call you...tomorrow. We can...argue...then. What hotel...are you...at?"

She could've sworn he was fighting a grin. "I'm not staying at a hotel."

"Where...you...staying?"

"With you."

Whatever was in her IV must be stronger than she thought, because it *sounded* like Gabe said he was staying with her.

Frowning, Ellena forced her eyes open again. With the most serious glare she could muster, she said, "Did the nurse...give you...drugs...too?" No way was he serious.

It was hard enough being in the same *room* with him. Ellena considered herself to be a pretty strong woman in most rights, but sleeping under the same roof with Gabriel Dawson again?

That was one challenge she'd lose, hands down.

Hands down...pants down...

Gabe chuckled, the sound both sweet and painful to hear. "Close your eyes, Elle," he ordered softly. "We can discuss it later."

Ellena wanted to discuss it *now* but talking was pretty much impossible at this point. Unable to fight it any longer, she did as he said and closed her eyes.

A second later, something warm and a little wet pressed gently against her forehead. It lingered there for a moment, and somewhere in the back of her clouded mind, she recognized the sensation as a soft, sweet kiss.

The last thing Ellena heard before she relinquished herself into the narcotic bliss was Gabe's whispered voice.

"Sleep tight, sweetheart. I'll be here when you wake up."

CHAPTER 4

"Absolutely not."

Standing in Ellena's small entryway, Gabe stared back at his beautiful, determined wife. He wasn't at all surprised by her refusal to accept his idea.

Especially since they'd been having this same argument for the past several hours.

It had been two days since the accident, and this morning, after another thorough examination, her doctor had assured him she well enough to be discharged.

Gabe's focus slid up to the area near her left temple. The skin there was bruised, but the thick bandage had been replaced with a two small butterfly strips covering the cut there.

Could've been so much worse.

"Stop."

He met her gaze once more. "Stop what?"

"You heard what the doctor said, Gabe. I'm good to go, so… thanks for the ride." Offering up a forced smile, Elle looked over his shoulder at the door behind him. "Have a safe trip home."

Refusing to take the not-so-subtle hint, Gabe sat his duffle bag down onto the small section of tiled flooring next to his feet. "Like I said, I'm staying here."

"And like *I* just said…" Using her good arm, Ellena reached down, picked the bag back up, and held it out for him. "Absolutely not."

It was good to see the fire come back into her eyes. When he'd gotten the call about the accident, Gabe was terrified he'd never get the chance to see it again.

When he took the bag from her hand, his fingertips brushing against hers. Though brief, the contact sent a shockwave of electricity up his left arm and straight to his heart.

He somehow managed to keep himself in check, but the tiny hitch in Ellena's breathing was a dead giveaway. That and the way the blues surrounding her pupils had darkened.

It had always been that way with them. They touched; they ignited.

She let go of the strap as if it had burned her, and Gabe knew...

She still feels it, too.

Though it didn't change anything, the knowledge that she still reacted to him so strongly made his dick stand up and take notice.

Clearing his throat, he held the bag at his side. "You should go lie down. I can make us something to eat."

"I've been lying down for three days, and I can make myself something to eat. *After* you leave."

Her tenacity damn near had him smiling, but Gabe held back knowing it would just piss her off even more.

"I'm not leaving you alone, Elle." He set the bag down again.

With a low growl, Ellena turned and headed for the split staircase behind her. She talked as she continued walking away.

"You know, just because you're the one saying the words doesn't mean it's the end-all-be-all of the conversation. I mean, I get that you're *the* Gabriel Dawson, Decorated Navy SEAL and all-around badass, but—"

"Former SEAL." Gabe couldn't resist goading her.

She looked back at him as though she were ready to spit nails. "You seem to forget we're not together anymore. A choice *you* made, remember?"

She put the hand not held in the sling on one hip, making it even harder for Gabe not to smile because, damn. She was still cute as hell when she was angry.

"I remember."

"Good." Ellena tilted her pretty little head and smirked, her twin dimples deepening. "Then it should be easy for you to accept the fact that you have absolutely no say in what I do, nor do you have the right to just barge in here and try to take charge of my life."

"I'm not trying to take charge, Elle." He took a step forward. "I'm trying to keep you *safe*."

"It was an accident!" She winced, and it was clear her raised voice had caused her pain.

It took every ounce of strength Gabe had not to go to her. "You know, you really shouldn't yell like that. It's not good for your head."

Ellena laughed humorously. "You just can't help yourself, can you?"

Not when it comes to you, sweetheart.

"Let me make something very clear," Ellena continued on with what appeared to be a forced calm. "I don't need you to tell me what is and isn't good for me. I also don't need you to protect me from a threat that doesn't exist."

A part of him even felt like he should apologize, but for what?

Upsetting her?

Caring enough to want to keep her out of harm's way?

For everything.

Later, when this was all over and Gabe knew with complete certainty that she was safe, he *would* apologize. What mattered now, however, was making her understand the seriousness of the situation.

A man like Adrian Walker wouldn't have taken the time to seek him out as some sort of sick joke. And though Gabe still didn't know the man's motives behind warning him of the danger Elle was in, the incident with the bike and the car wreck only added a terrifying validity to Walker's story.

"Look, Gabe." Ellena sighed, her voice having softened slightly. "I appreciate your making the trip here. I really do. I also appreciate you staying with me at the hospital the last few days, and I'm grateful for the ride home. But as you can see, I really am okay. So, I'm going to go upstairs and take a much-needed shower. After that, I'll probably grab a bite to eat, or I might go ahead and lay down for a bit. Maybe both. Either way, I'll be perfectly fine by myself, so thanks again. Feel free to see yourself out."

The beautiful, stubborn woman turned and started for the stairs again.

"I'm not leaving you here alone, sweetheart."

"No." Elle spun back around, the fury in her blue eyes burning even brighter than before. "You do *not* get to call me that. Not anymore."

"Sorry." Gabe quickly threw his hands palms-up. "Habit."

A drop of sadness mixed with her anger, and her eyes glistened with what he prayed weren't unshed tears.

"One you've had more than enough time to break."

Gabe didn't respond right away, mainly because she was right. He'd put this void between them a long damn time ago. Didn't matter that his decision to leave had stemmed from his need to keep her safe.

"I don't know who this source of yours is," she continued on, "but I can assure you, there is absolutely no reason for anyone... good, bad, or indifferent...to want to physically harm me. The car accident was just that, Gabe. An accident. So please believe me when I say I appreciate the offer, but I don't need you to protect me."

The woman had no idea... *I'll always protect you, baby. Even if it means hurting us both in the process.*

"Do you remember what happened to cause the wreck yet?" he challenged. When she remained silent, he said, "I'm guessing you don't, which means you can't possibly know for sure that it wasn't intentional."

Responding to neither his question nor his remark, Ellena's sad gaze stayed on his a second longer as she whispered, "Goodbye, Gabriel." Turning away, she made her way up the L-shaped staircase.

That time, Gabe didn't say a word. He just stood in the entryway and watched as she walked away.

Part of him wanted her to keep fighting with him but only because that meant she was still talking to him. He thought about spouting off some sort of smartass comment to prod her into coming back down, even if it was simply to continue the argument.

Instead, he let her go, taking the time to enjoy the view of her perfect, heart-shaped ass as she went.

Gabe knew it was wrong, but *fuck*. Her body had always made his mouth water, and the thin hospital scrubs the nurse had given her to wear home hugged every delicious curve with each step.

Ellena didn't bother looking back before disappearing around the corner at the top of the stairs. He was still standing there, trying to ignore the disappointment in his chest when his phone began to ring.

He pulled it from his pocket and looked at the screen before answering. "Hey, boss. I was just about to call you."

"How's it going?" Jake asked.

"It's…going." Gabe glanced back toward the top of the stairs.

"How's Ellena?"

Beautiful and feisty as ever. "Good. Mild concussion and a banged-up shoulder, but otherwise okay. They discharged her a little while ago, and we're at her place now."

"Glad to hear it," his boss commented sincerely. "Any sign of Walker?"

"Not yet." Gabe ground his teeth together. "Should've taken him down when I had the chance. I know I could've gotten him to talk."

"Told you before, Dawson. Beating yourself up isn't going to do you or her any good."

"Yeah, well, that's easy for you to say. You wouldn't have let him walk away."

"Maybe. Maybe not. No one knows how they'll react to a

given situation until they're actually in it, including me. Hell, your time with the SEALs should've taught you that."

His boss was right. Kicking his own ass wasn't going to get him any closer to finding the threat against Ellena. Using his free hand, Gabe dug his fingertips into the tense muscles at the back of his neck.

Jake spoke up again. "I've got your guys doing what they can to figure this shit out as quickly as possible."

Though he was grateful Jake had taken Walker's ominous warning as seriously as he had, the acid in Gabe's gut began to churn.

He fucking hated the thought of his teammates knowing what a fraud he was. That he'd spent his entire adult life protecting complete strangers but had failed to keep those closest to him safe.

Of course, Jake already knew everything there was to know about his past. The guy never offered a job to anyone without running the deepest background check available.

But having dealt with demons of his own past—ones that nearly cost Jake the woman he loved—the man had also understood Gabe's need for privacy.

Hope he still does.

"I can practically hear those fuckin' wheels of yours spinning." Jake's deep voice broke through his thoughts. "And no, I haven't told the team anything about what happened with you and Ellena. They know you two got married five years ago and separated after two. Figured the rest was yours to tell."

Well hell. "Thanks, Jake. Appreciate it."

"We all have things we'd rather keep buried, Dawson. The only problem with that is our pasts always seem to have a way of coming back to bite us in the ass. Best thing you can do is be honest with the team and Ellena. But most importantly, you need to be honest with yourself."

That all sounded good in theory, but if he *were* completely honest with himself, he'd have to accept the fact that he'd fucked up beyond all redemption.

That I'd give anything for a second chance with her.

Not feeling up to a touchy-feely moment with his boss, Gabe pushed everything else aside and changed the subject.

"It's probably a waste of time but have Nate access the security footage at my apartment complex. I'm sure Walker's too slick to be caught on camera, but he might catch something we can use."

"Wouldn't be the first time Walker's shown his face."

His boss had a point. During a botched attempt to abduct Gracie—R.I.S.C.'s office manager who was now married to one of Gabe's teammates—the security cameras outside the company's office building had caught a glimpse of Adrian Walker's face.

Since then, the son of a bitch seemed to be everywhere and nowhere all at the same time.

Gabe wasn't sure why the guy had such a hard-on for Bravo. He did know he was damn tired of always being one step behind the bastard.

Another reason he was still pissed at himself for letting the man stroll right out of his fucking apartment.

But damn. When Walker said Ellena's name…that she was in *danger*…all thoughts of ending the guy's life vanished. From that moment on, all Gabe could think about, all he *cared* about, was getting to her and keeping her safe.

He'd pretty much guessed how she'd react to seeing him again, but the one thing Gabe hadn't stopped to think about was how their reunion would affect *him*.

Seeing her in that damn hospital bed had brought an eerie feeling of Deja vu. As if time had stood still, allowing his soul-crushing memories to come rushing at him, all at once.

For three years, Gabe had worked damn hard to put it all behind him and move on. Lately, however, he'd begun to realize it was an impossible feat. The day his former teammate tried to kill Ellena, his entire world was changed forever.

It was the day he'd lost everything.

Despite his efforts against it, Gabe often found himself thinking about what his life would've been like had he stayed in bed with her that morning instead of going for his morning run.

Questions that would never be answered still occupied his mind at the most random of times.

Would they still be living in the city, or would they have moved to the peaceful quiet of the country like the two of them had talked about? Would they have had another child by now?

Would the son we lost have had Elle's eyes?

"Dawson? You still there?"

Shit. "Yeah." Gabe shook his head to clear the cobwebs from his past. "Sorry."

"You know, there's a chance Walker's just screwing with you for the fun of it."

"That's not what's happening here, Jake."

His boss paused a moment. "You seem very sure of that."

"I am."

"Because?"

"Because a few weeks ago, she told a friend of hers she thought she was being followed. Since then, someone's taken a shot at her while she was riding her bike and now the car wreck. That's two so-called accidents in as many weeks. Plus you and I both know that asshole isn't the type of guy to waste his time on some bullshit prank." *Not to mention my gut is screaming like a fucking banshee.* "Someone's after her, Jake. I just need to figure out who."

"We also need to figure out why a man like Adrian Walker would give you a heads up about it," Jake added with a curious tone. "Do yourself a favor and call your team. Tell them everything you know up to this point."

"So we're going forward with this?"

Understanding what Gabe was asking, his boss said, "I've officially assigned this as Bravo's priority. Until you figure out what the hell's going on with your wife, it's the team's *only* job. Be sure to update them with any pertinent intel as the situation changes and keep me in the loop."

"Yes, sir."

"In the meantime, sit down with Ellena. Have her tell you everything she can remember about the two accidents, as well as why she thought she was being followed."

"Copy that." Gabe thanked his boss one last time and ended the call. Then he thought about his team.

They already knew about his fucked-up marriage, but they didn't understand just how much Elle truly meant to him.

Gabe knew the only way for that to happen was to tell them the truth. The *whole* truth.

The pressure in his chest increased.

Get the fuck over yourself and focus on what's important.

Goddamnit. The voice in his head was right. This wasn't about him. It was about keeping Ellena safe.

Glancing toward the stairs, Gabe thought about the stubborn woman who'd just stormed her way up them. She'd made it abundantly clear that she didn't want him here. Although that shouldn't come as a surprise, it still hurt like a motherfucker.

It didn't matter. Her safety still trumped everything, including his own pride.

With that in mind, he tapped in Nate's number and put the phone back to his ear. The other man answered on the first ring.

"Hey, Dawson. I was wondering when you were gonna call."

"Find anything?"

A loud sigh hit Gabe's ear. "You're always such a peach when you call, you know that?"

Gabe bit his tongue and indulged the prick. "Hello, Nate. How are you?"

"I'm great, actually," Nate responded cheerfully. "It was so sweet of you to ask."

"Nathan…"

The man's snort filled the phone's speaker. "How's it going with the missus?"

"Fine," Gabe barely controlled his rising temper. "It would be even better if you'd quit being such a dick and just answer the fucking question."

"That good, huh?" Nate chuckled.

"Seriously, Nate. I am not in the mood for this shit."

"Just playing, man. Keep your panties on." There was a slight hesitation before Nate added, "On second thought, maybe you should take them off. Probably be a lot less grumpy if you did."

"Nathan, I swear to Christ…"

"Okay, jeesh." The smartass sighed loudly. "I pulled up the feed showing every entrance and exit into your apartment complex, as well as the building you live in. Walker is clearly seen driving a dark, four-door sedan through the east entrance, parking next to your assigned spot, and then leaving the way he came a little over an hour later. Guy didn't even try hiding his face."

Motherfucker. "Traffic cams pick up where he went to after he left?"

"Sort of."

"What the fuck do you mean, sort of?" Gabe cringed at the harsh bite of his tone. He had no business taking it out on the guy. Not when all Nate was trying to do was help.

But other man didn't miss a beat. "I was able to follow Walker for about half a mile, but I lost him when he turned down a side street where there aren't any cameras installed."

"What about after? No one just vanishes into thin air."

"Except our guy. That's what the asshole does, right? Drops in, stirs shit up, and then disappears without a fucking trace?"

He had a point. Still, something told Gabe this time was different. "I think he's close."

"To us?"

"To me."

A few seconds passed before Nate asked, "Why do you say that?"

"The way Walker acted when he was at my place left my gut twisted into goddamn knots. Like maybe this time is…different somehow." Gabe scrubbed his chin. "Fuck, I don't know. Maybe I'm seeing shit that isn't there."

"Doubt it. I just wish like hell I'd been with you. I'd love the chance to dole out some payback on the bastard."

Another rush of guilt settled like a lead ball in the pit of Gabe's stomach.

"Yeah, about that." He raked his fingers through his hair. "I fucked up. I had him, and I let him go. But I promise you, it won't happen a second time."

"Dude fuck that apology bullshit. Separated or not, she's still your wife. And while I plan on putting a bullet into Walker's head the first chance I get for what he did to Gracie, I understand why you didn't."

I'll be damned. "Yeah?"

"Hell yeah. Listen, Gabe. I don't know the whole story with Ellena, or why you never told any of us you were married, and I'm not asking for it."

"Why not?"

After what Walker did to Nate's wife, the man sure as hell had the right to know. They all did.

"Figured you'd share that interesting tidbit if and when you're ready."

The pressure in his chest began to ease. "Thanks, man."

"No thanks necessary. Just know if you ever do want to talk about it, Bravo's here for you."

Gabe closed his eyes and nodded. "Appreciate it."

"Any time, brother. I mean that."

Damn, he loved his team.

Clearing the emotion threatening to clog his throat, Gabe opened his eyes and got his head back in the game. "I'll call you when I have more to go on. In the meantime, keep digging. Walker's message to me was cryptic as fuck, but I got the feeling there are some big players in this latest game of his."

"Copy that."

Gabe shoved his phone back into his pocket and filled his lungs with a long cleansing breath. After holding it a few seconds, he blew it out as he contemplated his next step.

He could hear the water running and did his damnedest not to think about what it meant. But the harder he worked at trying to ignore it, the harder *he* became.

Despite his Herculean efforts, the image of Ellena upstairs, lathering up her wet, naked body…

Jesus.

With his cock feeling like a fucking steel rod shoving against his zipper, Gabe adjusted himself as best he could. Desperate for a distraction, he decided to take another look around the place while he also tried to figure out how he was going to convince her to let him play bodyguard for the foreseeable future.

Try to remember that's why you're here, asshole.

Once again, the voice of reason was right. No matter how much he'd missed Elle, or how badly his body still yearned for hers, he needed to stay focused on protecting her, rather than remembering how combustible they'd always been between the sheets.

Several minutes later, Gabe had gone through every room on the main floor. Using a skill he'd fine-tuned during his time with the SEALs, he'd mentally catalogued the placement of the furniture, picture frames, houseplants…anything he or Ellena likely notice if they were moved.

When that was finished, he opened the set of French doors leading from the living room to the secluded space outside.

Overlooking the San Diego Bay, the small patio and fenced back yard offered a beautiful, private oasis. It was also the perfect spot for someone to enter the home without being seen by the neighbors.

Set on the coastal end of a quiet neighborhood, Ellena's two-story townhome was cozy and full of charm, but as far as security was concerned, it didn't have jack shit.

Adding to his list of mental notes, he thought about the number of cameras needing to be installed as he made his way back inside. That and one of R.I.S.C.'s state-of-the-art alarm systems.

Christ, just thinking about her being in this house alone and vulnerable all this time scared the shit out of him. It also pissed him the hell off.

Protective instincts running in full gear, Gabe headed straight for the stairs. He could no longer hear the water running, which was good. Because after he pointed out how fucking foolish it was for a woman to live alone in this day and age without so much as an alarm system, they were going to discuss the changes he was planning to make.

This should be fun.

When they were still together, he and Ellena hardly ever

fought. In fact, the guys on his SEAL team used to constantly give him shit about how well he and his wife got along.

The only time they *did* argue was when Gabe's overprotectiveness would clash with Ellena's independent nature. Those arguments were few and far between, but damn.

When they disagreed about that shit, the sparks flew like fucking Fourth of July. Then later, when they'd make up, their entire world would become a magnificent explosion of pleasure.

Ellena definitely wasn't a 'my way or the highway' type of woman. She'd gracefully accept his help when she thought she needed it.

The problem was he sometimes thought she needed it more than she actually did.

She was right when she'd said he couldn't help himself. From the second they met, Gabe had felt an instant, almost primal need to protect her.

Being a psychologist, Ellena would try to get him to talk each situation out rationally. The issue with that was when it came to her, his rational thinking flew right out the goddamn window.

Gabe was so afraid of losing the best thing that had ever happened to him, he was constantly doing everything he could to keep her safe.

The one time he ignored his gut and let his guard down, they'd lost their baby. He also came damn close to losing Elle, too.

You did lose her. Just in a different way.

By the time Gabe made it upstairs, he'd remembered she'd just been released from the damn hospital. They'd definitely have to have a talk about everything eventually.

For now, she needed food and rest, not someone jumping her ass about her home's lack of security.

Pushing all that shit aside, Gabe refocused his energy on checking out the setup of the other rooms. He steered clear of the room with the double doors, assuming that was Ellena's bedroom.

If she were any other woman, he wouldn't even be tempted.

But walking in on her while she was getting dressed…that was the one enticing image he'd be powerless against.

Like she'd let you anywhere near her, anyway.

There was a time when all he had to do was give her a look and she'd start stripping down for him. But the cool indifference with which she looked back at him when she'd said goodbye was telling.

Ellena Dawson wanted nothing more to do with him, and he couldn't blame her.

Not. One. Fucking. Bit.

Gabe finished checking a spare bedroom that looked like it never got used, a full bath in the hallway next to it, and a small linen closet between the bathroom and the master bedroom. The door across the hallway from the guest room appeared slightly ajar, grabbing his attention.

Pressing a hand against the painted wood, Gabe started to push it open just as the door gave way, and Ellena came barreling through. A tiny squeal of surprise escaped the back of her throat as she slammed into him.

"Whoa." On reflex, Gabe grabbed her shoulders to keep her from tumbling backward. Her *bare* shoulders.

He swallowed hard.

Wearing nothing but a towel, Ellena's widened eyes locked with his. Her face was free of makeup, the soft skin appearing even more fresh and youthful than before.

Her sandy blonde hair was damp from her shower, its thick strands tickling the tops of his fingers, and electricity burned the skin on his palms.

Jesus, she's beautiful.

He dropped his gaze to her mouth. Unable to keep from it, he found himself wondering if she still tasted the same as before.

The tip of her tongue peeked out, wetting the delicate skin there. That one small, innocent movement sent a painful ache through his already swollen dick.

Her lips parted slightly the way they used to right before they were about to kiss. Gabe started to lean inward, more than ready to savor all that he'd been missing, and…

"Sorry," Ellena blurted, jumping backward just out of his reach. "I-I thought maybe you were already gone."

With a quick glance at the space behind her, he noticed she'd set this room up to be her home office.

Inwardly cursing himself, Gabe let his hands drop back down to his sides. "Look, Elle. I know I'm the last person you wanted to see, let alone have as a houseguest. But I can't leave here until I know for sure you're safe."

"Okay."

"You can be pissed if you want, and if I have to, I'll sleep in the damn driveway, but..." He cut himself off as her response finally sank in. "Wait. Did you just say *okay?*"

She shocked the hell out of him by nodding. "Yes. You can stay here." Ellena licked her lips nervously. "That's what I was coming to tell you."

Well, that was a hell of a lot easier than he thought it would be.

Too fucking easy.

Gabe studied his wife closer. Concession to his demand to stay had filtered into her baby blues, but that wasn't all he found there.

Something was definitely up. Something *other* than his dick, which was currently throbbing like a motherfucker.

His eyes narrowed into a suspicious gaze. "Why the sudden change of heart?"

"What do you mean?"

"I mean, twenty minutes ago you were hell bent on throwing my ass out the door. Now I find you practically sprinting out of your office like your ass is on fire. I also saw the look on your face when you realized I was still here. You were relieved, Elle. I'm asking why."

Her shoulders sagged a little, drawing Gabe's attention to the bruises on her upper left arm. Bruises caused by the accident she'd nearly died in.

Shit. She hadn't acted like he'd hurt her, and he didn't think he'd held on too tightly, but still.

Way to go, asshole.

"You're right." Ellena agreed. "I didn't want you staying here. But that was before."

"Before what?"

"Before I came in here to check my email." She glanced back at open laptop on her desk, and when her eyes met his again, they were filled with an unmistakable fear.

One that sent his heart racing.

"What is it? What's wrong?"

"There are…p-pictures."

The quiver in her voice kicked his ass into high gear. Stepping past her, Gabe spoke as he made his way across the room.

"Pictures of what?"

"Me, mostly." Holding the towel in place, she followed him slowly. "But there are some of me with Jenna, and with you. There's also a message."

Sonofabitch.

Reaching the desk in three large strides, Gabe grabbed the top of the computer and spun it around so he could see. His stomach dropped when he began clicking through the images still opened on the screen.

There were several pictures of Ellena appearing to have been taken over the span of at least a few weeks. Some showed her walking to and from her car in the hospital parking lot. A few were of her riding her bike on the Old Mill trail.

A couple were of Ellena having lunch with Jenna, and though those pictures showed both women talking and laughing, the person behind the camera was clearly focused on one woman in particular.

Ellena.

The most recent images the bastard sent were of both Gabe and Ellena, and they'd been taken earlier today. Those showed the two of them leaving the hospital together and getting into his rental car.

The final image was of a bruised and bloody Elle slumped in the front seat of her mangled car.

"What the fuck?"

"You were right." Ellena's soft voice shook from beside him. "It wasn't an accident."

Filled with a murderous rage, Gabe quickly found the warning she'd mentioned. He read the message aloud. "They can find you anywhere."

"I-I don't understand."

Gabe looked back up at her, wanting to kill whoever had put that damn fear in her eyes. Fury burning brightly, he pulled his phone from his pocket and thumbed Nate's number.

"Are you calling the police?"

He waited for Nate to pick up. "Nope."

"Then who?"

Gabe put the phone to his ear, his deep voice turning deadly as he locked his eyes with hers. "I'm calling my team."

CHAPTER 5

Someone had been watching her.

Ellena had suspected it the other day when she and Jenna had met for lunch but had quickly abandoned the notion. Because that was crazy, right?

Except it wasn't crazy. It was real. And whoever sent that email had done a hell of a lot more than just follow her.

Why would someone do that? *Why is any of this happening?*

That was the million-dollar question, wasn't it?

She wasn't anyone important. Wasn't involved in anything illegal or nefarious. She couldn't even blame it on some crazy ex who couldn't live without her.

Gabe had clearly been doing just fine without her.

"You finished?"

His rugged voice started Ellena out of her thoughts, and she realized she had no idea what he'd just said.

"What?"

Wearing the same, concerned look he'd had since she'd woken from her nap, Gabe nodded toward her plate. "Grilled cheese used to be one of your favorites, but if you don't like it anymore, I can make something different."

"No, I still like them." She picked at the buttery crust. "I guess I'm just not very hungry. Sorry."

"You don't need to be sorry, Elle. But you do need to eat something."

Ellena brought her gaze back up to his and sighed. "I can't stop thinking about those pictures. And every time I do, my stomach starts to turn."

"We're going figure out who sent them. I promise you that."

Gabe's tone became edgy, his eyes filling with cold hardness she recognized all too well. It was the same look he had when he'd walked into their kitchen to find Victor Campbell holding a gun to her head.

An uneasy feeling slowly grew from somewhere deep inside, the abrupt emotions catching Ellena by surprise.

She wasn't only scared for herself. She was also scared for the man who had broken her heart in two.

"What is it?"

Her eyes lifted to meet his. "I think I made a mistake."

"What mistake was that?"

"Asking you to stay."

Frowning, Gabe leaned forward, resting his elbows on the table. "I know our past is...complicated. But I promise you, there are no ulterior motives here. The *only* thing I'm focused on is keeping you safe."

The comment stung, even though Ellena knew it shouldn't. "I know. I just think it would be best for everyone involved if I hired someone else to look into this."

"No."

Her brows rose. "No?"

"I don't trust anyone else to protect you." The comment came off very matter of fact.

Standing, Ellena grabbed his empty plate along with hers and headed for the kitchen. "It's not your decision, Gabe."

"Damn it, Ellena." Gabe sat back in his chair. "We already talked about this."

"That was before."

"Before what?"

"Before I had some time to think." She put the dishes in the sink a little harder than necessary.

"When?" The pitch of his voice rose to an incredulous tone. "While you were napping?"

"Does it matter?" She grabbed ahold of the porcelain edge and rolled her lips inward to keep from shouting. Looking back at him, Ellena willed herself to speak with a calm, cool voice. "Look, I just think that maybe…maybe we're blowing this whole thing out of proportion."

"Someone has been stalking you." He stood abruptly. "They left you hurt and bleeding in the fucking car."

"That doesn't mean they were the one to actually hit me."

"You can't be serious."

"I'm very serious."

Are you?

With a shake of his head, Gabe began moving in her direction. "For argument's sake, let's say it was the same person. And that same person purposely rammed his car or truck or whatever the fuck it was into the driver's side of your car. Then what?"

"Then I don't want you getting hurt because of some misguided obligation you feel toward me!"

Gabe stopped walking. His dark eyes blinked several times, and it was obvious he was as surprised to hear the admission as she was to have said it aloud.

At first, he didn't say anything more. He just stood there, staring back at her as if she were some sort of great mystery needing to be solved. When he finally did speak, his harsh tone had softened.

"Is that what you think?" he asked quietly.

Terrified she'd say something even more revealing, Ellena shrugged but remained quiet.

He continued forward, not stopping until he was standing right in front of her. "You think I'm here because I feel obligated?"

"I know you still blame yourself for what happened with Vic, but…" Ellena licked her dry lips and swallowed. "You don't owe me anything, Gabriel."

He needed to know that. Needed to understand she wasn't

trying to use their past to guilt him into staying to protect her. Because if something happened to him, too…

"Don't I?"

Gabe's broad shoulders fell slightly, the cold wall he'd erected cracking just enough to reveal a sliver of emotion. Despite the pain his leaving had caused, the torment behind his eyes broke her heart.

"Gabe…"

He reached out, his hand inching toward her face. Unable to move, Ellena held her breath as he slid his callused palm against her cheek. His eyes dropped to her mouth.

He's going to kiss you.

A million thoughts raced through her mind all at once. The one that stood out amongst the rest…

I really want him to.

It was a mistake. One that would no doubt haunt her forever. She didn't care.

Ellena lifted her chin as she braced herself to feel what she'd been missing for so long. Gabe leaned in, his lips brushing against hers in a barely-there caress.

The doorbell rang.

Sucking in a breath, she looked away. At the same time, Gabe's wall was back, a cold indifference refilling that damn crack as if it were never there.

"I'm sorry." He took a step back. "That shouldn't have happened."

For some reason, his apology—and the ease with which he dismissed what almost happened—renewed her anger in record time.

"Don't worry." Ellena stepped around him and headed for the door. "I'll make sure it doesn't happen again."

The same hand that had been resting against her face shot out, his thick fingers wrapping around her wrist to halt her forward progress.

She swung her head around, her chest ballooning with hope.

"Let me." His jaw tightened. "You stay here."

That balloon popped in a spectacular explosion.

What did you expect?

Her subconscious was right. What did she think? That one almost-kiss was going to fill the giant void between them, and they'd be able to pick right back up from where they'd left off?

For a second there, that was exactly what she'd thought, and Ellena was disappointed in herself because of it.

She was stronger than this. And *smarter*. She'd filed for divorce, for Pete's sake, so this back-and-forth indecisiveness needed to stop. Now.

This wasn't her. She wasn't some wishy-washy woman who couldn't make up her mind about who and what she wanted. What she deserved.

Her husband might be back, but it was only temporary. The second they figured out who sent those pictures and why, he'd be gone, and they'd be divorced.

Something Ellena would do well to remember.

Gabe checked the peephole, his muscles becoming visibly relaxed when he saw whoever stood on the other side.

His team.

Lost in her thoughts since waking up from her nap, she'd completely forgotten they were even coming.

"Hey, Dawson." An attractive man with short, brown hair stood on her front stoop. "Nice digs."

"Nate." Gabe held out his hand. "Thanks for coming."

The man returned the gesture. "No thanks needed."

"Come on in, guys."

Stepping aside, Gabe held the door open. The one named Nate entered her home first, followed by three other men. Though they were a few years younger, all three had the same military vibe as Gabe.

"Nice place." Nate nodded approvingly.

"Thanks." Ellena shook off her wavering feelings about Gabe being there and stepped forward. "I like it."

All five men turned her way.

Gabe's expression was hard to read. "Ellena, this is my team." He went down the row, gesturing to each man as he went. "Nate

Carter, Kole Jameson, Matt Turner, and Zade King. Guys, this is Elle."

Wearing a wide grin, Nate stepped toward her with an outstretched hand. "I have *got* to shake the hand of the woman who actually agreed to marry your sorry ass."

The man's playful demeanor immediately put her at ease. "It's nice to meet you, Nate." After greeting him, Elle went down the row, shaking the hands of each of the other men. "Thank you all for coming. Would any of you like something to drink? I have tea and soda. Or if you prefer it, I could make us all a fresh pot of coffee."

"Coffee sounds great, actually." Gabe offered her a ghost of a smile.

She slid her gaze to his. Something told her the coffee was his way of getting rid of her so he could talk to his friends alone. Forcing a smile, she said, "I'll get that started. Please"—Ellena motioned to the living room—"make yourselves at home."

"Thanks, sweet…" Gabe stopped himself short. Clearing his throat, he started again. "Thanks."

"Sure."

As she headed back to the kitchen, Ellena heard him mumble something to his team as he led them into the living room.

Part of her wanted to balk at the way she'd practically been dismissed like the good little wife, but the other part…a bigger part…was more than happy to have a moment of privacy to clear her head before dealing with his team.

By the time everyone's cups were filled, Ellena felt a bit more centered. But as she stood there, waiting for someone to say something, she couldn't help but wonder why any of this was happening. One minute her life was normal…

Normal. Lonely. Whatever.

The next, someone was watching her. Taking *pictures* of her and then sending them along with a vague warning. But for what purpose? To scare her or was it something more?

They can find you anywhere.

A shiver ran down her spine as she thought of the email's chilling words.

"Elle?"

Ellena blinked, realizing too late that everyone was staring at her expectantly. She looked back at Gabe, who'd clearly been trying to get her attention. "I'm sorry, what?"

Concern flittered across his handsome face. "You okay? Do you need to lie down?"

"No." She offered him a shaky smile. "I'm good. This is all just…"

Surreal.

"A lot to take in." His eyes softened. "I know."

He was right. It was a lot. And scary as hell.

"Why don't you have a seat." Gabe motioned to the empty chair next to where he stood.

"Okay," Ellena agreed. Because really, what else could she do?

He'd told her a little about his job with R.I.S.C. after he'd called his team in. Knowing what Gabe did for a living and who he worked for now, she was confident he and the rest of Bravo Team had a much better chance at catching this guy than the local authorities would.

So as hard as it was to be around him again, Ellena knew if she wanted the person behind the email—and quite possibly her accident—these were the best men for the job.

Besides that, the San Diego police department had a lot on their plate these days. Cases that were much more important to them than some random stalker.

What's happening to you isn't random.

Ignoring the annoying little voice, Ellena took a seat in one of two matching chairs positioned around her living room space.

With two other chairs, a couch, and a loveseat, there were more than enough places for everyone to sit. Even so, Gabe chose to stand next to her.

Using a memory technique she learned in college, she already knew the others' names and what their specialties were.

Nate was Bravo Team's technical guru, Kole and Zade were snipers, and Matt was the team's medic. And of course, Gabe was the team leader.

A fact that didn't surprise Ellena in the least.

With his large arms crossed at his chest, her estranged husband gave her a tip of his chin. "Why don't you tell them everything that's been happening to you."

He'd given Nate the cliff notes version when they'd talked earlier, but he wanted the team to hear it from Elle's perspective.

"I don't even really know where to start." She looked around the room. "I had no idea any of this was happening. I mean, there was one day where I felt like someone was watching me, but other than that…"

"When was that?" Nate asked.

"Um…" She thought back. "A couple of weeks ago."

"What made you think you were being watched?" Zade asked.

"Honestly, I'm not even sure. I'd been walking to my car to go to lunch, and all of the sudden the tiny hairs on the back of my neck stood on end, and I got this weird feeling in my stomach." Ellena chuckled nervously. "Saying it out loud, I hear how ridiculous that sounds."

Kole offered her a kind smile. "Not ridiculous at all, actually. Gut instinct is a very real thing. It's gotten us through some pretty hairy situations."

Each of the men nodded in agreement.

"Logically, I know you're right." Ellena sighed. "I'm always telling my patients to listen to their instincts. I guess I should've listened to mine more closely. If I had, maybe I would've seen the person following me. Found out what it is they want."

"How?" Gabe frowned down at her. "By confronting them?"

"Well…yeah." She tipped her head back to meet his gaze. "I mean, if you saw someone taking pictures of you without your permission, wouldn't you want to talk to them?"

"She has a point, Dawson." Matt grinned.

"No, she sure as hell doesn't have a point, Turner," Gabe nearly growled at his teammate before bringing his focus back on her. "You see someone you think is watching you, you don't even look at them. Let alone *talk* to them."

Wrong. "If I have a chance to confront the asshole who sent me those pictures, you'd better believe I'm going to take it."

"Even if it means getting yourself hurt? Or worse?"

Ellena offered him a sugary-sweet smile. "I thought the whole point of you insisting on staying here to be my personal bodyguard was to keep that from happening."

A few snickers traveled through the tense air, causing the scowl on Gabe's face to deepen.

"You're right." He turned his body in order to fully face her. "My job *is* to keep you safe. But I can't do that if you go and make stupid decisions like walking right up to a goddamn stalker just so you two can have a nice little chat."

"Whoa…" Zade—whom Ellena quickly pegged as the peace-keeper of the bunch—put a hand up, attempting to diffuse the rapidly intensifying situation. "Easy there, big guy."

At least Ellena was pretty sure it was Zade. She couldn't be certain, because she was too busy using her good arm to push herself to her feet.

Facing off with Gabe, Ellena placed her good hand on her own hip and stared him square in the eyes. "I'm sorry, did you just call me stupid?"

The room grew silent as his dark eyes closed. He then drew in a deep breath in an obvious attempt to calm down before letting the air out slowly. Gabe opened his eyes again before speaking.

"No, Ellena." His voice sounded calm and controlled. "I did not call you stupid. I said the *idea* of you approaching a suspect is stupid. Two different things, sweetheart."

Her insides filled with anger…and another feeling she chose to ignore. "I told you last night not to call me that."

"Uh, guys?" Someone else piped in. "Do we really need to be here for this conversation?"

Without taking her eyes off of Gabe, Ellena bit out a sharp, "No!"

At the exact same time, Gabe released a growled, "Yes!"

Sensing they were headed for an impasse, Ellena regained

her composure and turned to the others. Attempting to smile, she said, "Gentlemen, would you mind giving us a moment?"

The men shared a few awkward glances with each other before mumbling their agreements and excusing themselves from the room. Making their way through the doors leading to her backyard, Ellena watched and waited until they were all outside before speaking again.

The second the door shut, her eyes slid back to his. "If there's even the slightest chance this is going to work, we need to get a few things straight."

"You think?"

With his hands resting low on his denim-clad hips, Gabe looked every bit the strong leader that he was. Tall, tattooed, and more than ready to go toe-to-toe with her, the man screamed sexy-as-hell alpha male.

Even now, despite his overbearing ways, just looking at him made her knees weak and her panties wet. But physical attraction had never been an issue for them.

Not even close.

Ignoring those unproductive thoughts, Ellena drew in a cleansing breath of her own and did her best to make him understand where she was coming from.

"I'm not trying to be difficult, Gabe." She crossed her arms in front of her, refusing to react to the painful pull in her left shoulder. "I promise, I'm not."

His dark brows rose. "Really? Could've fooled me. Why else would you even consider approaching someone who clearly intends on causing you harm?"

"Oh, give me a break." She rolled her eyes. "I was talking hypotheticals, and you know it."

"This isn't a hypothetical situation, Elle. This is your *life*."

"My point, exactly. You said you weren't trying to come in and take over, but that's precisely what you're doing. I can't even make an off-handed statement without you going all caveman on me."

The muscles in his handsome face relaxed some. "Damn it, I

wasn't trying to...I didn't mean..." Gabe blew out a breath, raking a frustrated hand through his hair.

The move made Ellena think of all the times she'd run *her* fingers through his thick, wavy locks.

Refusing to become distracted once again, she forced herself to stay on track. "I know you said it's your job to keep me safe, Gabe, but..."

"Damn right, it is," he cut her off brusquely.

"*But* we don't even know who or what I need protection from."

"Why do you think I had the team fly here, Elle? We're trying to figure that shit out."

"Then let's focus on *that* and leave our personal baggage out of it."

His dark brows furrowed. "What the hell is that supposed to mean?"

"Yesterday was the first time we'd seen or spoken to each other in a very long time. It's only natural for unresolved feelings about our past to rise to the surface."

He studied her a moment. "You goin' all shrink on me, Doc?"

With a shake of her head, she answered, "No, Gabe. I'm not going all *shrink* on you. I'm trying to be reasonable and have an adult conversation about all of this." She paused, her voice turning a bit softer than intended. "You left, and I didn't hear a word from you until you showed up in my hospital room."

I still need to ask Jenna about that little surprise.

"I heard from you, though, didn't I?" Gabe chuckled humorlessly. "Wait, that's not true. I heard from you through your lawyer."

"It's been three years, Gabriel." Ellena jutted her chin even as a stab of guilt pierced her heart. "What did you expect me to do? Wait forever?"

Regret filled his dark eyes. "No." He clenched his teeth together. "That shouldn't have been put on you. It was my decision to leave. I should've been the one to file."

"So why didn't you?"

Breaking eye contact, Gabe hesitated a beat before answering. "Just never took the time to do it, I guess."

Ouch.

Though his words weren't totally unexpected, they twisted the invisible knife even deeper. As unrealistic as it was, Ellena had allowed herself to believe he hadn't filed for divorce because he still loved her.

Guess you were way off base on that one, huh, Doc?

Not wanting to continue the painful conversation, she switched back to the original topic.

"First things first, right?" She jutted her chin up. "Let's figure out who sent those pictures and whether or not there was any truth to your mysterious friend's warning. We can deal with everything else after that."

Gabe's expression hardened. "Trust me, Adrian Walker is no friend of mine. But you're right." The corners of his lips turned upward just a tad. "First things first."

Interesting.

Making a mental note to ask him more about this Walker character, Ellena glanced over his large shoulder to the men talking beneath her veranda. "We should probably let them back in."

He followed her line of sight and began walking toward her back door. "I'll get them."

Before she even realized she was moving, Ellena snaked her right hand out to grab his thick wrist. "Wait."

He stopped, his eyes lowering to where she was holding him before raising up to meet hers. "Yeah?"

She licked her lips. "Thank you."

"For what?"

"For still caring enough to help me."

"Ah, sweetheart." His intense stare locked with hers. "I've never stopped caring."

Stunned into silence, by both the emotion in his eyes and the sincerity in his voice, Ellena let go of his wrist and watched as he headed for patio door.

I think I liked it better when we were fighting.

In a way, the fighting made his being here easier. At least when they argued, she could pretend she didn't care. But that's all it was, really.

Pretending.

Because she *did* care. Far more than she should. But when he looked at her the way he just had and said the things he just said, there was no denying it.

The man still owned every jagged piece of her shattered soul, and deep down, Ellena knew...

He always will.

CHAPTER 6

Gabe stood in Elle's living room, waiting quietly beside her as she started over, telling his team everything she knew about the situation. Unfortunately, it wasn't much.

As he continued listening, his mind wandered back to earlier, when they'd been standing in her kitchen. He still couldn't believe he'd almost kissed her. Even more unbelievable was that she'd almost *let* him.

And if that damn doorbell hadn't rung…

I'd have stripped her down, picked her up, and taken her right there by the kitchen sink.

Not that she would've let him. He and Elle may be staying under the same roof, but in all the ways that mattered, they may as well be worlds apart.

As if to prove that fact, she'd actually *thanked* him for caring enough to want to protect her. That shit still burned his ass.

The woman obviously had no idea what she meant to him. *Maybe you should tell her.*

Since coming here, Gabe had told himself over and over that he was here to protect her. That was it.

But he'd been fooling himself.

Truth was, he missed her like crazy. Missed her smile. Her laugh. Hell, he'd even missed the way she was quick to call him out on his bullshit.

It had always been a huge fucking turn-on, and *Christ*. When she'd done it earlier—in front of his team, no less—Gabe had worked damn hard not to grab ahold of her and kiss her senseless.

"So you don't remember anything from the wreck?"

Nate's question had Gabe returning his attention to the conversation at hand.

"No." She sighed, shaking her head. "I keep trying to, but the last thing I remember from that day is driving to work that morning. Everything between that and waking up in the hospital is still a blur."

He could tell she was frustrated, and he understood why. A huge piece to the puzzle they needed to solve could be locked away somewhere inside her, but she couldn't seem to find it.

She'd get there eventually. Gabe had complete faith in that. Because he had faith in *her*

"Don't try to force it, Elle," he told her softly. "Your brain just needs time to heal. You'll get there."

She lifted her head to meet his gaze. "Hopefully I get there sooner rather than later."

"You will."

One corner of her mouth turned upward in a half-smile. The movement was just enough to show off one of her adorable dimples, and damn if he didn't want to kiss it.

"So basically, we don't have shit…err…crap to go on." Zade gave Elle an apologetic grin. "Sorry, Doctor Dawson. I meant no disrespect."

"I told you before to call me Elle, Zade." Her smile grew wider. "And as surprising as it may seem, I have actually heard the word 'shit' before today."

Her smartass comment left the guys chuckling, but all Gabe could focus on was the fact that *both* dimples were showing now. God, he missed seeing those.

He shoved his hands into his pockets to keep himself from doing something stupid like yanking her out of that damn chair and hauling her upstairs to her bedroom.

"I'm sure you heard a hell of a lot worse when you were married to this guy." Matt jutted his chin toward Gabe.

"We're still married, dickhead." The comment was out of Gabe's mouth before he could stop it.

"Oh, that's right." Matt raised a brow. "Sorry. Hard to keep track."

Shit. Gabe knew he'd have to clear the air with the guy soon. Back when Matt's woman had been taken and was being held captive, he'd told him about Elle. Sort of.

Instead of giving Matt the truth, Gabe had shared the rehearsed version of why he and Elle weren't still together. One involving a fictional bank robbery and Elle blaming the Teams for keeping him away from home.

Why go through the trouble of inventing such a story? Because he was a chickenshit bastard.

Elle's eyes shot up to his, then awkwardly skittered away.

Seriously, Dawson? Why the fuck did you bring attention to the fact that you're still married?

He wished like hell he knew. From the second he'd stepped foot into her room two days ago, Gabe had been all over the fucking map.

Just like her switching between having a cool indifference toward him to thanking him for wanting to protect her, his own conflicting thoughts and emotions had been bouncing around inside him like a goddamn pinball machine.

And he fucking hated it.

As if that wasn't bad enough, he'd apparently lost control of his goddamn mouth, too, because...Jesus. Had he really thrown the fact that she'd filed for divorce back in her face?

Yeah, asshole. You really did.

Gabe knew full well it was a total dick move. One he regretted making the moment it happened.

Not only did the woman have every right to divorce his ass, she should've done that shit a long damn time ago.

A nauseating churn formed by years of regret filled his gut.

Despite the fact that he'd been the one to leave, it still killed him to know Elle was finally moving on without him. And God, the thought of her being with someone else made him want to pick her up and carry her away from every other male on the planet.

But she deserved to be happy. To be free to live the life she wanted. The life she *deserved*. There once was a time Gabe thought that life would include him.

Maybe it still can.

He worked to school his expression, because what the fuck? Those thoughts were pointless and had no place here.

Ellena didn't need him in her life. Not for anything other than a bodyguard, anyway.

What she needed was a man whose job wouldn't put her at risk. Someone she could count on to always be there when she needed them.

Someone who's not me.

Speaking of her being with another guy...

Gabe looked back down at her. With a surprisingly steady voice he said, "You told me about your friends and co-workers, but I also need a list of anyone you've been involved with recently."

As much as he *didn't* want to know about any other men she might have been with, Gabe couldn't risk missing something because he was a jealous asshole.

She'd already been hurt once because of him. He was going to make damn sure he did right by her this time in keeping her safe. Once that was done, he'd walk away from her for good.

You sure you'll be able to leave a second time?

"Oh." Elle licked her lips nervously in response to his request. "O-okay."

Shit. It wasn't the reaction he'd been hoping for, despite her earlier comment.

It's been three years, Gabe. What did you expect?

Clearing his throat, Gabe quickly moved on. "We'll also need a list of your patients. Past and present."

She frowned. "You know I can't give you that information."

"This isn't the time to be worrying about policy, Elle."

"Patient confidentiality is a hell of a lot more than just some policy, Gabe."

This was one argument he'd known was coming. But it was one he was damn sure going to win.

"I get that your job is to protect your patients, but you've got to look at this from all sides. You spend your days with people who've seen the worst the world has to offer. Going into battle... that shit can screw with those guys in a lot of ways. Sometimes it messes them up inside. Makes them do things they wouldn't normally do."

"Like becoming fixated on the one person trying to help them," Kole chimed in.

As expected, Ellena didn't back down. "I'm well aware of the traumatic effects war and combat can have on an individual, Gabriel. It's kind of what I do."

"Then you also know sometimes soldiers return home a shell of their former selves. That sometimes, something happens to them over there and a switch gets flipped. One that can't be undone."

"He's right, Elle," Nate agreed. "When that happens, it makes those men and women a danger not only to themselves but also to others. In this particular case, it's possible one of your patients has, for whatever reason, made you their target."

Determined to get through to her, Gabe softened his tone before adding, "I've seen it happen, Elle. We both have."

With a knowing stare, she nodded. "I haven't forgotten."

"I know you haven't, sweetheart."

Taking a chance, Gabe squatted down in front of her and took her hand in his. Ignoring the same electrical pulse he'd felt when they'd collided in her office doorway earlier, Gabe said a silent prayer of thanks when she didn't pull away.

"Listen to me, Elle. I know how important your job is to you. But I also know the law protects mental health professionals if they believe their patients are a danger to themselves or others."

"He's right," Matt backed him up from his spot on the couch. "If you believe one of your patients is a possible threat, you're allowed to share that information with someone who can keep the endangered party safe."

Piggybacking on Matt's point, Gabe added, "You also have a duty to warn the person in danger of any possible threat. Baby… this time *you're* the one who's in danger, and the only way I know to protect you is to rule out every possible suspect until we've found the person who's after you."

"Gabe." His name escaped as a whisper. A plea to not ask her to go against everything she stood for.

He continued on, determined to drive his point home.

"I promise I'm not trying to strong-arm you on this, Elle. You know I wouldn't ask for this information if it wasn't important. I hope you also know there isn't anything I wouldn't do to protect you." He'd walked away from her three years ago for that very reason. "Sweetheart, I know what I'm asking is a pretty tall order, but no one's looking to ruin your career, here. We just want to keep you safe."

He watched and waited as Elle's baby blues left his to take in each member of Bravo. When her gaze returned to his, Gabe saw something he never thought he'd ever find shining there again.

Trust.

Still, instead of giving in completely, she thought for a moment before asking, "Compromise?" She looked down at her lap then back up at him. "We used to be pretty good at those, as I recall."

Gabe's heart thrummed hard inside his chest as memories from their time together made their presence known. This was the way they'd settled most of their disagreements when they were still together.

"That we were." He smiled his first real smile in a long damn time. "What's your offer?"

"I look through all of my patients' files, and if there are any red flags I think are worth looking into further, I'll give you a name."

"Counteroffer," Gabe replied with a sideways smirk. *God, I've missed this.* "You look through the notes for any red flags, and let

Nate run your patients' names for anything that might come up in his system."

"His system?" Elle slid Nate a glance.

Nate's 'system' was complex as hell, and Gabe didn't understand any of it other than the end result, which was all he cared about, anyway.

The other man jumped in to try to explain. "I enter a name, DOB, and social security number, and the program's algorithm, which I created, searches for a criminal record and at the same time connects all sorts of dots."

"Dots?"

The skin between Elle's delicate brows bunched together, and Gabe had the sudden urge to kiss her confusion away.

Not the time, dickhead.

He gave himself a mental shake of his head and focused on what Nate was saying.

"For example"—the former Naval Intelligence officer continued on—"my program will tell me a person's known associates, any business transactions, illegal or legitimate, that might raise a red flag. Known dealings with less than savory characters…stuff like that."

"Wow." Ellena's brows rose to form twin arches. Blinking, she looked back at Gabe, who was still squatted before her. "When you said he was a genius, you weren't kidding, were you?"

"Nope." He grinned.

With another slight squeeze of her hand, Gabe pulled his free and rose to his feet. If he didn't put at least a little distance between them, if he didn't stop *touching* her, he was liable to do something monumentally stupid like lean up and kiss her.

There was a time when he was free to do so. Unfortunately for him, that time had long since passed.

Had your chance, Dawson. And you fucking blew it.

Big. Time.

Giving her—and himself—some much-needed space, he waited quietly while she turned her negotiating tactics to Nate.

"I hand over my patients' names if and only if I find something I think is worth looking into further. In turn, you give me your word any list I give you will be destroyed once you've completed your search, along with any trail of the search itself."

Nate's eyes shifted to Gabe's. The two men shared a knowing glance before Gabe gave Elle trustworthy smile.

"Agreed."

With a slight hesitation, Ellena nodded. "Okay. I'll need to go to my office." She turned back to Gabe. "I didn't bring my work computer home with me, plus I need to go through the physical files, as well."

She'd told him long ago how she'd jot down notes on paper while listening to her patients, then type them up in the system after the fact. Not every note she wrote made it into her final electronic files, which meant there could be something in writing she'd inadvertently glossed over.

"I can take you first thing in the morning."

"Actually, I'd rather go now. I still have some empty boxes in the garage from when I first moved in here. We can use those to bring the files back here. I can go through a few tonight before bed, and Nate could get started on running the names through his system. If there are any to run."

"You sure?" Gabe glanced at his watch. "It's getting late, and you've had a couple of rough days."

"I'm sure. Besides, if we don't go now, I'll just be up all night thinking about it."

"Okay, then." He looked at the others. "You guys can follow us to the hospital and help us carry them."

"I'd prefer it just be you and me. No offense," she quickly offered his team. "It's just that, if someone from the hospital sees me going into my office late at night with one person, no big deal. They see me go in there with the A-Team, however..."

"They could get suspicious," Gabe finished the thought for her.

"At the very least, it would draw unwanted attention to us that could possibly stir up questions I really don't want to have to answer."

As usual, she was right.

"Fine." To his team, Gabe said, "You guys can go to the hotel for the night while we head to her office. I'll call if we need anything."

As all four men muttered their agreements, he turned and gave his wife a pointed look. "We'll do this, but you're not carrying a single box."

"I can handle a few files, Gabriel."

"You heard the doctor. That shoulder needs time to heal." He ran a glance over her arm and frowned. "Speaking of which, where's your sling?"

Ellena rolled her pretty eyes but let one corner of her kissable mouth curve upward. "I don't need the sling, and I promise I won't carry anything other than my purse and my phone. Besides." She exhaled loudly. "It's late, so it's not like I'm going to get through them all tonight, anyway. We can take a few files now and then bring them back tomorrow and swap them out for the rest. Deal?"

"Deal."

Out of the corner of his eye, Gabe saw Zade give Matt a sideways grin.

"You got something to say, King?" he asked his teammate.

Zade snapped his head back to meet his gaze. "Nope."

"Don't worry, big guy." Matt's mouth curved into a goofy grin. "He just loves it when a plan comes together."

"Nice." Ellena's smile stretched wider. "Best TV line ever."

"Here I thought I was the only one old enough to remember that show," Gabe chuckled.

"Are you kidding?" Elle's eyes met his as she and the others stood to leave. "I used to pretend my older cousin's Big Wheel was the black van with a red stripe painted down the side."

Headed for the front door, Kole slapped Gabe on the shoulder as he passed by. "Wait, wasn't 'The A-Team' a movie that came out several years ago? Something about a group of misfit Vietnam vets?"

"Yeah." Zade nodded. "It starred Liam Neeson and Bradley Cooper, and...shit. What's that one chick's name?"

"Jennifer Biel," Ellena smirked. "But it was an eighties TV series before it became a movie several years later.

"Eighties?" Kole asked, clearly surprised. "And you remember it? What were you, like two?"

Ellena chuckled. "Four. And I started watching when it was on as re-runs after the series had ended. It played on one of the seven channels the tv in the room I shared with my brother picked up. We'd turn the volume down low so our parents couldn't hear it because it was always on after our bedtime."

"Sneaky girl," Matt teased.

Everyone laughed, including Elle. The woman had barely smiled since she'd woken up in that damn hospital bed, so he was more than a little glad to see it.

Gabe always said her smile could light up a room. But when she laughed...

The sound made Gabe's heart tumble over itself inside his chest.

"Wait." Kole stopped as he was reaching for the door. "What's a Big Wheel?"

Damn. Gabe shook his head. Sometimes he forgot he was over a decade older than his younger teammate.

His dormant heart stirred when Kole's most recent question had Elle's laughter growing even louder. And as he followed her out the door, Gabe wondered how the hell he was going to leave that sound—and her—behind once this was all over.

CHAPTER 7

"Why the fuck is she still alive?"

Adrian Walker stared out the window to the city below. "Bitch got lucky."

"Lucky? You've tried to kill her twice and have failed miserably both times."

Taking a slow sip of his whiskey, he turned and faced the man who'd hired him. "Maybe she's a cat. They do have nine lives, you know."

"You think this is funny?" The prick slammed his own glass down onto one of the suite's accent tables.

Adrian shrugged. "It's a little funny."

The other man's clean-shaven face grew beet red. "I told you what needed to happen. I explained how time-sensitive our situation is, and I—"

"You didn't explain shit."

Adrian moved toward him. As usual, the chicken shit backed up a half a step. *That's right, tough guy. You should be fucking scared.*

"You gave me my mark and said to make it look like an accident. I tried while she was on her bike, but she somehow managed to keep the damn thing on the road. So she gets lucky one damn time, and you hand the job over to your boy, Hall. Behind my back. The guy didn't even check to see if she was actually fucking dead after he smashed into her car. *He's* the reason she's still alive. Not me."

"You said you were the best." The idiot went back to his glass, swallowing the rest of its contents in a single gulp. "It can't be that fucking hard. Just toss her down a flight of stairs and be done with it."

Jesus fucking Christ. Adrian shook his head. "You really are a clueless bastard, aren't you?"

He slapped his chest. "I took care of the reporter, remember? *I* did that."

"Because you were desperate and lost your shit. Let's not forget who helped you clean up that mess."

Unable to admit he'd fucked up by letting his temper flare and pushing the poor reporter a little too hard, the other man bypassed his mistake and moved on.

Jutting his chin, he said, "People fall down the stairs every goddamn day, Walker. It's a known fact."

"About a million falls every year, last time I checked," Adrian agreed. "But do you know how many of those people actually *die* from their injuries? Twelve thousand."

With his pointed nose in the air, the asshole smirked. "Exactly."

"No, dipshit. *Not* exactly. Twelve grand is barely a tenth of a percent of a million. So no, throwing someone down a flight of stairs is *not* the most believable way to cover up a murder."

The man made a ticking sound with his tongue. Obviously disappointed, he shook his head. "All those stories I've heard about you. All the rumors and whispers around DC about the great and powerful Adrian Walker. The second my boss came to me with this little problem, I thought…he's the man I want for this. *Walker* is the one who will get the job done." The asshole chuckled. "What a load of shit."

Before the man could blink, Adrian threw his glass down and covered the distance between them.

His thick fingers wrapped around the idiot's throat, and he shoved the mouthy prick against the table. Its marble top dug into the man's back as the arrogant fuck choked and sputtered, fighting for air Walker refused to give him.

Not until I'm done with him, anyway.

"You listen to me, you stupid fuck." Adrian felt the man tremble beneath his palm. "I *am* the best. I've done things you can't even imagine. Things that would make the Devil, himself, piss his pants. In fact, I could kill you right now and dispose of your body in a way there wouldn't be enough left to run a fucking DNA test on your sorry ass. So you might be paying me for this job but don't mistake that for you being in charge."

Adrian shoved the guy away and took a step back, continuing on with his version of Murder 101.

"You want someone executed, I'm your guy. But passing a death off as accidental is a lot fucking harder than it looks in the movies. And if she has another accident now, after two failed attempts back-to-back, there's no way the cops will buy it. They'll start digging, which is exactly what we don't want."

Cowering like the well-groomed pussy he was, the crooked bastard coughed. He had to suck in several breaths before he was finally able to speak again.

"You know the man I work for." His voice shook as he rubbed his bruised throat. "What he's capable of."

"I do."

"Then you also know what will happen to both of us if you fail." In an attempt to regain his composure, the dick ran his hands along his chest, smoothing the front of his suit jacket. "She's one helpless woman, Walker. Honestly at this point, I don't give a shit how you do it. Accident or not, you need to take care of her soon. Otherwise, we're both done."

Without another word, the man left, and Adrian went back to the window where he'd been standing before. The one overlooking San Diego's Naval Medical Hospital.

Pulling his phone from his pocket, Adrian opened the tracking app to check his target's location. *Perfect.*

A plan began to form. One he prayed would work.

As he gathered his things, Adrian thought about the best way to proceed. He'd have to be careful. Very careful.

Because despite what that asshole and his employer thought, Ellena Dawson was far from helpless.

* * *

Ellena slid her ID badge along the card reader. When the tiny light turned green, a loud click let her know the employee access door was unlocked.

She reached for the metal handle, but Gabe stopped her by placing his hand over hers. "Let me go in first."

Her heart did that little thing in her chest again. The way it always did when he touched her. No one else had ever made her feel that way.

Only him.

It was so irritating, knowing the man still had such a strong effect on her.

"Seriously?" Ellena raised her brow. "You really think someone's waiting for me in the hallway on the other side of this door, hoping I might decide to stop by my office at"—she glanced down at her watch—"nine twenty-seven on a Sunday night?"

Her tone and incredulous look did nothing to persuade him. Not that she actually expected it to.

The frustratingly handsome man simply shrugged one of his broad shoulders and said, "Stranger things have happened."

Reminding herself that he meant well, Ellena stepped to the side, biting her tongue to keep from popping off another smartass reply.

The corner of Gabe's mouth twitched. "Thanks."

With a wink that caused a familiar tingling in her lower abdomen, he opened the door and looked ahead. Pausing to check for any boogie men that may be lurking around, he held the door so she could go past.

"You still in two twenty-two?" He asked from behind her.

Ellena's step faltered slightly. "You remembered my office number?"

"Of course, I remember." He slid her a sideways glance. "It was our lucky number."

To most, two hundred twenty-two would probably be a strange number to consider lucky. But it was theirs all the same.

For starters, February twenty-second was the day they met. Gabe had been texting someone on his phone when he ran into her—literally—as he was walking into the hospital to visit a teammate who'd been injured on an op.

As if it were yesterday, Elle could still remember the funny way her insides swirled around when she'd caught her first glimpse of him. That and the way his deep voice reverberated through her when he'd apologized.

Once he learned the number on her office door was two-twenty-two, he'd officially declared it their lucky number. When she asked him why, he'd explained it was the day they met, her office number, and his old locker number in high school.

He'd said fate must've known even way back then that she was the one he'd end up with. Elle had laughed and told him he was crazy, but deep inside she'd found it sweet and endearing.

When they'd checked into their hotel the night of their wedding and she discovered he'd reserved room two twenty-two, she fell in love with him even more than she already had.

So, from that point on when either of them happened to see that time displayed on their phones, watches, or a clock on a wall, they'd text each other. No words…just 222.

Then one day, the texts stopped.

Guess our luck ran out.

Ignoring the ache in her heart, Ellena slid her badge along her office door's sensor. Turning the knob, she held the door open for Gabe before flipping on the light switch.

Gabe bit out a low curse causing her to swing her head around. She gasped, the scene before her stealing every ounce of air in her lungs. "Oh, my god."

The place was in shambles.

As he pulled his phone from his pocket, Gabe instructed, "Call hospital security."

Feeling almost as if she were on autopilot, she made her way to her desk, doing her best to keep from stepping on the strewn files and papers covering her office floor. From her peripheral, she could see Gabe taking pictures of the mess.

As soon as she was off the phone, Ellena stood by her desk and looked around as she spoke. "Security's on their way up here now. I can talk to the staff. See if anyone saw anything."

"I have that covered." Gabe looked at her from across the room. "When was the last time you were in here?"

She took a moment to consider the question, shock from what they'd found slowing her thought process.

"I'm assuming right before the wreck. According to a couple of other doctors I work with, I came to the hospital, saw my appointments for that day, then went home at the usual time. You know the rest." She stared at the mess covering her office floor. "I-I don't understand why someone would do this." Meeting his gaze, she crossed her arms, hugging herself as best she could with a sore shoulder. "Or why is any of this happening?"

"Neither do I, sweetheart." Sympathy mixed with the anger filling Gabe's dark eyes. "The man who came to see me—"

"Adrian Walker," Ellena interrupted. "That's his name, right?" When he shot her a look, she reminded him, "You mentioned the name earlier."

Gabe's brows turned inward as he gave a slight shake of his head. She'd seen that look before, could tell he was mentally cursing himself for the apparent slip-up.

Though she was scared of the answer, she asked him, "What exactly did this Walker guy tell you?"

He shoved his phone back into his pocket, the defining line between the muscles in his arm deepening with the movement. "The knowledge she has could help stop them. Those were his words."

"Them who? And what knowledge?" Uncrossing her arms, Ellena's voice rose with frustration. "I'm a freaking psychologist, Gabe. I help my patients work through issues affecting their daily lives. I help them learn to open up about their troubles and then teach them ways to cope with it all. That's it."

He stepped forward. "Clearly, someone thinks you know something. And whatever it is, it's worth going through the trouble of breaking in here and doing this." He glanced around the room. "Which only affirms our theory that one of your patients is also involved."

"You said Adrian Walker wasn't a friend."

A muscle in his strong, sexy jaw twitched. "He's not."

"Then who is he?"

"No one you need to worry about."

"Don't do that." Ellena shook her head.

"Do what?"

"Shut me out."

"I'm not."

"You are," she challenged back. "You're doing what you always do."

"What I always do?"

"You're trying to protect me by leaving me in the dark." Ellena crossed her arms again. "It didn't work when we were together, and it's not going to work now."

"Now's not the time, Ellena."

"You're right." She smiled sadly. "Of course, it's never the right time to talk about it, is it?"

"Elle…"

"Dr. Dawson!" Howard, the head of the night security staff, barged in. "I came as soon as I heard." Huffing a breath, his worried eyes shifted from the mess on the floor to her. "Are you okay?"

Gabe started to put himself between her and the older man, but she put her hand up to stop him. "It's okay. It's just Howard."

Recognition flittered behind her protector's eyes. "Howard. Right. It's been a long time." Gabe held out his hand.

When the other man hesitated, Ellena said, "You remember Gabe, don't you?"

"The husband." Howard straightened his shoulders and took Gabe's hand in what appeared to be a strong hold.

The man was in his early fifties, shorter than average, and about fifty pounds overweight. He'd worked for the hospital longer than she had and was known for being the father-figure type amongst the female employees.

Someone messed with them, he was right there, ready to step in and help.

From the look he was giving Gabe, Ellena knew he was gearing up to defend her honor.

She put a hand on Howard's shoulder and made sure that didn't happen. "Gabe came back to help me."

The older man grunted but dropped his hand. With a narrowed gaze he asked, "Help, how?"

"Someone's trying to hurt Ellena. I'm here to make sure that doesn't happen."

Howard's silver brows rose high. "Hurt her?" His light blue eyes bounced back and forth between her and Gabe. "Why on earth would someone want to hurt Dr. Dawson? She's one of the nicest women I know."

"That's why we're here," Gabe told him. "To try and figure that out."

Ellena could practically see the man's wheels turning as he looked at the mess surrounding them. "You think one of your patients did this? But why?"

"I don't know the answer to either of those questions, Howard."

"You can help us find them, though," Gabe told him. "If you're willing."

"Of course." Howard looked at her then back to Gabe. "I'll do anything I can to help."

"I was hoping you'd say that because there's something I need from you."

"Name it."

And just like that, the two men were on common ground.

"I need access to the security footage. Everything from three days ago to tonight. I also want a guard posted outside Dr. Dawson's office."

"Shouldn't we call the cops first?"

"Once I see the tapes, I'll know whether or not we should get the local authorities involved."

Howard tilted his head. "You still a SEAL?"

"No sir."

"Who did you say you work for now?"

"I didn't."

"Gabe works for R.I.S.C.," Ellena chimed in. "It's a private security company based out of Dallas."

"I've heard of it." The other man nodded. "They do good work, from what I hear."

"Better than good," Gabe stated bluntly. "We're the best, which is why I need to see that footage."

With a curt nod, Howard got on his radio and instructed one of the other officers to come to his location immediately. Three minutes later, a young man in a uniform appeared.

"Jamie, this is Dr. Dawson. Her office was broken into, and I need you to stand guard until Mr. Dawson and I get back."

"Yes, sir."

To Gabe, Howard said, "Follow me."

Howard walked out the door, but Gabe didn't follow. Instead, he looked at her and said, "Stay here. See if anything's missing. We need to figure out what it was they were looking for."

Ellen glanced down at the floor and sighed. "This is going to take forever to straighten out, but you're right. The answer's here, somewhere. I just have to find it."

"We will." He reached out as if he were going to touch her but dropped his hand back to his side. "Lock the door behind me, and do not let anyone in but me."

"Okay."

"I mean it, Elle. I need you to trust me on this."

"I heard you, Gabe." She glanced at the mess once more. "And right now, you're about the only person I do trust."

An emotion she couldn't quite place reflected off his eyes, but then he turned to the young guard. "No one comes in or out of this office until I get back. No. One."

The man's eyes skittered nervously to Howard then back to Gabe's. "Y-yes sir."

With a final glance back at her, Gabe shut the door, leaving Ellena alone to deal with the mess. Knowing she had to start somewhere, she picked up one folder, then another. And another.

As she worked to sort through the papers, she made three stacks. One for the patients she knew, without a doubt, were not a threat, a second for those who had something in their notes that gave her pause, and a third area was reserved in case she found any notes she felt were cause for alarm.

An hour later, Ellena's office was back in order, and every loose note or document had been put back into the files in which they belonged. All except one.

A yellow sticky note with the word 'monarch' written on it.

Sitting crisscrossed on the floor amongst the three groups of neatly stacked files, she studied the tiny note more closely.

It wasn't wrinkled or faded and didn't appear to be very old. For some reason, the word struck a chord, but for the life of her, Ellena couldn't remember why she'd written it down. She also had no idea which patient she'd been talking with when she did.

My computer.

She'd been so busy dealing with the paper mess, she hadn't thought to look for it before now.

Rising to her feet, Ellena quickly made her way over to her desk. She looked around its top, opened drawers. She searched every possible space, all the while knowing in her gut...

"Damn it."

Without really thinking about what she was doing, Ellena pulled her cell phone from her purse with the intention of calling Gabe but stopped short. He was busy in the security room, and would be back soon, anyway.

She started to put the phone away but halted her own movements. This time for an entirely different reason.

There was a tiny red box at the corner of her voicemail icon reminding her she had several voicemails she'd been ignoring. Between her hospital stay and everything else that had transpired since, she hadn't bothered to check her messages since the accident.

Hoping there might be something there to help put the pieces of her lost day together, Ellena tapped her screen and began scanning the list. It was a long shot, but it was also the only thing she had to work with until Gabe came back.

Most of her messages were from the last couple of days. Co-workers and acquaintances who'd heard about the wreck and were most likely calling to check up on her. With enough on her plate, she'd purposely ignored the incoming calls.

Skimming past those, Ellena was about to give up and close her phone when she saw a number she didn't recognize. One with a Texas area code.

She pressed play and put the phone to her ear. Her heart thrummed against her ribs when she heard Gabe's voice...

"Hey, Elle. It's me. Listen, I know it's been a long time, and this is going to sound crazy, but I think you're in danger. I'm sorry to drop this on you out of the blue, and I promise I'm not trying to scare you, but...look, I'll explain more when I get there, okay? I'm leaving Dallas tonight, and I'll call you as soon as I land. Do me a favor and don't go anywhere. Keep your doors locked and don't answer them or the phone unless it's me. Call me when you get this...please."

He'd called her. Someone had told him she was in trouble, and the first thing he did was call to warn her.

She listened to the voicemail again. And again.

He sounded so worried.

For some odd reason, that made her feel good inside. Cared for in a way she hadn't been in so long.

Ellena was in the middle of listening to it for a fourth time when someone knocked on the door. Startled, she fumbled and nearly dropped the phone before closing the screen and putting it back into her purse.

"It's me," Gabe's voice traveled through the wooden door.

She unlocked it and swung it open. "Did you find anything?"

"Yes and no." He let the door close behind him. "You?"

She motioned to the stacks of folders on the floor. "I went through the mess and got everything back where it belonged. I may have found a few things worth looking into. The ones in those stacks there." She pointed to the two piles on the end. "But I'm not sure they'll be of any help, since I don't really know what it is I'm looking for. Plus, there are still several files in those cabinets over there. Those don't seem to have been touched, though."

"I'd say if whoever did this didn't bother looking in there, whatever they did come for wasn't in any of those."

"That narrows them down then, at least." Ellena blew out a breath. "Oh! I almost forgot. My computer is missing. I looked everywhere, but they must've taken it."

"No, they didn't."

Between the exhaustion settling in, the headache that was determined to make its presence known, and being flustered from listening to Gabe's voicemail, she didn't hear what he'd just said and continued talking.

"Which is going to be a logistical nightmare. All of my patient files have now been compromised." She started for the door. "I need to let Howard know, and I also need to call the department's director. He'll have to notify the state, and—"

"Elle!"

"What?"

Gabe held up a laptop. *Her* laptop.

"How did you...where did you find that?" Ellena went to him, taking the computer from his hand.

"Howard had it."

She frowned. "Why?"

"He said they installed an updated spyware program on all the staff's computers the night of your wreck. When he found out you'd been injured and were a patient here, he decided to hang on to it for safe keeping."

"Thank God." Ellena exhaled loudly. The staff was notified of the update by email last week, but with everything going on, she'd completely forgotten about it.

Closing her eyes, she took a moment to rub her fingertips against her aching temple.

"Headache?"

"Getting there."

"Come on." Gabe walked over to the stack of folders. "Tell me again which of these you want to take home so I can get you out of here and into bed." He swung his head around, eyes shimmering with that deer-caught-in-the-headlights look. "Because you're hurting, and you need sleep."

Ellena grinned. "It's okay. I knew what you meant."

"Good." He appeared relieved. "I didn't want you to think... not that I wouldn't want..." His eyes closed, his brawny chest rising and falling with a deep, cleansing breath. "You know what? I'm just going to stop talking."

Ellena's shoulders shook with silent laughter as she pointed to the floor. "Those two piles there." Sliding the strap of her purse over her good shoulder, she gave him a lazy smile. "And normally I'd argue and say we need to look those over more before I go to bed, but I'm too tired."

"Good." Gabe leaned down and picked up the folders. "You have to take care of yourself, Elle."

What if I want you to take care of me?

She coughed away the unspoken question and headed for the door. Those kinds of thoughts weren't helpful. Nice, but not helpful.

"Here. Let me carry that."

Gabe started to grab her laptop, but Ellena shifted to the side so it was out of his reach. "I've got it."

"Elle..."

"I'm fine, Gabe. It's in my right hand, not my left. Besides that, it's not even heavy."

One corner of his mouth twitched. "You know, I don't remember you being this stubborn."

"Being stubborn is like having a penis. It can be good or bad, depending on how you use it."

Gabe barked out a laugh, the sound vibrating to her soul. "God, I've missed you." His eyes widened slightly, as if he hadn't meant to say those words out loud.

Feeling a sudden urge to put him at ease, Ellena smiled up at him, admitting, "I've missed you, too."

Dark, powerful eyes lingered on hers a second longer before he turned and opened the door. With his head on a constant swivel, Gabe escorted her from the hospital.

Sticking close to her side, they started across the parking

lot toward his rental car. Resting her computer in the nook of her elbow, Ellena held it against her chest as they walked.

His car came into sight several spaces down, and she grinned.

"What's so funny?"

"Nothing."

He raised a brow. "Then why are you smiling?"

"It's just sort of comical."

"What is?"

"You. Driving such a compact car."

He grunted. "It was either this or an eight-passenger van."

As they continued walking, Gabe's hand slid protectively against her lower back. Heat from his palm seared her skin through her t-shirt's thin cotton barrier.

Ellena wondered if he even realized he'd pulled her closer to him, and though it was probably a masochistic move, she let him.

"At least with a van, you'd have plenty of space for those long legs of yours," she teased.

"No shit." He shook his head. "I feel like a damn contortionist trying to climb into that tiny thing."

"I'm sure it's not *that* bad. From what I recall, you used to be pretty flexible." Her cheeks became instantly hot, and Ellena slid him an embarrassed glance. "Sorry."

Smooth, Elle. Really freaking smooth.

Gabe pulled his keys from his pocket. "Anytime you want to test my flexibility, sweetheart, you just say the word."

Ellena's footing stalled but she recovered quickly. She knew he was kidding.

Of course, he was kidding.

What if he's not?

A car turned into the parking lot, its headlights causing her to squint. It drove slowly along the aisle on their right, as if the driver was searching for a place to park.

Mumbling a curse, Gabe pulled her to a stop. "I shouldn't have said that, Elle. I'm sorry."

Ellena tilted her head back to look at him. "We're adults, Gabe. Adults who used to be married."

His expression intensified. "We're still married."

"You know what I mean."

"Yeah." He ran a hand through his hair. "I do."

"We've been through a lot together." She gave him a ghost of a smile. "Too much to have to walk on eggshells, don't you think?"

Gabe stared down at her, his lips parting sightly as if he wanted to say more. Instead, he continued walking. Half a beat later, he asked, "What if I wasn't joking?"

"What?"

"Like you said, we're both adults. Not like we'd be doing anything wrong."

Her feet stopped moving. Her heart stopped beating. "That's probably not a good idea." She wanted to be with him again. God, did she want to.

"Why?" He glanced at her from over his shoulder as he rounded the rear of his car.

Ellena frowned, unable to come up with an appropriate response.

It was a crazy idea.

A crazy, wonderful idea.

"Just something to think about." Gabe opened the passenger door for her and waited.

Thoughts and enticing possibilities whirled around inside her needy brain. Hugging her computer even closer to her chest, she began moving again.

Her eyes stayed glued to his as she approached the vehicle. And the way he was looking back at her...

He still wants you.

The thought had barely entered her brain when she heard Gabe yell for her to get down.

A heartbeat later, something slammed into her with the force of a rocket, throwing her backward and onto the cold, hard ground.

Pain filled her chest making it impossible to breathe. Several loud explosions mixed with the sound of shattering glass and squealing tires. Silence filled the air, and then suddenly, he was there.

Gabe fell to his knees beside her, terror filling his eyes. His mouth was moving, but she couldn't quite make out was he was saying.

As the world began to fade around her, Ellena finally heard him. He was begging her. Just like that day three years ago, her strong, fearless Gabe was begging her not to leave.

CHAPTER 8

"That's enough." Standing next to Ellena's bed—another *fucking* hospital bed—Gabe stared at the other man in the room. "You've asked, she's answered. We both have."

Sgt. Puett, the man in charge of San Diego's Major Crimes division, slid a glance from Elle to him. "Your wife was shot at tonight, Mr. Dawson. I'm asking questions because I'm trying to figure out who pulled the trigger and why. I'd think you'd want to do everything you could to help us find them."

I'll find him. Then I'll fucking end him.

Gabe looked down at Elle, her delicate fingers giving his hand a squeeze. He still couldn't believe how close he'd come to losing her. If it hadn't been for her computer, he would have.

Can't lose what you don't have.

"You're probably right, though," Puett's deep voice cut through his thoughts. "Chances are this wasn't personal. Probably gang initiation or something like that."

His tone gave Gabe pause, making him study the other man more closely. "Or something."

"It's a shame we weren't able to at least find the bullet." The other man put his notebook back into his jacket pocket. "Damn thing must've bounced off the computer when it hit."

"That would be my guess." Gabe nodded. He had a feeling the cop knew exactly what had happened to the bullet.

Sgt. Puett glanced Elle's way. "I hate to admit it, Dr., but in a city this size, the odds of solving a case like this aren't very high. Without any hard evidence, it's pretty much impossible for my department to see it through to the end." Puett came closer, his seasoned eyes shifting to Gabe's. "Even so, justice sometimes has a way of hunting these criminals down. You like to hunt, Mr. Dawson?"

You'd better fucking believe it. "I do my fair share."

There was another brief pause before the guy nodded. "I'll let you know if I have any more questions." Puett held out his hand, his sudden change in direction telling.

Gabe shook the man's hand. "Thanks."

"Take care of yourself, Dr. Dawson." The man headed for the door but turned back just before it. With one last look at Elle, his eyes landed on Gabe's. "Tell McQueen I said we're even."

A second later, Gabe and Elle were alone.

"McQueen?" She frowned. "Isn't that your boss's name?"

"Yeah."

That explained the guy's cryptic comments about hunting. If Puett knew who Gabe worked for, the man damn sure knew what he was capable of. Not only that, the guy had just given him the green light to handle the situation the way he saw fit.

I'll be damned.

"What did he mean when he said they were even?"

"Puett knows I have the bullet, but he's looking the other way." Gabe glanced back at Elle. "How are you feeling?"

She put a hand to her chest. "Like I was punched by Mike Tyson."

He stared at the spot where she was hit. Opening his mouth, Gabe started to apologize for not protecting her better but was interrupted by a frazzled Jenna rushing into the room.

"Oh, my god! So it's true?"

"Before you blow a gasket, Jen, I'm fine," Elle assured her friend.

"You were shot, Ellena." The fiery redhead shot him a glare before practically pushing him aside to get to her friend. "Don't tell me you're fine."

"I *am* fine. And actually, he shot my computer. Not me."

Despite the woman's angry demeanor, she carefully wrapped her arms around Elle and held her closely. "Shut up and give me a hug." A moment later, Jenna pulled away and shook her head. "I swear, if you'd gotten yourself killed I would've been so pissed."

"I'm sorry I scared you." Elle's eyes skittered to his then back to her friend's.

"Trust me, it wasn't something I planned."

Gabe's heart gave a hard thump as his mind played through the night's most recent events again. The entire scene had been running on loop in his head like a fucking horror film.

He saw the gun. Hollered for Elle to get down. Heard the shot a fraction of a second before he saw her fall. It made him want to fucking puke.

Seeing her go down like that...hearing her gasping for the air her lungs refused to accept...she hadn't just scared him. She'd fucking *terrified* him.

"You did a helluva lot more than just scare me," Jenna parroted his thoughts before diverting her anger onto him. "Tell me you killed the sonofabitch."

"Jenna!" Elle admonished her.

Jenna threw her hands on her hips, her long red ponytail nearly hitting him in the chest as she shot Elle a look. "Don't you 'Jenna' me. Someone literally tried to kill you tonight, Ellena. Please, for the love of *God*, tell me you don't still think I'm being paranoid about all of this."

"No." Looking at Gabe from over Jenna's shoulder, Elle whispered, "I believe you."

"Good." After exhaling a long puff of air, Jenna studied her friend with a nurse's eye. "So what did the doctor say?"

"I got the wind knocked out of me, and I have a pretty good bruise." Elle pulled at the hospital gown's paper-thin neckline. "Other than that, I'm fine."

Bile churned deep in Gabe's gut as she exposed the darkening area below her right clavicle.

"Shit." Jenna cringed. "That had to hurt."

"Could've been a lot worse. Just ask my computer."

Neither Jenna nor Gabe laughed at Elle's attempted humor.

"Jesus, woman." Jenna shook her head. "I've never seen anyone get as lucky as you have, lately. You should think about buying a freaking lottery ticket or playing the slots or something."

Elle chuckled, then winced. "Damn, that's sore."

Jenna's green eyes filled with concern. "Are they keeping you overnight, or do you get to go home?"

"Neither," Gabe answered before Elle had the chance. His gruff tone had both women looking up at him. "She's not going back to her house."

"I'm not?"

He stared back at her. "The email was right. The people behind this know where to look for you. Hell, the pictures they sent were proof enough."

"It's my home, Gabe. If I run, they win."

"They tried to kill you tonight, Elle." His teeth clenched together. He took a step toward the bed. "Not in a way that could be blown off as an accident, but with a bullet to the fucking chest."

"What email?" Jenna's green eyes bounced back and forth between he and Elle. "Wait, someone sent you pictures?"

Ignoring the woman's questions, Gabe kept his eyes locked with his wife's. "Three attempts now, sweetheart. This last one was too fucking close."

The image of her being thrown back from the bullet's impact flashed through his mind for what felt like the millionth time.

His words must've sunk in, because rather than argue, Elle asked, "Where will we go?"

"Dallas."

Her brows shot up. "*Texas?* Gabe, I can't just drop everything and fly to another state. I have a job. Patients who—"

"Can see another doctor or maybe even set up virtual visits with you."

"It's not the same, and I can't ask them to do that. They need me."

"So do I." *Shit.* He hadn't meant to say it out loud.

Gabe took a deep breath and regrouped. Resting his hands on his hips, he softened his voice. "You're no good to your patients if you're dead, Ellena."

"He's right."

Elle looked over at Jenna.

"Sorry, but I agree with Gabe on this one. You should get as far away from here as you can. The other doctors can divvy up your patients while you're gone, same as they do when staff takes vacations."

"Some vacation," Elle mumbled low.

"It's only temporary, Elle." Gabe reminded her. "I'll bring you back as soon as I know you're safe. Promise."

Unless I can convince her to stay with me.

Gabe schooled his expression, silently cursing his overeager subconscious.

"Listen to him, honey," Jenna pleaded. "Please."

Elle stared up at him, fear and confliction dimming the light in her beautiful eyes. "What's to keep them from following me to Texas?"

"Nothing," Gabe answered honestly. "But at least then we'll be on my turf."

"Listen to him, sweetie." Jenna squeezed one of Elle's hands. "Homefield advantage is always a good thing. And since he's the one who'll be doing the fighting..."

Unshed tears filled Elle's gaze, but she blinked them away. "I-I'll need to pack. Make arrangements for the patients I have scheduled. How far out should I go?"

Forever. "A couple of weeks, to start."

Her shoulders fell, but she didn't argue. "I'll call the head of our technology department and have them get me another computer."

"You can't use the one you have at home?"

"The program we use for scheduling and electronic patient files is encrypted for confidentiality purposes. We're not allowed to have it installed on our personal devices."

"I can probably help with that."

All three swung their heads toward the doorway.

"Who are you?" Jenna shifted her body to block Elle from the man who'd just entered the small room.

"Stand down, Jen." Gabe put a hand to her shoulder. "He's with me."

"Hi, Nate." Elle peeked her head around Jenna.

A corner of Nate's mouth lifted in a half-smile. "Hey, Elle. Glad you're okay." To Gabe he said, "The others are waiting outside."

Gabe looked down at Jenna. "I need to talk to my team."

"Go." The redhead lifted her chin toward the door.

"You'll stay with her until I get back?"

"Don't worry." She grabbed Elle's hand. "Wild horses couldn't drag me away."

Moving around Jenna, Gabe went to Elle. He leaned down, pressed his lips to her forehead. "I'll be right outside." He pulled back, his eyes staying with hers a second longer before he grabbed the plastic bag holding her belongings.

The questions started the second the door shut behind him.

"What the hell happened?" Matt asked, sounding almost as pissed as Gabe felt.

Gabe ran a hand over his face and swallowed back his emotions. "Single shot to the chest. Shooter drove a dark two-door with tinted windows. Didn't get a look at the plates."

Kole frowned. "Nate said something about her computer saving her life?"

"Damn thing acted like a fucking vest." He still couldn't believe that shit. "She was holding her laptop with her right hand, cradling it against her chest like this." Gabe loosened the bag's drawstring opening and pulled out the damaged device. "Bullet penetrated the screen but got lodged here, between the keyboard and the back panel."

A wide-eyed Zade took the computer from Gabe. Turning it this way and that to study the bullet's effect, he shook his head in disbelief. "Jesus."

Matt rested his hands on his hips. "Wait. So she wasn't actually hit?"

Shoving his hands into his pockets, Gabe glanced back at the closed door behind him. "Got the wind knocked out of her. Chest is bruised all to hell. But the scans showed no internal bleeding."

"She was really fucking lucky," Matt stated the obvious.

The other men murmured their agreements. They were all well aware that a bullet didn't have to enter a person's body to do serious damage.

Damage Gabe couldn't even fathom his Elle having to endure.

"I should've seen it coming." He clenched his jaw shut. "I should've been right next to her, and I should've…"

"Don't do that to yourself, man." Matt shook his head. "Regrets and what-ifs are a waste of time. Trust me."

"Turner's right, Dawson," Nate agreed. "You could've been standing shoulder-to-shoulder with Elle. Wouldn't have changed the outcome."

"Other than you could've been the one to get shot, instead." Kole stared back at him. "And I could be wrong, but I'm willing to bet you weren't carrying a hunk of metal strong enough to stop a damn bullet."

Gabe's eyes moved down to the computer in Zade's hand. He could still feel the soul-wrenching fear racing through him when he realized there was nothing he could do to stop the inevitable.

"What now?" Nate's question ripped him out of his own personal hell.

"Doctor's supposed to be getting her discharge papers, so we should be good to go shortly.

The other man nodded. "I reserved the room across the hallway from mine, just in case." He handed Gabe two plastic keycards. "Room six thirteen. Double queen. But we can go straight to the airstrip from here if you'd rather."

"She's had a hell of a day." Gabe wanted to get Elle out of town as soon as possible but mumbled a curse when he checked his watch and saw it was almost midnight. Rubbing a hand down his face, he told them, "We'll stay the night and fly out first thing in the morning."

"Copy that." Nate tipped his chin.

"Have her put together a list of things she needs from the house," Zade suggested. "We can run by there now, throw whatever she needs in a bag, and meet you at the hotel."

"Sounds good." He dug into the bag for her purse. Unzipping it, he pulled out her keys and held them out for Zade. "I'll text you the list. Make sure you lock up when you're done."

Zade's eyes fell on the keys. "Uh...shouldn't you maybe ask Ellena first?"

"King's right, Dawson." Kole's expression turned leery. "I'm not so sure she's gonna appreciate us going through her things."

"Don't make me pull rank on you assholes." With the four men staring back at him expectantly, Gabe drew in a calming breath and silently counted to ten. "Just head to her house and wait for my text. Let me worry about my wife."

Matt rubbed his jaw with a smirk. "Damn, man. I still can't get used to hearing that."

Yeah well, you'd better get used to it.

Gabe cleared his throat, because shit. Thoughts like that were bound to get him in trouble.

"I'll take a look at this." Nate took the computer from Zade's hands. "With any luck, the motherboard's still intact. If it is, I should be able to recover the data that was saved on here. If not, I'm sure I can find a way into the program's backup system."

Of course, he could. The guy was a flippin' genius when it came to computer shit.

"That reminds me." Gabe slid his hand into his back pocket, pulling out the 'missing' bullet. Holding it between his thumb and forefinger, he held it out for Nate. "See if you can get anything off of this."

A slow smile formed on the guy's face. "You sly dog. I can't believe the cops didn't ask about it."

"The Sgt. in charge knows Jake."

With a shared a look of understanding, Nate slid the mangled piece of metal into his pocket. "I'll let you know what I find."

"Thanks, Carter." Gabe glanced over his shoulder. "I'm gonna get back in there. I'll shoot you a text in a few."

"Sounds good."

His team turned to leave, but Gabe quickly added, "Watch your six. If they came after her here, there could be someone waiting for her at home."

The others' eyes hardened as Matt spoke up. "If there is someone there, we'll be sure to give them a proper greeting."

With a single nod, Gabe slid the door open and returned to Ellena.

A little over two hours later, they were at the hotel. As asked, the guys had gotten some things from Ellena's house and had her bags waiting for her when they'd arrived.

Sensing she needed a few minutes alone, Gabe had insisted she take a hot shower while he ordered them some room service. Thankfully the hotel's kitchen was open 24/7.

He glanced at the narrow door. Their food had arrived a few minutes ago, but she still hadn't come out.

Torn between leaving her be and needing to have her in his sights every fucking second, Gabe went to the narrow door. Using his knuckles, he gave the wood a gentle tap.

"Elle?"

There was a second of silence before he heard a soft, "Yes?"

"Food's getting cold."

Another pause. "O-okay."

Her voice sounded thicker than normal, and when she opened the door, Gabe understood why.

She's been crying.

His heart broke. "Sweetheart…"

"Something smells delicious." Putting on fake-as-hell smile, she moved past him. "What did you order?"

She didn't want to talk about it. *Message received.*

"I wasn't sure what you were in the mood for, so I got a little bit of everything."

"I guess so." Ellena chuckled as she looked at spread of food covering the portable cart. "Have you eaten?"

"I was waiting for you." Gabe shook his head, willing himself to ignore how beautiful she looked.

Wearing a modest pajama set and no makeup, the woman shouldn't be so damn tempting. Still, it was all he could do not to reach for her and start unbuttoning her top.

Almost as if she could read his thoughts, Ellena's gaze remained locked with his a second longer before she picked up a plate and began making her selections.

"The weather's nice," she commented. "We could sit out on the balcony and eat."

Gabe grabbed a plate of his own. "I don't want you out in the open."

"Oh. Right." Her shoulders fell, making him feel like a giant prick.

Carrying her plate to the room's small table, Ellena pulled out a chair and sat down. Joining her, Gabe waited for her to take the first bite before digging in.

She grinned. "You don't have to do that, you know?"

"What's that?" He took another bite of his burger.

"Wait for me to start eating before you do."

Shrugging, Gabe swallowed the bite before responding. "Old habit."

"It seems you have a lot of those."

"Only when it comes to you." His words caused her eyes to widen slightly. Clearing his throat, he offered her a low, "Sorry."

"Don't be." Her expression turned wistful. "You always were good at sweet talking me."

"It's not sweet talking if it's the truth."

Shit. Feeling like he'd lost control of the words coming out of his damn mouth, Gabe was about to apologize again, but then he noticed the way her blue eyes had darkened.

It was the same look she used to give him just before they'd make love. His rising cock became uncomfortable behind his zipper, but he didn't dare adjust himself.

She was probably dealing with the after-effects of a major adrenaline overload, and after everything that had happened, the last thing she needed to deal with was his overeager dick.

"So what now?" Ellena took a sip of her water and swallowed. "I know we're flying to Dallas in a few hours, but what will happen once we get there?"

"I'll take you someplace secured."

"Secured." She glanced down at her drink. "Like a safe house?"

"Exactly like a safe house." Using the white cloth napkin, Gabe wiped his mouth and rested his elbows on the table. "Like I said before, Elle, this is just temporary. Once we figure out who keeps coming after you and why, my team and I will put an end to the whole fucking thing."

Abandoning her uneaten food, she stood and went to the room's floor-to-ceiling windows. Hugging herself, she stared down at the city below.

"You, uh...you should probably stay away from the windows," he told her quietly. "Just in case."

Despite his suggestion, Ellena remained in place for another minute before facing him again. She took a few slow steps in his direction, an emotion he couldn't quite place crossing over her beautiful face.

"I'm glad you're here."

Her whispered words surprised the hell out of him.

"So am I, sweetheart." He got up and walked toward her.

Gabe's eyes landed on the yellowing bruise and healing cut on her forehead. His gut churned when they fell to the spot where that fucking bullet damn near killed her.

I failed her. Again.

"Stop."

His gaze rose back up to hers. "Stop what?"

"Blaming yourself for what happened."

He swallowed, the fists hanging at his sides tightening. "Not possible, sweetheart."

It's all he'd been doing since she'd been hit.

"You had no way of knowing, Gabe."

"I should have." Rolling his lips inward, he barely kept from howling at the fear still pumping through his veins. "I should've been paying attention instead of..."

"Flirting with me?"

She smirked as he scowled.

"This isn't funny, Ellena."

"Yeah well, it's either laugh or start crying again, right?"

She started to rush past him but stopped when Gabe reached out, gently wrapping his fingers around her wrist. "Hey." He waited, but she kept her eyes on the floor in front of her. "Sweetheart, look at me."

A hesitant, watery gaze met his.

"I've failed you twice." His teeth ground together. "There won't be a third time."

"Oh, Gabriel." Ellena turned to face him fully. Blinking away fresh tears, she rested her free hand against his cheek. "God didn't give you those big ol' shoulders just so you could carry the weight of the world on them. You can't protect everyone all the time."

His heart kicked against his ribs when her eyes fell to his lips.

"Don't need to protect everyone, Elle. Just you." He released her wrist and cupped her cheek. "I'd die before letting anything else happen to you."

"Today wasn't your fault." She swallowed hard. "Neither was three years ago."

His stomach dropped, and his chest tightened. It was the same, familiar pain he always felt when he thought about that day.

Unable to go there, Gabe let his hand drop and put some distance between them. "We fly out in a few hours." He cleared his rough throat. "You should get some rest."

"Right." A flash of anger flittered behind her eyes. "I almost forgot. We don't talk about that, do we? Not now. Not back then."

"Elle."

"Why is that, Gabriel?" she demanded to know. "There are two of us, yet you're the one who chooses whether or not we talk about what happened. Of course, you're also the one who single-handedly decided we shouldn't be together anymore, so…"

"Damn it, Elle…"

"I needed you, Gabe." She swiped angrily at a tear that had escaped. "I needed you, and you just walked away like we were nothing. Like I *meant* nothing."

"Nothing?" He growled, closing the distance between them. "You meant *everything* to me."

"Yet you still left, despite my having begged you to stay."

"I was trying to protect you!"

"I didn't need your protection, Gabriel!" Elle's angry voice bounced off the walls. "I needed *you!*"

The two of them stood like that for several seconds, scowling at one another. By the time Gabe opened his mouth to break the silence, he was too late.

"You know what, you're right." She walked around him. Choosing the bed closest to the windows, Elle began pulling the comforter and top sheet back. "It's late, and I've had a really shitty day." She climbed under the covers and turned her back to him. "Wake me when it's time to leave."

"Elle—"

"Goodnight, Gabe."

Shit. Fuck. Shit.

Feeling as though he'd just taken two gigantic steps back with her, Gabe decided it was best to keep his mouth shut, for now. If he said anything more, chances were good he'd just end up digging himself an even deeper hole than he was already in.

You need to talk about it with her.

Ignoring the pain-in-the-ass voice, Gabe went to the door and double-checked the locks before heading to the bathroom for a shower. Standing beneath the water's hot spray, he wished he could man up and say what he should've said three years ago.

I'm sorry, baby. So fucking sorry.

CHAPTER 9

"This is nice." Ellena stood by Gabe's truck, taking in the small cabin before her. "Cozy."

"More importantly, it's safe." Gabe grabbed their bags from the back seat of his truck. "Kole and Sarah don't come here very often, and it's not listed in his name, so the property would be really hard to trace back to him."

Reaching for her good shoulder, she adjusted the strap of her computer bag which contained the files she'd taken from her office. "Have you used it as a safe house before?"

He nodded. "Not too long ago, actually. Matt's wife, Katherine, is a scientist. Before they were married, the work she was doing put her in danger. The two of them hid out here for a while."

"This all seems so surreal." Ellena shook her head in disbelief. "The attempts on my life, someone breaking into my office. Coming to a cabin in the middle of nowhere to hide from the bad guys...it's like something out of a movie."

One she wished she could turn off.

Unlocking the door, Gabe held the door open for her. "After you."

Ellena's brows turned inward. "Shouldn't you, I don't know... clear it first?"

For some reason, her comment made him grin. "Kole and

Nate came out less than half an hour ago to stock the fridge and check the area. There was no sign of anyone having been here recently, and they're too good to let themselves be followed."

"Oh. Good." She smiled up at him.

With an expectant look, Gabe remained in place. It took a few seconds longer for her to realize he was waiting for her to go inside.

"Right. Sorry." A blush crept into her cheeks as she stepped past him. She hated how awkward she felt with him, now.

Once upon a time, being with him—*loving* him—had been effortless. As natural as breathing.

But today, she'd woken up on edge. Conscious of every single word forming on her lips before she said them and moving around him as if she were walking through a mine field.

"The bedroom and bathroom are through that door." Gabe pointed to a door on their far right. "Towels and washcloths are in the closet there, and you're welcome to anything in the kitchen."

The bedroom? As in one?

"Don't worry," his voice rumbled. "I'll take the couch."

Ellena eyed the modest couch. She couldn't help but grin as she imagined his large frame trying to fit. "I think maybe you should take the bed."

"I've slept on worse." He set his bag down beside the small table on their left and headed to the bedroom with hers. "Besides. There's only one way in and out of this place, and I'll sleep a hell of a lot better knowing I'm between it and you."

And they say chivalry is dead. "I thought you said this place was secure."

Stopping just before the bedroom door, Gabe turned to look back at her. "I'm not taking any chances, Elle. Not with you."

She watched as he disappeared through the doorway, hating how confusing the whole situation was. They'd barely said two words to each other on the flight into Dallas or the drive here, but when he said things like that, her heart felt completely defenseless.

Images from last night flew through her mind. Gabe rushing

to her after that bullet had struck. Hearing him scream her name and then feeling him scooping her up into his strong, safe arms.

Amongst the pain and her struggle to breathe, Ellena had actually felt the utter terror seeping from his body into hers as he held her close and sprinted toward the E.R. entrance.

I've got you, Elle. You're going to be okay. I've got you, baby.

The tone of his voice had held the same fear she'd heard in his voicemail. Her strong, fearless man had been scared. Not for himself, but for her.

Then afterward, at the hotel, he'd been so sweet. Almost vulnerable. So much so, she'd damn near kissed him for it. Of course, then she'd gone and ruined the moment by opening her big mouth.

Ellena released a deep sigh. Being with him the last few days may have caused her to realize how much she still loved him, still wanted to *be* with him, but it was clear that Gabe had no desire to return to the past.

If he couldn't find a way to deal with the loss they both shared, they'd never have any chance at a future.

"You hungry?" His deep voice snapped her away from her bewildering thoughts.

Practically jumping out of her skin, Ellena looked up. "Uh... yeah. I could eat."

"Why don't you sit down and relax." Gabe headed for the small kitchen. "I'll see what I can find for us in here."

"Actually, I want to go through these files again." She walked over to the couch and slid her bag from her shoulder. "I meant to look them over on the flight here, but I dozed off."

"I'm not surprised," he spoke from the kitchen. "You were pretty restless last night."

Of course, he'd noticed. Unfortunately, the small nap she took on the plane hadn't done her much good, either.

She settled herself onto the couch. "Yeah, well. Apparently almost being shot can do that to you."

"Trust me, I get it." Gabe's voice had turned low. Solemn.

Shifting herself sideways, Ellena rested her head against the back cushion and glanced toward the other room. A new aching sensation made its presence known, her heart hurting for all he'd been through over the years.

Ellena felt her eyes growing heavy.

Despite not knowing the specifics, she'd been there for him after each of his SEAL ops. Had kissed every single scrape and bruise until his pain became a memory and their passion all-consuming.

With no way of knowing what he'd gone through while working for R.I.S.C., she could only assume he'd suffered more of the same. Had there been someone else to kiss away his pain since her?

No. Do not go there.

Her subconscious was right. Thoughts like that would only bring about unnecessary heartache, and that was the last thing she needed on her plate.

Ellena had just closed her eyes when Gabe poked his head around the corner.

"Spaghetti sound okay?"

She offered him a polite smile. "Sure."

Lips twitching, he nodded. "I'll get the water started."

As he vanished back into the kitchen, Ellena allowed her eyes to shut again.

Just for a minute.

Time slipped away until she heard Gabe's soothing voice again.

"Welcome back."

Sitting up straighter, she rubbed the sleep from her eyes and frowned. "How long was I out?"

Standing between the fireplace and one of the room's two windows, Gabe smiled down at her. "A couple hours."

Ellena looked at the files still waiting to be looked over. "You shouldn't have let me sleep so long." Belatedly remembering the lunch he'd been preparing, she muttered a curse. "The spaghetti…"

"Is ready and waiting for you." He slid his hands from his pockets and sauntered toward the kitchen. "I'll go heat us up some."

"Didn't you already eat?"

"I was waiting for you."

The wink he gave her as he walked past made her heart beat a little harder. Scooting to her feet, Ellena realized only then that, at some point while she'd been sleeping, he'd also covered her with a blanket.

The gesture was a small one. Simple. Yet to her, it meant so much.

Ignoring the sudden onset of burning in her eyes, she laid the blanket on the couch and went to see if he needed any help. Thirty minutes later, she and Gabe had finished their spaghetti lunch and had moved on to dessert.

In the chair across from him, Ellena swallowed a bite of chocolate pie before speaking.

"This is really good." She licked some whipped cream from her lips. "Thank you."

"I'd say you're welcome, but Kole's the one to thank for the pie." Gabe wiped his mouth and smirked. "Actually, I'm pretty sure Lexi Matthews is the one to thank."

"Lexi?"

"She's married to one of the guys on R.I.S.C.'s Alpha Team. Lex owns The Gardens. It's a pretty popular restaurant in the city."

"Oh." Elle took another bite of the heavenly goodness. "I bet she keeps you guys fed pretty well then, huh?"

He chuckled. "We don't often go hungry, that's for sure."

A few seconds of awkward silence passed before they both started talking at the same time.

"So I talked to—"

"Have you heard from—"

They both chuckled as Gabe gave her a nod. "You first."

Smiling, Ellena sat her fork down. "I was just going to ask if you'd heard anything from Nate about my computer."

"As a matter of fact, I did. He texted right after you fell asleep. He's pretty confident he'll be able to recover all of your files."

"Really?"

He swallowed his drink of water. "Said he'd bring it by later."

"Wow. I assumed it was a lost cause."

"With anyone else, it probably would be. But Nate's a..."

"A computer genius?" She finished for him with a smirk.

Gabe's shoulders shook with silent laughter. "Exactly."

"I'll go through those folders again after we're done eating, and then when Nate gets here, I'll start going through all of my electronic files. See if anything stands out."

Ellena took another bite of the pie, her mind wandering with the insanity of it all.

Here she was, hiding away in the middle of nowhere with a man she'd intended to divorce, all because someone wanted her dead. She had no idea who it was or why, and now she was tasked with trying to decide if one of her patients was the culprit.

Could it really be someone she knew? Someone she'd tried to *help?*

"I'm sorry." Gabe's tender voice broke through her thoughts.

"For what?"

His dark eyes softened with compassion. "I know this is hard, and I hate that you're going through it." He looked away, smiling sadly and shaking his head before locking eyes with her again. "I'm sure my being here doesn't help."

An emotion she couldn't quite pinpoint filled her tightening chest. "I told you before I'm glad you're here, Gabe. Besides..." She offered him a smile. "Who could protect me better than a badass former SEAL, right?"

A ghost of a smile formed on his lips as he stood and went to her. He cupped her cheek. "I'll protect you with my life, Ellena. Always."

"I don't want that, Gabriel." She stood, covering his hand with hers. "I never wanted that."

His fingers skimmed across her skin, their soft touch leaving a shivering wake in their path. Tracing her collarbone, he let his hand linger there a moment.

"You were my world, Ellena."

Her short intake of air seemed to fill the entire cabin. "You're still mine."

It was a confession Ellena hadn't intended to share, but now that she had, she couldn't bring herself to be sorry.

She rose up slightly, shifting her weight to her tiptoes as he leaned inward. Kissing Gabe may very well be a monumental mistake, but in that moment, it was one Ellena was more than willing to make.

Gabe pressed his lips to hers, his familiar touch filling her with a consuming excitement. And when she opened her mouth to let him inside, it felt like coming home.

Their tongues danced together as he pulled her tightly against his chest, Ellena's breasts pressed against his solid form. His well-trimmed beard tickled her skin.

Oh, how she'd longed to feel this again. To have him hold her in his arms. To taste him.

To love him.

Gabe took the kiss deeper, the low rumble of his deep moan sending shockwaves of pleasure throughout her entire system. Ellena dug her fingers into his biceps, terrified if she let go, he'd disappear.

"Ah, baby." Gabe moved his mouth lower to her jawline, his words escaping with panted breaths. "I've missed you so damn much."

Though the words had already been said, Ellena felt their power from her heart to her toes. "Gabe…"

He lowered his hands to her hips. Turning their bodies, he claimed her mouth once more as he slowly guided them toward the couch.

Once they were there, Gabe released his gun from his back waistband and placed it on the coffee table before easing them down onto the cushions. The weight of his body was a welcome feeling as he settled between her open legs.

Despite the thick barrier of his jeans—and hers—Ellena couldn't miss his solid erection pressing against her heated core. On reflex, her hips lifted, her body's natural instinct to get as close to this man as was humanly possible.

"This is a mistake." She breathed between kisses.

Gabe froze.

Carefully hovering over her, he shifted his body so most of his weight was being supported by one elbow. Looking down at her with all the love he used to show, he brushed some hair from her face and whispered, "Ah, sweetheart. Being with you has never been a mistake."

Her damaged heart swelled inside her chest.

Logically, she knew sleeping with Gabe again didn't mean he was back for good. Nor did it mean their situation had changed.

He was here to protect her, not reconcile the marriage they'd once shared. She knew that. The psychologist in her understood the situation was the reason for their reunion. The *only* reason.

And yes, she was also fully aware of the setback having sex with him could cause in her mission to move on without him. But even with all of that knowledge and all of her professional training…Ellena still couldn't find it in herself to care.

If this is all I can have of him, I'll take it.

"Make love to me, Gabriel." She smiled up at him, ran her fingertips through the silver and black hair at his temple. "Please."

He pressed his lips to her forehead. The tip of her nose. Her lips. His hot breath caressed her face as he stared back at her and smiled.

"You don't ever have to beg me for that, baby. Not ever."

CHAPTER 10

One second they were talking, and the next Gabe was slamming his mouth against hers.

In a frenzy of kisses, they began tearing at each other's clothes with no thoughts of stopping. She helped him pull off his t-shirt. He unbuttoned her blouse.

Ellena slid her hands between them, her fingers working to release his belt.

Though he hated to do it, Gabe broke away from another mouthwatering kiss and rose to his knees to give her better access. She pulled the leather strap through the buckle, released it from its clasp, and was reaching for the button on his jeans when an alarm began to blare loudly from somewhere behind him.

What the...

Both he and Ellena froze.

"What is that?" Her blue eyes grew wide. "Gabe?"

He stared down at his wife. Her cheeks had become flushed with arousal and her chest was heaving, eagerly pushing her breasts toward him. Gabe was so enthralled by the pointed nipples playing peak-a-boo through her white, lacy bra that it took him a few seconds to answer.

Shit. "It's my phone." He jumped off of her, grabbed his gun, and went straight for his phone, which he'd left on the kitchen table.

Taken off guard by his sudden movements, Ellena blinked quickly as she sat up and began re-buttoning her shirt. "That's one heck of a ring tone."

"Not a ringtone." He studied his phone's screen, frowning as he marched to the nearest window. "It's an alarm."

"You have someplace to be?" She gave him a tiny smirk.

Gabe pushed the curtain aside just enough to be able to see out. "Not that kind of alarm, sweetheart. It's a program Nate created. It's connected to a security system that lines the cabin's perimeter."

"Meaning?"

He looked back at her from over his shoulder. "Meaning someone's here."

"They found us?" Ellena shot up from the couch, her panic obvious. "W-what do we do?"

Gabe looked back through the window, his muscles relaxing a few seconds later when he recognized the truck—and its driver—headed in their direction.

"Nothing." Turning around, he shoved his gun back into his waistband and began re-buckling his belt as he made his way back to her. "It's just Nate."

Ellena blew out a breath of relief. "Oh, thank God. I thought…"

"I know." Gabe put his hands on her shoulders. "I'm sorry."

"Sorry I was scared, or that we almost…" She glanced back at the couch.

Using a gentle touch, he turned her chin in his direction, forcing her to look at him. "The only way I'd be sorry about that"—he motioned toward the couch—"is if *you* were sorry."

Her ocean eyes stared back into his. "I'm not sorry."

Thank God.

Gabe exhaled loudly and pulled her to him. "Good." He squeezed his eyes shut when he felt her arms tightening around him.

As much as he wanted to kiss her again—and do a hell of a

lot *more*—he relished in how good it felt to have this woman back in his arms. They continued to stand like that, holding onto one another, until there was a loud knocking on the door.

Fucking Carter.

"I should probably let him in."

Releasing him, Ellena bent over and picked up his shirt from where she'd thrown it on the floor. With a suddenly shy smile, she held it out for him.

"You should probably be wearing this when you do."

"Thanks." Gabe grinned as he slid his arms through the holes and pulled it over his head. Then, because he couldn't stand not to, he cupped her face and pressed his lips to hers once more.

Moving more slowly than before, he savored the sweetness of her taste, their tongues gently caressing each other's as if they had all the time in the world. When another round of pounding came from the door, Gabe growled.

"I'd better answer that before he decides to break the damn thing down."

Gabe made his way to the door and began disengaging the locks. Giving Ellena one final glance over his shoulder, he opened the door with a glare.

"What the hell are you doing here?"

"Easy, big guy." Nate held up a laptop. "I come bearing gifts."

He looked at the computer then back up to Nate. "You're finished already? I thought you said it would be later."

"That was almost three hours ago." The other man looked at him deadpan. "It is later."

"I told him to wait until morning, but he said it was important."

The sweet, feminine voice took Gabe by surprise. "Gracie?"

Peaking her head into the doorway from Nate's right, the tiny blonde came into view. "Hey, Gabe. Things were slow at the office today, so Jake said I could tag along with Nate. You know, keep him out of trouble."

Snorting, Gabe moved to the side to let the couple in. "Not sure that's possible."

"You're probably right." Gracie laughed as she and her

husband passed by. Making a bee line straight for Ellena, she held out her hand. "You must be Elle. I'm Gracie Carter. Nate's wife."

"Nice to meet you."

Gabe watched as the two women shook hands.

"Okay." Gracie shook her head. "I've got to say, I was a little more than shocked to find out Gabe was married. We all were."

Elle's eyes slid to his, her smile faltering slightly before she recovered. "It's kind of a...long story."

"One I'm dying to hear. But I have a feeling that story should wait to be told over a bottle of wine. When the other wives are with us."

"Other wives?"

"Sure. They're all *dying* to meet you, by the way."

"They are?"

"Uh...yeah." Gracie looked at Ellena as if she were crazy. "We always wondered why Gabe never dated anyone. We never *dreamed* it was because he already had a wife. Our only question is where the heck have you been all this time?"

"Gracie," Nate warned his wife.

The other woman swung her head around toward her husband and frowned. "What?"

"These two have more important things to worry about right now, don't you think?"

"Oh." Gracie looked back at Ellena with a chagrined expression. "Right. Sorry. I guess I just got overly excited to meet you."

"It's fine." Ellena gave Gracie a smile that didn't reach her eyes. "And I'd love to share a bottle of wine with you and the others sometime."

"Really?"

Great. The last thing Gabe needed was for the other R.I.S.C. wives to find out what a shithead husband he'd been.

Made your bed, asshole.

"I'm assuming that thing's fixed?" Gabe nodded toward the computer in Nate's hand, praying his attempt to change the subject was successful.

"Huh?" Nate frowned before his brows rose into high arches.

"Oh, right. Yeah. Well, sort of. The shell is different because, well, the bullet pretty much destroyed the other one. But the innards are almost all the same. Most importantly"—he shot Ellena a grin—"the hard drive was fully intact."

Walking over to where he and Nate were standing, she took the computer from Nate's hand. "That's incredible."

"The model's a little different than the one you had, so the keyboard will probably take a bit to get used to. But I installed a faster processor so it will work faster than your old one. You should be able to fire it right up and do your thing."

She set it on the table, lifted it open, and turned it on. Two seconds later, the screen lit up and after she tapped a couple of keys, Ellena smiled wide. "Oh, my gosh. It's all here! Nate, you really are a genius."

Nate slid him a smug smirk. "I know."

"And so modest, too." Gracie laughed as she walked over to them. Her teasing was obvious, but so was the love she felt for Nate.

Struck with a sudden dose of jealousy for his younger teammate's relationship, Gabe had to work to keep from squeezing his teammate's shoulder too hard.

"Thanks for bringing that by."

"No problem, brother. Glad to be of service."

The two women looked back and forth between him and Nate a few times before Gracie rolled her eyes and made her way over to them.

"He wants us to leave, Nate."

"You do?" Nate's brow furrowed right before a slow, knowing grin spread across the bastard's face. "Ah, I get it. Come on, baby." He reached for Gracie's hand. "Let's leave these two lovebirds alone."

Ellena's confused eyes shot to his, but Gabe blew Nate's comment off with a slight shake of his head.

"That's not..." He started to comment, but let his voice trail off. Because there really was no good way to end that sentence. Not when Ellena was standing right there.

"Um...thanks, again for fixing this for me, Nate." Her lips

curled into an uncertain smile. "And Gracie, it was really nice meeting you."

"You, too, sweetie." Gracie pulled a surprised Ellena in for a hug.

She mentioned a get-together with the other R.I.S.C. wives, which struck up a whole new conversation, and as the two women talked for a couple more minutes, Gabe seized the opportunity.

Turning his voice low enough for only his teammate to hear him, he kept his eyes on Ellena while he asked Nate, "You get it?"

"You even have to ask?" Nate's dark brow rose. "I'm running her patient list through my program as we speak. If there's anything there, we'll know by tonight. Oh"—he pulled a burner phone from his pocket and handed it to Gabe—"I almost forgot this."

"It's clean?"

"Dude, seriously." Nate scowled. "You act like this is my first rodeo"

Gabe slid his gaze to Ellena. "It's the first one involving her."

Just then, Gracie whispered something in Ellena's ear. He couldn't hear what it was, but whatever Gracie was saying had Ellena's eyes travelling straight up to his.

After another round of goodbyes, the other couple headed for the door. Just before Gracie walked through it, she looked back at Ellena. "Don't forget what I said."

Gabe studied his wife carefully, but her only response was a guarded smile and a soft, "Thank you."

With a 'who the hell knows' shrug, Nate led Gracie to his truck. As he was opening the passenger door for her, he hollered back at Gabe.

"Keep your phone handy, big guy. Just in case."

"Always." Gabe stared back at the other man with a deliberate smirk. "And the next time you decide to just pop by, use yours to send me a damn text or something so you don't get your ass shot."

Walking around the front of the truck to his side, Nate snorted. "And ruin the element of surprise? What's the fun in that?" Giving him a departing wink, Gabe's teammate climbed into his truck and shut the door.

For a moment, Gabe remained on the cabin's modest porch, watching as they drove off. He scanned the wooded area surrounding the structure and prayed that coming here was the right decision to make.

Make love to me, Gabe.

His heart thumped against his ribs as he pictured her lying beneath him, saying those whispered words to him again. The sweetest he'd heard in years.

He glanced back over his shoulder at the closed door and wondered what was going through her head. Was she in there right now, remembering that exact same moment?

Another image flashed, but this one was different. It was of Ellena's face when Gracie commented on how no one knew he was married.

I fucking hurt her.

Gabe rubbed his chest before turning on his heels and heading back inside. He needed to make this right with her. Explain why he hadn't ever mentioned her or their marriage to the guys and make her understand it had nothing to do with her.

The screen door creaked as he pulled it open. Ellena was still standing by the table where he'd left her, the computer now held snugly against her chest.

"I'm sorry," Gabe whispered softly.

"For what?"

"I should have told my team about you."

A set of guarded blue eyes shone back at his. "I don't know why I'm surprised. I shouldn't be. I was your wife, and you shut me out back then. Why would your new team be any different?"

"You're still my wife, Elle." He took a step toward her. "And I...I never meant to shut you out."

"Yes, you did." She smiled sadly. "And I let you. That was my mistake."

"Why do you say that?"

"Your entire focus back then was on protecting me. That's all you thought about, to the point you obsessed over it." Her swallow was audible, her voice barely more than a whisper. "But I didn't need your protection, Gabriel. I needed your love."

Heart pounding to the point of pain, Gabe closed the distance between them. Cupping her face with his palm, he stared down at her, willing her to understand.

"My love for you is the whole reason I left."

Ellena shook her head against his hand, a single tear falling down across her cheek. "You left because you were scared."

"I left because *I* was the reason you lost everything."

Another tear fell. "That's where you're wrong, Gabriel." She reached up, wrapping her fingers around his thick wrist. "I didn't lose everything until you walked away."

Removing his hand from her face, Ellena turned her back on him and walked quietly to the bedroom.

As she reached for the doorknob, Gabe said, "Ellena."

She stopped but didn't bother looking at him.

The words he wanted to say—things he *needed* to tell her— were right there, on the tip of his tongue. But when he opened his mouth, all he heard himself say was, "I need to do a perimeter sweep. Check outside and make sure the area is secure."

She gave him a resigned nod. "Okay."

Goddamnit.

Why couldn't he tell her everything he was thinking? Everything he felt?

"I'll lock the door behind me and let myself back in. I won't be far, but"—he sat the burner phone down on the table beside him—"this phone is for you to use in case of an emergency. It has my number already programmed in it. I'll only be gone a few minutes, but if you need something, call me."

Ellena looked over at the phone, but not at him. With another soft 'Okay', she walked into the other room, shutting the door behind her.

Resting his hands on his hips, Gabe closed his eyes and hung his head, hating that he'd taken yet another fucking step backward with her. How the hell they went from being seconds away from ecstasy to her barely speaking to him...

Fuck!

Full of pent-up anger—mostly at himself—Gabe yanked his keys from his pocket and headed outside. After making sure the door was locked, he stormed down the porch steps and started his perimeter check.

A cool, fall breeze blew through his short hair as he strategically walked around the cabin and through the trees. Elle's words ran through his mind, making his heart physically hurt.

I didn't lose everything until you walked away.

Didn't she understand? Not only had he failed to protect her from his world, he'd brought that shit into their home. How did she not get that?

Because you never told her.

Shit. That damn voice—and Ellena—were right. He hadn't wanted to talk about what happened back then. Didn't want to talk about it now. But as he continued walking through the surrounding brush and trees, Gabe came to the dreaded conclusion that he had to.

They needed to talk about it. She needed to understand.

With his keys in his hand and his heart on his sleeve, Gabe made his way around to the front of the Cabin. He unlocked the door and stepped inside.

The place was quiet. The bedroom door still shut. Nerves settled in the pit of his stomach as he slowly walked toward it.

He'd been neck-deep in the worst war had to offer. Had gone toe-to-toe with some of the most evil, dangerous humans on the face of the earth. Yet he was terrified of the conversation he was about to have with the woman who'd owned his heart for what felt like forever.

If the guys could see me now.

Reminding himself he'd survived a lot worse shit than this, he tapped his knuckles against the thick wood. "It's me."

"Come in."

Her soft voice had him reaching for the doorknob. Gabe drew in a long, deep breath, releasing it slowly before letting himself inside. Ellena was sitting crisscross on the bed with the computer Nate brought resting on the mattress in front of her.

"Everything's clear outside."

She stared back at him with a guarded expression. "Good."

"Listen, Elle." He reached back, his fingertips digging into the tense muscles on the back of his neck. "What you said before... about my never wanting to talk to you about what happened..."

"Yes?"

Gabe sighed. "You were right. I didn't want to talk about it. Still don't, if I'm being completely honest. But I know we need to, so..."

"Okay." Ellena closed the computer and set it on the nightstand with her folders. Leaning back against the headboard, she crossed her arms in front of her. "So talk."

CHAPTER 11

"I was an ass."

Ellena stared up at Gabe, his anxious demeanor a far cry from the fearless warrior she knew him to be. He may have finally decided to talk, but after years of waiting for this moment, she wasn't about to make this easy on him.

"Was?"

"Okay, fine." He blew out a breath. "I *am* an ass."

Though Ellena didn't verbally agree, she did raise one of her brows in a *tell me something I don't already know* look.

Gabe shook his head, adding, "But I need you to understand why."

"I know why, Gabriel." She'd always known. "You were scared."

"No, that's not..." He looked away, his dark brows turning inward before his eyes found hers once more. "You're right. I was scared. But only because I didn't want to be the reason you got hurt again. I couldn't stand to be the reason you lost anything more than you already had."

Barely holding back a growl, Ellena uncrossed her arms and legs and shot up from the bed. "Enough with that martyr bullshit!"

"Damn it, Elle. I'm not trying to play the martyr, here."

"Really?" She put her hands on her hips and looked at him from across the bed. "Christ, Gabe. Just admit it, already."

"Admit what?" He threw his arms in the air, his palms slapping against his denim-clad thighs.

"That you still haven't forgiven yourself for what happened."

He grew quiet, his tortured eyes staring back into hers. "Have you?"

"No." Ellena could tell her answer was crushing, so she quickly added, "Because there's nothing to forgive, Gabe. But you don't believe that, do you?"

His broken eye contact was his answer before he even spoke. "I brought him into our home, Ellena. I did that. And yes, leaving you was the last thing I ever wanted to do, but I couldn't risk something like that happening to you again. I couldn't risk someone hurting you because of me."

God, why couldn't she make him understand? Her entire career had been built on helping people, many of them men just like the one standing before her. But the one person who meant more to her than anyone was hurting, and she couldn't find the words to help ease his pain.

You have to keep trying.

"I'll tell you the same thing I told you back then, Gabriel. What Vic did that day was *his* doing. No one else."

"Vic honestly believed I betrayed him." A muscle in Gabe's strong jaw twitched beneath his scruff. "Maybe he was right. If I hadn't..." His eyes met hers again. "If I'd just kept my mouth shut, then..."

"What, Gabe?" Ellena *had* to find a way to get through to him. "Things would've been business as usual?"

"Maybe."

"Right," she scoffed. "So you would've continued leading your team into God knows where, a team of men you and I both cared a great deal for, knowing a member of that same team was unstable?"

"That's not what I'm saying."

"That's exactly what you're saying, Gabriel." Ellena walked around the foot of the bed. "But you know as well as I do if you had done that, if you'd kept your mouth shut about what Vic did to that prisoner, then you would've been putting yourself and every other man on that team at risk. Every single op you went on from that point forward would've been compromised."

Regret poured off him as he shoved his hands into his pockets. "Vic wasn't..." Gabe rolled his lips inward and shook his head. "He wasn't himself, Elle. Hadn't been for a while."

"I don't disagree," she said truthfully. "Vic was obviously dealing with the fallout from the job, but it wasn't just that."

"What do you mean?"

"Victor Campbell was a classic narcissist who refused to take responsibility for anything he did."

"That's not fair."

"Not fair?" Ellena laughed humorlessly. "What happened that day wasn't fair, Gabe. Not for any of us. But it was a result of the choice *Vic* made. Not you."

"Elle—"

"Do you blame me for what happened?" She cut him off, refusing to listen to him berate himself any longer.

Gabe tore his hands from his pockets and flinched back, almost as if she'd struck him. "Fuck no, I don't blame you."

"Why not? You had the situation under control."

"No."

"I could see it in your eyes, Gabe." She took a step toward him. "You knew I was planning to make a move, and you didn't want me to. But I didn't listen. Instead, I panicked. I chose to fight back, and then I threw myself to the ground."

Gabe's eyes began to glisten with unshed tears, which meant her words must have struck a chord. At the very least created a picture from his memory of that day. Either way, Ellena knew she was finally making progress.

"What happened was *not* your fault, Elle."

"Wasn't it?" She covered another few inches. "I could've waited. I *should* have waited."

He shook his head but said nothing.

"You and I both know I shouldn't have fought Vic off like I

did. And if I hadn't, if I'd given you more time to talk to him, he might have realized that what he was doing was wrong."

"No. You're wrong."

"It's okay to admit it, Gabe. It's okay to say the words out loud." Heart racing, she offered him a sad, watery smile. "*I'm* the reason we lost our baby."

"*The fuck you are!*"

One second he was standing a few feet away, and the next, he was right there. His hands cupping her face in a gentle hold as a tear streaked down his rugged cheek.

"Victor Campbell stole our baby from us the second he put that gun to your head. That bastard did this to us, baby. *He* did it."

His voice cracked on that last part, and despite her best efforts against it, twin tears fell from the corners of Ellena's eyes.

"I know that, Gabriel. I just needed *you* to see it, too." She reached up, her thumb wiping his tear away. "Things happen, baby. I mean, look at what's going on with me right now. Someone's trying to kill me, and it has absolutely nothing to do with you." Ellena stared into his eyes, willing him to see.

She knew the exact moment it happened. The second Gabe realized how mistaken he'd been, it was as if a wall came tumbling down. With it came more tears.

"Oh, God." His hands slid from her face, and he stumbled back a few steps. "I fucked everything up. I..." His watery gaze rose back to hers. "Jesus, I fucked everything up."

"You had really good intentions, but yeah. You fucked everything up." Ellena gave him a little smile as she went to him. "Question now is, what are you going to do to fix it?

His dark brows scrunched together, the skin between them bunching with confusion. "What do you mean?"

"Well, you finally understand what I've known all along, so... I guess I'm wondering what happens now?"

"With what?"

God save me from hard-headed men.

"With us, Gabriel." Ellena stopped when her socked toes

touched the tip of his boots. "I'm asking, what's going to happen with us."

Still looking adorably taken off guard, he used one of his large hands to wipe his face dry. With a sniff, he said, "You filed for divorce, Elle. So that's it, right?"

"You haven't signed the papers, have you?"

"No."

"Okay, so let's look at our options. The way I see it, we have two."

"Two?"

"Mmhmm." She nodded. "Option one, you sign the papers, I give them to my lawyer, and we go our separate ways."

His Adam's apple bobbled up and down with an audible swallow. "And option two?"

"We tear them up and act like they never even existed."

Ellena held her breath as she waited for him to respond. Her heart had never pounded so hard before in her life, and she was certain if he didn't say something in the next two seconds, it would explode from her chest.

Thankfully he spoke up before that could happen.

"Compromise?"

Well it isn't a screw you, so...

"Your offer?" she asked quietly, hating how shaky her voice sounded.

Gabe put his hands back to her face, sliding them against her flushed skin. "We burn the damn papers."

Oh God. Was he saying what she thought he was saying?

"So...option one is for sure off the table?

Say yes. Please, God, let him say yes.

Gabe's intense gaze reached deep into her soul, his image blurring behind a new onslaught of tears forming in her eyes. He leaned in, his deep voice low and determined as he said, "Baby, I fucking hate option one."

* * *

Ellena barely had time to suck in a breath before Gabe's lips were on hers. She knew they still had a lot to work through, but they'd just leapt over their biggest hurdle.

Finally, *blessedly*, Gabe had come to the realization that the loss of their child wasn't on him.

Her mind raced to catch up to what her body was feeling, and her broken heart began healing itself with every touch. Every nibble.

Thank you, God.

"I love you, Ellena." Gabe's mouth ate at hers greedily. "God, I never stopped loving you."

The remaining fissures from his leaving grew together, the scars there making her heart beat even stronger than ever.

"I love you, too, Gabriel. Only you."

She thought he'd kiss her longer. Deeper. He broke away.

For a moment, she wanted to scream her denial but then he bent at the waist and scooped her up in his arms. Turning them toward the bed, he gently laid her on the mattress, following her down as she went.

She thought he'd ravish her. Take her like he was starved for her. *Like I'm starving for him.* But he kept his weight on one elbow to keep from crushing her and simply stared.

"Gabe." Her hips involuntarily lifted.

"Shh…"

He pressed his index finger to her mouth, letting it trail languidly down over her chin.

Her neck.

Her top button.

"I've waited so long for this, sweetheart. So fucking long." He carefully pulled her earlobe between his teeth before whispering, "There's no way in hell I'm rushing it."

Ellena's insides tingled, the muscles there clenching in anticipation. They'd barely gotten started, and her body was already desperate for relief.

But her soul…her soul was more than willing to wait because this was Gabe. The man of her dreams. The other half of her heart.

The one I was born to love.

Despite their past and the baggage that came with it, surrendering herself to him was one of the easiest decisions Ellena had ever made.

She smiled up at him, relaxing her body beneath his. "Take all the time that you need."

Gabe's lips curled into a slow, smooth grin as he leaned down, dropping a warm kiss in the hollow of her throat. He moved lower, his hands working to release the rest of her shirt's buttons as he went.

Soon her blouse was off, and he was staring down at her as if she'd hung the moon.

"You're so beautiful." He kissed the swell of one breast and then the other. His coarse whiskers brushing across her sensitive skin.

"Gabe," Ellena whispered his name again.

Her lower body pressed against the hard bulge between his thighs. She sucked in a breath, her body trembling with need. Or nerves.

Probably both.

It was silly to be this nervous. He was her husband, for crying out loud. It wasn't like they'd never slept together before. Still…

"Don't worry, sweetheart." Gabe pushed himself back up, his lips meeting hers in a barely-there kiss. "I've got you."

Ellena's breath hitched. "Promise?"

"Always."

She wasn't just asking about the sex, and from the way his dark eyes had locked with hers, Gabe knew it.

All the pain and heartache she'd felt the last few years began to vanish, and a deep-seated warmth began to spread throughout her chest. It was as if the love he still felt for her had reached inside and grabbed hold of her heart.

Doing some reaching of her own, Ellena slid her bra's front clasp open, freeing herself for Gabe to see. His audible hiss made her smile. It also made her insides quiver with satisfaction.

"You said I never had to beg…"

Gabe moved his head slowly from side to said, his entranced

gaze frozen on her bare breasts. "No, ma'am." He gave her a boyish grin. "You most definitely do not."

His mouth went to one nipple, the hot, wet flick of his tongue sending shockwaves through her system. Ellena threaded her fingers in his short hair, grasping tightly when he used his teeth to gently tease the rock-hard nub.

She moaned, and he continued on. First licking and sucking one breast before giving the other the same exquisite attention.

"Gabe," she panted his name, her hips rising to meet his.

"I know." He moved lower, his lips leaving a trail of fiery kisses along her midsection.

He stopped when he reached her waistband, his fingers expertly releasing the button. The sound of her zipper coming undone filled the room, and Ellena was more than happy to help when Gabe began pulling her jeans and panties down her legs at the same time.

When he had them off, he tossed them aside as she did the same with her bra, neither caring in the least where any of it landed. And when he stared back down at her, she felt like the most beautiful, desirable woman in the world.

"Even better than I remember," Gabe muttered, more to himself than her.

"Miss this, did ya?" Ellena teased.

His heated gaze found hers. "More than you can ever imagine."

Every second she spent with him like this made it harder and harder to breath. Her chest was so full, Ellena thought she'd never catch her breath.

Then Gabe stood to remove his own jeans and boxer briefs, and she began to seriously wonder if she was going to survive this.

She already knew what he looked like naked. Was intimately familiar with every curve and indentation of his broad shoulders and six pack abs. Her mouth had been on every inch of his delectable body, and still the sight of him took her breath away.

His defined muscles and strong physique were incredible, and the tattoos were works of art. But the swollen shaft protruding between his thighs was, honest to God, a thing of beauty.

Her mouth literally watered, which was silly given that this was her husband. For two glorious years, they'd spent every moment they could together. Never taking for granted those times when he was home and between ops.

Ellena had made love to this man countless times before in just about every way imaginable. Still, in some ways, this felt like the first time all over again.

Better than that, this was almost like a rebirth of their union. A renewal of their love. One she could no longer wait to start.

"Now, Gabe." She let her legs fall open. "I need you inside me. Now."

Despite the low groan rumbling inside his chest, Gabe took his time. Kneeling on the mattress, his smile grew.

"Patience, baby." He leaned down. "Need to taste you first."

In the next second, Gabe's mouth was on her. Ellena cried out, her body jerking beneath his face as his tongue entered her body.

"God, I've missed this." A slow lick of her slit. "So good." Another lick.

She moaned loudly as Gabe continued to consume her in a way only he could. The man knew every sweet spot on her body, and with each and every subsequent lick, he drew her closer and closer to implosion.

"Oh, Gabe," she praised him. "That feels so good."

"Yeah?" He looked up at her from between her thighs.

Ellena nodded, unable to formulate another word.

"What about this?" He inserted a finger. "This feel good?"

"Yes!" She pressed her body against his hand.

"And this?" Another finger. He pumped them in and out at a torturous pace. "This what you wanted?"

Yes!

He knew exactly what she wanted. Always had.

"More," Ellena ordered, closing her eyes and letting her head fall back. Her fists clutched at the bedding beneath her as he began thrusting his hand a bit harder.

"That better, baby?"

Yes! No! She was already so close.

She cried out again when she felt his other fingers press against her clit, and when Gabe began rubbing against her swollen nub while also pumping the two fingers in and out of her wet heat, Ellena thought she'd die from the pleasure.

Her body began to shake. "I'm so close."

"That's it, baby." He continued to move in slow, agonizing circles. "I want to see you come undone for me."

Almost there!

Gabe's fingers began moving faster. Rubbing harder.

"Come on, Elle. I love watching you come."

Oh, my god!

"That's it. Let it all go, baby." More pumping. More rubbing. "Let it all go."

"Gabe!"

Ellena flew, her body careening into a tidal wave of pleasure as her climax slammed into her with explosive power. She was so lost in her mind-blowing orgasm she almost missed Gabe's mouth on her once more.

His lips were around her opening, his tongue savoring her essence as her inner muscles contracted over and over again. Through heavily leaded eyes, Ellena watched with overwhelming satisfaction as Gabe licked and sucked every last drop of pleasure from her body.

Seeing his head there, between her thighs, was a sight she never, ever wanted to forget.

When the pressure became too much, Ellena reached for him. Pulling on his shoulders, she guided him up the length of her still-trembling form.

"I want to feel you inside me," she said again. "Please."

Gabe put his mouth on hers in a hard, fast kiss. "Whatever you want, baby." He positioned himself at her sensitive entrance. "Whatever. You. *Want.*"

He entered her in one, long thrust. Ellena threw her head back with a loud cry. His body stretched hers to a point it hadn't been in a very long time—almost to the point of pain—and it took her a few seconds to adjust.

"Shit. Did I hurt you?" Gabe froze, obviously aware of her sudden stiffness.

"No," she assured him. "It's just been…"

"A long time."

Ellena stared up at him. "Yeah."

"For me, too, sweetheart." Gabe brushed some hair from her forehead. "We can go as slow as you want to."

The words he spoke were sincere, but it was obvious he was holding back.

She didn't want him to deny himself. They'd both been denied far too much for too damn long. No, she didn't want this beautiful man holding anything back.

Not ever again.

Ellena cupped his face and brought his mouth to hers. Kissing him softly, she lifted her hips from the mattress, silently urging him to start moving.

He did.

Gabe's low moan matched her own as he slid his cock in and out of her body slowly. For the first few thrusts, they kept the same unhurried pace. The feel of his body molding together with hers was one she'd missed at an indescribable level.

"So good," Gabe spoke between kisses. "So fucking good."

"You, too," she panted.

Their breathing increased. They began to move faster. And as it always did with this man, Ellena felt her body preparing for a second, glorious eruption.

"Elle." Her whispered name was a warning.

"I'm there."

With full understanding, Gabe reached between their bodies and began rubbing her clit with perfection.

He thrust harder. Faster. The room filled with the sound of their bodies slapping together until…

"Ellena!"

She cried out again, her body jerking when she came with even more force than before. Gabe joined her a second later.

He grunted loudly, his large body becoming stiff with uneven thrusts. This continued on until the last of his climax had been spent. His hot seed filling her womb.

Heavy breaths filled Ellena's ears, and it took her a minute to find the energy to even speak. When she did, all she managed to utter was a breathy, "Wow."

A low, deep chuckle vibrated against her chest. Keeping his weight from crushing her, Gabe leaned back just enough to look down at her with a smile. "That was definitely a wow."

He kissed her slowly, as if he never wanted their time together to end. Ellena knew she didn't. Not now. Not ever.

She finally had him back, and in that moment, she realized his reasons for returning didn't matter. All that mattered was that he was here. With her.

No matter what happened from this point forward, Ellen knew one thing with utter certainty.

I'm never letting go of him again.

CHAPTER 12

"Three strikes, Walker. You know what that means."

"Well, damn." Adrian stared back at the clueless prick and sighed. "Guess I don't get to see what's behind door number two, now, huh?"

"You think this is funny?" The vein in Daniel Price's forehead began to bulge. "Is this all a big fucking joke to you?"

I think you're *a joke.* "Look, man." Walker shrugged. "I get that your boss is pissed, but it is what it is."

"It is what it...Jesus Christ." The guy ran a hand through his hair, mussing up his perfect politician hair. "You said you were the best. *Everybody* said you were the best."

"What can I say? Even superstars have their off days. I mean"—he chuckled—"who knew a MacBook could stop a fucking bullet?"

"You should have!" Price took a large step toward him. "The deadliest assassin around shouldn't have *off* days. That sort of thing makes me and my boss very suspicious."

His boss. That would be the man favored as the frontrunner against President Russell in next year's election.

Price was the crooked bastard's Chief of Staff, and the kiss-ass was hellbent on making sure his boss's secrets remained silent. Secrets he believed Ellena Dawson knew.

"Fine." Walker turned his back on Price and began walking

toward the door. Despite the gun he'd just seen the fucker pull from his back waistband, he raised his left hand in a half-assed wave. "I'm sick of this bullshit, anyway. See you around, Price."

"Freeze."

With a roll of his eyes, Walker halted his movements. Exhaling loudly, he turned back around, nearly snorting when he saw the way the idiot was standing there.

Gun pointed out in front of him. Legs spread too wide. Arms shaking like a leaf in a fucking windstorm.

Dumbass has probably never even shot a gun before.

"I can't let you leave." Price swallowed hard. "Not knowing what you know."

Sweat was already beading on the man's forehead, and Walker would bet money he'd probably piss his pants if he actually did end up pulling the trigger.

"So...what?" Walker raised a brow as he began walking back toward Price. You're going to shoot me?"

"I told you." Price's voice trembled. "I-I don't have a choice."

A few more steady steps. "Oh, there's always a choice, Danny Boy."

"Not with this, there isn't. I have to protect him."

"And you think by killing me you're protecting him?"

"I've killed before, you know." Price licked the sweat from his upper lip. "Just two nights ago, in fact. Shot a man in cold blood."

"Oh?" *This should be good.* "And who, pray tell, did you kill?"

The wimp finally grew a set of balls—or, at least, he tried to. Jutting his pointy assed chin up a notch, Price said, "Someone who knew too much."

Shit. Walker was really hoping for a name. "Isn't that what you hired me for?"

"It was an...unexpected opportunity. But I handled it. All by myself. Besides, you were supposed to be focused on finding the Dawson bitch."

Meaning whoever Price killed, it was done so out of pure panic and without any sort of planning.

Fucking amateur.

"Right. Well, as fun as this has been"—Walker started to turn back around—"you and I both know you're not going to pull the trigger. Frankly I've grown tired of your and your boss's games, so I'll see you aroun—"

A loud explosion filled the abandoned warehouse as Price did, in fact, pull that trigger. The shot went wide, but surprisingly, not by much.

"Seriously?" Walker shot the man an incredulous look. In one, smooth motion, he drew his own weapon from the shoulder holster hiding beneath his somewhat tattered jacket.

"The second shot won't miss," Price warned. He readjusted his hold on the gun.

Walker didn't hesitate. He fired, hitting his target exactly as intended.

"Ah!" the stupid fucker cried out as his gun went flying. Blood dripped from where the bullet had grazed Price's hand.

Gun still raised, Walker stormed toward the other man. "Second shot goes in your empty goddamn head."

The man's expensive-as-shit pants darkened with a stream of fresh urine. Glancing down at the man's wet crotch, Walker tsked. "You're gonna play hell trying to explain that one to your *boss*."

"P-please," Price begged like the little bitch he was. "Please, don't kill me."

"Ironic, coming from the man who just took a shot of me."

"I told you, I had no choice."

"Well, you do now."

"What?" the injured man cried. "Tell me what to do. I'll do anything, just please…don't shoot me again."

And that, ladies and gentlemen, is how quickly the tables can turn.

"I want you to let me do my fucking job."

"B-but my boss…" Price grimaced in pain as he kept hold of his injured hand. "What am I supposed to tell him?"

"Tell him I have things under control."

"But y-you don't. You don't even know where the Dawson woman is."

"No, but I know how to bring her out of hiding."

Pushing through his pain, Price studied him a moment.

"How?"

"First rule of professional assassination. You can't go to the target, you make the target come to you."

"H-how you plan on doing th-that."

"Same way you catch a rabbit." He forced a smug smile. "By dangling a carrot in front of its nose."

Two minutes later, Walker got into his car and drove away. His gut tightened as he thought of the gorgeous redhead he'd been watching closely over the last few weeks.

Even from afar, the sexy nurse's spitfire personality had turned him on faster than any woman he'd ever met. She made him wish he'd chosen a different path. He'd wished that same wish a billion times before, but never for the reasons *she* put into his head.

Who knows? If he had chosen a different life for himself, maybe he and the little firecracker could have...

Another time. Another fucking life, man.

Walker blinked away the pointless daydream. That kind of life—that kind of *world*—had no place for an asshole like him.

Picket fences, two-point-four kids...all that shit was for other guys out there. Men who had normal, nine-to-five jobs. Men who didn't kill other men for a fucking living.

No, a spunky, vivacious woman like Jenna Shaw deserved better than some sick fuck sitting here, fantasizing about the two of them together...while he was on his way to kidnap her.

* * *

Gabe traced a fingertip along the dip of Ellena's spine, causing tiny goosebumps to spread across the smooth skin covering her back.

"That tickles," she mumbled from beside him.

He smiled. He'd actually done little else this past week, which was how long they'd been holed up here, in Kole's cabin.

Good didn't even come close to describing how it felt waking up to her gorgeous face every day. He just needed to figure out a way to make the rest of his days begin the same way.

Neither had broached the subject of the future yet. Gabe suspected Ellena wanted to but was afraid he'd change his mind.

Not in this lifetime, baby.

Gabe hadn't started that conversation yet, because he thought it best to get their current situation figured out first. Then they could focus solely on their future.

Together.

So far, there'd been no further signs of trouble, which was both good and bad. No trouble meant Ellena was still safe, but the sudden inaction made Gabe very nervous.

It had been too long since the last attempt on her life. In his experience, that meant something was brewing. Something bad.

Unfortunately for them, Nate's assessment of the hospital security tapes from the night of the break-in resulted in a dead end. The fucker who'd broken into Ellena's office hadn't shown enough of his features to get a hit.

Nothing had really stood out from her files, either. She'd gone through them more than once, both on the computer and the ones they'd found on the floor, and still …nothing.

Even more disheartening was the gap still in Ellena's memory. Gabe had hoped the events from the day of the accident would have returned by now, but that was still a blank slate, as well.

Though he had no way of knowing what, his gut still said something important was locked away inside that beautiful brain of hers. Speaking of beautiful…

A set of sleepy blue eyes opened to meet his, her dimples growing deeper with her lazy smile. "Good morning."

His heart swelled inside his chest, the way it always did when she looked at him that way. "Morning, sweetheart."

"What time is it?"

"A little after nine."

Closing her eyes, Ellena stretched her arms above her head but remained on her stomach. "I feel so lazy sleeping in like this."

"Nothing else to do, so I say we take every advantage while we can."

She opened her eyes again, the smile crossing her face one

filled with mischief. "Oh, I don't know about that. I'm sure we could think of something else to do besides sleep."

Gabe's cock twitched beneath the sheets. They'd made love so many times in the past week he felt like they were on a second honeymoon.

In a way, they sort of were. It may not be the ideal situation, but he couldn't think of a better way to reconnect with his wife than to be tucked deep inside the woods, away from everyone and everything.

Scooting himself closer, Gabe planted a kiss on her back, just below her shoulder blade. "You have anything particular in mind?"

"I thought I'd leave that part up to you."

"Well in that case…"

He kissed her back again, a little lower this time. Shifting so he was hovering over her, Gabe pulled the sheet down, exposing the small of her back. Bending down, he placed another light kiss there, just above the top of her crease.

Ellena drew in a short breath, her lower half inadvertently lifting toward him. Pulling the sheet down even further, Gabe's dick began to throb to the beat of his heart when he took in the sight of her perfect, heart-shaped ass.

Running a palm over one of the perky globes, he pushed to his knees and moved between her thighs. Using both hands, he began massaging her rear end, his fingers pushing and digging into the toned muscles there.

A low moan escaped from Ellena's throat, telling him she liked what he was doing.

You ain't seen nothing yet, sweetheart.

Sliding one hand over, Gabe traced the length of her crease with his middle finger, letting it slip between her cheeks as he went. She gasped when his fingertip hit her puckered entrance there.

They'd never ventured into that territory before, and he didn't really think now was the time, either. But someday…

Ellena lifted her bottom toward him again, this time spreading her legs as she moved. Knowing what she wanted,

Gabe slid his finger down to her entrance, his throbbing dick leaping again when he found her already wet and ready.

"Jesus, baby." He slid that finger inside. "You're soaked."

"Mhmmm…" She moaned, pushing her body back against his hand.

"This all for me?" Gabe added a second finger, loving the way her greedy channel sucked him in.

He watched as she clutched the sides of her pillow and nodded. "Only you."

"That's right." In and out. In and out. "Only me." In and out.

Gabe withdrew his fingers. Ellena whimpered in protest, but when he grabbed her hips and lifted her to her knees, her whimper turned into a heady grin.

"Grab ahold of the headboard," he ordered softly.

She did so without hesitation.

He hadn't bothered to put his boxers back on after they'd made love last night, which only served to save them both some time. Looking down, Gabe fisted his cock, nearly shaking his head at how angry the damn thing looked.

Not angry. Hungry.

He lined himself to her entrance, nearly losing it when he rubbed his swollen tip against her there. Jesus, he felt like a fucking teenager again. Like he couldn't get *enough* of her.

Because you can't.

It would never be enough. Not when it came to his Elle.

"You ready?" he asked, his eager voice rough. When she looked back at him and nodded, he told her, "Hold on tight."

Gabe slammed himself inside her, his eyes rolling in the back of his head from the pleasure. Between the woman he was with and the position they were in, he had to hold still to keep from coming, right then.

Ellena had always loved sex like this. She'd once told him it was because she felt fuller somehow. That this position allowed him to go in even deeper than all the others.

For Gabe, it made the sex raw. Primal. He wasn't sure why that was, exactly.

All he knew was that he had to be very careful when he took

her from behind. If he wasn't, if he went too fast too soon, it would be over before it barely began.

Ellena wiggled her hips, letting him know it was time to start moving. With grin on his face and his hands holding onto her hips, he was more than happy to oblige.

He pulled back, nearly withdrawing completely, and then hammered into her again. She cried out, the familiar sound telling him she was enjoying herself as much as he was.

Gabe did it again. And again. Soon, he was like a piston, moving in and out of her welcoming core with such force the headboard was slamming against the wall.

Thrust after thrust, he drove deep, his grip tightening to the point he knew he'd probably leave bruises. The idea increased his primal urge to mark this woman, to make her his forever, was damn near overwhelming.

"Gabe!"

Thank God, she was close. His spine tingled and his balls were pulled in tight. His knees shook from his efforts to try to hold back a little longer.

She would always, *always* come first. In every way possible.

Releasing one hip, he reached around, his fingers immediately finding her swollen bundle of nerves. He wasn't slow this time. Wasn't gentle.

Instead, Gabe swirled his fingertips in small, tight circles, putting just the right amount of pressure to send her into oblivion.

Ellena threw her head back, her blonde hair splaying across her bare back as she screamed in ecstasy. A rush of hot liquid covered his cock, and when her inner muscles clamped down on his, Gabe lost all sense of control.

In rough, uneven thrusts, he jerked behind her. His orgasm hit with the force of a freight train, and Gabe held on tightly until the zing of electricity ebbed, his body completely depleted.

Weak with pleasure, Gabe leaned down, resting his head against the dip in her back. His chest rose and fell with harsh, heaving breaths.

"Holy shit, woman." He eased out of her body and dropped

onto the mattress beside her.

"I'd say I'm sorry, but I'd be lying," Ellena teased.

Blue, sated eyes stared back at him. Knowing he'd been the one to put that look on her face filled Gabe with a primal sense of pride.

"You hungry?"

Just then, a low rumbling sound came from Ellena's stomach.

Her shoulders shook as she laughed. "I guess that answers your question."

"I'll go make us some breakfast." With a playful smack, Gabe's palm landed on one of her bare cheeks as he rolled over and off the bed.

"Gabe?"

"Yeah?" He stopped by the doorway and turned around.

Covering herself with the sheet as she went—which was a damn shame—Ellena pushed herself up into a sitting position. Something about her expression bothered him, but he wasn't sure why.

She hesitated half a second before asking, "What are we doing?"

He frowned. "I thought you were going to take a shower, and I was going to make us some food."

"No." She shook her head, the smile she now wore not reaching her eyes. "I mean...this. Us."

"I don't understand. I thought we already settled all of that."

Sighing, Ellena looked down at her lap before meeting his gaze once more. "Being here with you, like this...it's been great. More than great."

A gnawing feeling began swirling low in his gut. "But?"

"No but." Ellena's silky blonde hair swayed across her shoulders as she shook her head. "Not really. I guess...I guess I'm just wondering what happens next?"

"Next?"

"Yes, Gabe. Next."

Clearly frustrated, Ellena held the sheet to her body as she stood from the bed and faced him. He watched as she wrapped the thin cotton around her as best she could. She bunched a section of the material between her breasts and held on to keep it from falling.

"Despite our reason for being here, playing house with you this past week has been...fun."

"Fun?"

"Better than fun." She blew out a breath, appearing to gather her thoughts. "The way things have been going these last few days makes me think maybe we can really"—she cut herself of abruptly, then gave a quick shake of her head—"but I can't help but remember how things ended before. How hard it's been trying to get over you. I know what you said about burning the papers, but I just need to know if..." She looked away, the weary look in her eyes nearly breaking him. But then, she lifted her chin and locked her blue eyes with his. "I need to know if this is real."

Gabe was stalking back toward Ellena even as her voice was trailing off. He'd already told her how he felt about her. How sorry he was for having walked away.

Knowing she still doubted his love for her--for even a *second*—tore his heart to shreds.

"Let me clear all that up for you." He spoke low and with purpose as he slowly made his way around the foot of the bed. "First, I haven't been *playing* at anything. Second, I know I screwed up by leaving before, but I'm here. Now." Gabe stopped moving when their toes were about to touch. "I'm here, sweetheart, and I'm not going anywhere again. Not unless you ask me too. Third, I can't tell you what's going to happen tomorrow or next week, because until I know you're safe, that's all up in the air, but fourth...and it's really important you hear this last part... as far as I'm concerned, this"—he motioned a hand between them—"is as real as it fucking gets."

Ellena's chest rose with a stuttered breath. Her eyes glistened with a well of tears, and Gabe held his own breath waiting for her response. Thankfully he didn't have to wait long.

"It's real for me, too." Her whispered voice was shaky and thick with emotion. "I just needed to know I wasn't alone in those thoughts."

"You're not alone, baby." Gabe framed her face with both hands. "You'll never be alone, again."

"Gabe..."

He kissed her slow and deep, pouring every ounce of love he felt for her in that one, sensual gesture. Then he said it again, just to make certain she understood.

"I love you, Elle." They kissed again, the saltiness of her tears hitting the tip of his tongue. "I love you, and if you give me another chance, I swear to you I will never, *ever* let you down again."

"I love you, too, Gabriel." Letting go of the sheet, she rose to her tiptoes, wrapping her arms around the back of his neck. "So much."

The sheet fell to the floor with a soft whoosh. With breakfast momentarily forgotten, Gabe wasted no time hoisting her into his arms, his heart swelling even more when her legs instinctively wrapped around his hips.

Carrying his precious cargo into the bathroom, Gabe held on to her luscious body with one arm while he used his other to start the shower. Once the water was warm enough, he was careful not to slip as he carried her with him into the small space.

With her back pressed against the slick shower wall, he then proceeded to show her—for the second time that morning—that he meant every single word.

* * *

Ellena sat on the couch, flipping through the handful of channels the antenna on Kole's cabin picked up, thinking of how deliciously sore her muscles were. Muscles that had been ignored for a very, *very* long time.

All of the sweet, loving words Gabe had spoken over the past few days playing over and over again in her mind.

I never stopped loving you. This is as real as it fucking gets. You'll never be alone, again.

In spite of the situation, Ellena's cheeks hurt from smiling so

157

much. She understood Gabe's hesitation in discussing their future until things settled down otherwise, but she couldn't help but go there.

Between their lovemaking and sweet, honest conversations, Ellena's lovestruck mind was already making plans for the two of them. Big plans.

She just hoped Gabe was okay with them once she finally got up the nerve to tell him.

That conversation could wait, though. Because he was right. Even though they seem to have lost the trail of whoever had tried to kill her before, Ellena knew they were still out there somewhere. Waiting for the chance to catch up with her.

"Blueberry or plain?"

Glancing away from the T.V. she wasn't really paying attention to, Ellena found Gabe standing in the kitchen's entryway wearing a red apron with the words *I Turn Grills On* printed on the front.

She barked out a laugh. "Where on earth did you get that?"

"Found it in one of the drawers." He looked down at himself and grinned. "What do you think?"

God, she loved this man. "I think grills aren't the only things you can turn on."

"Yeah?" He raised a cocky brow and started swaying his hips back and forth like he was doing a slow striptease. "What do you think? You wanna try a taste of my...meat?"

As he continued with his provocative moves, she laughed even harder. Waggling his brows up and down, Gabe started toward her. The closer he got, the more overtly sexual his gaze became.

The sound of Ellena's growing laughter filled the cabin as she watched the amusing show from her place on the couch. *Bless his heart.*

Her sweet, charming hunk of a husband had hunted some of the world's worst enemies. He could kill a man with a bullet or with his bare hands. The guy could seriously do just about anything he put his mind to...

Except dance.

"Come on, baby." He leaned over the back of the couch, his whiskers creating goosebumps as he nestled his lips against the curve of her neck. "You know you want it."

"You're ridiculous." Ellena chuckled, doing her best to pull away from the ticklish sensation.

"Admit it." He continued on relentlessly. "I set *all* your grill parts on fire."

With a squeal, she leaned down against the other couch cushion, doing her best to escape the playful torture. They both laughed, but then Ellena screamed for him to stop when Gabe's wiggly fingers were heading for her ribs.

Looking away, she caught a glimpse of the T.V. and her laughter came to an immediate stop.

"Oh, my god." She pushed against him as she sat up. Her hand flew to her opened mouth. "No."

Gabe pulled away instantly, picking up on the alarmed tone of her voice. Without hesitation, he came around the couch and sat down beside her. "What is it?" His strong hand reached out for hers. "What's wrong?"

"Shh!" She held a hand up, motioning for him to get quiet so she could hear.

Focused on the picture filling the screen, Ellena could hardly believe what she was hearing.

"Tragically, the number of deaths among United States Veterans due to suicide is still rising. The country's most recent loss, a young soldier by the name of Mark Ellis. Just this week, a relative discovered Mr. Ellis's body in his San Diego apartment after she hadn't heard from him in several days. The medical examiner's official cause of death? Self-inflicted gunshot to the head. As the number of suicides within the veteran community shows no sign of dropping, those of us are left wondering, what will it take to end this tragic trend?"

"Jesus," Gabe muttered beside her.

The anchorwoman moved on to the next story, but Ellena was still frozen by the one she'd just listened to. Bits of memories flashed through her mind, tiny slivers she couldn't quite put together to form the whole picture.

She wasn't sure how long she sat there, staring at the screen from behind her tears before Gabe finally spoke again.

"Who was he?" he asked, his voice low and filled with sympathy.

"Mark's a..." Her voice cracked. Clearing her throat, she tried again. "Mark *was* a patient of mine."

"Ah, Elle." Putting his arm around her shoulders, Gabe pulled her close and kissed the top of her head. "Sweetheart, I'm so sorry."

"Thanks." Ellena wiped her face dry with her palms. "I knew he was troubled, but I never pegged him as suicidal. Even at his worst, he never mentioned wanting to harm himself or acted as if he were giving up. If anything, he was scared to die and doing everything he could to *live*."

"What do you mean?" Gabe asked, the question immediately followed with, "When was the last time you saw him?"

"The day of my wreck." The words were out of her mouth before she knew what she was saying.

Gabe stiffened beside her. "You remember?"

Ellena swung her widened gaze to his. "I do. I didn't even realize it until just now, but...I remember seeing Mark that day. He came in unexpectedly. Showed up right before I left the hospital."

Shifting to face her more directly, Gabe frowned. "He didn't have an appointment?"

"No. We weren't scheduled to meet until the following week. I mean, I can check the computer, but I'm almost certain of it."

"Do you remember what the two of you talked about?"

Ellena hesitated, but then another memory hit. A very clear memory of Mark begging her to help him. To go to the authorities...to tell *someone* what he'd told her so they could both be safe again.

By doing that, he'd very clearly given her permission to share what they'd talked about during that last session. That meant, by law, she was free to do so.

"He thought someone was following him."

"He what?" Gabe's brows rose high.

"Mark suffered from a pretty bad case of PTSD. His biggest issue was suffering from paranoid delusions. He and his team were cornered by a group of insurgents. They were being picked off, one by one, when reinforcements were finally able to get to them. Mark and another young man were the only two to make it out alive.

"Shit."

"Yeah." She nodded. "Almost immediately after, Mark began suffering from night terrors. Things progressed quickly from then on. He seemed to be getting better. At least, I thought he was. But then, when he burst into my office that night…" Ellena trailed off, swallowing back the outpouring of guilt Mark's death had caused before continuing on. "I thought that's all it was. Just another episode of his manic paranoia."

"I take it you don't think that anymore?"

Ellena shook her head. From the look on Gabe's face, neither did he.

"I…I'd forgotten until now, but I remember the fear in his eyes when he came to me that day. It was different than the other times before."

"Different, how?"

"It was real." She met Gabe's worried stare. "Oh, God, Gabe. What if Mark didn't really kill himself? What if someone had been after him the entire time?"

"Baby, stop." He cut her off, giving her hand a supportive squeeze. "You know better than most not to let yourself go down the what-if trail. Trust me, you'll drive yourself crazy doing that shit."

"Logically, I know, you're right, but…" She used her free hand to swipe at another fallen tear.

"The best thing we can do for Mark now is focus on what we know. What else do you remember from that day?"

"Everything." Her watery eyes stared back into his. "I remember everything."

CHAPTER 13

Excitement and dread intertwined inside Gabe's gut as he waited for Ellena to tell him about the day of her accident.

"Take your time, Elle." He took her hand in his. "Start with the first thing that comes to mind."

Her baby blues were filled with trepidation as she looked over his shoulder and into the recent past. She spoke softly, listing off the day's events as she recalled them.

"I went to work like normal. Saw all of my scheduled patients. Had lunch with a couple of the other doctors in the hospital cafeteria." Ellena rubbed her temple as if the effort to remember was causing her physical pain. "I'd just finished up the final notes from my last patient and was about to leave when Mark barged into my office with a panicked look on his face."

"Tell me about the conversation you had with him."

"It was jumbled, really. I could tell he was in a heightened state of paranoia. Much greater than the previous times we'd met. He kept saying 'they're after me'. I remember him being worried about me, too. He said he'd brought them to me, too."

Gabe's heart physically hurt for the pain and guilt he saw pouring from her self-deprecating eyes.

"Sweetheart, listen to me. No matter if Mark committed suicide or if it turns out he was somehow connected to what's been happening to you, neither of those things are your fault."

"I blew him off."

"I'm sure you did everything you could as his doctor to help him."

"No, I mean that night." Her shoulders fell with regret. "I was tired and ready to go home, and I…I blew him off. I told him to come back the next morning. That I'd had a cancellation, and I could fit him in during that timeslot."

"What did he say to that?"

Ellena huffed out a humorless laugh. "He told me I should leave. That I needed to go someplace far away and hide." She stood and walked over to the fireplace. Staring into the burning logs, she shook her head. "Hide someplace no one will find you. That's what he told me." Ellena turned back to him. "Guess he knew what he was talking about, after all."

Though Gabe wanted to go to her, he kept his ass planted on the couch. As hard as it was to watch, she needed to work through her last encounter with Mark in order to get to the rest of that night's events.

"He wasn't making any sense," she continued on. "Mark just grabbed my shoulders, begged me to go into hiding, and took off."

"What did you do, then?"

"I left. I remember feeling a little shaken by the conversation and wanting to get home as quickly as I could. So I left the hospital and drove home. Or started to, anyway."

"Do you remember the wreck?"

Ellena nodded. "I was on Florida Drive, the two-lane road that runs behind the hospital. I was driving past Balboa Park when out of nowhere, a set of headlights appeared on one of the dirt roads that intersects the road I was on. By the time I saw them, it was too late. The car hit me square on the driver's side door. Pushed me off onto the shoulder, tipping the car onto the passenger side."

Christ. The image her words created sent a renewed rush of fear through Gabe's system.

"I'd hit my head pretty hard, but I remember the blood. I

could feel it running across my forehead and into my eyes. It made it hard to see the man."

"The man?" Gabe stood then, unable to stay away from her any longer.

Ellena turned back to him. "H-he came up to my car. I thought...I thought he was going to help me, but instead he just stood there. Staring. I screamed at him to help me. Or, maybe it was only in my head. I was pretty out of it by then, but I do remember a blinding flash of light. Like from a camera."

"The email."

Gabe still hadn't been able to get the picture out of his head. His woman injured and completely helpless. Trapped inside her mangled car.

"He took my picture and then called someone. I remember him reciting our location and telling whoever it was to hurry. That I was hurt and needed help."

"He called it in?"

"I think so." Ellena blinked. "Yes. I remember hearing him on the phone. H-he called the police, reported the accident, and then..."

"Then what?"

"I don't know. That must've been when I passed out. The next thing I remember after that was waking up in the hospital. I was so frustrated because I couldn't remember anything from that day." She frowned. "Now I kind of wish I hadn't."

Gabe understood what she meant. Sometimes ignorance really was bliss.

He rested his hands on her shoulders, his eyes peering deep into hers. "We're going to figure this out, sweetheart. I promise."

"How? Everything's so messed up, and we're no closer to finding any answers than we were a week ago."

"That's not true."

"It's not?"

Head shaking, he said, "You got your memory back." When Ellena opened her mouth—no doubt to argue that her memories weren't actually helpful—Gabe quickly added, "Plus, we know about Mark."

164

"All we know is that I turned him away, and now he's dead."

"You're wrong." Gabe stared down at her pointedly. "He said someone was after you because of him. Makes perfect sense, given the timing."

Elle's so-called accidents, the wreck, the email she'd received...and now Mark Ellis's death.

"But why would someone come after me because of Mark? It's not like he revealed state's secrets to me during our sessions."

"What if he did?"

Her brows turned inward again. "I counsel my patients, Gabe. It's not like they come into my office, lie down on a couch, and share top-secret information with me."

Even as he considered what she'd just said, a familiar churning began to swirl around in Gabe's gut. It was the same feeling he got when he was on the right track.

"What if they did?"

"Right." Ellena scoffed, giving him an incredulous look.

"Just hear me out." Gabe put up a hand to interrupt her attempt to argue. "What if one of your patients revealed top-secret intel without your realizing it."

"You're serious."

"Think about it. What better way to let someone in on something without them actually knowing it. Maybe Mark Ellis wanted to let the cat out of the bag but was afraid of what would happen to him if he went to the authorities."

"Okay..." Ellena began to follow his train of thought. "You think Mark had something he needed to get off his chest but was afraid of the consequences if he did?"

"Makes sense. He can't go to the authorities himself because he either doesn't trust them or is afraid whoever's watching him will see. So he does the next best thing."

"He tells me."

"Exactly."

She stepped out of his reach and began pacing the length of the living room. "Okay, but like I said...Mark never actually revealed anything to me about, well, anything. He spent most of our sessions either not talking or rambling about things that didn't make much sense. I always got the feeling he was holding something back, but I get that a lot with my patients. Especially new ones, and especially the ones who suffer from paranoid delusions." Ellena stopped by the edge of the couch and turned back toward him. "Those patients don't trust *anyone*. Certainly not enough to share something major. Not even with me."

"But the people watching Ellis wouldn't know that." Gabe walked over to her.

"If anyone was actually even watching him."

"I think that's a pretty solid assumption at this point, sweetheart."

Her shoulders fell, her head nodding with a reluctant acceptance. "So they know Mark meets with me on a regular basis, and assume he feels protected by doctor-patient confidentiality enough to tell me whatever it is they don't want me to know."

"The knowledge she has will help you and your team stop them." Stopping in front of her once again, Gabe shoved his hands into his pockets. "That's what Adrian Walker said the night he broke into my house."

"But I already told you I don't know anything."

"You might know more than you think."

Blinking away more tears, Ellena huffed out a frustrated breath. "How am I supposed to figure out something I don't even know that I know."

"If anyone can do it, it's you." Gabe pulled a hand free and rested it against her cheek. "What would you tell a patient if one of them was trying to recall something they'd forgotten or had locked away somewhere."

She opened her mouth but then clamped it shut. At first, Gabe thought she was going to continue pushing the fact that she didn't know anything to begin with, but she didn't. Instead, she inhaled a slow breath through her nostrils and let it out slowly.

"I'd tell them to retrace their steps," she shared softly. "I'd tell them to go back through their memories one, small step at a time. That sometimes looking at things from a different viewpoint can make all the difference."

"What else?"

Determination returned to her electric blue gaze. "I'd tell them to not give up. To keep searching until they found whatever it was they were looking for."

"Good." He brushed his thumb back and forth across her smooth skin. "Then that's what we'll do."

She smiled, then, her dimples falling deep. Like she had a few times before, Ellena's delicate fingers wrapped around his wrist. "It means a lot that you said 'we.'"

We really need to work on your trust issues, baby.

"I told you before, and I'll keep saying it until you believe me. I'm not going anywhere, Ellena. Not this time."

Rising up to her tiptoes, she let her eyes fall shut and brought her lips to his. Gabe barely had the chance to taste her when the alarm on his phone alerted him of another perimeter breach.

"Damn it." He pulled back and dug his phone from his pocket. "If those assholes didn't tell me they were coming again, I swear to Christ..."

"Go." Ellena gave his chest a weak push. "I'm sure whoever it is just forgot."

"Yeah, well"—Gabe pulled his gun free from his waistband—"they won't forget a third time after I put a bullet in their ass."

"Be nice." She chuckled, following him to the door. "Besides, they could be bringing us another chocolate pie."

With his hand on the doorknob, he stopped and gave her a grin. "Chocolate pie would definitely be grounds for a pardon." Leaning down, he gave Ellena a quick peck on the lips and reminded her, "Lock this behind me and whatever you do—"

"Don't open it for anyone but you. I remember."

"Good girl. Oh, I almost forgot." He went over to his go-bag he kept in the corner by the door. Unzipping it, he pulled out his Glock and held it out for her. "Here."

Ellena looked at it as if it were a snake ready to strike. "What's that for?"

"Just in case." He lifted her hand and placed the weapon in her palm. "It's a Glock, so there isn't a safety. The mag is loaded, and there's one in the chamber. All you have to do is point and shoot."

"Gabe, I haven't shot a gun since you took me to the range and practically forced me to learn how to shoot. And that was over four years ago."

"Just like riding a bike."

"You know how I feel about guns."

"And you know how I feel about you." He cupped the back of her neck. "Like I said, it's only a precaution, but I don't know how long I'll be gone, and I'll do a better job at staying focused if I know you have a way of defending yourself if you have to."

Gabe kissed her again, simply because he wanted to. "Be right back."

"Be careful."

"Always." With a wink, he left her safely tucked away inside the cabin.

While he hated leaving her for even a minute, he knew his Elle. If it came down to it, she'd shoot. He just prayed she never had to.

Checking Nate's app on his phone, Gabe studied the electronic map. Nerves sparked to life when he realized the breach showed in the trees on the backside of the property. If it was his team, they'd be coming down the driveway, on the front side of Kole's land.

Praying it was just a deer or some other animal big enough to trip the sensors, he held his gun steady and began making his way through the timber, moving as quietly as he could. It wasn't easy given all the dried leaves that were already starting to cover the ground, but thankfully Gabe's training had taught him ways to move silently through some of the toughest terrains around.

Several minutes later, he was about to chalk the tripped sensor up to a wandering animal when he spotted something off in the distance. Check that…some*one*.

The trespasser was twenty yards to his south, squatted down behind one of the area's larger trees. If the guy was trying to hide, he was doing a shit job of it. He must also have a death wish.

Anyone who knew anything about Texas—or any other area of the country where property like this one existed—should know better than to sneak around on someone else's land. Around here, some landowners were likely to shoot first and ask questions later.

So whoever it was, was either stupid or had a fucking death wish. And if they were dumb enough to come after what was his, Gabe wouldn't hesitate to pull the trigger.

Closer and closer, he crept through the trees and brush. Knowing it would be impossible to get right up on the bastard without being detected, Gabe waited until he knew he'd hit his target without fail to stop moving and let himself be known.

From his position behind him, all Gabe could see was the man's dark hair, dark jacket, and dark jeans. It was impossible to see the man's face, but it didn't matter. No one hid in the fucking woods unless they were up to no good.

Arms taut and gun steady, he gave the intruder one chance to stay alive. "Show me your hands. Slowly."

The man didn't startle. He didn't turn around to see who Gabe was. Instead, he began to move slowly, just as Gabe had instructed.

"Now stand up."

Again, the man did as he was told.

"Turn around. And you so much as breathe in a way I don't like, you'll be dead before your body hits the ground."

"I believe you." Familiarity rang through the man's voice as he faced Gabe. "I've seen you do it."

The air left Gabe's lungs in a loud huff. "Ryker?" Gabe stared back at Jason Ryker—R.I.S.C.'s Homeland Security handler. "What the fuck are you doing out here?"

"Came to see you." The strait-laced bastard tilted his lips into a slight grin. "Can I put my hands down now."

Realizing he was still holding the government agent at gunpoint, Gabe cursed under his breath and shoved the weapon back into his waistband.

"Thanks." Ryker lowered his hands to his sides. "I was beginning to think you weren't gonna come out here."

Forcing his heartrate back to a normal level, Gabe nearly growled at the other man. "Why the hell didn't you come to the front door like a normal person?"

"Normal's overrated." He brushed some leaves from his ass. "Besides, I didn't want anyone to see me pull onto the road. Can't be too careful."

"Speaking of careful, how the fuck did you even know I was here?"

One of the man's dark brows lifted. "You've worked for Jake McQueen for how long, and you still have to ask that question?"

Shit. The guy was right. He may not be CIA, but he sure acted like a damn spook.

"Whatever." Turning on his heels, Gabe started back the way he came. "Talk and walk. Ellena's waiting for me back at the cabin."

"Ah, yes. The ex-wife. How is she?"

"She's not a fucking ex, for one."

"She filed for divorce a few weeks ago."

The comment stopped Gabe in his tracks. "How did you... never mind." Of course, the guy knew about that shit. He knew fucking everything. "We've worked things out."

"Congratulations," the brown-hair, brown-eyed agent offered.

Gabe couldn't tell if he was being serious or facetious. "You never answered my question."

"What question is that?"

"Why are you here?"

"Told you. I came to see you."

Spinning around, Gabe got into the agent's face. "Cut the bullshit, Jason."

The other man didn't so much as flinch. "Fine. I came to update you on a new development in our ex...your wife's situation."

"If you're talking about Mark Ellis, we already know."

Ryker's lips curved. "Been watching the news, I see."

"Yeah." Gabe turned and began walking again. "We saw the fucking news. You know something they didn't report?"

To this, the other man snorted. "You ever know a news station to report everything they know?"

The man had a point. The media often left bits and pieces of the truth out to better sensationalize their stories. The sexier— or bloodier—the story, the better their ratings.

"So tell me what *you* know, other than the fact that Ellis didn't eat his own gun."

"How did you know that?"

"I didn't." Gabe smirked. "Not for sure. But thanks for the confirmation."

Ryker's sport-coat covered shoulders shook. "Well played. Guess you have learned a few tricks over the years."

"Several." The two men continued walking. "Another skill I have is being able to tell when someone is stalling."

Ryker focused on the direction they were walking. They were close enough, now, they could clearly see the cabin through the trees.

"Fair enough," the other man finally spoke up. "There's a lot about this particular job you're unaware of. Things that, before now, were 'need to know.'"

"Let me guess. The powers that be have finally decided to read me in."

"Pretty much."

"So tell me, Ryker. What is it I need to—"

A loud scream cut his question short.

No!

Yanking his weapon free, Gabe took off in a dead sprint. Pulse racing with fear, his heart kicked painfully against his ribs as he pushed himself to get to her as fast as he could.

Dodging limbs and hurdling downed logs, he didn't bother to see if Ryker was keeping up. Didn't matter. Nothing mattered, other than getting to Ellena.

"Dawson, wait!" Ryker called from behind him.

Not a fucking chance.

Gabe moved even faster, then. The muscles in his thighs began to burn from their effort to take him to the one place he needed to be. Despite the cool, autumn air, a thin sheen of sweat began to bead on his forehead, but Gabe ignored it and continued on.

"Damn it, Gabe. Hold the fuck up a second!"

He was about to tell the pansy-assed agent to go to hell when a deafening bang echoed through the trees. The few birds that hadn't flown south yet scattered, their caws and chirps muffled by the rush of Gabe's blood through his ears.

"Ellena!"

His primal, protective instincts allowed him to move even faster. Barely registering the low curse coming from the man behind him, Gabe pushed on. With only a few feet left between him and the cabin, he forced his body to its limits, covering the distance in record time.

Skipping the wooden steps completely, he flew up to the porch and kicked in the door. His heart stopped cold when he saw the splatter of blood on the wall next to the small table, and the body on the hardwood floor in front of him.

CHAPTER 14

Ellena ears were ringing, and she was shaking so badly the gun nearly fell from her hand. The man who'd broken in was still on the floor, fresh blood seeping past the hand he had pressed to his injured shoulder.

I don't even remember pulling the trigger.

She'd been in the kitchen trying to decide what to make for dinner when she heard what sounded like someone unlocking the front door. At first, she assumed it was Gabe. But when she heard his voice, she knew it was someone else.

A different voice. A *familiar* voice.

It's him.

"I-it was you." She stared down at him. "You ran your car into me."

"Wasn't me," he ground out past his pain. "But, yeah. I was there. Damn. I forgot how much getting shot hurt."

He'd been shot before? Who was this man?

I think I'm going to be sick.

"Easy, Doc. Slow, deep breaths. In through your nose, out your mouth."

Ellena's eyes flew to his.

The guy had broken in here to do only God knows what. He'd quite possibly caused her wreck, and most definitely took her picture and sent it—along with several others—to her as a warning. She'd *shot* him, and he was giving her advice on how not to throw up?

"Wh-who…" Ellena swallowed back the burning bile. "Who are y-you?"

Grimacing in pain, the man opened his mouth to tell her, but before he could answer, an extremely panicked Gabe burst through the door.

Weapon in hand, his terror-stricken gaze moved from the blood on the wall behind the table, to the man on the floor. His entire body seemed to nearly crumble with relief when his eyes landed on her.

Keeping his weapon pointed at the intruder, his eyes softened as he slowly began walking toward her.

"Ellena?"

She could see his lips moving. Could make out what he was saying, but the ringing from the gunshot and the sound of her own heart racing muffled his voice.

Ellena wanted to go to him. To grab hold and never let go. But for some reason, she couldn't get her legs to move.

"Hey, Dawson." The man on the ground groaned. "You mind telling your wife to quit pointing her gun at me?"

"Actually, yeah." Gabe slid the man a narrowed glare. "I do mind."

Another man came rushing through the opened door. One she'd never seen before. He took in the unthinkable scene then shook his head and cursed.

A shot of renewed fear hit her system, and Ellena swung her hand in his direction, instead.

"Ellena, no!" Gabe held up his free hand. "It's okay. He's with me." Moving slowly, he began walking toward her. "Sweetheart, I need you to give me the gun."

She was confused by his sudden change in demeanor. He appeared to be approaching her with caution, almost as if he was afraid of what *she* would do.

That's not right. None of this is right.

"H-he broke in here. I-I didn't…" Ellena licked her desert-dry lips. "I didn't m-mean to shoot him. It just…h-happened."

"I know, baby." Gabe came a little closer, his voice becoming more and more clear as the incessant ringing began to dull. "It's okay. You didn't do anything wrong."

"It's him." She slid the man on the floor another glance. "H-he's the one."

"The one?"

Ellena nodded woodenly. "He was there. Outside my car."

Fury burned behind Gabe's darkening eyes. Spinning around, he used both hands to steady his gun as he started for the stranger on the floor.

"You were the one who crashed into her? She could've been killed, you son of a bitch!"

In an unexpected—and terrifying—move, the other man she didn't know put himself between Gabe's gun and his intended target.

"Dawson, wait!"

"Get the fuck out of my way, Ryker."

Ryker...Ryker...Why does that name sound familiar?

While Ellena's shock-filled mind worked to remember where she'd heard that name before, Gabe and the man called Ryker continued their standoff.

"Listen to me, Gabe." Ryker stood with his hands up to keep Gabe from going after the other guy. "I know how it all looks, but Walker's not who you think he is."

"Walker?" Ellena's eyes went to the man she'd shot. "Adrian Walker?"

The man gave her a pained smirk and a wink. "In the flesh, sweetheart."

"Don't call her that," Gabe spoke through a set of clenched teeth. "Better yet, don't even fucking look at her."

"Seriously, Gabe." Ryker moved into Gabe's line of sight again. "You don't want to do this."

"The fuck I don't!"

Ellena watched as Gabe got right into Ryker's face.

"That bastard went after my *wife*, Jason."

"I get that, but—"

"No." Gabe shook his head. "You don't fucking get it. You

175

heard her. She remembers the night of the accident." He slid his murderous gaze—and his gun—back onto the man on the floor. "She remembers *you*. You rammed your car into hers, and then you left her there for dead."

Ellena couldn't believe it when the injured man actually began to laugh. "You think you have it all figured out, don't you?"

"Oh, I know I do."

Gabe sidestepped Ryker, stopping directly in front of Walker. Ellena felt like her heart was going to explode with fear as she watched him point the gun directly at the other man's head.

Oh, God.

The sweet, fun-loving man who'd been joking and dancing around in the silly apron he was still wearing had been replaced by someone else. A warrior, ready and willing to kill to protect her...again.

"No!" Ellena lowered the Glock to her side and went to him. Carefully, she wrapped her fingers around his taut forearm as best she could. "Don't."

"He almost killed you, Elle."

"I didn't cause the fucking wreck!"

Ellena turned her gaze on Walker. She wasn't sure why, but something in his eyes made her want to believe him.

"I think he's telling the truth."

Walker's dark brows rose with surprise, his gray-blue eyes shifting to hers. "Thanks, Doc." He looked back to Gabe. "You really should listen to your wife. I wasn't the one who hit her, but...I know who did."

"My *wife* just put a bullet in your shoulder." Gabe stared down at him. "You really think she's on your side?"

"Can't really blame her for shooting me." Wincing, Walker used his good arm to push himself up into a more upright position. He huffed a few breaths before adding, "She thought I came here to hurt her."

"And I'm supposed to believe that you didn't?"

"Gabe." Ellena tried getting through to him again. "Please."

"It's the truth." Ryker put a hand on Gabe's chest in an attempt to talk him down.

With a deadly tone to his voice, Gabe glanced at his chest then back up to Ryker. "You're gonna want to remove that hand."

Deciding now was not the time to push the limit with Gabe, Ryker dropped his hand but refused to step aside.

Keeping his eyes—and gun—on Walker, Gabe spoke to her next. "Did he touch you?"

"No."

"Did he threaten you in any way?"

"No."

"She got spooked when she heard my voice," Walker explained for her. "Thought I was here to kill her. Didn't think she had it in her, but..." He glanced down at his bloody wound. "Should've known better."

"I'm sorry," Ellena heard herself say.

Gabe's incredulous expression immediately followed. "He breaks in here, and you're *apologizing* to him? What the fuck is happening right now?"

"He's right," Ellena answered his rhetorical question. "I got scared. He didn't even have a weapon, but I...I don't know. He started to walk toward me, and I guess it was just...reflex."

"Helluva reflex you've got there, sweetheart."

Gabe's head moved on a fast swivel. "I told you not to fucking call her that." He looked back at Ellena. "And trust me, he has a weapon."

"Look. We all just need to take a breath and calm down."

All eyes turned to Ryker. The clean-cut man was standing at Gabe's side looking like he was ready to pounce if Gabe made another move toward Walker.

An alternate reality. That's where I am. It's the only explanation for the amount of crazy happening in this room.

"Here." Ellena held Gabe's Glock out to him. "Take it. I-I can't even look at it anymore."

Sympathy warred with his anger as Gabe took the weapon from her hand. "You sure you're okay?"

"Not sure okay is the correct description for what I'm feeling at the moment." She let out a sarcastic laugh. "I don't really know how I'd describe my current state of mind, actually."

In shock would probably be a good place to start.

"He didn't hurt you? 'Cause so help me God, if he laid a finger on you…"

"He didn't." She put a little more pressure on his arm, a tiny bit of tension releasing when he began to lower his weapon.

Walker blew out a breath and stared up at Ryker. "Feel free to jump in anytime."

The other man shoved his own gun back into the side holster next to his badge—a badge Ellena just now noticed.

"Are you with the police?" she asked, still unable to put a finger on where she'd heard his name before.

"Homeland Agent Jason Ryker." He held out his hand. "Nice to finally meet you, Mrs. Dawson."

"Doctor," Gabe corrected him gruffly.

"My mistake."

"Ellena's fine." She shook the man's hand, finally remembering what Gabe had told her about this man. "You're Bravo Team's handler, aren't you?"

"I work closely with both of R.I.S.C.'s teams, actually. Just happen to be in on Bravo's current case, at the moment."

"You mean me."

"Yes." Agent Ryker turned to Gabe. "We need to talk."

"You think?"

The man sighed. "I promise I'll explain everything. Just…put the damn gun down."

Gabe glared down at Walker again, but after a long moment's hesitation, he finally lowered his weapon. "Fine. You can start with why you're protecting this low-life piece of shit. And he stays right there while you do."

"Gabe…" Ellena frowned. "He's hurt. We need to get him to a hospital."

Walker surprised her by chuckling again. "Thanks, Doc, but hospitals aren't really my thing."

She crossed her arms at her chest. "And bleeding to death on the floor is?"

The corner of his mouth curled upward. "I like her, Dawson." He lifted his focus to Gabe. "Smart, beautiful, can obviously take care of herself. Why the hell would you ever walk away from a woman like that?"

Gabe took a menacing step toward Walker, but Agent Ryker slid back into his path. "Enough!" His authoritative voice boomed. He looked down at Walker. "How bad is it?"

"Through and through." The guy actually seemed to blow it off as if it were no big deal. "Hurts like a bitch, but I'll be fine."

"Good." Turning to Ellena, Ryker spoke in much softer tone, "Could you please find a clean towel or something to put on his wound?"

"Oh, well...might as well get him a nice cup of hot fucking tea while we're at it."

Ignoring Gabe's understandably angry comment, Ellena went to the small linen closet on the wall behind the couch. Grabbing the first towel she saw, she went back to Walker, feeling a bit awkward trying to help a man she'd just shot.

"Here." She held out the towel.

"Thanks, sweet...uh..." Taking the towel, he shot Gabe a quick look before finding her eyes again. "Thank you, Dr. Dawson."

"You're welcome."

Holding her stare a second longer, the man Gabe clearly disliked turned his attention to Agent Ryker. "We should probably move things along."

"What's the rush, Walker?" A muscle in her husband's jaw bulged. "Got someplace else you need to be? Another woman you feel the need to terrorize today, or have you met your quota?"

"Nah." Walker shook his head. "Two a day's my limit."

Elle's heart thumped loudly. "Two?"

"Don't worry, sugar. She's tucked safely away. Like a bug in a rug. Although, she'd probably prefer I get back to her sooner, rather than later."

She couldn't tell if he was being serious. "You're holding another woman hostage?"

"Well when you say it like that, it sounds much worse than it actually is. Like I said, your friend's just fine, for now. Although, I gotta tell ya. That tiny little thing's a giant ball of fire when she gets mad. Must be the red hair."

"My friend?" Ellena's blood turned cold. Her eyes flew to Gabe's. "Jenna?"

Gabe started for his pistol, but once again, Ryker intervened.

"Goddamnit, Adrian." The man glared back at Walker. "Are you trying to get yourself killed? And put the fucking gun away, Dawson. The Shaw woman is fine."

The Shaw woman. They *were* talking about Jenna.

"Where is she?" Ellena demanded to know. "Why did you even involve her in any of this?"

"Same reason I aimed for the computer instead of your pretty little head," Walker answered casually. "To buy you some much-needed time."

It took a second for his words to resonate. "You were the one who shot me?"

"No. I shot your *computer.*" Walker held up his bloody hand to stave off Gabe's impending attack. "Relax. It was a small round, and I knew the laptop would act as a vest."

"You knew?" Gabe growled. "How the hell could you possibly know that?"

"It's called the internet, Dawson. You should try it sometime. Can learn about all kinds of shit on there, these days."

"Jesus Christ." Gabe ran a hand over his face. "If that bullet had hit even a centimeter higher…"

"I hit what I aim for, Gabriel." Walker smirked. "And I don't miss. Just ask your teammates. What are their names? Oh, yeah. Carter and King."

Gabe *did* pull his gun, then. "Get the fuck out of my way, Ryker." He shoved the other man to the side. "I'm done playing games with this asshole."

"Gabe, no!" Ellena's heart leapt into her throat as she tried grabbing for his arm.

At the same time, Agent Ryker fisted the front of the red apron, using both hands to push Gabe back.

"Stand down, Dawson!" Ryker yelled. "You shoot him, you'll be charged with murdering a United States Federal law enforcement official."

Ellena could actually see Gabe's muscles go into lockdown as a *what-the-fuck* expression quickly spread across his face.

The cabin fell eerily silent. It stayed that way for several seconds.

"You'd better start talking, Jason." He pinned the Homeland agent down with his stare. "Right the fuck now."

CHAPTER 15

"Where's Jenna?"

Gabe looked down at his shaken wife, hating the trembling in her voice. Standing behind where she was sitting on the couch, he placed his hands on her shoulders and gave them a gentle squeeze.

Directly across the room from him stood Ryker. The man Gabe and his team—the man *both* R.I.S.C. teams—had trusted with their lives. On more than one occasion.

Jason Ryker was someone Gabe had begun to think of as more than their Homeland handler. He'd considered him a friend. But now...

I don't even know who the fuck he is anymore.

"She's fine," Ryker assured her. "Scared but fine."

"Told you."

Fury still burned within Gabe as he looked toward the man sitting at Kole's small table.

With both legs zip-tied to one of the chair's wooden legs, Deep Cover Special Agent Adrian Walker—or at least that's what he was calling himself—was surprisingly quiet as he held the bloody towel to his wound.

After a thorough pat-down—because yeah, Gabe didn't trust the asshole any further than he could throw him—he'd secured Walker to the chair and called in his team. Now they were all waiting for Ryker to fill Bravo Team in on whatever the fuck was going on.

Gabe glanced around the packed room. "Gang's all here, Ryker. Just like you requested."

"Thanks for coming out on such short notice." Ryker eyed the other men in the room. "Makes things a hell of a lot easier if I only have to explain this shit once."

"You've got about two seconds to explain why that motherfucker is still breathing," Nate pointed over to Walker. "Any longer than that, I start shooting."

And Gabe was more than ready to let him after Gracie, Nate's wife, nearly drowned when Walker delivered her to the cocksucker who wanted her dead.

"Stand in line." Zade spoke up from where he stood at the end of the couch. "I still owe him for shooting me in that fucking car and leaving me for dead."

"Don't worry, King." Walker tipped his chin to Zade. "Doc Dawson already took care of your revenge."

"He's kinda right." Kole gave Zade a smirk. "Wrong shoulder, but still..."

Matt growled beneath his breath. "Yeah, well I'd be happy to put a hole in the other one for him." He shot Walker a glare. "Kat damn near died in that goddamn lab all because the man you were working with wanted her formula."

Gabe clenched his jaw, his teeth grinding together. When he thought of the pain and suffering Adrian Walker had caused his team. His *wife*.

And now poor Jenna.

Ellena had used Gabe's phone to try to call her, but it went straight to voicemail. When the hospital confirmed she didn't show for her shift today, they knew Walker had been telling the truth.

The bastard had taken Jenna. Had her stashed away someplace. They just didn't know why.

"Get to it, Ryker. Jenna's waiting."

"Yes, Jason." Walker spoke up again. "My little fireball is waiting."

"Say another word, Adrian," Gabe warned. "I dare you."

"You heard Ryker." The asshole actually looked smug. "I'm untouchable."

"I'll fucking touch you, you murdering son of a—"

"Can we please stay focused?" Ellena raised her voice, her gaze lasering in on Ryker's. "What's going on, and why did he take my friend?"

Ryker blew out a breath and began the unbelievable story.

"A little over ten years ago, the president at the time contacted the US secretary of Homeland Security. He requested our agency put together a special task force working side-by-side with the CIA."

"We already know what your task force does, Ryker." Matt cut him off. "Jesus, man. R.I.S.C. has been working with you for how long?"

Kole chimed in, too. "Yeah, we don't need a goddamn history lesson. Just get to the point, already." He slid a glance in Walker's direction. "It's gonna take forever to get that asshole's blood off my floors as it is."

"Fine." Ryker started to get pissed. "You want the short version? Here it is. Ten years ago, Adrian was part of a Fleet Anti-terrorist Security Team. Same one as Matt, I believe."

The men in the room all looked in Matt's direction.

"Sure was," Matt confirmed. "Until his deserting ass turned traitor."

"And hit-man," Zade bit out harshly.

"Will you guys just shut the fuck up?" Walker's raised voice bounced off the cabin walls. "Christ, Jason. I don't know how you work with these guys. It's like being in a room full of middle schoolers."

"Middle school?" Matt shot to his feet. "I'll show you fucking middle school—"

"Sit down, Turner," Gabe ordered Matt. All eyes turned to him. "You're all pissed. I get it. I'm not happy about whatever this is either, but an innocent woman's being held against her will, and someone is after my wife. We need to find out why and how to help her. I know it's hard, but we need to put our personal shit aside and let Ryker talk."

"Thank you."

Gabe shot the other man a *don't fucking push me* look.

Clearing his throat, Ryker picked up where he left off. "Like I was saying, Walker was a Marine working in the same FAST as Matt when the special, deep-cover task force was formed. During that time, Adrian's sister went missing. Authorities believed she'd gotten caught up in a sex-trafficking ring preying on young runaways and prostitutes."

"Bree wasn't a fucking prostitute," Walker said in a low, emotionless voice.

Ah, shit.

Gabe started to get a bad feeling about where Ryker was going with all this but decided to let him finish rather than make assumptions.

"Is that true?" Ellena asked, sitting on the couch in front of where Gabe stood. "Did you really have a sister?"

Gabe saw the first hint of real emotion haunting the grays in Walker's eyes as the man gave a single nod.

"We learned one of the sex trafficking victims was the sister to an American soldier," Ryker continued on. "A decorated soldier with specialized skills. We also learned this particular soldier had no other family or real roots planted anywhere, so we—"

"Used him," Ellena finished the man's thought. Sympathy mixed with worry for her friend as she turned her head toward Walker. "They used the love and concern you had for your sister and your dedication to your country to manipulate you into giving up your life. Probably offered you the chance to help take down the men who took your sister."

The look Walker gave Ellena revealed her assessment was spot on.

"We *utilized* him," Ryker tried covering his ass.

A humorless laugh came from Walker's direction.

"Utilized. That's good, Jason. I'll have to remember that one." To the group, he said, "Enough with the PC bullshit. You want to know what happened? I'll tell you. The government was looking for an easy target, and they found one. As far as the world knows, I'm a traitor and a ruthless murderer." He scoffed. "At least they've got it half-right."

"You're not a murderer, Adrian." Jason looked over at him. "You're an asset. And a damn good one."

"I'm every bit the gun for hire I claim to be. The only difference is Uncle Sam signs my paychecks instead of those bastards I pretend to work for."

"And your sister?' Ellena asked Walker. "Did you ever find her?"

A muscle in Walker's jaw twitched. "Yeah. I found her."

Something akin to sympathy made its way into Gabe's chest. He couldn't stand the thought of any woman or child being subjected to the horrifying world of sex trafficking. And though Walker didn't come right out and say it, he could tell from the man's expression his sister's story didn't have a happy ending.

"Whoa, whoa, whoa." Nate stood. "You expect us to believe you're a deep cover agent working on some off-the-books task force for the CIA? You fucking shot me, you prick. Then you kidnapped my wife and handed her over to that fucknut Bukhari."

Zade, who was usually the more reserved one of the bunch, had a vein in his forehead that looked like it was about to pop. "You murdered an innocent police detective in cold blood less than two feet away from me. Then you put a bullet in my shoulder and took Matt's wife against her will."

"Okay, look. I'm sorry I shot you." Walker looked first at Zade and then Nate. "Sorry for shooting both of you. I was doing my fucking job, and I had to make that shit look legit in order to keep my cover. The fact is, if I'd wanted you dead, you'd be dead, and as for the women…" A look of regret crossed over his pained face as he glanced in Elle's direction. "I know how it looks, but I did everything I could to keep them safe while they were with those bastards. If you think I enjoyed kidnapping them, you're wrong. I just didn't have a choice."

"You didn't…" Gabe fisted his hands at his sides to keep from strangling the man with his bare hands. "There's always a fucking *choice*, Adrian."

Walker's gray eyes lifted to meet his. "Not when they own you, there isn't."

"You're saying our government...owns you?" Elle asked, studying the man with an intense stare.

"For the last ten years." He nodded.

Matt scoffed. "Right."

"Y'all know how it is with the CIA. Hell, every alphabet agency, for that matter."

"No, Adrian." Nate glared at the other man. "We don't know. So why don't you enlighten us. Go on, tell us how rough your life's been."

"Anyone got some popcorn?" Kole sat back in his seat. "'Cause this story has *got* to be good."

"Fuck you, Jameson." Walker glared back at Kole. "Fuck all of you. You have no idea the shit I've done to help you." His eyes landed on Elle. "All of you."

"This is a waste of time." Zade stood and started for the door.

Ellena reached out and grabbed Zade's wrist to stop him. "Let him finish."

Zade's eyes went to hers.

"Please."

With a silent nod, Zade returned to his spot and waited.

All eyes were on Walker as he shifted in his seat, the movement causing him to wince. "Nothing is ever how it seems with agencies like that. One minute they're spinning their stories, filling your head with a bunch of honor and duty bullshit. Making you feel like you matter. Like what they're asking you to do will make a difference in the world. Then one day, you wake up and you realize you've signed your entire life away without even knowing it. By that point, you're so far under, there's no way you're getting out."

"Oh, spare me the fucking sob story." Nate shook his head. "You expect us to believe our government would sanction a job that would allow you to not only shoot an operative who works with Homeland, but they'd also be okay with you kidnapping innocent women for the sole the purpose of putting them in harm's way?"

"You're kidding, right?" Adrian blinked, looking back at everyone as if he were truly dumbfounded. "You were in the military, Turner. You've seen more shit than most people can ever imagine."

"What's your point?" Gabe asked.

"My point is, you know the lengths certain agencies will go to in order to take its enemies down. You think they give a shit about you? About your women?"

"And the detective you killed back when you shot me?" Zade asked, his voice flat. "What was that? Collateral damage? You'd shoot an innocent man to help validate your cover?"

"That *detective* was far from innocent."

"What are you talking about?"

Walker looked to Ryker who tipped his head in a single nod.

Staring back at Zade, Walker said, "The cop I shot that day was on a list."

Gabe frowned. "What kind of list?"

"The kind the CIA keeps for agents like me. We cross paths with someone on that list, we're duty-bound to eliminate them."

"You're telling us that cop was some sort of enemy of the state?"

"If you consider a sexual predator involved in kidnapping and trafficking young girls an enemy of the state...then sure."

Ellena gasped as the room erupted. It was clear Gabe's men didn't believe Walker's story.

"He's telling you the truth." Ryker spoke up again. "About all of it."

The room fell silent.

"Fine." Gabe stared back at Ryker. "Let's say we buy the story that Walker's been working undercover this entire time. Why take the women?"

"What do you mean?"

"I mean, why kidnap Nate's and Matt's wives and hand them over to the very person the CIA wanted to capture? Why not just use the intel Walker acquired, while supposedly working for the bastards to take them down?"

"Because I'm supposed to be a ruthless killer," Walker piped in. "I'm a traitor, remember? *I'm* the enemy of the state. Only a handful of people even know about my cover, and if it came down to it, they'd ship me off to Leavenworth without blinking a fucking eye. Part of the fine print written just above that dotted line I told you about."

Jesus.

"He's right." Ryker backed him up. "His cover is too deep, and his work is too clandestine."

"So his cover gets blown…" Zade trailed off.

Walker gave them all a sad smile. "I'm on my own."

"You've all worked ops like that before," Ryker told them. "You know the drill."

Sonofabitch.

As the pieces began to fall into place, Gabe ran a hand over the scruff on his jaw. "So the CIA, and whoever else is involved in this, spins a bullshit story about you having deserted your post with the Marines and going off on your own. They use their other contacts and assets to build you up to be the best in your field. The gun for hire everyone wants on their payroll. You do their dirty work, taking out targets our government wants to eliminate but can't without risk of an upheaval within our allies, and in the meantime, you're collecting intel on the men who hired you."

"Like a double agent," Ellena commented softly.

"That's exactly what I am, Doc." Walker offered her a sad smile.

"That's a horrible way to live."

Gabe couldn't miss the pity crossing over his wife's face. Of course, she had no idea the hell this man and his *job* had rained down on his team and their wives.

His job. His life. And Walker had chosen both.

"I get the double-agent shit"—Matt spoke up—"but that still doesn't explain why you'd hand over our women to the men who wanted them dead."

"We almost lost them." Nate swallowed hard. "Gracie and Kat damn near died because of what those men did to them. Men *you* delivered them to."

"Your women were my employees' targets." Walker slid Ryker a sideways glance before looking back to Nate. "They were going after them, and it was either me or some other asshole. We made sure *I* was the one they hired so I could protect them as best I could without blowing my cover."

Gabe shot Ryker a look. "So it was all a setup?" Betrayal churned like acid rain inside his gut.

The agent sighed. "Gracie and Kat were already in those bastards' crosshairs. We just made it so Walker was their only real choice. Listen, I get how fucked up it all is. But the CIA and Homeland had been after those guys for a long damn time. We had to make sure there was irrefutable proof that they'd done something to warrant their deaths by American hands. Reliable witnesses, victim statements..." Ryker slid Walker a sideways glance. "Something other than the word of a man everyone believes turned his back on our country."

Shit. As much as he hated to admit it, what Ryker was saying made sense. "So kidnapping and attempted murder of innocent women—*American* women—gave you the justification you needed."

Walker groaned when he moved his shoulder again. "Those two agencies sure know how to work the system, don't they? It's all about the greater good."

"We knew R.I.S.C. would do whatever it took to get their women back," Ryker further explained. "And I wanted to make sure that happened, which is why I first put you in contact with Ghost and his Delta team. I wanted to make sure you got your girls out of there alive."

Gabe gave the guy a deliberate stare. "You also knew by the time we were done with those bastards they'd no longer be a problem for our government."

"Or anyone else," Walker quipped.

"Jesus." Kole sat back in his seat. He glanced over at Walker. "The

CIA and Homeland used you to make sure *we* got involved in those cases." His pissed-off gaze shifted to Ryker's. "Then you used our connections to Gracie and Kat to finish the jobs you didn't want to."

"Jobs we *couldn't* do," Ryker corrected him. "Not without a global scandal."

"Goddamnit!" Matt's fist landed hard on the arm of his chair. "I fucking *hate* bureaucratic bullshit."

"Why are you telling us this, now?" Zade directed his question to Ryker.

"Because I'm done," Walker answered for the other man.

Gabe raised a brow. "Done?"

"Done. You know, I'm out. Finished. Finito."

"Just like that?" An *I'm not buying it* scoff sounded in Gabe's throat. "I thought you just said there was no way out."

A slow, grin spread across the smug bastard's face. "There wasn't until now. I've done a lot of shit over the past decade. Dark, dirty shit that's helped some very important people. When this last guy contacted me, I knew I'd found the best bargaining chip around."

"You blackmailed the CIA?"

"I like to think of it as more of a negotiation. I agreed to do this one, final job and help keep a lying sleazeball like Radcliff out of the White House, I walk away free and clear."

"This last job..." Ellena looked to Walker. "Were you really hired to kill me?"

"Yes."

Gabe felt her entire body tense beneath his hands. "No one is killing you, Elle. Not this asshole or anyone else."

The expression on Ryker's face was dead serious. "They will if we don't stop them."

"Them who?" Ellena demanded the agent tell her.

The bastard actually had the nerve to sidestep his answer. "This is where it gets tricky."

"Give us a fucking name, Jason."

Releasing a slow, steady breath, Ryker finally did. "Daniel Price ring a bell?"

"Price." It took Gabe a few seconds to process the name. "Henry Radcliff's chief of staff?"

"Hold on." Nate put up a hand. "You mean *Governor* Henry Radcliff?"

"The man, the myth...the mass-murdering asshole," Walker answered dramatically.

Ellena frowned. "Mass murderer?"

"I thought that guy was a shoo-in to replace President Russel at the end of his second term next year," Zade commented.

"He is." Ryker looked first to Zade and then Gabe. "Unless we can stop him."

Walker cleared his throat to get everyone's attention. "I can see the questions burning in your minds, and it's going to take this asshole forever to get there, so I'll try to make this one short and sweet. For those of you who didn't already know, Radcliff was a strategic combat Airforce pilot back in his hay day. He also liked to drink. A lot. His unit was given orders to bomb an abandoned village located on the outskirts of the Central Plateau as a warning to our enemies nearby."

"Let me guess." Kole sat up straighter. "They missed."

Walker nodded. "By a hundred miles. Radcliff was sauced, gave his guys the wrong coordinates. Ended up hitting a fully populated village, instead. Women, children. Everyone was wiped out instantly."

"Oh, my god." Ellena put a hand to her chest.

"Why haven't we heard about this before now?" Gabe posed the question to Ryker.

"Radcliff comes from old money. Not to mention, his father was a four-star general at the time who cared more about his rank and reputation than anything else. He made sure the media never caught wind of it. The incident was written off as a result of bad intel from local assets. Coincidentally, those assets, along with the other members of Radcliff's unit, didn't make it out of the war alive."

"Coincidence, my ass." Gabe saw exactly where this was going. "So Radcliff comes out of the war with a clean slate. Goes on to make his way up the political ladder, but now that he's

White-House-bound, the son of a bitch wants to make sure those ghosts stay hidden."

"Exactly." Walker nodded.

"But Vietnam was a really long time ago." Ellena looked up over her shoulder to Gabe. "If the others in his unit were killed back then, how would anyone else even know about what happened? And what does any of this have to do with me?"

"Not you, directly, Doc," Walker intervened again. "Unfortunately, one of your patients discovered the truth."

Gabe cursed beneath his breath. "Mark Ellis."

Walker nodded. "Dumbass actually showed up outside Radcliff's office one night. Waited for him to come out, and when he did, Ellis started spouting off all kinds of shit about how Radcliff was a murderer. Said he knew all about Radcliff's fuckup with Operation Monarch."

"Monarch?" Ellena's eyes flew to Gabe's. *That's* what Mark was talking about when he came to see me. He kept rambling on about monarchs. I thought..." She swallowed hard, her guilt obvious. "Damn it, I thought he was talking nonsense about butterflies."

"Not your fault, Elle," Gabe assured her.

"Your hubby's right." Walker actually took his side on something. "Ellis and I had a nice, long chat in a corner booth of a secluded coffee shop the day before he died. I 'accidentally' bumped into him, spilled his coffee. Offered to buy him a new one. Dude was paranoid as shit, but thankfully I knew that ahead of time. Played on conspiracies and managed to talk him into sitting down for a bit. He even told me about the reporter he'd gone to. One who was stupid enough to go to Price himself."

Shit. Gabe rolled his lips inward. "Price have him killed, too?"

"Would you believe the dumbass got pissed and pushed the guy down the stairs? Called me to help him clean up his mess." Walker returned his focus to Elle. "Of course, your boy, Ellis suspected something when the reporter suddenly stopped returning his phone calls. I gotta say, you really had your work cut out for you with that one, Doc. Guy was loonier than a crack whore on Christmas."

"He'd been traumatized from his time in the field," Ellena quickly defended her deceased patient. "Mark's altered state of mind wasn't his fault."

"Not saying it was. Just stating the facts. Unless he actually showed you the letter and explained what was going on, there's no doubt in my mind the guy came off to you as simply being paranoid. So again, Gabe is right. None of this is your fault. You just happened to get caught in the middle of the whole mess."

Ellena huffed a breath. "No shit."

Despite the seriousness of the conversation, Gabe had to work not to grin. Most women he knew—and some men— would've fallen apart completely after shooting someone at point blank range. Even ones they thought were out to do them harm.

Ellena may have been a bit shaken up at first, but she was her usual, tough-as-nails self now. Damn, his woman was something else.

"Anyway"—Walker continued—"Daniel Price was with Radcliff the night Mark Ellis approached him, along with Radcliff's security guys. When they began strong-arming Ellis back to his car, the guy shouted out that he had proof of what Radcliff had done."

"Wait," Ellena chimed back in. "If Mark made all these accusations in front of Governor Radcliff's staff and security team, wouldn't he be worried about those guys finding out the truth, too?"

"Men like Radcliff deal with nutjobs all the time," Matt commented. "No offense to your patient, but if the guy didn't know better than to publicly accuse a presidential candidate of committing mass murder, they're not going to take anything he says seriously. Neither will local authorities."

"Agreed." Ryker looked to Elle. "Especially if that same guy has a medical record like the one Mark Ellis has."

"How do you know about Mark's medical record?"

Walker snickered. "You decide to stay with your hubby, Doc,

you'll figure out the answer to that question real quick." When Gabe shot the man an angry glare, Walker raised a bloody palm. "Sorry, Dawson. Didn't mean to overstep my bounds."

The fuck you didn't.

"Focus, Adrian." Ellena's firm voice snapped the asshole's attention back to her. "How did Mark find out about Radcliff's past?"

They'd just learned the man was a government assassin, but she'd just spoken to him as if he were a child in need of redirecting.

Jesus, I love this woman.

"Funny story, actually." Walker's mouth curved up a bit, clearly as amused by Ellena's gumption as Gabe was. "Turns out Mark Ellis was the grandson to one of the men in Radcliff's old unit. Before the elder Ellis was KIA—not that I'm buying that bullshit for a second, mind you—the guy wrote about what happened to his wife."

Ellena's brows bunched together. "She never said anything to anyone?"

"She never knew. A few weeks back, Mark inherited the woman's house after she passed. He was going through her attic and found an old tin filled with letters from his grandfather. One letter in particular was left unopened. It was postmarked the day his grandad died. Apparently, Mark's grandmother couldn't bear to read it, so she put it with all the others."

"And you know about this how?" Gabe asked Walker.

"How do you think? Mark told me about it."

"Mark Ellis didn't trust anyone, but he told you?" Ellena clearly thought the story was bullshit. "A stranger he'd just met?"

"I'm good at what I do, sweetheart." Walker immediately looked at Gabe. "Sorry. Just slipped out."

"Yeah? I'll *slip* my fist down your throat if it happens again."

"I'm so confused." Elle stood and walked toward the kitchen. "And I need coffee. Anyone else?"

"I'd love a cup, Doc." Walker winked as she passed by.

A few of the other men in the room muttered their desire for some of the hot brew.

Asking the question burning through his mind, Gabe looked at Walker. "Did you kill Mark Ellis?"

"No," he answered immediately. "But I know who did."

"Was it the same person who ran me off the road?" Ellena appeared in the kitchen's small entryway.

"Yes."

"You want to share with the rest of the class?" Matt prodded, his voice still laced with thick disdain.

"Guy by the name of Chris Hall. He's a piece of shit criminal who'd do his old lady in for a quick buck."

"Funny." Matt offered him a disdained smirk. "That's what we always said about you."

"Then I guess my cover story worked."

While Matt flipped the restrained man off, Gabe asked, "So Chris Hall works for Radcliff?"

"Hall works for *Price*."

"I thought *you* were Price's golden boy, Walker," Nate goaded him.

"I am. Hall is Price's plan B."

Gabe thought for a moment. "If you don't get the job done, they send Hall in?"

Walker nodded. "That's why he went after her with the car that night. In Price's eyes, I failed on my first try, so he went behind my back and hired Hall. I suspected the asshole may pull something like that, which is why I was keeping an eye out on her."

"The bicycle," Ellena muttered more to herself than anyone else. "You shot my tire, didn't you?"

Walker didn't bother to deny it. "I'd been watching you for a while. Knew how steady you were on that thing. I waited until I knew you could make it to the railing before taking the shot."

A low, menacing noise hit Gabe's ears, and it took him a second to realize it was coming from him.

"Down, boy." Walker shot him a look. "She's okay, isn't she?"

"No thanks to you, dickhead."

"See that's where you're wrong." Walker shook his head. "If I hadn't continued to follow her even after Price chewed my ass for my supposed fuck-up, your wife would've been stuck in that car a hell of a lot longer than she was. If that had happened, she very well could've bled out."

"Why didn't Hall just shoot her then and get it over with?" Zade's eyes shifted to Ellena's. "No offense."

"Because the idiot saw all the blood and that her eyes were closed and assumed she was dead. As soon as he left, I approached the car. Saw that she was alive and called it in."

"And took my picture," Ellena added curtly. "Then you sent it to me, along with other pictures and a warning."

"Yeah, what the fuck was that all about?" Matt asked. "You develop some sort of crush on Gabe's woman? Followed her around so long you became fixated on her?"

That same animalistic growl escaped Gabe's throat again.

Walker shot a narrowed Gaze in Matt's direction. "No, I didn't become fixated on her, asshole. I sent that email to try and scare the shit out of her." Walker looked over at Ellena. "It was the only way I knew for you to agree to have Gabe and his team protecting you."

"Why didn't you just come to me?"

"Uh…I did come to you, remember? In fact, I seem to have a very clear memory of you pulling a gun on me in your apartment not too long ago."

"You showed up with your riddles, acting like you're Jason Fucking Bourne. You could've told me all of this then. Now that I think about the timing, you had to have gone straight from the scene of the accident in San Diego to the airport, because the hospital didn't even call me until after you left."

"That's exactly what I did. And I *would* have told you, but the powers that be gave me strict orders not to."

"Why?"

"Why do they ever do anything? Because they can." Walker ground his teeth together and groaned through his pain. "It's just like every other fucking time I've had to deal with your team. They want you involved, but they can't officially ask you to be involved, because then they'd have to reveal classified intel that goes even above your level. Part of my job is to make sure you know what's going on without actually spelling it out for you. So you can go after the bad guys, and I keep my cover and my reputation as the badass assassin everyone thinks I am."

"Jesus H. Christ." Nate shook his head. "That's some fucked up shit."

"Fucking CIA and their need-to-know bullshit," Matt bit out harshly.

Rather than let loose with a string of curses—something he'd really love to do at the moment—Gabe asked Walker, "So why do you all of a sudden have their permission to tell us now?"

"He doesn't, actually." Ryker's deep voice interrupted the two men's back-and-forth argument. "Neither do I. Which is why we were never here, and this conversation never happened."

"See?" Matt chuckled angrily. "Just more spook worthy bullshit."

"You've got to be kidding me." Gabe looked to Ryker.

"I wish I were, Dawson." The other man didn't crack a smile. "Really, I do. I fucking hated not being able to tell you all the under-the-table bullshit that's gone on. Especially when it's personal."

"Does Jake know?" Gabe asked about their boss and close friend of Ryker's.

"I called him on the way here."

Kole let out a low whistle. "Bet he was pissed."

"He wasn't happy, as you can probably imagine." Ryker shrugged. "But he also understands how these things work."

Yeah, right.

Drawing in a deep breath, Gabe let it out slowly. "Okay, so just to recap so that everyone's on the same page...A much younger Radcliff gets drunk, screws up his target's coordinates, and kills a bunch of innocent people. He thinks everyone who knew the truth has been taken care of until Mark Ellis comes along several decades later. Governor Radcliff tells Daniel Price, his Chief of Staff, to clean up the mess for fear the scandal will cost him the upcoming election..."

"Then Price hires Hall to follow Elle's patient and make sure he stays quiet," Nate joined in. "When Price realizes Ellis is in counseling, he gets scared. Worried Ellis has shared either the letter or the story or both with his psychologist"—Nate motioned to Ellena—"and decides she needs to be taken out, as well."

Taking a turn at the helm, Matt continued with the unbelievable scenario. "What Price doesn't realize is the assassin he hired is actually...I can't believe I'm even saying this...an undercover government agent working for a super-secret task force formed by the CIA and Homeland."

"And since Ellena isn't on the government's hit list, you've been making it look like you're trying to kill her, when actually you've been trying to help her." Zade tilted his head to the side, his brows turning inward as he stared back at Walker. "And us."

"Finally." Walker let out an exaggerated sigh. "You know, I'd clap if I could, but..." The smartass glanced down at his wounded shoulder. "Now, seeing as how y'all know I'm not really the bad guy, what do you say you cut me loose? Break out some of those pain meds, some gauze, and that Quick Clot I know guys like you keep handy."

"I still have one more question." Ellena took a step closer to him.

"Shoot, Doc. Oh, wait." Walker snickered. "You already did."

"Shut your mouth, Walker," Gabe warned. "Before I shut it for you."

"You never answered me when I asked why you involved Jenna in this."

Though he couldn't swear to it, Gabe thought he saw a swarm of regret swimming behind Walker's gray eyes. "Price still thinks I'm on his payroll, Doc."

"Which means?" Ellena crossed her arms in front of her chest, almost as if she were hugging herself.

"Like I said before, I've been trying to buy you some time. It's worked up to this point, but Price is getting antsy. Really antsy. And Radcliff's getting almost as paranoid as your boy, Mark."

A sinking feeling settled deep in Gabe's gut. "Get to the fucking point, Walker."

The other man's steel-colored eyes met his. "Price wants me to bring him Ellena."

"Ah, shit," someone in the room cursed.

"But Jenna—"

"Is his bait," Gabe told Ellena bluntly.

She frowned. "Bait for what?"

"You, Doc." Walker finally found the balls to admit it. "I've been able to hold Price off as long as I could, but I gotta give him something."

Ellena's eyes grew wide. "So you're going to give him *me?*"

"The fuck he is." Gabe took a step toward Walker.

"Take a breath, Dawson," Ryker ordered him. "Of course, we're not just going to hand her over and walk away."

"Why not?" Nate challenged the Homeland agent. "Isn't that what he did with Gracie and Kat? What makes Ellena any different?"

"Because I'm done with that shit!" Walker's voice boomed throughout the room. Chest heaving, pain etched all over the man's face, he met everyone's gaze before landing on Ellena's. "Look, I'm supposed to be the best of the best when it comes to being a hitman, but my two 'attempts' on your life resulted in squat. I had to talk a huge load of bullshit just to convince Price to give me one last chance so he wouldn't have Hall shoot my ass. That happens, my plan to protect Ellena and Jenna gets shot to hell. Problem is, the second chance Price gave me came with a condition."

"What's the condition?"

"I made him think I was going to use Jenna to draw you out. You show up to save your friend, I take you for her, we go see Price. Together."

"Not happening." Fuming with anger, Gabe walked over to Ellena, standing protectively in front of her. Eyes locked on Walker's, he made sure the prick understood. "She's not doing this so get that idea out of your head right fucking now."

With a grimace, Walker tried looking around Gabe. "You don't do this, Doc, Jenna will be dead within a week."

"Gabe?" Ellena's worried eyes shot to his.

"Don't," he warned Walker off. The tips of his fingernails dug into his palms as the fists at his sides tightened.

"She deserves to know what will happen, Dawson." Refusing to back down, the other man shifted his gaze to Elle's. "They'll kill Jenna, Doc. They'll kill her, and then they'll come after you."

"Shut the fuck up!" Gabe snarled. "They're not touching either one of them, and neither are you."

"Don't be naïve, Gabriel. You know I'm right on this."

He didn't get it. How could he? A soulless, coldhearted bastard like Adrian Walker would never understand the lengths a man will go to in order to protect the ones he loves.

I'll die before seeing her hurt again.

Voice low and flat, Gabe made sure he understood. "They'll have to go through me."

"Eventually, they will." Walker glanced around the room. "That's what I've been trying to get you to see. Radcliff and his men will do whatever it takes to win next year's election. They'll use whoever they have to in order to keep this shit buried. Your women. Your families." When Walker's gaze landed on Gabe's again, there was a level of sincerity Gabe couldn't deny. "I don't blame you for not trusting me, but I'm telling you the truth. If you don't let me do this my way, we'll lose them both."

Something flashed behind the man's eyes. The coldness in his concrete stare darkened, and if Gabe didn't know any better, he'd think the pain he saw there had nothing to do with the man's wound.

What the hell?

"I need some air." Gabe started for the door, pointing to Walker as he walked past. "He tries anything while I'm gone, shoot him."

"Your wife already did that, remember?"

Not bothering to look back at the prick, Gabe gave him a low 'Fuck You' before walking outside and slamming the door behind him.

CHAPTER 16

Storming across the crisp, fall grass, Gabe was halfway to the tree line before he was able to fully fill his lungs. With his hands on his hips, he hung his head and closed his eyes, doing his damnedest to make sense of it all.

Walker wasn't the backstabbing criminal they believed him to be. Ryker had known this entire time and didn't tell them. Both men had conspired to kidnap Jenna under the guise that she would be bait, and now...

They want me to willingly send my wife into the lion's den.

Gabe drew in another slow, deep breath, barely managing to keep the vomit from working its way up at bay. All he'd ever done was try to protect her. He'd fucking *left* to keep her safe and away from the evils he knew existed. But they'd found her, anyway.

I can't do this. He opened his eyes and looked up at whisps of clouds etched across the graying sky. "I can't lose her."

"You won't."

The unexpected sound of Kole's voice startled him. Turning only his head, Gabe struggled to speak for the emotion clogging his throat. "I will if I let her go along with this crazy plan."

"Let?" The other man chuckled. "Dude, if your wife is anything like mine, you'd better pray she didn't just hear you say that."

"You know what I mean." Gabe faced him directly. "No offense, man, but you don't get it."

Kole's brows arched high. "No? You must've forgotten what happened to Sarah."

Shit. "I don't mean to downplay what you two went through with that psycho stalker from her law firm. I just meant..." Gabe blew out a breath and grabbed the back of his neck. Pushing hard against the tight muscles there, he tried to make his teammate understand what he was trying to say. "You're the only one on the team who hasn't had to deal with that asshole on a personal level."

"Which is why I'm the one out here."

"You defending him, now?"

"I'm not defending shit." Kole scowled. "I just have a more objective outlook than the rest of you do, so I can see this for what it is."

"Look, Gabe...I get what you're saying. I do. But you're wrong to think I don't have a personal stake in this, too. No, Walker didn't take Sarah from me, and no, he didn't shoot me. But he did shoot my friends, and he did put their wives...*your* wife...in harm's way. So don't think I'm not as pissed at him as everyone else on the team. I'm beyond pissed. At him and Ryker."

Gabe studied his younger teammate closely. "But?"

"But I think they're right." When Gabe shook his head and started to argue, Kole cut him off at the pass. "Just hear me out. After that, you don't like what I have to say, you can tell me to fuck off."

Begrudgingly, he gave Kole a curt nod.

"You're the team leader. You're like our—"

"Swear to God, you say the word 'dad', your ass will be on the fucking ground."

Kole chuckled. "I was going to say big brother. And with that role comes a sense of responsibility."

"You gonna make your point sometime today, or..."

"You feel responsible for us, Gabe. Something happens to one of us, you take that shit on. And don't try to deny it, because I've seen it. After what happened to the others, and now with your wife's involvement in all of this, it's no wonder you can't wrap your mind around working alongside Walker."

"No." Gabe raked a hand through his hair. "I can't."

"Unfortunately, I don't think we have much choice." Regret filled Kole's expression. "Walker's right. One way or another, Radcliff is coming after Ellena. At least if we go this route, we have a say in how shit goes down. We'll be there, ready to take the fuckers out before they can have a chance to hurt anyone else."

"He's right."

Both men turned to see Matt walking toward them.

"You, too?" Gabe was surprised. "Figured you'd be fighting tooth and nail to tell Walker to shove his plan right up his ass."

"Believe me, I'd like to." He stopped next them. "But what Kole said makes sense. Last time, Walker took us all by surprise. Doing it this way, we'll be able to keep an eye on Ellena and him. He tries to double-cross us, we'll all be there, ready to take his ass down."

"And Ryker?"

Matt shrugged. "Like it or not, the man was just doing his job. We know what guys in those positions are like. Hell, most of us got out of the military for that exact reason. All that red tape, need to know bullshit drives me insane, but it's the price we pay for doing business with a government agency like Homeland."

Staring back at him, Gabe asked Matt, "Can you honestly say you'd be okay working with Walker on this?"

"*Okay* may be a bit of a stretch. Do I trust him?" Matt shook his head. "Hell no. But your girl's in there right now, talking with him and Ryker. She wants her friend back and out of this mess as soon as possible, so she's already agreed to the plan."

"Fuck." Gabe rubbed his palm over the scruff on his jaw.

"Look, man. I may not know her very well, but from what I've already seen, your wife is one brave woman." Matt grinned. "I mean, she shot Adrian Fucking Walker without blinking an eye. Pretty sure she's strong enough to handle whatever else comes her way."

"She is strong enough," Gabe admitted. "She's survived more pain and heartache than you know."

"I figured as much."

The two men shared a look. One Kole picked up on immediately.

"I have a feeling you two need to talk." Kole slapped Gabe on the shoulder. "I'll leave you to it."

Gabe waited until Kole was out of earshot before speaking again. "Look, Matt. The story I told you back when Kat was in trouble...about why my marriage to Ellena didn't work out—"

"Was bullshit." Matt smirked. "Yeah, I sorta got that impression when I found out you were still married."

Feeling chagrined, Gabe tried to explain. "A little over three years ago, Ellena found out she was pregnant." He smiled sadly. "We were ecstatic. Not long after, we had a name picked out and the room all painted and ready to go. I couldn't wait to be a dad. But then a couple months into the pregnancy, I came home from my morning run to find Vic, a former SEAL teammate of mine, in our kitchen. He had a gun to Elle's head."

"Ah, shit."

"He, uh..." Gabe swallowed. "He'd been having a lot of issues. Erratic behavior on missions. Going off half-cocked and not following orders. Vic had a couple close calls early on, and he didn't handle it or the aftermath well. I tried talking to him about it. Offered to get him help, but he blew me off. Said he was fine. For a while, that seemed true, but then while we were on a particularly bad op, Vic ended up executing one of our prisoners in cold blood."

"Damn."

"Yeah." Gabe could still see the man's face right before the bullet entered his brain. "Of course, I had to remove him from the team. He was brought up on charges and was set to go to trial. His JAG attorney was planning to use Vic's PTSD as his defense, but either way, Vic's military career was done."

"And he blamed you, so he went after Ellena in retaliation."

Gabe nodded. "Ellena fought him off long enough for me to get a clear shot. Vic died instantly, and we thought it was over, but then about an hour later, Ellena started having these pains…"

"Shit. I'm sorry, brother."

His heart ached, the pain still as raw and fresh as the day it happened. "I couldn't bear the thought of another enemy of mine using her for retaliation, so I left." Gabe looked out into the trees. "I also didn't want the men I'm supposed to be leading to know what a chickenshit I was."

This made Matt laugh. "No more than the rest of us. We've all got our own shit, Gabe. You should know that by now."

"I do." He met his friend's stare. "Now."

Matt offered him a tip of his head. "So you and Ellena. All that time apart and you stayed married."

"I couldn't file." Gabe shrugged. "I couldn't bring myself to sign a piece of paper stating I didn't want to be married to her anymore. It would've been a lie."

"Lucky for you, she felt the same way." Matt grinned. "Otherwise she would've been the one to—"

"She did." Gabe cut him off. "I got the papers a few weeks ago."

Matt blinked. "Oh. Damn. So uh…what does that mean?"

"We've had some time to talk since coming here." Gabe shoved his hands into his pockets. "Elle says she wants to give it another go."

"That's great!" Matt slapped him on the shoulder. "Congratulations, man."

"Thanks. It would be a helluva lot easier to celebrate if someone wasn't hell bent on killing her."

"We'll figure it all out, man." Matt blew the concern away with confidence "That's what we do. The important thing is she still loves you and is willing to give you a second chance. Believe me, I know what a gift that is."

Gabe thought back to everything his teammate had to go through to finally get his happy ending. Maybe he should listen to the guy. After all, Matt and Katherine were proof that second chances really could work out.

"Fuck me." Gabe grabbed the back of his neck again. "I can't believe I'm actually considering letting her do this shit."

"There you go, using that dirty word again."

"Shit?"

"No." Matt chuckled. "*Let.*"

Despite the situation, Gabe let out a little chuckle. "Guess I'll have to watch that, huh?"

"If you plan on keeping her around for very long, you will."

I'm keeping her with me forever.

"I do have one other question, though."

Gabe slid Matt a glance. "What's that?"

The other man eyed him up and down slowly. "What the fuck are you wearing?"

"What?" Gabe glanced down at himself, realizing only then that he still had that damn apron on. "Shit."

Ignoring his teammate, who'd just busted up laughing, Gabe reached around to his back, yanking the tie loose before pulling it up and over his head.

"I'm surprised Walker didn't jump at the chance to razz me about it."

"He was probably too busy making sure your wife didn't shoot his ass again. Come on, man." Matt punched him in the bicep. "We'd better get back in there before they decide to plan World War Three."

Wadding the thick material into a ball, Gabe fell in line with Matt, and the two men began walking back to the cabin. When they walked inside, he was surprised to see Walker standing next to the kitchen sink, Ellena carefully cleaning the area around the bullet hole she'd inflicted.

Hearing them come in, Walker sent him a wink. "Your girl's got the magic touch."

He's on our side...he's on our side...

"You really don't want to push me right now, Adrian."

"But it's so much fun. Ah!" Walker groaned, wincing from the extra pressure Ellena had suddenly used.

"Oops." She looked up at him with a sugary sweet smile. "Sorry."

"No, you're not." Despite his words, Walker chuckled. "Damn, Gabriel. Your wife's almost as ruthless as you are."

"Worse." Ellena smiled again. "If you catch me on a bad day."

"No wonder you and Jenna are friends. You're just alike."

"Nah." Ellena shook her head. "She's even more ruthless than me. Which is why I'm looking forward to watching her take a go at you when she realizes what's really going on."

"I'm looking forward to it." A funny look crossed over Walker's face, but then it was gone as quickly as it appeared.

Whatthefuckever.

"Turner." Gabe turned to Matt. "There's a med kit under the sink in the bathroom. Take care of that, would ya?"

"You got it, Boss."

Once Matt went into medic-mode with Walker, Gabe grabbed hold of Ellena's freshly washed hand and led her into the living room.

He needed her by his side. Needed to be touching her. Because what they were about to discuss would no-doubt send his raging fear racing through his veins again.

If she was here, right by his side, Gabe might be able to control himself and not decide to kill Walker, after all.

CHAPTER 17

"Who are these men again?" Ellena whispered softly so no one else could hear.

Nate tilted his head toward hers. "That guy there is Ghost. He's their team leader and a total badass. The man standing next to him is Coach, those two over there are Fletch and Hollywood, and the big one at the end is Truck."

While Gabe, Ryker, and Walker gave the new team a rundown on the situation, Ellena studied them closely.

When Gabe first told her they were meeting up with another group of guys, she'd had no choice but to go along with it. She knew he was doing everything he could as quickly as he could, but for Ellena, it wasn't nearly fast enough.

An image of her friend's smiling face flashed through her mind, striking a match to the pile of guilt burning inside her stomach. Aside from being her friend, Jenna had *nothing* to do with any of this. But yet, she'd been taken from her home by a man posing as a world-renowned assassin, having no idea he was actually working undercover for the CIA.

When Ellena discovered Walker hadn't bothered to share this little tidbit with Jenna, she'd nearly come unglued.

Knowing the friend who'd been there for her through everything—the good, the bad, and all of her many, ugly cries— was locked away somewhere, terrified and probably thinking she was going to die, made Ellena physically ill.

Walker claimed he needed Jenna's fear to be genuine so she wouldn't do or say anything to tip off the man keeping watch over her. When Ellena asked him who that was, he'd said Chris Hall.

The same man who caused my wreck.

The thought of Jenna being anywhere near someone like him...or Adrian Walker...was terrifying. But Walker had assured them all that he'd do whatever it took to keep Jenna safe, and there was something about the way he'd said it that made Elle believe him.

After Matt had finished cleaning and sewing up Adrian's wound, they'd all gathered back in the tiny living room to hash out the details of Walker's crazy plan. Halfway through, after even more back and forth bickering and finger-pointing than before, Gabe told Ryker they weren't going through with it unless they had more men there to help protect both her and Jenna.

They'd all waited while Ryker called the man Nate had just pointed out as Ghost, informing him that his team's services were needed ASAP. Though Ryker had done his best to say the last part quietly, Ellena had still heard the mysterious man's whispered words.

Off the books.

After a few more phone calls—to whom, Ellena had no idea —a meeting had been called at the location they were in, now. When Ellena had asked why they couldn't stay at the cabin, Nate had laughed and told her she'd understand once she saw who they were meeting.

So, here they were. Standing inside an old barn in the middle of nowhere with some other team. A team Gabe assured her was every bit as good—and deadly—as Bravo Team.

"Hey."

Gabe's soft voice made Ellena jump. She looked around and realized he'd finished bringing the others up to speed.

"Hey." She offered her ruggedly handsome husband a hint of a smile. "Sorry. Guess I got lost in my thoughts for a minute."

"Understandable. You doing okay?" His concern for her obvious as he slid a comforting hand against her cheek.

"Yeah." Her smile grew slightly as she covered his hand with hers. "I'm just worried about Jenna."

"Walker gave us his word that she's safe."

"I thought you said you couldn't trust him."

"I don't." One corner of his mouth twitched. Resting both hands on her shoulders, he attempted to reassure her. "But I've worked with Ryker long enough to still trust him, and he backed up Walker's claim, so…"

His unspoken *What choice do we have?* hung in the air between them.

Wrapping her arms around his waist, Ellena closed her eyes and held on tightly, just long enough to send up a silent prayer that her friend would be okay.

"This will work, baby." Gabe pressed his lips to her forehead. "I promise."

She wasn't sure who he was trying to convince more. Her or himself.

With a nod, Ellena dropped her hand and stepped out of his reach. "Are we about done here?" The sooner they could put their plan into action, the sooner this would all be over.

"Almost. Walker is outside right now calling Price to let him know he made contact with you. He's setting up the details of the trade, and as long as Price agrees with the plan, we'll head out as soon as we can."

"What if he doesn't? What if Price doesn't like Walker's idea, or he doesn't—"

"He will." Gabe cupped the sides of her neck. "As much as I hate the guy, Walker's good at getting what he wants."

Yeah, that seemed pretty obvious.

"And Ghost and those guys?" Ellena motioned toward the men talking intently with Agent Ryker and the rest of Bravo. "You sure they're up for this?"

A low chuckle reverberated from his chest. "Oh, I'm sure. Those guys are as solid as they come. Trust me."

"Who are they? I mean..." Ellena licked her lips taking in the large, intimidating men again. "Are they former SEALs like you?"

"No. They're not SEALs, but they are still active duty. I'm not allowed to say what unit they're with, but I can tell you those men over there are top notch."

"Active duty?" She found that to be both surprising and worrisome. "Are they going to get into trouble for helping us? When Agent Ryker first called Ghost, I overheard him say this whole thing was off the books."

With a shake of his head, Gabe followed her gaze to the other group. "No need to worry about that. Ryker and their commanding officer go way back. In fact, when Gracie and Kat were taken, these guys helped us get them back. They also helped us rescue Gabby and her sister."

"Really?"

"Yep. Ryker was the one who helped make that happen, which is the only reason I'm inclined to give him some slack on the whole Walker deal."

Wow. Her heart hurt for all Gabe and his friends had been through. And while she didn't know the specifics, she knew enough to understand the danger each of those situations had created. Danger the man she loved had purposely put himself in, in order to help his teammates save the women they loved. And in any one of those scenarios, this incredible, fearless man of hers could've been killed.

And I never would have known.

"Elle?"

Blinking away tears she hadn't even realized were forming, Ellena shook off the macabre thoughts and rejoined the conversation.

"Gabby." Ellena thought for a moment. "She's engaged to Zade. Right?" At least she thought that was the name he'd mentioned earlier in the week when they'd been talking about his team.

Brows turned slightly inward, Gabe held her gaze a moment longer before nodding. "And when Gabby's sister was taken and nearly sold, Ghost and the others also helped us get her back."

"Sold?" Ellena felt her eyes grow wide. Though he didn't say it, she understood exactly the kind of people who *bought* young, terrified women. "That's horrible. But Gabby's sister is okay?"

"Zade says she is. Had a rough go of it right after, but according to him and Gabby, Samantha's doing much better."

"Good." Her heart ached for the poor girl. "I hope she's been talking with someone."

"She has." He gave her another squeeze before dropping his arms. "Come on." Grabbing one of her hands, he linked their fingers together and kissed her temple. "Walker's back. Let's go see what the asshole has to say."

Feeling even smaller than her petite frame already made her feel, Ellena stood amongst the group of musclebound warriors, wondering how the next few hours of her life were going to go.

"Listen up." Ryker got everyone's attention. "We got the final word, and Walker and I both believe it's a solid plan."

"Well, as long as Walker thinks so…" Zade mumbled beneath his breath.

A few of the men muttered their agreements, including a couple from Ghost's team.

"Enough." Ryker shot Zade a look. "I get that your pissed, King. You're all pissed, and I can't say I blame you. But we've already been through that shit, and frankly, we're running low on time. So, for the next couple of hours, you men need to get the fuck over yourselves and work together on this so we can end this bullshit and get on with our day. If anyone here doesn't feel capable of doing just that, there's the goddamn door." Ryker pointed behind him. "Feel free to use it."

"Actually, it's not really a door, per se." Nate pretended to study the barn's decrepit entryway. "More like a few pieces of rotted wood that's just hanging on by…"

Ellena was amazed at the power Agent Ryker had over these men. Even now, after having kept what she considered to be vital information from them, the formidable man didn't even have to say anything. He just *looked* at Nate, and the guy stopped talking.

"As I was saying," Ryker continued. "We've come up with a plan we believe will ensure the safety of both Ellena and the Shaw woman."

"Jenna." She gave the man her own look before glancing around to the others. "Her name is Jenna. She's sitting some-place right now, scared to death, and the *only* reason she's there is because she's friends with me." Ellena's voice cracked, and she wiped away an escaped tear. "So please. Help me get Jenna out of this mess...and help me find justice for Mark Ellis."

"We will." Ghost's dark eyes met hers. "We'll do both of those things and make sure Henry Radcliff pays for what he's done."

Truck's voice was deep as he added, "And anyone else who's been helping him cover up his crimes."

Once again, Ellena met each of the men's gazes. With a nod and a slight smile, she whispered a sincere, "Thank you."

She shouldn't be surprised at how these men had all come together the way they had. Though she'd only just met them, Ghost, Truck, Hollywood, and the others put off the same good guy-warrior vibe she'd gotten from Gabe the first time they'd met.

Men like the ones surrounding her now were all made from the same cloth. Good. Honest. Fierce. And when it came to righting the wrongs this crazy world sometimes doled out on innocent souls, they were the first to step up. Ready and willing to lay it all on the line in the name of God, country, and the ones they loved.

A sense of dread began building in the pit of her stomach, and she said a silent prayer asking God to watch over them all. Including Adrian Walker.

* * *

"So that's it." Adrian looked back at the others. "Any questions?"

They'd gone over the plan ad nauseum, and he was chomping at the bit to get back to Jenna. He fucking hated leaving her in that house with Hall—the guy was such a prick—but like everything else in his mess of a life, he hadn't had much choice.

"I have a question." Zade spoke up.

Of course, you do. Speaking in his best, most well-mannered teacher's voice, Adrian smiled a little too wide at the other man. "Yes, Zade?"

"I'm cool with the plan as it sits, except for one part."

"Which part is confusing to you?"

"The part where you leave us here to go get Jenna. Alone."

"Oh, that's easy." Adrian gave the pissed off R.I.S.C. operative a smirk. "You see, I'm going to walk out the door that isn't really a door anymore, get into my CIA issued, non-descript vehicle, and then I'm going to...are you paying attention, because this part is tricky...drive that vehicle to the location where Jenna is being held."

A muscle in Zade's jaw twitched as he turned his glare onto Ryker's. "You seriously expect us to trust this asshole to do what he says he's going to? I mean"—he ran a hand over his short hair —"he could be sending us all into a fucking trap."

The phone call Adrian had made earlier was to Price. He'd convinced the prick he'd found and made contact with Ellena and convinced her to trade herself for her friend. Adrian then talked Price into flying his ass from D.C. to a small airstrip not far from where they were now to make the trade.

The airstrip in question was located on a piece of land owned by the federal government. Government officials, federal agents, and politicians often used it—and the hundreds just like it spread around the country—to avoid being mauled by the press when they landed.

What Price didn't know was that Bravo Team, along with the Delta team Ryker had brought in, would already be on location and in position. The plan was to take the asshole down the first chance they got. After that, it would be up to Ryker to get Price to turn on Radcliff, effectively taking both men down in one, fell swoop.

"King does bring up a good point," the guy they all called Truck rumbled his opinion. "We've all tangled with Walker a time or two. What's to say there won't be a shitload of guys waiting to take us all out as soon as we get there?"

"You've got to be fucking kidding me with this shit." Adrian threw his hands in the air. "*Hellooo*. Look around, gentlemen. You're closer to each other right now than you will be at the trade sight. It'd be a helluva lot easier to take your asses out here as opposed to when you'll be spread out along the airstrip like a bunch of fucking cockroaches."

"Nah, Truck's right," Zade pressed on. "You went outside earlier to make that phone call. Alone. How do we know you weren't setting us up, then?"

"You don't." Walker stared back at him. "Guess you'll just have to trust me."

"Trust the man who put a fucking hole in my shoulder?" Zade scoffed. "Don't think so."

"Dude, you really need to play like Elsa and let that shit go. Besides..." Adrian stared down at the makeshift sling Matt had concocted for him before giving the other man a wink. "We're twinsies now. Hey, maybe when this is all over, we can take a selfie together. Use one of those cute little filters and show off our matching scars. What do ya say?"

Zade went for him, then, but several arms reached out all at once to stop him. While the other man growled and struggled to get loose, Adrian casually glanced down at his watch.

"And on that note, I'm going to go pick up the hot little nurse and that dipshit Hall. As soon as Price has landed, I'll head to the hanger. The guy's already a suspicious bastard as it is. If I'm late, it'll only cause more problems. And speaking of problems"—he shot Gabe a look—"I suggest you get your man King, there, under control. I'd hate for this thing to go sideways because he's still butthurt over something that went down months ago."

"Fuck you, Walker!" Spittle flew from Zade's angry lips as he continued fighting to free himself.

Ignoring him and the others, Adrian offered them a smile and a two-finger salute as he turned to leave the barn. Anxious to see Ellena's friend again, it was all he could do not to haul ass to his car.

He was fully aware that he shouldn't even be *thinking* about the feisty redhead beyond using her to get the job done. Shouldn't care about the fear he'd seen in her eyes when he'd gotten the jump on her in her apartment's parking lot. Or how soft and tender Jenna looked after the injection he'd given her had knocked her out cold.

With everything going on, and everything still left to do, he had to do, the last thing Adrian should've been worried about was leaving Jenna unconscious and alone with that Hall fucker.

But he *was* worried. And he *did* care. Far. Too. Much.

Adrian didn't know what it was about the fist-slinging, ball-threatening tiny bit-of-nothing woman. All he knew was, ever since he'd first laid eyes on Jenna Shaw, he hadn't been able to get her out of his head.

Adding more pressure to his accelerator, he increased his speed as he made his way down the gravel road leading away from the old barn. The sudden need to see her, to make sure she was okay had become a living, breathing thing inside him.

Ironic, given the fact that he'd been dead inside a long damn time.

Half an hour later, he was pulling up to one of the CIA's numerous safe houses in the great state of Texas. For this particular job, Adrian had picked one that was on an isolated piece of land and had intentionally been left to appear neglected and run-down.

After all, if one wants to stash away a kidnap victim, one needed the assurance of privacy in order to keep that little secret safe from prying eyes.

Shoving the car in park, Adrian got out and began walking up the broken sidewalk toward the paint-chipped front door. He started to use the key, then realized Hall had left the damn thing unlocked.

Fucking idiot.

Walking inside, Adrian had just opened his mouth to holler out for the dipshit when he heard a sound coming from the back bedroom. The same room he'd locked Jenna in a few hours before.

He stopped and listened closely. Silence met his ears, but then there was a loud crash and a muffled scream.

Sonofabitch!

Adrian took off with a vengeance, covering the narrow hallway's length in two seconds. Not bothering to turn the knob, he lifted his foot and kicked the damn door in. His vision filled with red.

Jenna was on the floor next to the bed he'd left her cuffed to. One of the cuffs was still attached to a wrist, the other had been unlocked. And Chris Hall—the motherfucker—was on top of her, holding her down by the wrists.

One second, Adrian was standing there, mentally cataloging the many ways he knew how to kill with his bare hands. The next, his body was slamming into Hall's with enough force to send them both flying.

A searing pain spread throughout his injured shoulder, but he ignored it and pushed on.

"What the fuck?" Despite his being trapped beneath him, Hall somehow managed to pull his gun from his waistband. He started to bring it around, but Adrian knocked it out of the man's hand before he could pull the trigger.

The weapon skittered across the dull, hardwood floor, but Adrian was too busy punching Hall's lights out to pay attention to where it went. All it took was one hard, right hook and the man was out cold.

Without giving it another thought, he shot to his feet and started toward Jenna. It was only then that he realized she'd picked up the gun...and was pointing it directly at his head.

"Whoa!" Adrian threw his hands up. "I'm not going to hurt you."

Using her free hand, she clumsily crab-walked herself back toward the bed. Shaking her head wildly, she spewed what he could only guess was a long line of curse words from behind the duct tape covering her full, rosy red lips.

"Are you okay?" Adrian made his way toward her slowly. "Did he hurt you?"

Shoving the mass of red, unruly hair from her flushed face,

Jenna's auburn brows turned inward with an angry scowl. Her perfectly proportioned breasts rose and fell with each of her heaving breaths, and the metal cuffs he'd used on her dangled from the hand holding the gun.

Never taking her eyes off of him, she used the bedframe to push herself up into a defensive stance. Bringing the other hand around, Jenna's arms shook as she kept the weapon trained on him.

"Easy." He kept his hands up. "I'm not going to hurt you."

The sounds coming from behind the tape told Adrian she wasn't buying it.

Yeah, I wouldn't either, sweetheart.

Doing the only thing he could think of to prove he wasn't lying, he went back to Hall who was starting to stir. With another fist to his jaw, Adrian ensured the guy stayed out for at least the next several minutes and then grabbed the small set of silver keys from his pocket.

Taking caution, he began walking toward Jenna once more.

"Here." He showed her the keys. "I'm going to take those off of you and put them onto him."

Her gorgeous, emerald eyes rolled, and damn if Adrian wasn't tempted to smile. As if suddenly realizing her hands were free, she used one to rip the tape quickly from her lips.

With a wince, she threw it onto the floor next to her feet then brought the hand back up to help steady the gun. "Don't you fucking touch me."

"I don't want to hurt you, Jenna." He spoke quickly, taking another step closer. Worried the dickhead on the floor may still be able to hear him, he mouthed to her, 'I'm undercover.'

"Right." Skin reddened by the sting of the tape, Jenna gave him a look that said she wasn't buying it for a second. "Because I'm *that* stupid."

Damn, she was something else.

The woman had been kidnapped, held captive, and had come damn close to being sexually assaulted seconds before. Most women would be cowering down in a puddle of tears, but not his Jenna. She was as fiery and as full of sass as ever.

Not yours, dumbass.

Fuck. That tiny voice was right. There wasn't a woman on the planet who'd want anything to do with a guy like him. Especially not the one whose mesmerizing eyes were currently shooting daggers back into his.

"Fine. Here." He gave the keys a gentle toss. "You do it."

Without blinking, Jenna caught the keys with one hand. She took all of two seconds to look away from him and start working the cuffs.

Letting them fall from her wrist, the metal bracelets clinked together when they hit the floor. "Now what?" She sneered back at him. "Am I supposed to say, 'thank you'?"

"No." He shook his head. "But I do need you to listen to me very carefully." Adrian glanced over her shoulder at Hall, who still appeared to be unconscious. "He's going to wake up very soon, and when he does, he's going to be pissed."

"Guess it'll be a party, then, because I'm not particularly happy right now, either."

Jesus, she got his blood pumping in ways it hadn't in years. But he blocked it all out and stayed focused.

"I'm going to pick those up." He motioned to the cuffs. "Then I'm going to put them on him so we can talk."

"Newsflash, asshole. I don't want to *talk*. I want you to give me the keys to your car so I can get the hell out of here."

"Can't do that."

"Uh...this little guy right here"—she wiggled the gun—"says you can."

Adrian's lips twitched, but then he flattened his lips and turned his voice lower. "Not if you want Ellena to live."

The breath escaped her lungs in a low huff. "I knew it. You're the one, aren't you?" She rolled her lips inward. "You're the one who's been stalking her."

"I'm one of them, yes." He took a step closer. "But not for the reason you think."

She barked out a laugh. "So you *do* think I'm stupid."

"No. I think you're scared. And you should be."

Just a little closer.

"Really?" Jenna glanced down at the weapon in her hand. "Because the way I see it, you're the one who should be—"

Adrian snaked his hand out and grabbed her wrist. Surprised by the sudden move, she cried out, immediately going all hellcat on him as she attempted to keep hold of the gun.

Nice try, sweetheart.

Given his training and background, it didn't take much for him to gain control of both the woman and the weapon. Still, she fought back with a vengeance.

"Stop," Adrian ordered, his voice loud and sharp.

Not surprising, Jenna continued kicking and fighting to break free of his hold.

"Goddamn it, Jenna! I said *stop!*"

Adrian pushed against her flailing wrists to keep her from hurting either one of them. The move was unintentional, but the momentum of his body's strength fighting against hers left them both tumbling backward onto the bed.

Using his elbows to keep his weight from crushing her, he instinctively felt the need to protect her in all ways possible. He was much bigger and stronger than her, and now was not the time for this shit...but damn if he didn't find himself loving the way her soft, feminine curves felt beneath his hard body.

And he was getting harder every second.

Jenna froze beneath him, their heavy breathing filling the tiny room. Her eyes locked with his, and it was obvious she'd felt his growing erection pressing between her splayed legs.

For a split second in time, Adrian couldn't help but imagine this woman looking up at him while they made love. Then he noticed the tears welling in her terrified eyes.

"Please," Jenna spoke softly. "L-let me go."

It was the first sign of vulnerability she'd shown, and damn if it wouldn't have broken his fucking heart. If he still had one.

Way to go, asshole.

"I told you before. I'm not going to hurt you," he promised her quietly. "But I need you to listen to what I'm telling you before that asshat over there wakes back up. That happens, you, Ellena, and I are all dead. Got it?"

Seas of green swirled with fear as she continued to stare up at him. Adrian fully expected her to keep fighting, but instead she nodded shakily and asked, "W-who are you?"

With a quick glance back at Hall, he whispered, "I'm the man trying to take down the assholes who've been terrorizing your friend. That guy over there?"

Jenna nodded again.

"He works for the man trying to kill Ellena."

"So do you." Her voice came out a little stronger. "You kidnapped me and brought me here, just so you could use me to set a trap for Elle."

Shit. Hall had a big fucking mouth. "I know it seems that way, but—"

"It sure as hell does *seem* that way." Her ample breasts vibrated against his chest as she let out a humorless laugh. "Do you honestly think I'd believe a fucking word coming out of your mouth, right now?"

He got an idea.

"No. I don't think you'll believe me." As much as he enjoyed feeling her luscious body beneath his, Adrian let go of her wrists and pushed himself off the bed. Pulling his phone from his pocket, he dialed Ryker's number. When the other man answered, Adrian said, "Put Elle on the phone."

There was a pause before Ryker asked, "Why?"

He wanted to growl with frustration. Why did everyone involved with this job seem hellbent on making it so fucking hard?

"You really want me to waste time explaining?" Adrian asked in a hushed whisper. "Just put her on the goddamn phone."

After a brief pause and some rustling, Adrian heard Ellena's soft voice. "Hello?"

"I need you to talk to your friend, Doc. Get her to trust what I'm telling her, or this whole thing gets blown to hell."

"Put her on." Ellena didn't hesitate. "I'll explain everything."

Thank fuck.

Adrian slid Hall another sideways glance. "Do it quick. We don't have much time." He handed a weary Jenna the phone. "It's

Ellena. Try to keep that pretty little mouth of yours shut and let her do the talking."

Pushing herself into a sitting position, Jenna's narrowed eyes glared up into his as she yanked the phone from his hand.

"Elle?" There was a slight pause before her eyes widened, and her shoulders fell with relief. "Oh, thank God you're okay." Another pause. "What's going on? I was abducted when I got home from work, and then I woke up here...although, I'm not even sure where here is..."

Clearing his throat, Adrian made a circle motion with his hand to remind her they were on borrowed time. To his surprise, she actually stopped talking and listened to Ellena explain the situation.

"Oh, my god. Really?" Jenna's guarded eyes lifted to his again. "Yeah." She huffed another breath. "That is hard to believe." A few seconds of silence passed before Jenna's shoulders fell, and her expression softened. "It's not your fault, Elle. I know you'd never purposely involve me in something dangerous. Although I should probably warn you, there will be a hefty dose of I-told-you-so's when I see you again."

Jenna smiled then. The sight caused something to stir inside Adrian's chest. Refusing to identify the strange feeling, he held out his hand and wiggled his fingers. "That's enough. Tell her bye."

With a snarky scrunch of her face, Jenna huffed out an exaggerated sigh. "The asshole's telling me I have to go. Take care, Elle. I love you."

Adrian took the phone from her hand. Ignoring the electric pulse striking his skin when his fingers inadvertently brushed against hers, he put the phone up to his ear and muttered a low, "Thanks, Doc," before ending the call.

"So what now?" Jenna crossed her arms at her chest.

Pretending not to notice how the move pushed her breasts together beneath the thin scrub top, Adrian put on a forced smile and said, "First, I'm going to deal with him. Then you and I are going to get ready to make a trade."

CHAPTER 18

"What if this doesn't work?" Ellena looked up at Gabe. "What if I do something that pisses this Price guy off and he hurts Jenna? What if—"

Gabe was walking across the grass pulling her into his arms before she could finish. "Shh... Told you before, Elle. The what ifs will just tear you up inside."

She relished in the warmth of her husband's strong embrace. Once everything had been hashed out, she'd come outside for some fresh air and to try and clear her thoughts. Gabe had followed, and they'd been out here, together, ever since.

It had been several hours since Adrian had called so she could explain things to Jenna. She'd never heard her friend sound so utterly terrified, and it killed Ellena to know she was the reason.

No, not you. Daniel Price and Henry Radcliff are to blame. Not you.

She'd been telling herself that over and over again since her conversation with Jenna. It was an exercise she often had her patients practice, because there was validity in the old wives' tale.

If you tell yourself something enough times, eventually, you start to believe it.

But now that *she* was the one needing to believe the unbelievable, Ellena was starting to realize it wasn't as easy as she'd always thought it would be.

"I know you're right. Logically, I understand that line of thinking is a waste of time, but if anything happens to Jenna..." Her voice cracked. Heart aching, she rested a palm against his cheek. "God, Gabe. If anything happens to you or any of the others...I couldn't live with that."

"Baby, stop." Dark eyes pierced into hers as Gabe gently brushed his hand along her hair. "Don't do this to yourself. Ghost and his team are already in place, and Ryker's there, too. My men and I are trained for this sort of thing. It's what we do. I promise you we're not going to let anything happen to you or Jenna, or anyone else."

He kissed her forehead, the tip of her nose, and finally her lips. Resting his forehead against hers, they stood like that for the next several minutes, until Gabe raised his head, and said, "It's time to go."

Ellena stared back at the man who meant everything to her. There was no sign of fear or doubt in his eyes. He truly was the bravest man she'd ever met.

Now it was time for her to be brave, too. She had to be. For everyone's sake.

Taking in a long, deep breath, Ellena let it out slowly and smiled. "What are you waiting for? Let's get this show on the road."

The drive was painfully quiet until Nate finally turned on the radio. He purposely found a station playing up-beat, big hair bands. Ellena guessed it was his way of pumping himself up for what was coming. She had to admit, it was better than silence.

Sitting in the back of a blacked-out SUV Ryker had provided, Ellena kept her head resting on Gabe's shoulder the entire way. Matt was in the passenger seat next to Nate, who was behind the wheel. Kole and Zade were following behind them in an identical vehicle.

Ellena had brought up the idea over lunch, suggesting that if they had two cars, then once Jenna was out of harm's way, one of the guys could take her back to Kole's cabin so at least they'd know she was safe.

Gabe decided Zade would be a good man for the job, citing his softer nature and ability to show empathy and compassion. Ellena knew the real reason Gabe had chosen him was because the guy was still too amped up over what went down between him and Adrian a few months back, and Gabe wanted his teammate away from the volatile situation as soon as possible. Just in case.

Zade wasn't happy with the idea, but since Gabe was the team leader, he didn't really have much choice.

As they turned onto the road leading to the small airstrip, Gabe sat up straight. He instructed her and the other men to put in their earpieces while he did the same. He'd shown her how to use the tiny device back at the cabin, which only added to the surrealness of the situation.

The hangar and small parking lot came into view and Ellena's heart pounded hard against her chest. Sensing her fear, Gabe squeezed her hand and said, "What do we got, Ghost?"

Ghost?

Startled, she jumped at the sound of the other man's voice in her ear.

"Price and Jenna are next to the runway about twenty yards outside the hanger's entrance. Miss Shaw appears to be fine. Pissed, but fine."

Ellena smiled. If Jenna was, in fact, pissed off enough they could tell just by using their binoculars, she really must be okay.

She and the others listened as Ghost continued describing what he could see. "Walker and Hall are standing a few feet behind Price. They're both armed, and Hall keeps glaring at Walker. My guess is it has something to do with the fresh shiner Hall's sporting."

Gabe cursed below his breath. "Leave it to Walker to go to blows with the guy who's supposed to be on his side."

A few chuckles broke through, and it took Ellena a bit to adjust to hearing so many other voices in her ear at one time.

"There's a plane and two other men standing on either side of the hangar's opening. Both heavily armed."

"Price brought them along because he knew Ellena wouldn't be coming alone," Gabe pointed out. "Fucking Walker must have given him a heads up about us."

"Maybe, maybe not," Ghost commented through the coms. "Guy like Henry Radcliff isn't going to take any chances. Not with the White House at stake. That means his man, Price, needed to be prepared."

"Any sign of Governor Radcliff?" Gabe asked the other team leader.

Once again, Ghost's deep voice tickled Ellena's ear. "Negative."

"Radcliff is back in Washington meeting with some heavy lifters on his campaign contribution list," Ryker answered Gabe's question.

"Makes sense," Zade commented. "Guy like that would want to be as far away from this mess as possible."

Matt decided to add in his two cents, too. "Can't say I blame him. This plan goes sideways, it's bound to be a total shitstorm."

A plan that, as far as Price was concerned, included her handing herself over in place of Jenna so she could be questioned by Radcliff before they killed her. But what Price—and Gabe and his team—didn't know was that she was going to try to do a little more than that.

Ellena's nerves sparked and sputtered as she thought back to the conversation she'd had with Agent Ryker a few hours before.

The Homeland official had pulled her aside earlier when Gabe's team and Ghost's team were hashing out all the details after Adrian had left the barn. When she'd questioned him about why he wasn't filling the others in on this part of the plan, Ryker had told her Gabe would never agree to it.

She'd tried arguing against that assumption, but when Ryker told her this was the only way to make absolutely certain everyone involved paid for what happened to Mark Ellis, Ellena had agreed. And she'd stayed quiet.

For Mark and all the other innocent men and women Radcliff and his goons had hurt.

Please, God. Let this work.

Gabe was going to have her hide if she made it out of this thing alive.

Almost as if he could read her mind, Ellena felt his muscles tighten against hers once more. She squeezed his hand, this time trying to offer her *own* reassurance.

They pulled in, and Ellena saw the car Walker had driven away in parked directly behind the hangar. Both Nate and Zade parked their vehicles several feet back. Ellena assumed it was so they'd have a clear getaway when the time came.

Nate and Matt got out of the SUV, and while they talked outside, Gabe turned to her. A sliver of fear had made its way into his confident stare, and he brushed his knuckles softly against her cheek.

"You don't have to do this," he rumbled low. "We can still find another way. We can—"

Ellena stopped him with a kiss. When his mouth responded instantly, hungry and desperate against hers, she knew he was thinking the same thing she was.

This could quite possibly be the last moment they would have alone together. Although, technically they weren't alone since everyone—including Ghost and his men—could hear them. But it didn't matter.

The moment still belonged to them. It was their last chance to say goodbye before she risked everything to save her friend, and she was going to take full advantage for as long as she could.

Much too soon, a knock on the SUV's window brought that moment to a halt.

Gabe pulled back, taking her face into his hands.

"I love you, Ellena. You know that, right?"

She threw her arms around him. Squeezing her eyes shut, she held on as tight as she could. "Of course, I do. I love you so much, Gabriel. So, so much."

When she opened her eyes and looked through the window

behind him, Ellena saw the other men waiting impatiently outside. As much as she hated letting him go, she knew it needed to be done.

Letting her arms fall down the length of his shoulders, she pulled away. "Let's do this."

Gabe opened the door and stepped out. He held the door open for her, waiting while she slid across the smooth leather, slamming it shut a bit harder than necessary once she was out.

Ellena knew he was on edge. They all were. The situation sucked, and she was more than ready to get it over with.

Gabe put his hands on her shoulders. "We'll be here the whole time. Just like you heard, Ghost and his team are in place and already have Price's men in their sights. Ryker's around somewhere, too, and is watching Hall closely to make sure he doesn't try to hurt you or Jenna. Just listen to us and do as you're told, and you'll be fine." He pulled her in for a hug. "We've got your back, sweetheart. Don't worry."

Easy for you to say.

With Gabe's hand on the small of her back, they walked into the hangar. Despite having already been told about them, Ellena inhaled sharply at the sight of the men and their guns.

For a moment, she began questioning her sanity for agreeing to do this. But as they continued to walk toward the opening, she saw Jenna standing by Adrian.

Ghost was right, she was beyond pissed, but having known the woman for years, Ellena also recognized the stark fear hiding in her friend's eyes. It was in that moment she knew without a doubt this was exactly what needed to be done.

She looked up at Gabe, his eyes glaring toward Adrian and the other man. His jaw was clenched tight, and she feared, if given the chance, he'd kill either man without any regret.

"That's far enough," one of the men with the guns said. "You." He looked at Ellena. "Come with me."

"Like hell," Gabe growled.

"Boss said only the girl comes out."

Not wanting the situation to escalate from the get-go, Ellena turned to Gabe. "It's okay. We knew this would probably happen, right?" She leaned up and kissed his cheek, rubbing her thumb across the salt and pepper stubble she loved so much. "I'll be okay. I love you." Before giving him—or herself—a chance to change her mind, Ellena turned to the man, held her chin up, and said, "Let's go."

"After you." The terrifying man smirked. The second man stayed at his post, pointing his large, automatic rifle at Gabe and his team.

Ellena let go of Gabe's hand, her heart dropping into her stomach as she allowed herself to be taken away.

* * *

Gabe's gut was screaming like a banshee. Nothing good ever came from ignoring his instincts, but right now, he had no other choice but to stand back and watch.

Once Ellena was only a few feet from Price, her escort grabbed her arm. Through his earpiece, Gabe heard the bastard tell her, "That's close enough."

Gabe's fingers itched to go for his gun.

Doing as she was told, Ellena didn't move any closer to Price or Jenna. Price, the smug bastard, shooed his man away. The lacky obeyed, walking back toward the hangar. Once he was there, he regained his position at his side of the opening, opposite their other guard.

Gabe took the opportunity to signal to Nate. Using the fingers on his right hand, which was down at his side, he pointed to his own leg with his index finger. Then he pointed it and his middle finger at Price and Hall, indicating that if something bad went down, he would take out those two.

Once he was sure Nate understood, Gabe used the same gesture to show his teammate which man he was responsible for. Once they were squared away, Gabe used the same motions with his left hand to communicate with Matt, Kole, and Zade.

The movements were so slight, a civilian probably wouldn't pick up on it. They'd come in handy more times than he could remember as a SEAL, and Bravo Team was very familiar with them, as well.

He refocused on Ellena, who stood with her chin up and shoulders back. Damn, she was tough. Much tougher than he'd ever given her credit for.

A pang of regret tried worming its way in, but Gabe refused to let it. He'd owned up to his fuck-up, and the past was the past. He may have underestimated his wife's strength and tenacity to overcome the shit life had thrown at her before.

Not anymore.

She could do this. *They* could do this. Together they could damn well do anything.

Price gave Jenna a shove, and the other woman ran toward Ellena. The two nearly tumbled over as they wrapped their arms around each other and cried.

"I'm so sorry, Jenna." Ellena's thick voice came through the coms.

In pure, Jenna fashion, she simply said, "Shut up and hug me tighter."

The two women laugh-cried for a few seconds more before Price nodded to Ellena's escort. The dickhead growled out, "That's enough." Then, much like he'd done to Ellena, he wrapped his meaty hand around Jenna's upper arm and pulled her along with him.

"Wait!" Jenna tried fighting against his tight grip. "What about Elle?"

"Go with him. I'll be okay."

Gabe could tell from the sound of her voice she was fighting back more tears. Ellena didn't take her eyes off of Jenna, not until she was inside the hanger and tucked safely behind Gabe.

"Stay behind me," he ordered the shaken woman. "We'll get you out of here as soon as we can."

"W-what about Elle? Why is she still out there? I thought the plan was to—"

He grabbed her hand and squeezed. "Just trust me, okay? I'm not going to let anything happen to her."

She gave him a shaky nod, so he let her hand go and turned back to where Ellena and Price were still standing.

The plan was for her to act like she was going to follow him onto the plane so she could be interrogated by Radcliff about whatever he thought Mark Ellis had told her in their sessions.

Once Price turned his back, Gabe and his team would take the asshole out, along with the other men standing guard. Ghost and his team, along with Ryker, were there to provide backup and spot any surprises Price may have in store for them.

Come on, asshole. Get this shit going already.

Right on cue, Price looked at Ellena and smiled. "Well, now. Isn't that sweet? What a good friend you must be to offer yourself up like that for Miss Shaw."

"What do you want, Daniel?" Ellena asked smoothly.

"Straight to the point. I like that in a woman."

"Is it bad that part of me hopes this prick pulls something just so I can shoot his ass?"

Ghost's rhetorical question damn near made Gabe smile, but then he heard Price's voice again and all signs of humor vanished.

"There are so many things I want to discuss with you, Dr. Dawson. My associate, Mr. Walker, assured me you were brought up to speed on how this was going to work?"

"He did."

"Excellent. Shall we?"

Price held out his arm toward the plane, but Ellena didn't move. Instead, her calm voice filled Gabe's ears again.

"I need to know something first."

Something in her tone told Gabe she was talking more to him than Price.

Shit.

Price glanced down at Ellena with an innocent smile. "And what would that be?"

Gabe kept his voice low, his lips barely moving as he spoke to her through their earpieces. "Baby just walk toward the plane. We're right here with you. Walk toward the plane, and we'll take care of the rest."

"I want to hear you say it." Ellena's voice became flat.

"What is she doing?" Kole asked on a whisper.

A new sound hit Gabe's ear, then. A low, humming sound. One he and the others recognized immediately.

He and Nate shared a look, his gut screaming at him to get her the hell out of there. "We need to move," he said for everyone's benefit.

Confirming his thought, Truck's deep voice piped in next. "We've got an incoming bird. Chopper approaching from the south."

"I need to hear you say it, you murdering son of a bitch." Ellena continued pushing Price. "You killed Mark, didn't you?"

Unphased by the sound of the nearing helicopter, he answered her calmly. "Actually, no. I didn't." Price used his thumb to point to Hall. "He did."

"Holy shit." Matt's eyes shot to Gabe's. "She's getting him to spill his guts! Maybe we should go ahead and let her meet with Radcliff. Guy might confess all his deadly sins."

Gabe clenched his jaw to keep from ripping into his teammate. No way in hell did he want her anywhere near that son of a bitch.

She shouldn't be here, now.

Nate grinned. "God, I love that woman of yours."

"Hall takes care of all of my employer's problems," Price admitted openly. "And he and the others are going to do the same to you and your friends if you don't start walking. Now."

Gabe watched as his wife looked up toward the now-visible chopper. The humming grew into a more succinct thumping sound, and the closer it got, the more anxious he felt.

"Problems?" Ellena took a step toward Price. "Is that what you called him? A problem? Mark Ellis was a human being. A hero who fought for the same country your boss wants to be in charge of."

"Ellena, stop!" Both Gabe and Nate warned simultaneously, neither bothering to keep their voices down.

The two guards took a step in their direction, shifting their guns a little higher as a warning.

Price sneered back at her. "My boss is going to be the greatest president this country has ever seen."

"Who else has died because of your boss?" Ellena prodded. "Tell me their names, and I'll get on that plane with you right now."

She's trying to get him to confess to more.

"Your girl knows we're listening." Ghost agreed with his silent thoughts. "She wants us to hear him say it. That way, we can all be witnesses. Pretty damn smart."

"And fierce." Matt nodded.

They were both spot on with their assessments, but right now, Gabe didn't need her to be either. He just needed her back in his arms, safe and away from these bastards.

"Careful, Dr. Dawson." Price swayed his index finger back and forth. "You seem to forget who's actually in charge."

"Not you." She jutted her chin. "You follow orders, just like these guys do. Only difference is, you wear a fancy suit and designer shoes."

Goddamn it. "Ellena," Gabe said her name sharply. "Just walk toward the fucking plane."

"I don't understand." Jenna spoke up from behind him. "What's she doing?"

Trying to get herself killed, apparently.

Price's patience was gone. "You have no idea who I am or what I'm capable of." He got into Ellena's face. "And unless you want a front row seat to that particular show, I suggest you get your ass on that plane. Now."

"Fine." Ellena blew out a breath. "Let's go."

Gabe released the air he'd been holding in his lungs, his stomach churning with nauseating bile. Christ, that woman was going to be the death of him, yet.

"Get ready," he ordered the others quietly. To Ellena, he said, "Okay, baby. Just keep walking toward the plane. Don't look back at Price or at us. Just keep walking."

"Chopper's coming in hot." Ghost sounded alarmed, but then he said, "Too much of an unknown to engage."

Damn it, the Delta leader was right. Even though Gabe's

instincts were telling him otherwise, this airstrip was used by too many innocents to assume the people in the helicopter were involved in what was going on.

Dust lifted and swirled as a gust from the chopper's blades covered Ellena, Price, Walker, and Hall. Using their hands, they all turned their heads, protecting their eyes from the assault.

Gabe glanced at the two men with the guns who looked as confused as he felt. "This is wrong." Pulse racing, he looked over at Nate and then the others. "It's all wrong."

Just as Gabe went for the gun at his lower back, Price reached for Ellena in an attempt to pull her toward the plane.

A shot rang out, sending Gabe's heart into this throat. Price's blood showered one side of Ellena's face as a second bullet passed through the man's skull.

Her scream traveled through Gabe's ear and into his soul as she stood shell-shocked, watching Price's lifeless body fall onto the asphalt below.

"Ellena!"

Gabe and his men had their weapons drawn, but more shots rang out before they could take aim. Back-to-back, the two guards dropped where they stood as several bullets pinged against the sides of the metal building.

"Oh, my god!" Jenna cried out from behind him.

The sound of gunfire increased. Gabe grabbed Jenna by the wrist as he and his men took cover inside the hanger.

He assumed Ghost's team was responsible until they heard Ghost shout out, "We're taking fire! I repeat; we're taking fire!"

The panic Gabe felt for his wife nearly consumed him. He leaned out from the metal barrel he'd ducked behind, eyes scanning the chaos to find her.

There!

She was lying on the ground next to Price's body, her hands covering the back of her head. Somehow through the cloud of dust, their eyes met.

"Ellena, run to me!" Gabe yelled, praying she could hear him. "I'll cover you!"

He raised his gun toward the helicopter. At the same time, a man dressed head to toe in black combat gear pointed an ATAS —or Air-to-Air Stinger—shoulder missile launcher right at them.

Sonofa—

"Take cover!"

Gabe and his men dove to opposite sides of the hangar's opening. He hunched over Jenna's crouched body to give her some added protection as the ominous whistling sound flew past. A large explosion took out the back wall of the building, along with Walker's car.

"Ellena, stay down!" Gabe quickly recanted his earlier order.

Ghost's pissed-off voice came over the receiver again. "I can't get a visual on our shooter. Too many shots coming in!"

"Damn it! I'm hit!"

"Hollywood?" Truck shouted from his position on the roof. "How bad, man?"

"Just a scratch. I'll live."

Thank God.

Matt looked to Gabe. "Who the hell are these guys?"

Gabe shook his head. He had no idea, and he didn't have time to give a single fuck.

All he cared about was getting to Ellena and keeping her safe.

There was a lull in the gunfire, and the chopper turned as if it were finally retreating. Risking a glance, he looked back out to where he'd last seen Ellena, shocked to find Walker hovering over her—protecting her—the same way he had Jenna.

I'll be damned.

Making a mental note to thank him later, because he was damn well going to make sure there was a later, Gabe knew he needed to take advantage of the uncertain reprieve.

Standing, he walked over to where he knew she'd be able to see him motioned for her to come his way.

"Come on, Ellena. Run, this way, baby! Run to me!"

Hearing this, Walker pushed himself off of her and helped her to her feet.

"That's it, baby. Hurry!"

She'd just taken her first step toward him when another loud, whistling sound reached his ears. Gabe's gaze followed another ATAS, its smoke trail crossing in front of the hanger's opening just before a second explosion tore through the north section of the building's roof.

Ghost!

He and his team had been on that roof.

"Ghost, do you copy?" Gabe held a hand to his ear as he and his team all waited with bated breath. They were met with a deafening silence. "Ghost! Talk to me." Another silent stretch. "Truck? Fletch? Hollywood?"

He'd just started to assume the worst when Ghost and the others came through the new hole in the wall behind them.

Coughing, the Delta Force leader said, "We're here." More coughing. "Saw it coming just in time to haul ass over the edge and into the grass."

Truck and Fletch flanked a limping Hollywood. "Our boy took one to the leg. A graze," Fletch explained. "Other than that, we're good."

"Fucking miracle," Hollywood mumbled low. "Kass is gonna kick my ass."

"Nah." Fletch freed his arm from his teammate's shoulders. "Your sweet wife will probably kiss your pretty new boo-boo."

"Fuck off."

"Gabe, look!" Jenna caught his attention.

Turning, he followed her line of sight. Ellena and Walker were standing once again, and Ellena was starting to run to him.

"Shit. Are we clear?" He went to the hangar's large opening and looked up at the sky. "I hear them, but I can't see them."

He'd no more gotten the words out when another round of gunfire rained down on them. Shoving Jenna to the side, Gabe made sure she was safe before making his way to an area he could fire from.

Both teams took shots when they had them, all the while trying to keep from getting their asses hit in the process.

Gabe emptied his second mag and replaced it with the only

one he had left. He pulled the trigger several more times, trying —and failing—to hit a vital part of the moving chopper.

Fucking bastards!

He looked out to Ellena who was running with all her might to get back to him. She'd only made it a few steps when Hall came up behind her and reached around her waist.

He yanked her back against his body, using her as a human shield. Ellena kicked and hit, but the man held on tightly as he pulled her back towards the plane.

"No!"

Ellena screamed, and even through the blasts from all of the guns, Gabe felt it in the depths of his core.

He instinctively stood up and away from cover, determined to get to her—or die trying. Matt ran over to him, nearly knocking them both on their asses before pulling him back down.

"Get the fuck off of me!" Gabe yelled as he tried to push his teammate aside.

"You're no good to her if you get your damn head blown off!"

"I can't let them take her!" He fought to get loose. "If she gets on that plane, she's as good as dead!"

"Gabriel!"

He looked out just in time to see Hall hit her on the back of the head with the butt of his gun, knocking her out cold.

"Where the fuck is Walker?"

With a quick scan, Gabe realized some guy he'd never seen was forcing Walker onto the airplane by gunpoint.

Ah, God.

Not far behind, Hall was dragging Ellena's limp body up the airplane's steps. The shots from the helicopter increased, forcing Gabe and the others to take cover once more.

At the first sign of the slightest break, he tried for another shot, but he was too late. The door to the plane closed, and the helicopter took off as the plane began to move down the runway.

"Ellena!"

Almost immediately, the gunfire ceased, and the chopper

disappeared. Gabe pushed out of Matt's loosening hold and ran out onto the tarmac. To do what, exactly, he wasn't sure.

He couldn't risk shooting the plane. Not with Ellena on board. So he just stood there...helpless.

Watching as the plane took flight, going God knows where, with his entire life on board.

CHAPTER 19

Gabe's knees nearly gave out, his entire body feeling the impact of what he'd just lost. He looked down at Price's body, which was lying less than three feet away from where he now stood.

He pulled the trigger until his gun was empty.

Numb, he turned and walked woodenly back to the hangar.

"Oh, my god!" Jenna was crying. "They took her. They took Ellena!"

"Come on, Jenna." Zade tried to gently pull her away. "Let's get you out of here."

"No!" The stubborn woman yanked her arm free. "I'm sick to death of men who think they can order me around." Anger replaced anguish as she marched up to Gabe. "We have to get her back. You have to get her back!"

Gabe understood the emotions Ellena's friend was feeling. He was feeling them, too.

"I will," he promised her with everything he had. "If it's the last thing I do."

Ryker had rejoined them, too. He'd been watching from a car parked out of sight on the north side of the building. From the looks of things, the somewhat disheveled man had gotten in his fair share of the fighting.

"What the hell just happened?" Kole asked no one in particular.

"We'll get her back," Ryker spoke with confidence.

Opening his mouth, Gabe started to respond but clamped his jaw shut. He wasn't sure if he wanted to cry, yell, howl out at the universe or the men standing in front of him, now.

His emotions were all over the fucking place, and...*Jesus*. Is this what his men had felt when their women had been taken from them?

He ripped his earpiece out of his ear and looked back at the other men. Apparently, they were waiting for him to take the lead.

Glancing down, the blood on Hollywood's pants reminding him, "You need to tie that up to stop the bleeding."

"Yeah, I know." The good-looking Delta operator pointed at himself with a smirk. "Medic, remember?"

"Right. Sorry."

"S'okay."

While Hollywood removed his belt to use as a makeshift tourniquet, Gabe zeroed in on Ryker. "How the hell did this happen?"

"You can get her back, right?" A noticeably shaken Jenna was looking to Gabe for the answer.

One Gabe wished like hell he could give.

"Of course, we will," Zade assured her in Gabe's place.

He knew the guy was only trying to help, but he couldn't seem to keep his temper at bay.

"How?" Gabe turned to Zade. He didn't yell or scream. Instead, his voice came out flat. Almost emotionless. "We don't know who has her. Where they're taking her. What they're doing to her right..."

His voice cracked and his eyes burned. The other men stared, not knowing what to say. Because there wasn't anything to say.

He'd lost her. He'd finally gotten her back, and then he fucking lost her.

I know where to find her." Ryker finally broke the silence. "Well, I will soon."

"What?" Gabe frowned. Surely, he'd misheard the agent.

For the first time since he'd known the Homeland agent, Gabe saw uncertainty shining behind the man's dark eyes.

"You know more than you're telling us, don't you?" Nate accused.

Ryker slid Nate a quick glance but stayed quiet.

"Goddamnit, they have Ellena!" Gabe stormed towards him. "What aren't you telling us?"

Ryker swallowed hard, the look on his face doing zilch to comfort Gabe's churning gut.

"I got here before Ghost and the others arrived. As Price's plane was landing, I shot a tracking device onto its underbelly. Once it lands, we'll know its exact coordinates."

"Wait a minute." Jenna joined in on the conversation. "When I talked to Ellena on the phone earlier, she told me the plan was for her to come out, pretend to trade herself for me. She said she was just supposed to make it *look* like she was going with that Price guy, and then y'all were going to swoop in and take him down. Ellena said you wanted to detain Price so you could turn him against Governor Radcliff."

"Your point?"

"My point is, if you planned to take Price down before he left the ground, why bother shooting the plane with a tracker? I mean, look around." Jenna's intelligent green eyes swept across the sea of men surrounding her. "Until the helicopter showed up, you had Price grossly outnumbered."

"It's called being prepared, Miss Shaw."

"It's called bullshit, Ryker." Ghost chimed in. Looking pissed, he glanced over at Gabe then back to the other man. "We know where Price lives. Where he works. That plane came straight from D.C., and given Price's position and Radcliff's campaign schedule, there was no reason to assume Price was going anywhere else but back home to Washington. Not unless you know something we don't."

"Ghost is right." Gabe stepped closer to the agent. "We were planning to take him and Hall down before he even got back on that plane. Way I see it, the only reason you put a tracking device on a plane is if you have reason to believe it might become lost."

"Not to mention, Price's brains are currently splattered all over the damn tarmac," Matt pointed out. "Pretty obvious whoever was in that chopper wasn't working for him."

"No." Ghost continued with Matt's train of thought. "Whoever that was, they worked for someone above Price. Someone who wanted him taken out."

Jenna crossed her arms at her chest and snorted. "Along with the rest of us."

Except Elle and Walker.

Gabe took a few seconds to think before asking Ryker, "Who was on that plane, Jason?"

Ryker hesitated to answer.

Wrong move, buddy.

He took another step toward the other man. "Someone took out Price and his men, and it sure as hell wasn't any of us. So I'll ask again. Who was in the fucking plane?"

Ryker looked to the others before bringing his gaze back to Gabe's. "We have reason to believe Governor Radcliff flew in with Price."

All of the air left Gabe's lungs with a whoosh.

Amidst the multiple what-the-fucks the guys were tossing at Ryker, he stared back at their handler with a barely controlled temper. "Why the hell didn't you say something?"

"I wasn't a hundred percent sure. I'm still not."

"Bullshit!" Gabe's roaring voice echoed off the metal walls. "You had a strong enough suspicion to put a goddamn tracker on him, yet you didn't think to share that shit with us? What the fuck?"

Ryker stared at Gabe a second longer before skittering his gaze to the side. He closed his eyes and shook his head, cursing under his breath.

Running a hand over his jaw, he opened his eyes back up and looked at Gabe again. "Okay, look. Radcliff was in D.C. this morning. If you called his people right now, they'd tell you his schedule was booked solid well into the night."

"But?"

"But we've had a guy watching him. Radcliff boarded a plane less than an hour after Walker called Price to set up the trade."

Jenna held up a hand. "If your guy was watching the governor, they should've seen Price board with him. Right?"

"We believe Price was already on the plane when my guy got there."

There was a stretch of silence while everyone processed, but Gabe's nagging gut said Ryker was still holding back.

"What aren't you telling us?"

Making his first smart move all day, Ryker didn't bother to lie. "Five minutes after Radcliff showed up, a chopper landed with a group of mercenary-looking assholes. They talked with the governor, then Radcliff boarded the plane and the chopper took off."

"Jesus Christ." Ghost ran a hand over his jaw.

"Are you serious, right now?" Jenna stepped into the agent's personal space. "I may not understand what the hell is going on, but I can smell a set-up a mile away."

"This doesn't concern you, Miss Shaw," Ryker tried dismissing her.

Oh, shit.

"Doesn't concern me?" Looking like she was ready to explode, Jenna's pointed finger damn near touched the man's nose. "Listen, asshole. I was drugged and taken against my will. The one guy would've raped me if the other guy hadn't shown back up when he did, and that's my best friend on that plane. So don't you dare say this doesn't concern me, you stuffy, suit-wearing prick!"

Several of the men hid their curling mouths with their hands. A few even had to cough to cover up the laughter bubbling up inside their chests. But Gabe wasn't amused.

"She's right." Gabe's narrowed gaze held Ryker's. "This thing stinks to high Heaven, and we just about got our asses shot to hell and back. So for once, just tell us the fucking truth."

Finally, with a deep exhale, Ryker gave him a reluctant nod. "The last bit of intel we received told us Price was talking about resigning as Radcliff's chief of staff."

"Resigning?" Hollywood grimaced in pain. "His boss is about to become President of the United States. Why the hell would he resign, now?"

"Who knows?" Ryker shrugged. "Maybe the pressure of always trying to clean up Radcliff's shit was getting to him. All we've been able to piece together is Price supposedly told Radcliff he'd take care of this one last problem, and then he was out. According my people, Radcliff agreed to pay Price enough to keep living the lifestyle he was accustomed to in order to keep the guy from spilling his guts. Radcliff then decided at the last minute to come along to make sure Price kept his word." Ryker glanced out to where Price's body lay. "Pretty sure Radcliff had no intentions of letting him go."

The longer Gabe listened to the agent talk, the more his anger built. The bastard was standing there talking about this as if it were just a normal day at the office. As if Ellena hadn't just been abducted by one of the most powerful men in the world.

He wanted to hit something. Better yet, *someone*.

"You son of a bitch!"

Gabe's muscles tensed to the point of shaking as he stormed toward Ryker. His hands filled with the front of the guy's button-down shirt just before he slammed him up against the nearest wall. He brought himself nose-to-nose with the other man.

"You knew Radcliff would be here...that he'd hired fucking *mercenaries*... and you didn't tell me?"

"It was need to know, and--"

Gabe took a swing, punching Ryker square in the jaw. His other hand was the only thing keeping the bastard from completely falling to the floor.

"Need to know?" His words hissed through clenched teeth. "Are you fucking kidding me? *I* needed to know, Jason! My *team* needed to know! Ghost's team was damn near blown off the fucking planet, for Christ's sake! And now Radcliff has....you knew that she..." Gabe swallowed between frantic breaths, finding it hard to even say her name. "You knew that Ellena was going out there. You let her come here. Let them take her so she could, what? Get Radcliff to confess?" Gabe hit him again, this time letting him fall. "That's it, isn't it? You used her as fucking *bait* to try to trap him."

Ryker quickly stood to defend himself, wiping the blood from his split lip as he moved. "We didn't know for sure he'd be here, damn it!"

"But you thought he might be." Gabe fumed. "You *hoped* he would, because then you'd be able to make your big bust. You make sure we're in the dark about the fucking chopper so when it shows, we're caught off guard. We're too busy keeping our asses alive to keep that Hall fucker from getting Ellena on the plane."

Ryker stood silent.

Gabe threw up his arms in frustration. "Tell me I'm wrong."

"Fuck you, Dawson! Don't stand there acting all high and mighty. How many times did you do the same damned thing?"

"Why?" Gabe's voice boomed. "Why use Elle? You had Price dead to rights. You heard him confess to having Mark Ellis killed."

"And that's all we had on the guy! Daniel Price would've gone down for murdering Ellis. Maybe fleeing the scene of your wife's accident. That's it. Shit, Dawson. Start thinking like a fucking special ops soldier for two seconds, and you'll see we had no other choice."

"Bullshit." Gabe shot daggers at the other man. "You could've turned Price."

"Price wasn't going to give up Radcliff. Not when he knew how far the crooked bastard can reach."

"Guess someone should've told Radcliff that huh?" Jenna quipped.

Ignoring her, Ryker kept his eyes locked with Gabe's. "We needed to get Radcliff to talk, and Dr. Dawson is pro at getting people to open up. So yeah, I wired her before we came here. But come on, man. Surely you can see the bigger picture, here. Using a weaker link to get your man is like strategy one-oh-one."

His admission was like a punch to the gut. Ellena hadn't

mentioned anything about a wire or Ryker's plan. Why didn't she say anything?

Because she knew you'd never allow it.

Rage bubbled inside his veins as he continued throwing his anger toward the man responsible. "This isn't the Middle East, and it's not a goddamn war."

"The hell it's not!" Ryker's angry voice filled the space around them. "Are you really that naïve, or have you just been out so long that you've forgotten what it's like out there? This is every bit a war as the one you and your men fought in over there. And just like then, sometimes innocents get caught in the middle. It's the way things play out and you know it. We all make sacrifices. Sucks, but it's for the greater—"

Gabe went after him again, pushing him up against the same wall as before. "You're talking about sacrificing the woman I *love*, you bastard! She's my *wife*! Of course, a coldhearted bastard like you wouldn't understand what that's like, would you?"

Ryker flinched but stayed silent.

"Hell no, he wouldn't" Nate backed Gabe up.

"No." Gabe shook his head with a snide smirk. "You wouldn't. So don't you dare stand there and spout off that 'for the greater good' bullshit because there's no goddamn way busting Radcliff is worth more than Ellena's life."

"Or Walker's," Jenna added quietly. Her eyes rose to Gabe's. "I mean, I get that the jerk kidnapped me and all. But he also kept the other jerk from…" Tears welled in the woman's eyes as she let her voice trail.

Shit. Gabe had almost forgotten Walker was on that plane, too. Hearing Jenna recount how he'd protected her only added to his wavering opinion of the guy.

A sudden image of Walker covering Elle's body with his flashed through Gabe's mind.

He and his team had spent the past couple of years believing Walker was a traitor and a soulless murderer. But keeping Jenna safe, along with the selfless act he'd pulled on the runway with Elle, made Gabe think maybe they'd all been wrong.

About Walker…and possibly the man standing in front of him, now.

"What happens after Elle gets Radcliff to confess? You think he's just gonna let her walk away from that shit? Hell no, he's not. Radcliff will kill her the first chance he gets.

Ghost stepped up and put his hand on Gabe's shoulder, "I think he gets it. And we need to get busy tracking that plane. We don't want to stand around here wasting time when we don't know how long—"

The other man stopped himself short, but Gabe knew what he meant. They didn't know how long it would be until that plane landed. Once it did, they had no idea how much time Ellena had left.

With a pointed stare, he returned his focus to Ryker. "Do you have the equipment with you to trace the plane now?"

"It's in my car."

Gabe let go of the guy's shirt.

"I screwed up, Dawson," Ryker finally admitted. "I should've filled you in. Should've filled you all in. What's done is done, and I can't change that, but I *will* help you get your wife back."

Fury and betrayal boiled together, the combination bringing Gabe dangerously close to losing his shit.

"You're damn right you'll help us." He poked the Homeland agent in the chest. "And I swear to God, Jason…if Radcliff kills…" Gabe cleared his suddenly clogged throat. "He lays a hand on her, I will come after you with all I've got. And there's not a person on this goddamn planet who'll be able to stop me."

CHAPTER 20

Ellena woke to a pounding headache and a musty smell that reminded her of her grandparents' old cellar. Her mouth and throat were desert dry, and she felt like she had the mother of all hangovers, but when she tried opening her eyes, her lids refused to cooperate

Confused, it took her a moment to remember what happened. When she did, the fear she'd felt at the airstrip returned with a vengeance.

Gabe!

The last image imprinted in her brain was heartbreaking. She'd screamed for him. He'd tried to get to her. But then Matt had knocked him down to keep him from being shot.

She wanted to cry when the events leading up to that moment came back in spades. Though they were closed, Ellena's eyes stung as a painful knot formed at the base of her throat.

She had no idea if Gabe was okay or if anyone other than Hollywood had been hurt.

All she knew for sure was that Daniel Price was dead, and she'd been hit over the head. Now she was here. Except she didn't know where *here* was.

Ellena forced her eyes to open, only small slits at first. The light hurt too badly otherwise. After a few tries, she managed to focus on her surroundings. The second she did, her fear grew exponentially.

She was in a shack of some sort, her wrists and ankles bound to a chair with plastic ties. The small structure was made of wood, and her shoes dug into the dirt floor beneath her.

A man she'd never seen before was standing in front of her... and he was staring. Mid-thirties—maybe early forties—his dark, wavy hair was a bit too long. But it was his eyes that struck fear into her heart. Dark and emotionless, they reminded her of a cold, moonless night.

The man's automatic rifle rested loosely in his hands, but something told Ellena he'd have no trouble using it at a moment's notice.

Dressed in black, he reminded her of a special-ops soldier, except the vibe he put off was more cold-blooded killer than patriot. Staring back at her as if she were nothing, Ellena couldn't help but wonder if this was the man who would soon end her life.

"Who are you?" She shifted in the uncomfortable chair. "What do you want from me?"

Blatantly ignoring her, the man casually turned to look out the small window next to where he was standing. Anger over-took Ellena's fear, and she straightened her shoulders a little more.

"Where am I?" More silence. "Why did you kidnap me?" Again the man refused to acknowledge her. "Hey! I'm talking to you!"

Yelling at the man with the big gun probably wasn't the smartest move, but a person could only take so much. Ellena had reached—and surpassed—her breaking point.

"You're not answering me because you don't know, do you? You're just the muscle behind the man. Fine. Get Radcliff. He's the one you work for, right?"

Ellena wanted to scream at the jerk's frustrating silence. In fact, she opened her mouth to do just that when the door to her right creaked open and Radcliff, himself, walked in.

He looked taller on T.V. but still had that handsome face and square jaw. His silver hair was styled almost perfectly, and the smile he was giving her had probably melted the hearts of many.

This man walked into a room and people noticed. Over the last two years, he and his staff had convinced America he was a man of the people. Powerful yet understanding.

Any time Ellena had watched him speak, either during an interview or at one of his publicized rallies, she'd always thought of him as likeable. Approachable. Now she knew the truth.

Henry Radcliff is a monster.

"Hello, Dr. Dawson." Radcliff's smile grew a smidge. "May I call you Ellena?"

"You won't get away with this."

The infuriating man laughed. "But I already have."

"No. You haven't." Ellena pulled against the painful ties. "There are men who saw what you did. Important men who won't stop until they find me and destroy you."

God, I hope that's true.

"I'm counting on it. Well…not the destroying part." He chuckled again. "But I do hope your husband and his little group of toy soldiers join us soon. I have something very special planned for them. Oh, and I almost forgot." Reaching toward her ear, he pulled out the tiny com. "You won't be needing this."

Without another word, Radcliff turned and walked out the door. This time, Ellena did scream. She screamed and cursed and pulled against the plastic ties until they cut into her skin and made her bleed.

I have something very special planned for them.

It was another set-up. One Radcliff had created for Gabe and the others.

Tears fell down Ellena's cheeks when she realized the asshole had set another trap for the man she loved. And she was the bait that would lure him right in.

* * *

Gabe woke from an uncomfortable position in one of the chairs in the Kole's cabin, pissed for having dozed off for even a minute. Gabe knew he was running on fumes, but every time he closed his eyes, his tortured mind began to imagine the worst possible scenario of what Ellena might be going through.

His stomach was in a constant state of nausea, and he was terrified for his wife, but Gabe forced himself to focus on what needed to be done.

Several hours had passed since his world came crumbling down, but the rest of his team was still there, along with Jenna and Ryker. The Homeland agent had been on the phone since they'd left the demolished hanger, first smoothing things over with local authorities, and then running through his contacts and calling up favors owed him.

The guy knew he'd screwed up by not filling them in on his full agenda and had been trying to make up for it ever since by gathering as much intel as he could.

According to the blinking red dot on Ryker's laptop, the plane had landed somewhere near the southern tip of Mexico. Nate had immediately entered the GPS coordinates and began working up satellite imagery to give them the best, most accurate visuals to go by.

So far, they knew the plane was parked on a private air strip about an hour away from a one of Radcliff's many vacation residences. Ghost and the other Delta men took off almost immediately, preparing to gear up and fly there on one of Homeland's jets.

The plan was for Delta to get immediate boots on the ground and gain as much information as they could as quickly as they could. As much as he hated waiting back with the others, the SEAL part of Gabe understood they needed proof that Ellena and Walker were at the governor's ranch before implementing a strike and rescue mission.

To prepare, Ryker's people had somehow produced blueprints of Radcliff's property. Gabe and his team studied the layout of the modest, ranch-style house until they could each enter and maneuver their way through it with their eyes closed.

Gabe was surprised at the structure's simplicity and the fact that there was only one small, almost run-down shed next to it. No fancy outbuildings. No other structures of any kind.

The satellite images of the property gave them additional information needed to begin planning their approach. Ghost and his guys were already on their way to the property to do recon from the ground.

Matt came into the living room with two steaming cups and handed one to Gabe. "Here. Figured you could use this."

"Thanks." Gabe took the cup. To Ryker he asked, "Have you heard from Ghost? Have they seen Elle yet?"

"They're still ten minutes out. They'll need to get into position, his team will observe, and then they'll report in. Right now, all we can do is wait."

"This is bullshit." Gabe set his mug down and rose to his feet. "We know where they are. Why the fuck are we waiting?"

Apparently, the terrified husband in him had overridden the logical SEAL.

Zade's expression softened to a level of sympathy Gabe couldn't stand to look at. "We want to get her back just as badly as you do, man."

"No offense, King." Gabe shook his head. "But you don't."

"Fair enough." Zade stared back at him. "But you know as well as I do, an extraction like this takes time."

"We don't have time, Zade!" Gabe pointed to the satellite images of Radcliff's house that had been printed and laid out on one of the tables. "She's there right now, going through God knows what, while we're sitting here with our thumbs up our asses!"

"We don't even know she's there yet," the former Marine argued. "All we know is that plane landed *near* there. They could have stopped somewhere on the way to the ranch or landed there just to throw us off and then started back in the opposite direction."

"Zade's right, Gabe," Matt chimed in. "You can't go storming into Radcliff's place half-cocked, or you'll end up getting yourself killed. Which, by the way, won't do your girl a damn bit of good."

"They're both right." Kole stood as he defended the other two men. "You know as well as we do this kind of mission usually takes days to plan. We've only been at this a few hours."

"We know it's hard, man." Nate decided to join in on the gang-up-on-Gabe party. "But you've got to trust that every man in this room is doing whatever we can to get Ellena back."

"And Walker."

All heads turned to see Jenna standing in the kitchen doorway.

"And Walker." Zade assured her.

Gabe shifted his gaze back to Zade who had a look that was damn close to acceptance across his face.

They'd all witnessed the way Walker had risked himself to protect Ellena, and though Gabe wasn't quite ready to sing Kumbaya with the fucker, he was a step closer to admitting the guy may not be as bad as they'd been led to believe.

A teeny, tiny, baby kitten-sized step.

"Come on." Nate nudged Gabe toward the bedroom. "You're not going to be any good to Ellena, Walker, or any of us if you go into this thing running on empty. Take a shower, take a nap, and I'll come get you once we know more."

Gabe planted his feet and turned to face his friend. "I can't fucking sleep." His gaze skittered around the room and back to Nate's. "Every time I close my eyes, I see her. I wonder what she's going through..." His voice hitched, and he had to swallow twice to clear the lump in his throat.

"I know the waiting is pure hell. I understand the thoughts running through your head and the images you see when you close your eyes." Nate glanced at the other men in the room. "We all do. But we also know until we get that intel from Ghost's team, there's nothing more any of us can do."

"I know." Gabe rubbed a hand against the pain in his chest, fucking hating that Nate was right. "This whole thing just...sucks."

"Yeah, it does." Nate nodded. He didn't offer platitudes or empty promises, because he knew first-hand how pointless those were at a time like this.

Gabe took a deep breath and blew it out. "Come and get me if anything comes in. I don't care how insignificant it may seem."

"You got it, brother."

Gabe turned and made his way into the bathroom. For the next several minutes, he stood in the privacy of the steaming shower. Letting his head hang, tears for the woman he loved mixed with the rushing water, and he began praying harder than ever before.

When he was finished with his crying jag, he quickly dried himself off and climbed into bed. Forcing himself to ignore all the pieces of Ellena that were in the room.

Her brush and jewelry on the small dresser. Tennis shoes neatly placed by the wall. A baby blue robe hanging on the edge of the closet door.

Turning onto his side, Gabe faced the spot on the bed where he'd watched her sleep just that morning. When he stretched his arm out, his hand felt something smooth beneath her pillow.

He pulled it out, realizing it was the tank top she'd worn to bed the night before. He gathered the soft material in his hand, staring at it for what seemed like forever. Then he brought it to his face and inhaled.

Eyes closed, Gabe breathed in the sweet combination of vanilla, lavender, and...Ellena. He blinked away more tears, refusing to believe this was how their story would end.

I'm coming for you, baby. Please don't give up on me. I'm coming.

CHAPTER 21

Ellena's hangover was back. Like the other times before, she'd passed out in the shed and woken back up here, in the small, concrete room.

As she brought it into focus, the metal door opened. Her heart fell into the pit of her empty stomach. The dark-haired man had come for her again.

Was this it? Was he going to use the instruments on her now?

Despite her efforts against it, her body shook as he forced her to walk outside and to the other building again. Dizzy and weak, she could tell the drugs were starting to linger a bit longer in her system.

The man shoved her through the narrow doorway.

Please God, no.

Like all the times before, he forced her back into the chair, zip-tying her wrists and ankles so she'd be forced to sit there and stare at the tray. It looked like a tray one would find in an operating room—the shiny silver blades and instruments evenly spaced in a straight line across it.

Three times yesterday, she'd been brought here. Each time, she'd thought they were going to torture her with those instruments. Instead, she'd just been left alone, imagining the horrific things they might do to her.

When the big man would come back, he'd simply stick her

with the needle, the drugs rendering her unconscious once again. And each time, she would awaken in the small, concrete room.

It was a vicious, horrible cycle. One she prayed would end soon.

"Why do you keep doing this?" Her dry, rough voice rasped. "If you're going to kill me, just do it. Get it over with." As usual, the man didn't speak as he turned and walked away. "You bastard!" she screamed, her throat sore and dry.

He shut the door behind him.

Ellena pulled at the plastic strips encircling her wrists and ankles. But her efforts were in vain. Staring down at her raw, bloody wrists, she wept at the unfairness of it all.

Sometime later—she had no idea how much time had passed —the door opened. This time, when she looked up, she didn't see the dark-haired man. She saw Henry Radcliff.

Her breathing picked up, and her pulse raced as he approached her.

Stopping in front of her, he leaned down so they were eye-to-eye. "It's time."

Ellena drew in a deep breath, a futile attempt to calm herself as she waited for him to reach for the instruments. But he didn't turn away. Instead, his smile was pure evil as he reached for her neck and squeezed.

His grip was so tight, she immediately saw stars. Her head throbbed, her eyes watering as she struggled for a breath she knew wouldn't come. Oddly, several questions came to mind as she was being strangled...

Why go through the trouble of kidnapping me just to kill me?

Why make me come to this room and then drug me over and over?

Why kill me now when you said you were going to make Gabe watch?

Ellena's oxygen-starved mind pictured his handsome face. More tears spilled from her eyes as she thought about the precious time they'd been given and what a gift it had been.

The last thing she saw before everything went black was the way Radcliff looked into her eyes with utter enjoyment, and the sick feeling she got from knowing he enjoyed squeezing the life out of her.

Then he let go.

Ellena's wide eyes shot open. She gasped, coughing and sucking in as much air as her depleted lungs would take. Radcliff was still standing in front of her, smirking.

"Why are...you doing...this?" She spoke between coughing fits. "What do you...want?"

"I wanted to know what Ellis shared with you."

"I already told you." Ellena coughed again. "He didn't tell me anything."

"I know." Radcliff leaned down to her again, his fingertips brushing some wayward curls from her face. "I believe you."

Confused she asked, "Then why go through all of this?"

He stood tall, speaking with an eerie calm. "Because I can."

Oh, God. Radcliff wasn't just a crooked politician trying to cover his ass. He was *enjoying* this.

As her oxygen levels returned to normal, Ellena's professional training began to kick in. She studied the man with a psychologist's eye. Catalogued his behavior, demeanor, and speech. It didn't take long for her to realize she was staring back at a clinically diagnosable sociopath.

"Figure me out yet, Dr. Dawson?" He stepped back a few inches.

"Not that hard, really. You're a narcissistic sociopath with homicidal tendencies. You live for attention. Have an innate need to be admired and loved, even though you're incapable of expressing those same thoughts and emotions toward anyone else. You're like the perfect politician, really." Ellena snorted. "I can see why your party chose you to run. Of course, I'm sure they aren't aware of your hidden...passion, shall we say?"

"Passion?" he asked, appearing genuinely intrigued.

Of course, he is...you're talking about him. Keep it up, maybe it'll buy you some time.

"Yes, Governor. Passion. You enjoy doing things like this." Ellena glanced down at her bloody restraints. "I suspect it's always been there, hiding just beneath the surface. Tell me. Were you really drunk when you dropped that bomb on those poor people, or did you just use that as a cover?

She expected him to lash out at her, but instead his lips spread into a smile that revealed his picture-perfect teeth. Radcliff clapped his hands together at a slow, even pace as he looked down at her as if he actually *did* admire her.

"I'm impressed. Your diagnosis is almost word-for-word the same report the doctors told my parents when I was twelve. You must be very good at your job."

"I am. I'm also smart enough to know you can kill me, Gabe, and all the men on his team, and yet you still won't get away with what you've done."

"And why is that, Dr.?"

"Too many people know the truth. You're finished, Radcliff. Not only will you never be president, you'll most likely spend the rest of your miserable life in a maximum-security prison. My guess is, they'll put you in isolation due to your popular status. Can't imagine that will bode well with a man like you. Spending day after day with no one else around to feed your endless ego."

His smile faltered. "You don't know what you're talking about."

"Don't I?" Ellena continued pushing. "You killed your entire unit, then used the war to cover it up. You had Mark Ellis killed because he discovered the truth, and then you kidnapped my friend in order to force me into surrendering myself."

"The Shaw woman won't talk. As soon as I'm done with you, my men and I are heading back to Texas to make sure of it."

She schooled her expression. Gabe and the others would never let anything happen to Jenna.

Please let her stay safe.

"And what about my husband and his team? And the other team that was there. You planning to take them all out, too?"

"I told you. I'm waiting for them to get here, and then that little matter will be dealt with, as well."

"You know what? I was wrong. I should've added delusional to my list of diagnoses."

Moving lightning fast, Radcliff backhanded her, snapping her head to the side. A throbbing fire erupted along her cheek and jaw, and she tasted fresh blood.

"You'll watch your tongue when speaking to me! I will become President. And these....stories you think your friends will spread before their deaths...those will just be added to the endless list of rumors surrounding every president who's ever come before me."

Grabbing her throat, he squeezed like before. Once again, Ellena was pushed into the dark abyss.

* * *

Gabe and the rest of Bravo listened closely as Ryker spoke to Ghost on his encrypted phone. He never really slept, but the shower and time spent resting had recharged him more than he'd thought possible.

Ryker asked questions, scribbling information onto a note pad as Ghost relayed it. When he finally hung up, he looked directly at Gabe.

"They've seen Elle. No sign of Walker, yet."

Gabe's knees went weak, and he had to sit down. "Is she okay?" he asked anxiously.

"Ghost saw Radcliff, Ellena, and another man exit the vehicle and enter the house. About an hour later, the man escorted Ellena to the shed."

Gabe's stomach filled with lead. "And?"

Ryker hesitated. "The next time they saw her, the same man who'd taken her into the building was carrying her back to the house." His swallow was audible. "Ghost said she was limp and appeared to be unconscious. He said..." Out of character, Ryker hesitated again, almost as if he was afraid to say the last part.

"What?" Gabe looked back at the other man. "He said what, Jason?"

Ryker's forehead creased as he spoke. "He said that the pattern had repeated itself a few times today."

Gabe's hands fisted by his sides. Closing his eyes for a moment, he asked, "How many times?"

"Three so far."

So the bastard was taking her into that building, and each time she had come out unconscious. His imagination went wild, sending his fear racing into overdrive.

Grabbing the kitchen chair next to him, Gabe belted an echoing roar as he threw it at the cabin's front door. Pieces of wood splintered in every direction, the other men nearby ducking and hauling ass to get out of the line of fire.

In an attempt to calm him, Ryker squeezed Gabe's shoulder and said, "The good news is she's alive."

"But for how long?" Gabe raged, throwing the guy's hand off. "And whatever they're doing to her, it's making her fucking unconscious."

Unconscious.

Vulnerable.

Unable to defend herself.

"Fuck!"

He turned away. He raked his hands through his hair, tempted to pull every last strand out. Never before had he felt this helpless. Not even when Vic had held that gun to her head years before.

At least then, he could see her. Could talk to her and tell her everything would be okay. But they weren't okay. Not even fucking close.

Thanks to his time with both the Navy and R.I.S.C., Gabe knew better than most that some things—especially those done to women—were worse than death.

"Ah, God." He locked his fingers behind his head. "I can't lose her. Not now."

"You won't so long as you pull your head out of your ass and act like the goddamn operative we all know you to be."

His eyes flew back to Ryker's. "She wouldn't even be there if it wasn't for you."

"And we can play that particular blame game later. But right now, your wife and my asset are waiting for us to go in there and save their asses."

"He's right, Gabe." Jenna approached him with caution, tears glittering in her emerald eyes. "Elle needs you. Now, more than ever. Please."

Get yourself together, man. She needs you. They both do.

Letting his arms drop back to his sides, Gabe turned to Ryker. With his chest still heaving, he asked, "We have visual confirmation, so when do we leave?"

"Ghost's team is going to stay put. I got off the phone with Jake a few minutes ago. The R.I.S.C. jet is fueled and ready to go. I'll line up a couple of choppers to meet us near the border, and we can fly into Mexico from there." He pointed to one of the satellite images on the table. "That's where Ghost and the others landed theirs. We'll go through these trees through there and position ourselves here. It'll take us about an hour to get through these trees, less if we walk fast."

"When do we leave?" Gabe asked again anxiously.

After mentally running through the list of things that needed to be done before they could leave, Ryker said, "We should be ready to take off by this time tomorrow. Once there, we'll wait until dusk to go in. That time of day, their guard will be down some, plus the night sky will help conceal us. As soon as you and your men can get your shit together and drive to your boss's ranch."

CHAPTER 22

Bravo and Delta Teams watched and waited as Henry Radcliff left the small shed. Shortly after, the same man Ghost had seen earlier went inside, only to return minutes later carrying Ellena who lay limp in his arms.

Gabe's blood boiled with an unprecedented rage. One that was eating him from the inside out. But unlike back at the cabin, he forced himself to hold it at bay.

Every cell in his body screamed to run full-bore and take every one of the bastards out. Instead, he allowed his training to override his emotions and kept a steady head.

He had to, for Ellena's sake. And for Walker's.

If the guy's even still alive.

Once the man had Ellena back inside the house and out of the line of fire, Gabe gave the teams one final rundown, ensuring every man there knew exactly what they were expected to do. A few minutes later, they initiated their plan.

With their guns up and ready, Zade and Kole took out the two men standing guard at either corner of the house while Gabe took out the one guarding the front door.

Ghost's men were already in place around the perimeter with clear vantage points of the west side and back of the house. Surprising them all, Ryker had also suited up, and made the trip with them, and was just inside the tree line on the east side of the house.

From what Gabe could hear through his com, Delta had already taken out the two guards by the back door, and Ryker had eliminated a guy running out the east door, as well.

"I'm going in." Gabe growled as he started across the front lawn.

By now, the body count had most-likely alerted Radcliff, as was expected. Gabe was ready to face the bastard and make him pay for what he'd done.

They all were.

Matt, Nate, Kole, and Zade all moved as one, quickly forming a strategic stance in order to cover Gabe. Ghost's team remained in place, ready to take down anyone who came out the back door.

It was easy.

Too easy?

As if reading his mind, Zade said, "Something's off. This is too easy."

"You think it's a set-up?" Matt looked at the younger sniper.

"Say again?" Ryker said between gunfire.

"Something's off," Zade repeated a bit louder. "There aren't enough guards. No one's even firing at us. It's too fucking easy."

Gabe continued toward the covered porch and motioned for his guys to go low. "I'm going in."

"Pull back, man." Nate stopped walking. "Zade's right. It's a trap."

Gabe swung his head around. "We don't know that."

"Think about it." The man's analytical brain kicked in. "Why else would they allow your girl to have been seen so easily? Radcliff's been baiting us this whole time. Shit, we took out how many of his men and no one's come out to try and stop us?"

"I think he's right, Dawson," Ghost chimed in. "I think Radcliff is using us to get rid of his own fucking guys."

"No witnesses." Nate raised a brow.

"You're right." Gabe nodded. "You guys shouldn't get hurt because of me. Fall back and cover me."

"Wait. You're still going in?" Zade stepped toward him.

He stared back at his team…his brothers…and nodded. "I'm not leaving without her."

Gabe had no more stopped talking when a shot rang out, off to his right.

"Shit!" Ryker yelled through his com. "I'm hit."

Fuck. "Matt, go check it out."

"No!" Ryker ordered. "It's just a scratch. Keep your positions. I'm good."

Refusing to waste any more time, Gabe gave his team a final nod and headed for the house. He made it five more feet before the house exploded into a giant ball of smoke and flames.

The blast blew Gabe and his teammates off their feet. All five men landed in the grass several yards back. Ignoring the sudden throbbing in his head, Gabe immediately stood up and started running for the house.

"Ellena!"

God, no. No, no, no!

Matt caught up to him and tackled him to the ground. "It's too late, man. We need to pull back."

Blood ran into his eye, but Gabe didn't care. He pushed at his teammate, determined to get to Ellena. "Get the fuck off of me. That's my wife in there!"

"I know, but…" Matt's face filled with sorrow as he kept his hold strong. "There's nothing we can do now. Man, I'm sorry, but she's…gone."

Gabe's entire world stopped spinning. His heart stopped beating.

At first, he couldn't even breathe, but then a deep, gut-wrenching roar began building its way out of his lungs.

He'd just opened his mouth to release it when Ryker called out, "I don't think she is."

Gabe and the others turned to see the Homeland agent making his way to them from the east side of the ranch. Keeping his injured arm steady against his side, he looked angry. And determined.

"The whole damn place just blew to fucking bits, Ryker," Matt snapped. "No one could've survived that."

Ellena's face appeared in Gabe's mind. She was smiling. Laughing. Her blonde hair swaying in the wind.

Ah, Jesus. How am I supposed to go on without her?

Ryker walked past them, toward the trees from which they came. "Let's get back to cover and then we can talk." To the other team, he ordered, "Ghost, meet us over here. Keep your men in position, just in case."

Broken, Gabe shook his head woodenly. Unable to look away from the burning mass he ignored the tears rolling down his face as he told Ryker, "I'm not leaving her."

He started for what used to be Radcliff's house when a low curse hit his ears. "Goddamn it, Dawson." Ryker grabbed his arm to stop him. "Do you want to get your girl back or not?"

Gabe stopped, but he didn't look at the other man. "You heard them." Grief left his voice flat. "She's—"

"Alive would be my guess. But if she is, she won't be much longer."

A brief moment passed before Ryker's words finally sank in. Gabe frowned even as hope bloomed inside his aching chest. "What the fuck are you talking about?"

"Trees. Then we talk."

They immediately turned and followed the man as Ghost jogged over to join them from his previous post. The second Gabe's foot hit the tree line, he growled a low, "Talk."

Ryker stepped through the wiry brush, stopping a few feet in. Facing the small group, his eyes landed on Zade's."

"You were right. Radcliff set this whole thing up."

"No shit," Gabe groused. "If this is why you brought us in here..." He started to leave, but Ryker's next words stopped him in his tracks.

"There's a tunnel."

Gabe slowly turned back around. "What?"

Rather than answer the question, Ryker slid his gaze to Ghost. "You or your guys see Radcliff or anyone else flee the house?"

"No." Ghost shook his head. "We took out the two guards out back upon initiating the mission, but no one came out after that."

With a hand to his ear, Ryker then spoke through the coms to Ghost's men. "Delta, you copy?"

"We copy," Truck's deep voice came through.

"Any signs of movement on your end?"

"Negative. Nothing but flames as far as we can see."

"Keep your eyes peeled." Ryker began speaking to Gabe again. "That's what I thought."

"What?" Gabe demanded to know. "What did you think? Because *I* think Radcliff just torched himself along with..." He stopped, clearing the emotion from his throat before he continued. "Along with anyone else who was in that house."

"Think about it, Dawson. A guy like Radcliff isn't going to go through the trouble of killing off witnesses and setting up elaborate trades just so he can off himself a few hours later."

"Unless he knew there was no way out," Zade disagreed.

Ryker looked back at the group. "I think there *is* another way."

The same hope Gabe had started to feel before returned. "You mentioned a tunnel."

Nate sighed. "We all saw the blueprints, Ryker. There were no indications of any underground structures on this property."

Ryker gave the guy an incredulous stare. "You buy land and build an underground escape route, you really gonna turn that shit in to be approved?"

"The man makes a good point," Ghost agreed.

As far-fetched as the idea sounded, Gabe would believe in the fucking Easter Bunny if it meant there was a chance Ellena was still alive. "Let's say Radcliff does have an escape route somewhere. How the hell are we going to find it?"

"Not through there." Kole motioned toward the burning house. "It'll take at least a day for those flames to die down and that shit to cool off enough for us to touch anything."

"She doesn't have a day." Gabe shook his head, the need to search for his wife a living, breathing thing. "If Ellena and

Walker are somewhere underneath us, we need to find them now."

"Agreed. Which is why a chopper carrying an R2TD is headed this way." Ryker glanced down at his watch. "Should be dropping it within the next thirty minutes."

"Hold up." Nate spoke again. "You're telling me in the time it took that house to explode and for you to walk your ass back over to us, you've procured a bird and a sophisticated, ground-penetrating radar to be hand-delivered to us…a half hour from now."

The tech genius was clearly impressed with the agent's pull, and Gabe couldn't blame him. An R2TD—Rapid Reaction Tunnel Detection—was a tool created by the U.S. Army Engineer Research and Development Center. Using ground-penetrating radar, the system can pick up sounds and movement deep beneath the earth's surface.

"I have a contact who works near the border. A couple of their men will deliver the device and my contact will be on standby waiting to relay the data in real time."

Zade's brows rose high. "Just like that?"

Ryker shrugged. "They owe me a favor."

"Who doesn't?" Matt snorted.

Ready to crawl out of his skin, Gabe asked, "Where are they dropping it? We should go now so we're ready."

A thirty-minute wait may seem like a drop in the bucket to the others, but for him, it already felt like a lifetime.

"There's a small clearing two clicks south of here."

"Let's go." Gabe didn't wait for the others to start walking. To Ghost's team, he said, "Truck, you and the others watch that place like a fucking hawk until we get back."

Gabe knew full-well this could be a goddamn goose chase. The operative in him also understood the chances of Ellena and Walker still being alive were slim at best.

But he'd lived the past three years believing he'd lost any chance of being with Ellena again. By some miracle he'd never understand, he'd gotten her back.

Slim chance or not, Gabe would dig to the Earth's fucking core if that's what it took to hold her in his arms again.

CHAPTER 23

"Psst. Doc. Can you hear me?"

Ellena fought against her body's efforts to regain consciousness, again. If she stayed lost in the sea of black, she wouldn't have to face Radcliff or his goon again.

"Come on, Doc. I need you to wake up."

Doc? Ellena's sluggish mind processed the voice. Her heart beat a little harder when she realized it wasn't Radcliff. It was...

"Adrian?" The name came out a mumbled slur.

"Yeah, it's me. Can you open your eyes?"

It took a monumental effort to do so, but Ellena finally managed to peel her lids apart. She blinked several times to help rid her sight of the blurred image before her. When she did, Ellena found herself gasping in horror.

"Oh, my god." She stared back at Adrian's bruised and bloodied face. He was sitting directly across from her, his wrists and ankles tied to the chair. "What did they do to you?"

Through swollen eyes, he curved the corner of his split lip. "I'll admit it's not my best look."

"Adrian..."

"Don't worry, Doc. It looks worse than it is."

She didn't know how that was even possible. "I didn't know..." She cleared her dry, scratchy throat. "I didn't even know you were here. Why did they take you, too?"

"Funny story, actually. Turns out Hall can take a punch better than I thought." Adrian huffed a breath then winced. "Asshole pretended to be knocked out back when I was letting Jenna in on our little plan."

"He told Radcliff," Ellena surmised.

Adrian nodded. "Rat bastard ran his mouth the first chance he got."

"Was he the one who did that to you?"

"Yeah. Don't worry, though." He winked as best he could. "I'll take care of him."

"How?" Ellena looked around the same concrete room Radcliff had been bringing her back to. "We have no way out."

"There's always a way out, Doc. We just have to wait for the right opportunity. But when it strikes, I need you to be ready."

"We're tied to our chairs, Adrian." Ellena glanced down at her raw wrists. "What kind of opportunity are you expecting?"

The words had no more left her mouth when they heard an almost muffled booming sound coming from somewhere up above them. Despite their solid makeup, the walls and floors shook from the blast.

Ellena got a very bad feeling inside. "W-what was that?"

"Hard to tell from down here, but I'm pretty sure Radcliff's house just exploded."

"What?" She glanced around their makeshift prison cell. "So we're stuck down here?"

The door to the room opened and Radcliff walked in. This time, Chris Hall was with him.

"Good." Radcliff smiled. "You are awake. I was hoping you wouldn't miss the excitement."

"Nah, we heard it," Adrian told the twisted bastard. "Sounded kind of like fireworks. Mighty sweet of you to put on a show in our honor."

"Oh, it was most definitely in your honor. Well…more for the kind doctor, here." With a nod, Radcliff motioned to Hall who in turn handed him a small tablet. "And since you couldn't see the show in person, I thought I'd bring the show to you."

He walked toward her, and Ellena looked over at Adrian. The

sick feeling in her gut grew. If Radcliff was happy about whatever he was going to show them, it must be bad.

"Have a look, Dr. Dawson." Standing beside her, Radcliff held the small screen up for her to see.

The image appeared to be from a home security camera mounted by the cabin's front door. From its vantage point, Ellena could see the front porch steps and the central section of the manicured front lawn. At the edge of the camera's view was a line of thick trees.

"Why are you showing me this?"

"Patience, my dear."

Not wanting to play into his hands, she started to look away when Radcliff fisted the hair on the back of her head. Ellena cried out as a sharp, burning sensation penetrated her scalp.

"Eyes on the screen, Ellena."

"Don't fucking touch her!" Adrian growled.

Ellena cried out again, but this time, it was because Hall had just punched Adrian in the jaw. He grimaced, holding his breath through the pain before spitting a stream of blood at Hall's feet. Hall struck him again.

"Stop!" she yelled out. "I'll watch it! Just please…stop."

Radcliff must have given the man a silent order, because Hall stepped away from Adrian. He stood between him and the door while Radcliff restarted the security footage.

With his hand still holding her hair in its painful grasp, the crazed man said, "Watch closely."

As much as she hated to, Ellena slid her gaze from Adrian's to the screen. This time, after a few more seconds of what appeared to be nothing, she saw them. She saw *him*.

"Gabe! He's here." She looked up at Adrian and back to the screen. "They're here!" The sight of her husband and his team charging in with their weapons left her dizzy with relief. They'd come for her. For both of them.

"Ah, shit. Look away, Doc," Adrian ordered suddenly.

"No, they're really here, Adrian. They're right outside."

"Look the fuck away, Ellena. You don't want to see that shit."

But she kept her eyes glued to the screen. There was no way

she could tear them away from her incredible, brave husband and his friends. He was her own, personal hero.

They were going to come inside and take Radcliff and his men out. And then they were going to go home. Together.

As she continued watching, she saw them stop midway. Gabe and Zade appeared to be arguing about something. With no sound, Ellena couldn't be sure, but it almost looked like Zade was trying to keep Gabe from going to the house.

Why would he do that?

"Goddamnit, Doc." Adrian continued his plight for her to stop watching. Something else that didn't make any sense.

Ellena saw Gabe shrug Zade's hand away and started walking toward the house again. She let out a breath she hadn't realized she was holding when she saw the other men fall in line behind him.

"They're almost here." She smiled. "He's going to kill you, Henry. I hope you know that."

"Please, Ellena. Stop fucking watching—"

Ellena jolted in her chair as a sudden ball of flames and dust filled the screen. Stunned, she saw Gabe and the others get thrown up into the air just before the screen went black.

"No!" Her heart lurched inside her chest. Tears filled her eyes, spilling over in steady streams down her cheeks. Still, she didn't look away.

"You sick fucking bastard!" Adrian yelled at Radcliff.

Radcliff released her hair but kept the tablet where she could see it. Ellena couldn't yell. She couldn't say anything.

She just kept staring at the blank screen, replaying the image of her strong husband and his friends being tossed into the air like a bunch of rag dolls.

When she was finally able to speak again, her first words were for the man she wished had died instead.

"You bastard." His smug face filled her blurred vision. "You k-killed them."

"To be fair, they came here to kill me. I just beat them to the punch."

"I'll kill you," Adrian vowed with a deadly tone. "You and this pussy-assed bitch."

Ellena frowned. Shock, combined with the remnants of whatever drug they'd given her, slowed her ability to process.

"Why?" She spoke through her tears. "Your future is ruined. Why didn't you just leave the country? Why keep us alive all this time? Why bring Adrian here?

"You already know the answer to that, Ellena." A sick, evil smile spread across Radcliff's face. "Think back to your diagnosis. The answer to your question is right there, inside your own, brilliant mind."

You're a narcissistic sociopath with homicidal tendencies.

"You like toying with us." She looked up at him again. "Our pain brings you pleasure."

"I am enjoying this. Very much, as a matter of fact. You're also correct in your assessment that my life in America is over. It was a good run, and while being deemed the most powerful man in the world does have a certain appeal to it, I've decided to take my ventures elsewhere."

"I've decided to take my ventures elsewhere," Adrian imitated the arrogant man then laughed. "Give me a fucking break. You know your ass is grass, so you're tucking your tiny little dick between your legs and running like the little bitch that you are."

"You know, it's sad, really." Radcliff turned to Adrian. "We, too, have had a good run. Unfortunately for you and Dr. Dawson, this little soirée of ours has started to bore me."

"That's what I thought."

"However, I do think Mr. Hall is still owed something I promised him on the plane ride here."

Stepping out of the way, Radcliff stood next to the far wall as the other man approached her with a sickening grin.

"You've been a royal pain in my ass." Hall raised his foot, kicking Ellena's chair over onto its side.

She cried out, her entire body jarring as it slammed into the concrete floor. Adrian yelled a string of profanities as Hall drew a large knife from a leather sheath hanging from his belt.

Ellena knew her time was limited now. She silently prayed

Gabe hadn't suffered, and she'd find her way back to him soon. To him and their heavenly baby.

I love you. I'm so sorry.

Hall began pushing the tip of the knife against the skin at the base of her throat. She winced but didn't give him or Radcliff the satisfaction of screaming. Warm blood began to pool in the dip between her collar bones.

"Goddamn it, don't do this!"

She could hear Adrian's chair slamming against the floor as he fought against his ties.

An unexpected calm came over her as Ellena accepted her impending death. Being careful not to move her neck for fear the knife would cut deeper, she opened her eyes and looked over at Adrian.

"Don't. It's what he wants, Adrian. Don't let him win."

Hall pushed the tip in further. This time Ellena couldn't keep a small whimper at bay. She expected him to slice her throat completely, but instead the asshole laughed and pulled the knife away.

"Fuck you, Hall," Adrian ground out.

"You're not my type, Walker. She, however, will do just fine."

Oh, God.

"So nice and soft."

Hall spoke with a lustful tone as he dragged the knife seductively down her sternum and between her breasts. Pulling the t-shirt she'd thrown on—was that just this morning?—he tightened the material before slicing it down the center to the hem.

"Hall, you perverted son of a bitch!" Adrian went against her advice and continued screaming. "Why don't you cut me loose and fight like a man!"

Ignoring the outburst, Hall calmly pulled apart the two halves of her shirt to expose her white, lacey bra. Using the blade, he followed the lines of her bra, tracing down and around the bottom of one breast.

"Mmm...I bet these taste delicious."

Her breathing increased, her heaving chest inadvertently rising towards him. She couldn't see Adrian but could hear his chair legs shaking against the floor again as he continued to use his whole body in protest.

"Hold on, Doc. Just a little longer, okay? Hold. On."

Somewhere in the back of her mind, she wondered if he was trying to tell her something. A flashback hit. One from that day in her kitchen with Victor Campbell and Gabe.

She and Gabe had both communicated with each other in a way Victor wouldn't pick up. Was that what Adrian was doing now?

It didn't matter. There was nothing he could do. Nothing anyone could do.

Not seeing any way out of this situation, Ellena forced herself to stay strong. If this was how her life would end, she was damn sure not going to give either man the satisfaction of hearing her beg.

With her voice low and steady—or as steady as she could muster, anyway—Ellena looked Hall square in the eye and said, "You want me? Then you'd better just kill me now because I'd rather be dead than to ever feel someone as disgusting as you inside of me. So just do it." She licked her dry, cracked lips. "Kill me, already. Or don't you have the balls?"

Fury erupted behind the man's eyes. "I'll show you fucking balls, you bitch."

With a snarl, he raised the knife above her heart. When he started to bring it down, Ellena closed her eyes and pictured Gabe's handsome face.

His sexy, silver-fox hair and beard. His gorgeous brown eyes. His strong jaw and heart-stopping smile.

Ellena waited for the pain to come, ready to move on to the next world. To join her husband and child she prayed was waiting there for her. But the pain never came.

A deep roar filled the room followed by a loud crash. Less than a second later, the weight of Hall's body was lifted off of her as Adrian flew through the air, knocking the other man onto the floor beside her.

Pushing herself up, Ellena took in the unbelievable scene before her. She couldn't believe what she saw.

Adrian had somehow managed to get free from his restraints and had used the chair to take Radcliff down. The son of a bitch was lying in a heap amongst the pieces of broken wood. She couldn't tell if he was still breathing, but the guy definitely wasn't moving.

To her left, Adrian was already standing, leaving Hall's own knife in the guy's chest.

"Oh, God." Ellena swung her gaze in the opposite direction.

"Sorry, Doc. Had to be done. Come on." He held out a hand to help her up.

Feeling as if she were in some sort of dream—or, more accurately, the worst nightmare she'd ever had—Ellena slid her trembling hand into Adrian's palm and allowed him to pull her to her feet.

"We need to get out of here." She started for the door.

"Wait." Adrian rushed over to Radcliff's prone body and began digging through his pockets.

"What are you looking for?"

"Keys. Just in case." He then slid a hand behind the guy's back and pulled out a gun Ellena never knew he had. "And this."

Happy to let him lead the way—especially since he had the gun—she waited for Adrian to exit the room first.

Checking both sides of the hallway, he started to move forward when Ellena heard a shuffling sound behind her. Looking back, she screamed when she saw Radcliff coming for them.

With a crazed look in his eyes, he bellowed out, "You don't get to leave! That's not how this works!"

Ellena started to push Adrian out the door but stopped when a deafening sound blasted next to her ear.

She jumped. The same, incessant ringing she'd experienced from shooting Adrian—something she felt really bad about, now —made hearing anything else nearly impossible. But she didn't need her ears to see what had just transpired.

Radcliff's movements halted to a jerky stop. Confused, he looked down at the new hole in his chest...and laughed.

"Damn." He stumbled backward. "Well, it was a good ride, wasn't it?"

Ellena watched with horror and relief as Governor Radcliff, the man destined to be the next leader of the free world, dropped back down to the floor. She was still staring at the man who had caused so much pain to so many, when Adrian pulled on her arm.

"Come on." He motioned for the hallway.

At least she thought that's what he said. At this point, Ellena didn't care. She just wanted to get as far away from this place as she possibly could. She wanted to get to...

Gabe.

Grief slammed into her as they made their way down the dimly lit tunnel. While she needed to be free of this underground hell, Ellena didn't know how she'd survive seeing what awaited them outside.

CHAPTER 24

With Gabe in the lead, the men of Bravo Team, Ghost, and Ryker made their way through the tunnel in record time. Once the R2TD had been lowered to them, the men Ryker sent headed out of Mexico and back to the States.

Fucking Mexico.

The underground radar device had worked as designed, picking up on the hidden tunnel beneath Radcliff's property within minutes of use. And just as Ryker had claimed, the data recovered transmitted immediately to his contact near the border, who then called Ryker's SAT phone with exact coordinates to the tunnel's exterior entrance.

"How much farther?" Gabe asked Ryker who was a step behind him.

"The home's foundation should only be about twenty yards ahead of us."

"Fucking tunnels, man," Nate grumbled. "Does everyone in this godforsaken country have them?"

"No shit." Matt made a throaty sound of agreement.

Ryker smirked at the two men. "Only the criminals looking for a way out."

Gabe was thankful as fuck this tunnel existed. It brought him hope when he'd thought he had none.

Ignoring the throbbing pain in his head from where debris had struck him earlier, he vowed, "This asshole isn't ever getting out."

With their eyes peeled, the men kept their guns up and their trigger fingers steady as they continued down the cool, narrow corridor. Just up ahead, Gabe's tactical mounted light revealed what he thought at first to be a dead end. A second later, he noticed the shadowed entrance on their left.

"Stay alert," he ordered the other men. Through his com, he listened to Ghost's conversation with Truck.

"Hey, Truck. Any activity outside?"

"Negative." The big guy sounded bored.

"We're coming up on the house. Keep an eye out for runners."

"Copy that."

"Hey, Hollywood," Zade spoke up, too.

"Yeah?"

"How's the leg?"

Hollywood grunted. "Barely needs a band-aid, brother."

"Good to hear it."

It was good to hear. Gabe hated the thought of any of these men—his or any others—getting hurt on his watch. The thought made him wonder about Walker and whether or not he was still alive.

The bastard was like a bad fucking penny, always managing to get out just before all hell broke loose. But something told Gabe Walker's luck may have finally run out.

A month ago, the possibility would've damn near made him smile. Ironically, there was a part of Gabe who actually hoped the asshole was still alive.

Something moved up ahead. The sound was slight, but enough to tear Gabe from his thoughts.

He held up a fist to signal the other men to stop walking. They waited. Listened. Enough time went by, Gabe had all but convinced himself he was hearing things when a gunshot echoed down the tunnel toward them.

"The fuck?"

Ellena!

Gabe held his gun high, ready to shoot Radcliff or any of his bastards the second they came into his sights. The eight men clustered together...him in front, the others two-by-two, and Ghost picking up the rear.

Hurried footsteps and whispers reached Gabe's ear, and his heart pounded against his ribs as he prepared to take a shot. When he saw yet another tributary ahead on their right, his gut told him whoever it was would be waiting for them there.

A mental debate began...do they announce their presence, or no? He decided against it for fear that if it was Radcliff and Elle was with him, he'd shoot her and run.

If she's even still alive.

No. He couldn't start thinking like that. She was his world. His life. She had to be alive.

Please, baby. Please still be with me.

Less than a yard from the other entrance, Gabe used his shoulder to wipe some blood from his eye. He wanted to see Radcliff's eyes clearly when he put his bullet between them.

Signaling with his fist again, Gabe and the others stopped. Listening for anything that may give the bastard away, he was met with nothing but silence and decided they'd waited long enough.

Using the fingers on his right hand, he counted down from three. When his index finger fell, Gabe and the other men rounded the corner and began shouting all at once for whoever was there to drop the weapon they assumed they'd have.

Running on adrenaline and fear, it took them all a moment to realize who they were actually shouting at.

"Walker?"

Standing three feet away and looking beat all to hell, Adrian Walker was pointing the barrel of his gun right at Gabe's heart.

"Dawson? Oh, thank fuck." He lowered his weapon. "It's okay, Doc. It's just your boy."

Doc? Did that mean...

"Gabriel?" Hesitantly, Ellena came out from where she'd been hiding in the shadows. "Oh, my god! Gabe!"

She took off in a dead sprint, nearly knocking him on his ass when she jumped into his arms. "Ah, baby. Thank God you're okay."

"I thought you were dead," she sobbed. "H-he showed me the explosion. I saw y-you get blown up, and I thought…"

"Shh…" Gabe held the precious gift in his arms. "I'm okay. We all are."

"Got knocked on our asses pretty good, but it takes a lot more than that to take us down." Nate grinned from beside him.

"We saw you go into the house, and a few minutes later the whole thing went up in flames. I thought…" Gabe couldn't finish the sentence. Couldn't tell her he knew what it felt like to watch her die. "When we found the tunnel, I thought maybe there was a chance you were okay. But then we heard the gunshot, and—"

"Oh, that was me. Killing Radcliff. After I stabbed Chris Hall in the heart with his own knife."

"Jesus." Ryker shook his head. "What a fucking mess."

It was a mess. One that would no doubt cause Ryker a living hell trying to clean up before the media could catch wind of it all. But as far as messes went, Gabe was as grateful as ever for the way this one had ended.

He looked back down at his wife, only then noticing the bruises on her gorgeous face and the torn shirt and blood covering her front.

"What. The. *Fuck?*"

"It's okay, Gabe." Elle was quick to assure him. Resting a palm against his cheek, she tried calming the rising beast inside him by giving him a watery smile. "Just some bruises and a few scrapes. It would've been a lot worse, but Adrian saved me."

Adrian saved…

Gabe's eyes flew to the other man's. The two men shared a look, and Gabe instinctively understood. The man they'd all believed to be the worst of the worst had saved Ellena from something she may never have been able to get past.

Feeling too choked up for words, he gave Walker a single nod, relinquishing the final remnants of hatred he'd felt toward the other man.

After all, Walker had just saved his wife's life.

Glancing down at her once more, Gabe's jaw tightened with guilt and anger. Gently cupping her battered face, he said, "I'm sorry we didn't find you sooner."

"You found me." She smiled, her bottom lip quivering. "That's all that matters."

Threading his fingers with hers, they began walking back the way he and the others had come. Along the way, they listened to Walker give Ryker shit about not knowing about the tunnel ahead of time.

None of that mattered to Gabe, now. The only thing that mattered was the woman walking next to him.

Smiling for the first time in days, a huge weight lifted from his shoulders as he continued guiding them out the tunnel and into their future.

* * *

Gabe held the door at the end of the tunnel open, and Ellena realized she'd lost the entire day. Walking out into the night air, their only light came from the moon and the guys' guns.

In front of them was a large, grassy hill surrounded by trees, and when they reached the top, she saw Truck, Fletch, and Hollywood waiting for them.

After several handshakes and hugs, the other men began talking about what their next step was. Ignoring the conversation, Gabe stopped and turned her to face him, the move putting her back to what was left of their private hell.

Good riddance.

Leaning down, he kissed her. Not softly like she'd expected, but as if he'd been starving for her. Ellena's face and mouth hurt, but she didn't care.

He's alive. Thank you, God. He's alive!

Too soon, he pulled away. "Let me look at you." He pushed some hair from her face, running his shaking hands over her. "Are you hurt anywhere else?"

Ellena knew she wouldn't truly be okay until they were back in the States, safe and sound. But she didn't tell him that. Instead, she smiled and said, "I'm okay."

Shifting to her left a step, he allowed the moonlight to fully shine over her face. Carefully Gabe ran his fingertips over her swollen cheek and split lip. He touched the cut on her neck that had now stopped bleeding and traced what she assumed were bruises left by Radcliff's hands when he'd strangled her.

"I've never wanted to kill a man more in my life." His eyes found hers again. "I wish he was still alive so I could kill him all over again."

"I'm okay, now." She reached up and touched his cheek, her eyes falling on the cut on his forehead, just under his hairline.

"What about you?"

"Nothing a few stitches won't cure." He kissed her forehead. "So I guess we're both okay."

"Yeah." Ellena breathed her first full breath in what felt like forever. "Let's try to focus on that, yeah?"

Smiling down at her, Gabe whispered, "What do you say I take you home?"

She pretended to think about it. "Depends. Do you mean your home or mine?"

"Wherever you are, baby." His voice turned thick. "That's where I want to be."

Her heart melted. "Ditto, big guy."

Grinning, Gabe leaned down to kiss her again, but stopped suddenly. Looking at something behind her, his eyes grew wide as saucers.

"Gun!"

Ellena didn't have time to react before he grabbed hold of her shoulders and shoved her to the ground. Gabe grunted low as he covered her body with his.

Lying beneath him, Ellena heard several *what-the-fucks* followed by a barrage of gunfire. A strange warmth began to spread over her chest, and when the last shot had been spent, she pushed against Gabe in order to see what they'd been shooting at.

There, not far from the tunnel's entrance, Radcliff's body was sprawled out on the grass. This time, there was no doubt the bastard was dead.

Her heart gave a hard thump. "Holy crap. That was so close." Ellena glanced over to Gabe, who was still lying on his back beside her. He wasn't moving.

"Got the bastard that time," someone spouted off behind her.

"Gabe?" Ellena tried shaking him into consciousness. When he didn't move, she pushed even harder, this time shouting his name. "Gabriel!"

Hearing her panicked voice, Nate and Matt rushed over to her. The others followed.

"Oh shit!" Matt dropped to his knees next to her. "He take a hit?

"I-I don't know." She shook him again. "I can't see anything!"

"Here."

Nate shined his flashlight onto Gabe, the beam revealing a hole in his shirt, just above the top of his vest. The black fabric around it was soaked with blood.

Ellena felt along the front of her chest where she'd noticed the strange warming sensation seconds before. Something wet and sticky covered the palm of her hand.

"M-Matt." She tried getting the medic's attention.

He moved the light to her, his breath hitching when he saw the fresh blood on her chest. "Ah, fuck. Get my bag!"

Trembling, Ellena looked back down to her husband. "It's not...it's n-not mine."

She felt as if someone had kicked her square in the chest. She couldn't speak. Couldn't *breathe.*

Her hands flew to the where Radcliff's bullet had exited Gabe's body, just under his collar bone.

This couldn't be happening. Not now. Not when they'd finally found their way back to one another.

Ellena glanced around the dark sea of men talking and scrambling to help their brave leader and friend.

Someone tossed a bag on the ground next to Matt. He

pushed her hands aside so he could administer first aid, and Ellena fell back onto her heels.

Dazed, she continued looking at everyone around her, searching for some kind of explanation for what she was seeing. She needed them to tell her something—*anything*—other than what she knew to be true...

Gabe had been shot. Protecting her.

She sucked in a breath as reality kicked in. "No. Oh, God...*no!*"

She tried reaching for him again, but someone wrapped their arms around her and held her back.

"Let him work, Doc." Adrian's voice was like the hold he had on her...firm, yet gentle.

"He's hurt," she cried. "We have to help him!"

"Matt's trying to, honey. We've just got to give them the space to work."

The men watched silently as Ryker spoke to someone on the SAT phone with an authoritative tone, but it was all background noise to Ellena. Her focus was solely on Gabe.

"Look at me, Gabriel," she tried talking to him. "Open your eyes. Come on, baby. Please."

Matt's gaze rose to hers and then the others. "We need to get him to a hospital. Fast."

"Fucking choppers are miles away." Nate ran a hand through his hair.

"We'll have to carry him." Matt looked at no one in particular. "Help me get him up."

"I got him." Truck cut Matt off.

The big man bent down, scooping Gabe up off the ground as if he weighed nothing. Sliding him over his broad shoulders, Truck held Gabe's limp body securely and began walking toward the direction of the chopper.

As they all fell in line behind him, Ellena half-listened to the conversation between the other men, unable to focus enough to know who was saying what.

"How bad is it?"

"Don't know yet."

"Damn, man. He's lost a lot of blood."

"Fuck!"

"I've got contacts in a hospital just over the border in Texas." Ryker's voice stood out amongst the others. "I'll notify them we're coming, once we're in the air." Before anyone could ask, he added, "My men have used them in the past. There's a doctor there who is very discrete."

Discrete, meaning no cops.

What felt like hours later, Ellena was relieved to hear Kole holler out, "There are the choppers!"

They all picked up their pace. Once they reached the helicopters, Matt climbed into one and Truck handed Gabe off to him. Walker helped Ellena up and into the bird, then hopped in himself.

While she and Walker got situated in their seats, Ghost and his team headed to their own helicopter and started it up. With Ryker behind the controls, the others got buckled in, and soon, the blades began to twirl.

Matt motioned for Ellena to come down with him and Gabe. "You can sit there if you want." He pointed to the side opposite him. "There's room."

She couldn't unbuckle fast enough.

Sitting on the cold, hard floor next to her husband, Ellena prayed for the millionth time she wouldn't lose him. When she noticed Gabe's eyelids slowly beginning to close, she gave his thigh a little squeeze.

"Gabe, stay with me!" she yelled over the engine's loud roar.

His eyes appeared to be unfocused, but they found hers again. Swallowing, he rasped out, "I loved you so much. I'm sorry, Elle."

Loved? As in past tense?

"No." She shook her head. "You do not get to leave me. We're taking you to the hospital. The doctors are going to fix you up, and you're going to be just fine."

Gabe's eyes fell shut again, but this time a smile whispered across his face. "S'okay, baby. You're safe. That's all...matters. All I ever...wanted."

Every word ripped through Ellena's grieving heart. Tears streamed down her cheeks, but she didn't even notice.

"Shut the fuck up, Dawson." Matt intervened. "We didn't fly all the way to Bum Fuck, Mexico to save your girl, just to have you die on us now. Got it?"

Gabe's heavy-lidded eyes grimaced when Matt poked the needle into his veins.

"You stay with me, Gabriel," she ordered. "You hear me? You're *not* dying on me. Not today. So suck it up because you and I have a hell of a lot of time to make up for."

The pain meds must've worked through his system pretty quickly because his whole body seemed to relax, and he smiled at her again. Gabe opened his mouth to say something, but as the helicopter left the ground, Ellena had a hard time hearing him.

"What was that?" She bent down, putting her ear was next to her lips.

Gabe swallowed hard. "I've been…shot."

"I know, baby." She offered him a shaky smile.

"Then why are you…yelling at me?"

Ellena blinked. Frowning, she pulled back in order to look him in the eyes.

Is he actually trying to joke, right now?

Before she could ask, Gabe started talking again, his words slurring from either blood loss or the meds. Probably both.

"Shouldn't you be…saying sweet…loving things…to me? That's…what wives…do. Right? And you're…my…wife." He gave her hand a weak squeeze. "You're…mine."

Gabe smiled again, one eye closing in a slow wink. Through her tears, Ellena couldn't help but laugh. God, she loved this man.

Please don't take him away from me.

The prayer had no more whispered through her mind when Gabe's face went slack and his eyelids fell shut. His head lolled to the side, and for a brief, terrifying moment, Ellena began to panic.

But Matt quickly found his pulse and gave her a nod, assuring her the pain meds were doing their job.

Releasing a shaky breath, she leaned in and kissed her husband's rugged cheek. Resting her forehead against his temple, she made sure he knew, "Yes, Gabriel. I'm yours. Always yours."

EPILOGUE

Two months later...

Gabe gave his wife a quick kiss at the small of her back before easing himself out of her warm, wet entrance. He plopped down onto the mattress beside her.

"I think you killed me," Ellena mumbled against her pillow.

He chuckled. "Pretty sure I died right along with you, sweetheart."

"Well..." Ellena pushed herself up on one shoulder to face him. "You *are* named after an archangel."

God, she was beautiful after making love.

After making love. First thing in the morning. In the shower.

Always...

"Trust me, baby." Gabe's voice came out rough. Sated. "The only angelic thing about me is my name."

With a giggle, Ellena leaned over and pressed her lips to his. "I've always loved your name."

He tucked some hair behind her ear, his thumb brushing across her flushed cheek. "I've always loved you."

Round, blue eyes lit up with her smile, and Gabe couldn't help but to kiss each of her matching dimples. But then his gut tightened with nerves as he finally said what he'd wanted to since he'd woken up in that damn hospital.

"I never should've left you, Ellena." His stare locked with hers. "I know I don't deserve it, but... If you'll give me another chance, give *us* a chance, I swear I'll spend the rest of my life making it up to you."

"Gabe."

"I mean it, Elle." Gabe pushed himself up, so his back rested against the headboard. "I know we have a lot of shit to work out. The biggest being the fact that you live and work in California while I'm here in Texas. But if you'd give this place a chance, I really think you'd love it here."

"Okay."

"Or I can talk with Jake. See about moving to San Diego and dropping back to only working part..." He stopped talking, his brain finally processing with what she'd just said. At least, he *hoped* he'd heard her right.

"Wait. Did you just say 'okay'?"

More relaxed than he'd seen her in days, she smiled wide and nodded. Scooting herself up next him, she said, "I lost you for three years, Gabe. Then I almost lost you forever." She brought her hand to his chest, her fingertips tracing the scar there. "What we went through with Radcliff was beyond horrible. But it also made me realize we can do anything...*survive* anything...as long as we're together."

After the incident with Radcliff, Ellena's boss had granted her an extended leave. Since then, she'd been staying with him. First in the hospital and afterward here, in his apartment.

As usual, Ryker had taken care of the clean-up, somehow managing to head off any political fallout. Gabe still didn't know how—didn't want to know, for that matter—but as far as the public knew, Henry Radcliff, his chief of staff, and two of his personal security members were killed when his plane crashed due to mechanical malfunction.

Upon Ellena's insistence, Ryker also made sure the story about Radcliff's 'mistake' with the coordinates all those years ago was leaked, as well as his implication in the deaths of Mark Ellis and the small-time reporter Ellis had been in contact with.

They'd even had Adrian Walker over for dinner. Another thing Ellena had insisted. Some days Gabe still had a hard time believing that shit, but the man had risked his life to protect Ellena. Twice.

As far as Gabe and the others were concerned, the guy was no longer an enemy. That didn't mean Bravo—or Ghost's Delta team—were quite ready to call Walker a friend. More like someone they no longer wanted to torture slowly. Or kill.

In regard to what had happened to Ellena and Walker—and Gabe—Ellena had requested that part of the story be left out. He and Walker had wholeheartedly agreed, as had Ryker.

None of them wanted the extra attention a story like that would bring. Especially Elle. The only thing she wanted was to put it behind her and get on with her life.

A life that, thankfully, included him.

He kissed her, again, simply because he could. But there was still one more detail they needed to iron out.

"What about your job?"

"Well." Ellena's lips curled upward into a gorgeous grin. "I *was* going to surprise you at dinner tonight, but…I put in for a transfer to the VA hospital in Dallas."

"You did?" His heart swelled. "When?"

"Two days after we got to Kole's cabin."

Two days after…

Gabe's brows rose with surprise. "Really?"

Ellena simply shrugged. "There are just as many patients here who could use my help as there are in California. But most importantly"—she covered his cheek with her palm—"*you're* here." The sheets rustled as she slid her body even closer. "All I've ever wanted was to be with you, Gabe. To raise a family with you. That's my dream." Her lips met his. "That's always been my dream."

It was his dream, too. And Gabe couldn't be happier that it was finally coming true. Part of it.

His heart ached for the loss they both shared. For what he could never give her again.

"You deserve everything you've ever wished for, baby." He ran his palm along her silky hair. "The *whole* dream."

"And I've gotten it." Ellena's grin grew into a mischievous smile. "Actually, I should say *we've* gotten it."

Confused, Gabe stared back at her, waiting for more of an explanation. Instead, he watched as she rolled over and pulled something out of the top nightstand drawer. She handed him a white, plastic stick.

It took his brain several seconds to catch up to what his eyes were seeing.

Gabe's lungs quit functioning. His heart gave his ribs a hard thud. A giant knot formed deep inside his throat, and his eyes immediately began to burn.

There, on a tiny digital screen in the middle of the stick, was a word that nearly made his heart stop beating, altogether.

Pregnant.

His wide gaze shot over to hers. The same set of dark blue eyes that stole his heart years before were staring back at him, glimmering behind two wells of unshed tears.

"Is this...are you really..." His voice cracked, and *Jesus*. He couldn't even say the word for the hope he was feeling.

"Pregnant?" Ellena's smile lit up her entire face. She blinked, sending tears streaking down her cheeks. "Yes."

Gabe stared down at the home pregnancy test again, his mind working overtime to understand how this was even possible.

"The doctors." He looked back up at her. "They all said—"

"It wasn't possible," she finished for him. "I know." Placing the test on the nightstand, Ellena reached for his hand and threaded her fingers with his. "My doctor here said she couldn't really explain it, but somehow my body healed itself in a way that still allowed for conception and gestation."

"Your doctor here?"

She'd already seen a doctor?

"I probably should've told you sooner, but I didn't want to get your hopes up. Just in case."

"What about later? Will you still be able to carry the baby to term?"

"I'm considered high risk because of the previous miscarriage, but that just means I'll have more doctor appointments, and she'll probably order a few more ultrasounds over the next nine months to be safe. But she saw no evidence to suggest this baby will be anything but healthy."

Holy shit.

Oh so carefully, almost afraid he'd somehow hurt her, Gabe rested his palm over the womb carrying the tiny miracle God had granted them both.

"I'm going to be a dad," he whispered with amazement.

The statement felt odd falling off his lips. And really fucking good to say.

"Are you...happy about this?" Ellena asked hesitantly. "I mean, I know it's a lot to take in. The timing's not the best, and it means even more changes for us both. Since this is the only bedroom here, we'll have to get a bigger place soon, which means you'll have to give up your apartment and—"

He grabbed the back of her neck and slammed his lips to hers. Rolling them both over so she was on top, he kissed her until his lungs burned with the need for air.

"I'm not happy, baby." He stared up at her. "I'm fucking ecstatic."

Lips that were swollen and red from his kiss spread into the biggest smile he'd ever seen her wear. "Yeah?"

He kissed her again. "I love you, Ellena. Heart and soul, good times and bad." Gabe blinked against the sudden moisture in his eyes. "You and this baby are my entire world, and I will spend every day for the rest of my life making sure you both know that."

"We know, Gabriel." Ellena pressed her trembling lips to his. "We already know."

* * *

Adrian Walker stood across the street from Jenna Shaw's apartment, as he had off and on for the past two months. Yeah, it was a total stalker move. He owned it...but he couldn't bring himself to stop.

Somewhere along the way, what had started off as mere concern for a woman who'd been through a traumatic ordeal turned into a full-blown obsession.

And he was obsessed. In ways he'd never been before.

He ate, he thought of her. He showered, he imagined his hands were hers. He slept, he dreamed about her.

When all that shit when down with Radcliff, he'd waited to make sure Dawson was going to pull through, then he'd done like he always did. He'd vanished.

Adrian had damn near convinced himself he was fine going back to life as he knew it. No friends. No family. No one to talk to.

And then Ellena Dawson had called and invited him over for dinner. How she even got his number was beyond him. But she'd called. He went.

Things changed after that. A need deep inside him had begun to grow and fester until he found himself unable to fight it any longer.

He'd needed to see Jenna. Needed to see her beautiful face and that hair that set his libido on fire. Most of all, Adrian had needed to see her with his own eyes and know that she was okay.

The first night he'd come here, he'd had full intentions of knocking on her door. Just to check on her, he'd told himself. But something had stopped him.

Something *always* stopped him.

Maybe it was the fact that he didn't want to scare her. Remind her of everything that had happened.

Or maybe it was because a woman like her deserved a hell of a lot better than him. After all, his past was about as fucked as any one person's could be.

And it's not like they could have a real relationship, anyway.

Not with Jenna or any other woman. Not when he'd made countless enemies all over the fucking world.

Adrian flashed back to the day Jason Ryker had first contacted him about going under. Ellena Dawson had been right when she'd said they'd used his sister's disappearance and his need for revenge against him.

Wish I'd told Ryker and those CIA bastards to go to hell.

Shaking off the needless memory, Adrian waited until Jenna's bedroom light turned off before getting into his car and driving away.

As he made his way to the tiny house he'd recently rented not far from the spunky nurse's apartment—under one of his many aliases, of course—he began thinking of things he hadn't allowed himself to dream about in a very, very long time.

A life full of choices and freedom. A life that didn't revolve around fucking lies and death and destruction. A life filled with laughter and love.

Later, when he woke from a dream in which he had all those things and more, Adrian made a decision he hoped like hell he wouldn't regret. Before he could talk himself out of it, he got dressed, grabbed his keys, and headed for Jenna Shaw's apartment.

Nerves twisted in his gut for the first time since he could remember as he knocked on her door and waited. When she didn't answer, he knocked again, hitting his knuckles against the wood a little harder.

After giving her another minute, Adrian gave up and started to leave. He'd taken half a step when he heard the door open behind him.

"Adrian?"

The heart he thought was lost a decade before kicked his ribs. Sleep left her voice husky and deeper than normal, and he instantly wondered if she sounded that way after sex.

Jesus, man. Really?

He turned to face her, but he didn't say a word.

"What are you doing here?" Brows scrunched together, Jenna

glanced down the hallway as if she expected someone else to be with him. "Is everything okay?"

No. I can't stop thinking about you. You. Your eyes. Your hair. That smart mouth that drives me fucking insane every time you open it.

Adrian fisted his hands to keep from reaching out and touching her. Knowing he wouldn't get a decent night's sleep until he did this, he stared back into her sleepy eyes and asked, "Can I come in?"

* * *

If you liked this book, try out Anna's R.I.S.C. series, starting with Taking a Risk.

Want to read Kole & Sarah's story for FREE?

Click below to sign up for Anna Blakely's newsletter and receive your FREE copy of *Unexpected Risk-A Bravo Team Novella*

https://dl.bookfunnel.com/u3zicn7yhu

*Unexpected Risk was originally released as part of the Because He's Perfect charity anthology. It is now only available through this link, and brings you Kole & Sarah's trying experience while dealing with shocking news and a malevolent stalker.

ABOUT THE AUTHOR

Author Anna Blakely brings you stories of love, action, and edge-of-your-seat suspense. As an avid reader of romantic suspense herself, Anna's dream is to create stories her readers will enjoy and characters they'll fall in love with as much as she has. She believes in true love and happily-ever-after, and that's what she will always bring to you.

Anna lives in rural Missouri with her husband, children, and several rescued animals. When she's not writing, Anna enjoys reading, watching action and horror movies (the scarier the better), and spending time with her amazing husband, four wonderful children, and her adorable granddaughter.

FB Author Page: facebook.com/annablakely.author.7
Blakely's Bunch (reader group): https://www.facebook.com/groups/354218335396441/
Instagram: https://instagram.com/annablakely
BookBub: https//www.bookbub.com/authors/anna-blakely
Amazon: amazon.com/author/annablakely
Twitter: @ablakelyauthor
Goodreads: https://www.goodreads.com/author/show/18650841.Anna_Blakely

facebook.com/annablakely.author.7
twitter.com/ablakelyauthor
instagram.com/annablakely
amazon.com/author/annablakely

There are many more books in this fan fiction world than listed here,
for an up-to-date list go to www.AcesPress.com

You can also visit our Amazon page at:
http://www.amazon.com/author/operationalpha

Special Forces: Operation Alpha World
Christie Adams: Charity's Heart
Denise Agnew: Dangerous to Hold
Shauna Allen: Awakening Aubrey
Brynne Asher: Blackburn
Linzi Baxter: Unlocking Dreams
Jennifer Becker: Hiding Catherine
Alice Bello: Shadowing Milly
Heather Blair: Rescue Me
Anna Blakely: Rescuing Gracelynn
Julia Bright: Saving Lorelei
Cara Carnes: Protecting Mari
Kendra Mei Chailyn: Beast
Melissa Kay Clarke: Rescuing Annabeth
Samantha A. Cole: Handling Haven
Sue Coletta: Hacked
Melissa Combs: Gallant
Anne Conley: Redemption for Misty
KaLyn Cooper: Rescuing Melina
Janie Crouch: Storm
Liz Crowe: Marking Mariah
Sarah Curtis: Securing the Odds
Jordan Dane: Redemption for Avery
Tarina Deaton: Found in the Lost
Aspen Drake, Intense
KL Donn: Unraveling Love
Riley Edwards: Protecting Olivia
PJ Fiala: Defending Sophie
Nicole Flockton: Protecting Maria

Lynne St. James: SEAL's Spitfire
Dee Stewart: Conner
Harley Stone: Rescuing Mercy
Jen Talty: Burning Desire
Reina Torres, Rescuing Hi'ilani
Savvi V: Loving Lex
Megan Vernon: Protecting Us
Rachel Young: Because of Marissa

Delta Team Three Series
Lori Ryan: Nori's Delta
Becca Jameson: Destiny's Delta
Lynne St James, Gwen's Delta
Elle James: Ivy's Delta
Riley Edwards: Hope's Delta

Police and Fire: Operation Alpha World
Freya Barker: Burning for Autumn
B.P. Beth: Scott
Jane Blythe: Salvaging Marigold
Julia Bright, Justice for Amber
Anna Brooks, Guarding Georgia
KaLyn Cooper: Justice for Gwen
Aspen Drake: Sheltering Emma
Alexa Gregory: Backdraft
Deanndra Hall: Shelter for Sharla
Barb Han: Kace
EM Hayes: Gambling for Ashleigh
CM Steele: Guarding Hope
Reina Torres: Justice for Sloane
Aubree Valentine, Justice for Danielle
Maddie Wade: Finding English
Stacey Wilk: Stage Fright
Laine Vess: Justice for Lauren

Tarpley VFD Series
Silver James, Fighting for Elena

Deanndra Hall, Fighting for Carly
Haven Rose, Fighting for Calliope
MJ Nightingale, Fighting for Jemma
TL Reeve, Fighting for Brittney
Nicole Flockton, Fighting for Nadia

As you know, this book included at least one character from Susan Stoker's books. To check out more, see below.

SEAL of Protection: Legacy Series
Securing Caite
Securing Brenae (novella)
Securing Sidney
Securing Piper
Securing Zoey
Securing Avery
Securing Kalee
Securing Jane (Feb 2021)

SEAL Team Hawaii Series
Finding Elodie (Apr 2021)
Finding Lexie (Aug 2021)
Finding Kenna (Oct 2021)
Finding Monica (TBA)
Finding Carly (TBA)
Finding Ashlyn (TBA)

Delta Team Two Series
Shielding Gillian
Shielding Kinley
Shielding Aspen
Shielding Jayme (Jan 2021)
Shielding Riley (Jan 2021)
Shielding Devyn (May 2021)
Shielding Ember (Sept 2021)
Shielding Sierra (TBA)

Delta Force Heroes Series
Rescuing Rayne (FREE!)
Rescuing Aimee (novella)
Rescuing Emily
Rescuing Harley

Marrying Emily (novella)
Rescuing Kassie
Rescuing Bryn
Rescuing Casey
Rescuing Sadie (novella)
Rescuing Wendy
Rescuing Mary
Rescuing Macie (Novella)

Badge of Honor: Texas Heroes Series

Justice for Mackenzie (FREE!)
Justice for Mickie
Justice for Corrie
Justice for Laine (novella)
Shelter for Elizabeth
Justice for Boone
Shelter for Adeline
Shelter for Sophie
Justice for Erin
Justice for Milena
Shelter for Blythe
Justice for Hope
Shelter for Quinn
Shelter for Koren
Shelter for Penelope

SEAL of Protection Series

Protecting Caroline (FREE!)
Protecting Alabama
Protecting Fiona
Marrying Caroline (novella)
Protecting Summer
Protecting Cheyenne
Protecting Jessyka
Protecting Julie (novella)
Protecting Melody
Protecting the Future

Protecting Kiera (novella)
Protecting Alabama's Kids (novella)
Protecting Dakota

New York Times, USA Today and *Wall Street Journal* Bestselling Author Susan Stoker has a heart as big as the state of Tennessee where she lives, but this all American girl has also spent the last fourteen years living in Missouri, California, Colorado, Indiana, and Texas. She's married to a retired Army man who now gets to follow *her* around the country.

www.stokeraces.com
www.AcesPress.com
susan@stokeraces.com

Made in the USA
Coppell, TX
21 June 2022

79108859R00177